Cantonese for Everyone

大家嘅廣東話

dāai⁶ gāa¹ gẻ³ Gwóng² Dūng¹ Wáa²

(Jyutping version)

Chow Bun Ching

The Commercial Press

KEY TO PHONETIC SYMBOLS
Jyutping vs. Similar Pronunciation in U.K. English

Initial Consonants

Symbols	Sound
b	s*p*y
c	bi*ts*
d	s*t*y
f	*f*or
g	s*k*y
gw	s*qu*ad
h	*h*all
j	*y*es
-	
k	*k*it
kw	*qu*iet
l	*l*ine
m	*m*y
n	*n*o
ng	ha*ng*; si*ng*er
p	*p*an
s	*s*ee
t	*t*an
w	*w*est
z	bi*ds* (very similar but voiceless)

Six Tones

Six Tones	*bc* ① Marks	Pitch
1	−	high level
2	′	high rising
3	°	mid level
4	`	low falling
5	ˇ	low rising
6	˖	low level

① The diacritics are devised by the author, *Chow Bun Ching*

Finals

Symbols	Sound
aa	f*a*ther
aai	*ai*sle
aak	m*ar*ker*
aam	*ar*m
aan	*au*nt
aang	no equivalent ("aan" + ng")
aap	sh*ar*per*
aat	st*ar*ter*
aau	n*ow*

Finals

Symbols	Sound
(a~)	b*u*t
ai	f*i*ght
ak	tr*u*cker*
am	s*u*m
an	s*u*n
ang	r*u*ng
ap	s*u*pper*
at	b*u*tter*
au	sh*ou*t

Finals

Symbols	Sound
e	ch*e*rry
ei	d*ay*
ek	ch*e*cker*
eng	l*e*ngth

Finals

Symbols	Sound
(eo)	(French: *œ*il)
ai	(French: d*eui*l)
ak	L*o*ndon
am	no equivalent (p*u*t (but shorter))

Syllabic nasals

Symbols	Sound
m	"*mm*h"
ng	ha*ng*

Finals

Symbols	Sound
i	s*ee*
ik	th*i*cker*
im	s*ee*m
in	s*ee*n
ing	s*i*ng
ip	d*ee*per*
it	*ea*ter*
iu	f*ew*

Finals

Symbols	Sound
oe	h*er* (French: n*eu*f)
oek	j*er*k*
oeng	no equivalent ("l*ear*ni*ng*")

Finals

Symbols	Sound
o	l*aw*
oi	b*oy*
ok	l*o*cker*
on	l*awn*
ong	l*o*ng
ot	s*o*rter*
ou	g*o*

Finals

Symbols	Sound
u	m*oo*d
ui	r*ui*n
uk	c*oo*ker*
un	s*oo*n
ung	(German: ach*tung*)
ut	f*oo*ter*

Finals

Symbols	Sound
yu	(French: dess*us*)
yun	(French: *une*)
yut	(French: ch*ute*)

* non-aspirated at the end

CONVERSION TABLE OF ROMANIZATION

Initial Consonants

Jyutping	IPA	Yale
b	[p]	b
c	[tsʰ]	ch
d	[t]	d
f	[f]	f
g	[k]	g
gw	[kʷ]	gw
h	[h]	h
j	[j]	y
k	[kʰ]	k
kw	[kʷʰ]	kw
l	[l]	l
m	[m]	m
n	[n]	n
ng	[ŋ]	ng
p	[pʰ]	p
s	[s]	s
t	[tʰ]	t
w	[w]	w
z	[ts]	j

Six Tones

Jyutping	bc ①	IPA	Yale	
1	ˉ	˥	1	ˉ ˋ
2	ˊ	˧˥	2	ˊ
3	°	˧	3	
4	ˋ	˨˩	4	ˋ h
5	ˇ	˩˧	5	ˊ h
6	˺	˨	6	h

① *The diacritics are devised by the author, Chow Bun Ching*

Finals

Jyutping	IPA	Yale
aa	[aː]	a/aa~
aai	[aːi]	aai
aak	[aːk˺]	aak
aam	[aːm]	aam
aan	[aːn]	aan
aang	[aːŋ]	aang
aap	[aːp˺]	aap
aat	[aːt˺]	aat
aau	[aːu]	aau

Finals

Jyutping	IPA	Yale
(a~)	[ɐ]	(a~)
ai	[ɐi]	ai
ak	[ɐk˺]	ak
am	[ɐm]	am
an	[ɐn]	an
ang	[ɐŋ]	ang
ap	[ɐp˺]	ap
at	[ɐt˺]	at
au	[ɐu]	au

Finals

Jyutping	IPA	Yale
e	[ɛː]	e
ei	[ei]	ei
ek	[ɛːk˺]	ek
eng	[ɛːŋ]	eng

Finals

Jyutping	IPA	Yale
(eo)	[θ]	(eu~)
eoi	[θy]	eui
eon	[θn]	eun
eot	[θt˺]	eut

Syllabic nasals

Jyutping	IPA	Yale
m	[m̩]	m
ng	[ŋ̩]	ng

Finals

Jyutping	IPA	Yale
i	[iː]	i
ik	[ɪk˺]	ik
im	[iːm]	im
in	[iːn]	in
ing	[ɪŋ]	ing
ip	[iːp˺]	ip
it	[iːt˺]	it
iu	[iːu]	iu

Finals

Jyutping	IPA	Yale
oe	[œː]	eu
oek	[œːk˺]	euk
oeng	[œːŋ]	eung

Finals

Jyutping	IPA	Yale
o	[ɔː]	o
oi	[ɔːi]	oi
ok	[ɔːk˺]	ok
on	[ɔːn]	on
ong	[ɔːŋ]	ong
ot	[ɔːt˺]	ot
ou	[ou]	ou

Finals

Jyutping	IPA	Yale
u	[uː]	u
ui	[uːi]	ui
uk	[ʊk˺]	uk
un	[uːn]	un
ung	[ʊŋ]	ung
ut	[uːt˺]	ut

Finals

Jyutping	IPA	Yale
yu	[yː]	yu
yun	[yːn]	yun
yut	[yːt˺]	yut

Cantonese for Everyone (Second Edition)

大家嘅廣東話（第二版）

dāai⁶ gāa¹ gě³ Gwóng² Dūng¹ Wáa²

(Jyutping version)

Author   : Chow Bun Ching

Cover Design : Viann Chan

Publisher   : The Commercial Press (H.K.) Ltd.
                8/F., Eastern Central Plaza, 3 Yiu Hing Rd.,
                Shau Kei Wan, H.K.
                http://www.commercialpress.com.hk

Distributed by : The SUP Publishing Logistics (H.K.) Limited
                16/F, Tsuen Wan Industrial Centre,
                220-248 Texaco Road, Tsuen Wan,
                NT, Hong Kong

Printed by   : Elegance Printing and Book Binding Co., Ltd.
                Block A, 4th Floor, Hoi Bun Building
                6 Wing Yip Street, Kwun Tung
                Kowloon, Hong Kong

Edition   : Second Edition, Second Printing, August 2023
                ©2021 The Commercial Press (H.K.) Ltd.
                ISBN 978 962 07 0572 4

Acknowledgements

I am grateful to all the following people who had contributed to the publication of this book:

- ☆ *John Guest* for his input especially his suggestions for the First Unit and other parts of the book.

- ☆ *Monica Magcase* and *Justin Lam* who proofread the manuscript and gave me valuable suggestions and advice.

- ☆ My publisher, *Shin-Yee Cheung*, who trusted my ability and experience in the field of Cantonese teaching and learning, and supported me during the period of publication.

- ☆ *Chui-Man Wo* for her hard work in typing and preparation of the manuscript.

- ☆ *Jane Hui, Justin Lam & John Guest* who assisted me with the sound recording.

- ☆ The reviewers and The Commercial Press editorial team for their time, cooperation and graphic designs.

My gratitude also goes to my dear friends, several generations of students and colleagues who have supported me throughout the years. Special thanks go to *Richard Law* and his company, *Winstate Technology Limited*, for their excellent work in developing the romanization conversion tool from Yale Romanization System to Jyutping.

The preparation of any book entails an inevitable sacrifice in family life: I am very grateful to my husband, *P.C.*, and two children – *Wan Yeung* and *Wan Fung*, because without their patience and generous support, I would not have had the energy and time to finish it.

Chow Bun Ching

This short course is meant for people who have no prior knowledge of Cantonese but have a strong desire to learn and a need for its use as soon as possible. This book is principally designed for newcomers to Hong Kong (especially international students) who wish to overcome the language barrier in their new living environment.

The aim of the course is to introduce the fundamental structure of the Cantonese language, as well as common and useful Cantonese vocabulary, phrases and expressions that can immediately be put to use in daily life.

The emphasis will be on the practical side of the language use, so as to meet everyday needs while residing in Hong Kong. In a relatively short period of time, learners will grasp the most useful and practical phrases or expressions to make life here easier and more enjoyable. In addition, there are sections on the culture and life in Hong Kong that will hopefully help you in the transition stage.

Many people say that Cantonese is a difficult language to learn, but I believe that given the right learning material and environment, it is no more difficult than any other second language. I hope that this course will help in this regard.

Chow Bun Ching
BA, MA, Cert TJFL
Honorary Lecturer
University of Hong Kong

The Cantonese phonetic transcription in alphabetic characters in this book is based on the Linguistic Society of Hong Kong Cantonese Romanization Scheme (also known as Jyutping).

This book consists of five units. *Unit 1* is an introduction to the Cantonese dialect. There are 3 sections within the unit. Users are introduced to the language they are going to learn and how to learn it in the first section. The second section "Cantonese Sound System" describes how the sounds and tones of Cantonese should be pronounced accurately and how to transcribe Cantonese sound in romanization. Learners will soon know that the six tones are worthy practicing over and over again. You are suggested to have a quick look of this section first before going to the next section. You can always return to this section to look up any sounds or tones that cause confusion. There is a "Key to Phonetic Symbols" before the copyright page that can also help you get used to the Cantonese sound system. The third section "Immediately Useful Expressions" provides learners with practice exercises to get a feel of speaking the Cantonese language. Try out the learning formula: "Listen – Mimic – Practice – Use – Check" described in this unit to practice on the expressions and sentences until you can grasp the sounds and tones. At this stage, don't worry too much about the structure of the sentences. You will enjoy speaking Cantonese afterwards.

Unit 2 "Numerals" introduces the fundamental concepts of numbers and measure words of the Cantonese language. The materials in this section will be used in the situational conversations discussed in the following units. You may return to review the sections in this unit from time to time when you encounter the special topics discussed in later units.

Units 3, 4 & 5 play an important role in helping learners develop oral communication skills through situational dialogues, short speech, story, and questions and answers. The main character, Amy Smith, a new comer to Hong Kong and her friends in these units help you to memorize the converses and vocabulary that appear in the text.

Unit 3 consists of 4 lessons. This unit, discussed around the main theme "Arrival", aims at familiarizing students with basic sentence patterns and the basic needs after arrival in Hong Kong.

Unit 4 "Personal Information" consists of 4 lessons and meets the need of learners to make new friends with local people. Students will be able to use Cantonese to deliver a short speech to introduce themselves and make simple conversations with their new friends after this unit.

Unit 5 "Essential Basic Conversation" covers 7 conversations on special topics of situations in everyday life. Students will be encouraged to do role-play in order to familiarize themselves with real occasions in daily life.

There are 15 lessons spread over units 3 to 5. "**Learning Objectives**" are listed at the beginning of each lesson, which give you an idea of what you are going to learn and for checking if you have achieved these objectives after each lesson. The "**Main Text**" of each lesson, either a dialogue or narrative, accompanied with English translations, provides students a common platform to learn the language. When practicing the main text, extensive drills would help you to repeat and understand a sentence easier, e.g. hōk⁶ sāang¹ > hāi⁶ hōk⁶ sāang¹ > ngǒ⁵ hāi⁶ hōk⁶ sāang¹. To retain your memory, you need to review what you have learned time and again before you proceed to a new lesson. After managing the vocabulary and patterns, students may check to see if they can express the same meaning in Cantonese from its English equivalents. "**Vocabulary**" gives a thorough explanation of the new words that appear in the main text for the first time. Before practicing on the main text, it is suggested that you work on the vocabulary repeatedly first, until you are familiar with their meaning, speech sounds and tones. "**Sentence Structure**" is incorporated within each lesson for analysis of language sentence structures. Here, vocabulary from dialogues or texts will appear again in examples to reinforce memory. Some more commonly used words and phrases will be introduced in the examples as well. If the examples for these structures are not suitable for your own need, construct your own example(s) and write it down in the "**Your Example(s)**" space provided to help yourself to remember the sentence patterns.

In addition to text vocabulary, "**FYI** (For your information)" part in each lesson provides a large range of additional vocabulary covering Hong Kong customs and culture to widen your learning. You don't have to memorize all these words at one time but you can choose to use any of them whenever the right occasion occurs. Remember, "If you don't use it, you won't learn it."

The "**Exercise**" part of each lesson provides varied practices to support the learning objectives of the lesson and give you an idea of how well you have done with the lesson. Students are recommended to revise the lesson before working on the exercises and do it without referring to the text. Writing the Romanization is another method that helps you to master the sounds and tones of Cantonese. Since most of the correct answers can be found in the same or earlier lessons, there are no keys to the exercises provided.

All texts and vocabulary from Lessons 1-15 and parts of Unit 1 and 2 are recorded. The QR code indicates a recording is available.

Over all, Units 1-5 cover approximately 30-40 hours of class time. More time might be needed depending on individual class needs. When done with this course, students would have learnt more than 400 words of vocabulary and about 100 basic Cantonese sentence structures from the main texts. Around 1,100 extended words are introduced in the Sentence Structure and FYI as well. Students can use the *Quick Reference Matrix* and *Glossaries* as index to recall the structures and vocabularies. Equipped with the basic oral language skills and familiarization of the Cantonese romanization transcription after this course, learners can choose any other Cantonese textbook or materials written in the Jyutping to continue and extend their Cantonese learning.

CONTENTS

Quick Reference Matrix

Learning Objectives	FYI
● Lesson 1 Greeting at the airport	

1. To say "Hello" & "Welcome" (54)
2. To indicate possession with "**gě³**" (54)
3. To address people with title (55)
4. To introduce oneself or someone using the verb "**hǎi⁶**" (55)
5. To give one's name using the verb "**giu³**" (56)
6. To suggest how you prefer to be addressed (56)
	1. Arriving in Hong Kong (57)
	2. Naming in Chinese (57)
	   1) Chinese family name first (57)
	   2) One-syllable & two-syllable family names (58)
	   3) Given names (58)
	   4) English translation of Chinese names (58)

● Lesson 2 You are here	
1. To form plural personal pronouns with "**děi⁶**" (63) 2. To indicate "here", "there" and "where" (63) 3. To ask and tell where one goes using the verb "**hěoi³**" (64) 4. To ask and tell whereabouts using the verb "**hái²**" (64)	1. To and From the Airport (66) 2. Hong Kong's Major Urban Districts (67)
● Lesson 3 Accommodation & check in	
1. To ask about numbers (72) *(refer to Unit 2 Section 1)* 2. To ask and tell where one lives (72) 3. To tell where an event takes place (73) 4. To use an adjective as a comment (Adjectival Predicate) (73) 5. To tell what one wants using "**sóeng² jiu³**" (74) 6. To form an imperative sentence of suggestion with "**lāa¹**" (74)	1. Accommodation (75) 2. Rooms & Facilities (76)
● Lesson 4 Money exchange	

1. To indicate possession with the verb "**jǎu⁵**" & "**mǒu⁵**" (80)
2. To connect two items with "**tùng⁴** (and)" (81)
3. To express one's wish or desire to do something using "**sóeng²**" (81)
4. To do money exchange (82) *(refer to Unit 2 Section 4)*
5. To ask "how much" or "how many" (82)
	1. Currencies (83)
	   1) Hong Kong currency (83)
	   2) Other currencies (84)
	2. Necessities (84)

Learning Objectives	FYI
● Lesson 5 Self-introduction	

1. To talk about one's family (Intimate possession) (90)
2. To know how to use Measure Words (90)
   (refer to Unit 2 Section 7)
3. To tell one's nationality (91)
4. To tell one's age (Nominal Predicate) (91)
5. To tell one's major/subject of study (92)
6. To tell one's hobbies (92)
7. To ask "what" or "what kind of" using "**māt¹ jě⁵**" (92)
	1. Countries, People and
	   Nationalities
	   1) Names of countries (93)
	   2) People (93)
	   3) Nationalities (94)
	2. Major in University (95)
	3. Hobbies (95)

● Lesson 6 Getting to know a new friend	
1. To ask for someone's name (102) 2. To use "**m̀⁴**" to indicate negation of a verb or an adjective (102) 3. To ask a yes-no question (103) 4. To ask and tell one's know-how/ability with "**sīk¹**" (103) 5. To ask and tell where one comes from (104) 6. The elliptical question with "**nē¹**" at the end (104) 7. To ask and tell the clock time (105) *(refer to Unit 2 Section 6)* 8. To express necessity or obligation to do something using "**jiu³**" (105)	1. Languages (106) 2. Skills (107) 3. Sports (107)
● Lesson 7 My Chinese friend	
1. To tell one's occupation or working place (113) 2. To use the verb "**gåau³** (teach)" (113) 3. To know the function of "**dōu¹**" in a parallel situation (114) 4. To express one's likes or dislikes (115) 5. To ask a yes-no question with a disyllabic "**zūng¹ jì³**" (115) 6. To use "**tùng⁴**" to indicate doing something with someone together (116) 7. To indicate how often an action occurs (116)	1. Occupations (117) 2. Working Places (118)
● Lesson 8 Chatting with a friend	
1. To ask and tell when an event happens (123) *(refer to Unit 2 Section 5)* 2. To inquire about one's occupation or working place (123) 3. To tell if someone is busy or not with adverbs of degree (124) 4. To know the function of "**dōu¹**" expressing all-inclusive or no exception (124) 5. To express that an action/activity is not necessary using "**m̀⁴ sái²**" (125) 6. To ask and tell what one likes to do in one's free time (125) 7. To state a continuous action or activity with "**gán²**" (126) 8. To know how to respond to a compliment (126)	1. Common Activities (127) 2. Time Words (128)

Learning Objectives	FYI
● **Lesson 9 Looking for a place**	
1. To tell & ask the purpose of a motion/journey (135) 2. To ask politely with "**céng² mǎn⁶**" before a question (135) 3. To express "There is…" and "There isn't…" using "**jǎu⁵**" and "**mǒu⁵**" (136) 4. To ask the existence of something in a certain place with "**jǎu⁵ mǒu⁵**" (137) 5. To ask where something can be found using "**bīn¹ dōu⁶ jǎu⁵**" (137) 6. To know how to respond after being thanked for (137)	1. Position Words (138) 2. Neighbourhood (139)
● **Lesson 10 What is this?**	
1. To greet someone according to the situation using "**àa⁴**" (145) 2. To specify "this/these", "that/those" and "which" with "**nī¹**", "**gó²**" & "**bīn¹**" (145) 3. To ask and answer the question "what *is* this?" (146) 4. To call the name of something using "**gi̊u³ zōu⁶**" (146) 5. To express one's feeling or thinking with "**gȯk³ dāk¹**" (147) 6. To express an attempt or trial to do sth. with "**hǎa⁵**" (147)	Breakfast in Hong Kong 1) Chinese style (148) 2) Western style (148)
● **Lesson 11 Ordering food**	
1. To give an explanation of something using "**zīk¹ hāi⁶**" (153) 2. To state what one wants when ordering food or buying things using the verb "**ji̊u³**" (153) 3. To use an adjective to modify a noun (154) 4. To express the total amount using "**jāt¹ gūng⁶**" (154) 5. To give choices to the addressee using "**dīng⁶ hāi⁶**" in a question (154) 6. To know topicalization in Cantonese (155) 7. To make a polite request with "**céng²**" (155)	1. Drinks in Hong Kong style cafés (156) 2. Adjectives (157)
● **Lesson 12 Having a dim-sum lunch**	
1. To indicate that something has not yet been done by "**mēi**" (163) 2. To indicate that something has been completed by "**zó²**" (163) 3. To ask whether something has occurred or not (164) 4. To suggest doing something together using "**āa¹**" at the end (164) 5. To treat or invite someone to something with "**céng²**" (165) 6. To ask someone's agreement to your suggestion with "**hóu² m̀⁴ hóu² åa³?**" (165) 7. To express the sense of "in addition to…" using "**zūng⁶…tīm¹**" (166) 8. To give an alternative in a statement with "**wǎak⁶ zé²**" (166)	1. Chinese Tea (167) 2. Dim-sum Menu (168)

Learning Objectives	FYI
● Lesson 13 Buying and bargaining	
1. To request or invite the addressee to do as he/she pleases (175) 2. To express whether something is worth it or worth doing with "**dái²**" (175) 3. To express a higher degree than is expected with "**tåai³**" (176) 4. To state the comparative degree with "**dī¹**" (176) 5. To seek approval or permission using the tag question "**dāk¹ m̀⁴ dāk¹ åa³?**" (177) 6. To bargain and ask for discounts (177) 7. To use the verb "**béi²**" (to pay; to give) (178) 8. To emphasize one's gratitude using "**såai³**" (178)	1. Souvenirs (179) 2. Colours (180) 3. Sizes (180)
● Lesson 14 Taking public transportation	
1. To ask what kind of transportation one should take (186) 2. To ask and tell the method of moving from one place to another (186) 3. To ask "Do you know…?" (187) 4. To tell the route or terminus of transportation (187) 5. To inform the driver where to get off a car (188)	1. Transportation (189) 2. A Stop or Terminus (189) 3. MTR (190)
● Lesson 15 Finding your way	
1. To ask how to carry out an action using "**dím² jóeng²**" (200) 2. To give instruction to find one's way (200) 3. To coordinate/indicate a sequence of events with "**jìn⁴ hằu⁶**" or "**gān¹ zỹu⁶**" (201) 4. The ordinal numbers (201) *(refer to Unit 2 Section 2)* 5. To ask how long it takes to do something using "**géi² nŏi⁶**" (201) 6. To state the time duration of an event (202) 7. To state the possibility or likelihood that something will happen with "**wǔi⁵**" (202)	1. Directions (203) 2. Banks in Hong Kong (203) 3. Time Duration (204)

Unit One

Introduction

1. Cantonese, the Language
2. Cantonese Sound System
3. Immediately Useful Expressions

1. Cantonese, the Language

1. What is Cantonese?

1) A language spoken in "Canton" (the former English name for Guangzhou 廣州 City), or Guangdong 廣東 Province [①].

2) One of the many major "dialects" of the Chinese language. (It belongs to the "Yue 粵" dialect. In China, Mandarin, also known as *Putonghua* 普通話, is the official national language.)

3) Its written form shares a similar writing system of "characters" as other Chinese dialects.

4) A "tonal" language – the meaning of the word depends on the tone used to pronounce it.

5) There are various forms of Cantonese, with different accents in different regions. e.g. *Chungshan* 中山 form, *Xinhui* 新會 form, etc.

6) As a colloquial language, Cantonese is full of slang and non-standard usage. The language among the youth is rapidly evolving, and new slang and trendy expressions are constantly emerging.

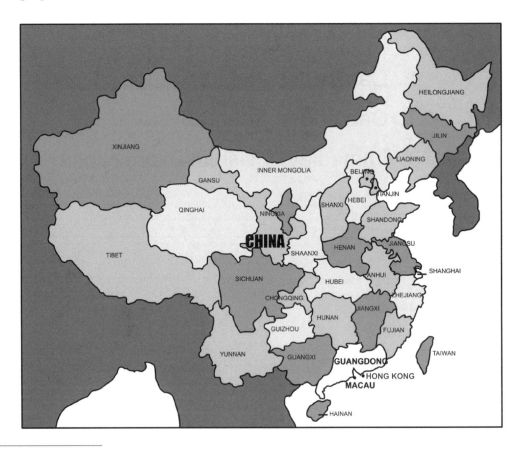

---

① Cantonese is not used in the whole Guangdong Province, but the accent in Guangzhou City was once considered as the purest form of Cantonese. Note that in this book, Cantonese spoken in Hong Kong is considered as the most common form of the language.

2. Where is Cantonese used or spoken?

1) Guangzhou 廣州 (or Canton), the capital city of Guangdong Province 廣東省 (a southern coastal province of China). The dialect spoken here was once considered the home of the purest form of Cantonese.

2) Western Guangdong Province 廣東省, including the Pearl River Delta.

3) Southern half of Guangxi Province 廣西省, adjoining the province of Guangdong to the west, e.g. Nanning 南寧.

4) Special Administrative Region of Hong Kong 香港特別行政區 – the common language of the majority of the ethnic Chinese population. Through years of mass media and pop culture influence, Hong Kong has now become the cultural center of Cantonese.

5) Special Administrative Region of Macau 澳門特別行政區

6) South-East Asia where Chinese communities have settled, such as Cambodia, Indonesia, Malaysia, Singapore, Thailand and Vietnam.

7) Overseas "Chinatowns" in major cities around the world such as London, San Francisco, New York, Vancouver, Toronto, Sydney, and many other places around North America and Europe. Due to the migration of Cantonese speakers from Hong Kong and the Guangdong area, Cantonese, not Mandarin, is the dominant language in overseas Chinese communities.

There are over 73 million Cantonese speakers worldwide, including speakers overseas. This makes Cantonese the 23rd most spoken language in the world in 2020.
(Source: https://www.visualcapitalist.com/100-most-spoken-languages/)

3. What do Cantonese speakers call the language they speak?

1) "Gwóng² Dūng¹ Wáa² 廣東話" – Guangdong speech; Guangdong Province vernacular

2) "Gwóng² Zāu¹ Wáa² 廣州話" – Guangzhou speech; Guangzhou vernacular

3) "Jy̌ut⁶ Jy̌u⁵ 粵語" – Yue language (Yue: another name for Guangdong Province)

4) "Tòng⁴ Wáa² 唐話" – Tang speech (Tang: a dynasty at 618-907)

5) "Bāak⁶ Wáa² 白話" – Plain speech (Plain speech is different from the speech used in ancient times in the imperial empire.)

6) "Hōeng¹ Góng² Wáa² 香港話" – Hong Kong speech; Hong Kong Cantonese

4. What are the similarities & differences between Mandarin and Cantonese?

Cantonese and Mandarin (also known as Putonghua, the "common" language in China) are similar in some ways but different in others.

1) They are both tonal languages – each syllable has a specific tone associated with it and the meaning of the word can change with a different tone.

2) They share much of the same written script of characters. In Chinese, one character represents one syllable. The majority of Cantonese and Mandarin words[②] are made up of two or more characters in combination.

3) Except for a number of special cases, Cantonese and Mandarin share much of the same grammar in their language.

However, there are several key differences between Mandarin and Cantonese.

1) Firstly, Mandarin is both a spoken and written variety of Chinese, which is used all across China, while Cantonese is generally considered a spoken dialect only used in a specific region of southern China.

2) Secondly, Mandarin has an officially recognized phonetic transcription system known as "Hanyu pinyin" that most educated people in China are able to understand/use. For Cantonese, while many different romanization systems are in use by foreigners, none of them is used commonly by native Cantonese speakers. Fortunately, The Linguistic Society of Hong Kong is in the process of introducing Cantonese Romanization Scheme (also known as Jyutping) in Hong Kong schools, I believe that it will become the most commonly recognized phonetic transcription system in future.

3) Finally, Cantonese shares a similar writing system of "characters" as traditional Chinese, but Hong Kong has kept what are called traditional characters. Mainland China has been using a set of simplified characters since the 1950s.

5. How essential is Cantonese in Hong Kong?

1) In Hong Kong, 95% of the population use Cantonese as their major means of communication. Although English is an essential subject in school, among many local Chinese circles, English may not be readily understood.

2) Cantonese is the major language used on radio, TV, live theater and cinema, popular songs and novels, cartoons and mass advertising, and some newspapers as well.

3) In Hong Kong, Cantonese is the medium of instruction in most schools. Children learn to read Chinese characters using standard Cantonese pronunciation too.

---

② Words are the smallest meaningful units of language, which can be used independently.

6. The advantages of knowing Cantonese in Hong Kong

1) Be able to communicate with local people.

2) Get your things done easier with Hong Kong people if you can speak Cantonese.

3) Especially useful where English is rarely used, such as wet markets, dim-sum restaurants, roadside stalls and the outlying islands.

4) Help "break the ice" at parties, among your local friends, colleagues and classmates, and will probably earn you respect for your efforts.

5) Make life much easier and more enjoyable in Hong Kong. The local people will certainly appreciate your trying to speak their language.

7. How to learn Cantonese

1) Join a Cantonese course and attend all the classes with good preparation.

2) Learn by yourself with the formula: Listen – Mimic – Practice – Use – Check

3) Take the recording with you and listen during your free time or while traveling around.

4) Try to mimic out loud (several times) the local sounds and tones of the words as closely as possible.

5) Study what you have learned and practice as often as possible.

6) Practice, practice, practice! Remember, "Practice makes perfect".

7) Don't be shy to make mistakes. Practice and use what you have learned at every chance you get. "If you don't use it, you won't learn it."

8) Check your new language with a teacher or a native speaker.

9) Keep your ears open and listen.

10) Be patient. Each individual has his/her own pace of learning. Just don't give up and persevere!

2. Cantonese Sound System

In this course, both Chinese script and alphabetic characters have been used to represent the syllables of Cantonese. The phonetic transcription in alphabetic characters (commonly referred to as romanization) provides an important tool for new learners to acquire the sounds and tones of Cantonese, even though it is not generally used by native Cantonese speakers (who simply use the Chinese characters itself to represent the language).

For the romanization, this course has adopted the "The Linguistic Society of Hong Kong Cantonese Romanization Scheme", or known as "Jyutping [3]" to transcribe Cantonese sounds into alphanumeric characters, with certain modifications [4]. The Chinese traditional characters included in the course are mainly for readers of Chinese and native Cantonese speakers; they demonstrate pronunciation to aid new learners.

Three important elements in the Cantonese syllable:

The basic characteristic of Cantonese pronunciation is that for each Chinese character there is a single syllable associated with it. The syllable in Cantonese language consists of three basic elements: initials, finals and tones.

1. **Initial:** The sound of the consonant at the beginning of a syllable, if any. There are 19 initials in total.

2. **Final:** The sound of the vowel sound plus final consonant, if any, at the end of a syllable. There are 51 common finals in total.

3. **Tone:** The relative pitch, or variation of pitch, of a syllable. There are 6 tones in total.

Note: There are two nasal consonants that can stand-alone without a vowel. These are consonants "m" & "ng", which are called Syllabic Nasals.

The syllables are made up of various combinations of 19 initial consonant sounds (initial) and 51 common vowels and vowel-consonant groups (final). In addition, a fixed tone pattern of fixed length is superimposed onto each syllable (tone).

Note that some initials or finals can be used independently and do not need to be in combination with others (see next topic: the combination of initial and final).

Note also that it is essential that the six tone patterns have to be mastered.

---

[3] Jyutping was designed and proposed by The Linguistic Society of Hong Kong in 1993 in order to standardize a simple, easy-to-learn and easy-to-use Cantonese romanization scheme. (http://lshk.ctl.cityu.edu.hk/)

[4] Tone mnemonics designed by the author are added as iconic notations of tones. Please refer to the section on the Six Tones on page 17.

Let's take "good morning" as an example for Cantonese syllable structure in Jyutping and diacritics devised by the author. The following two syllables form the phrase mean "good morning" in Cantonese:

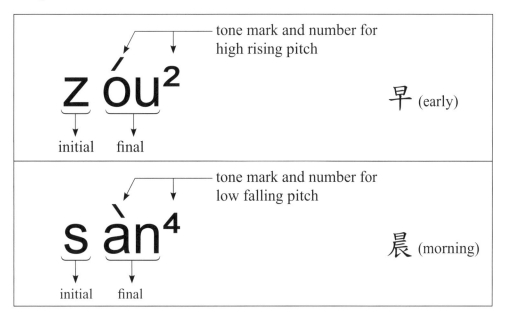

The combinations of initial and final (syllables in Cantonese)

	Element	Pattern* I	Pattern* F	Example
1.	One central vowel	—	V	ō¹ *(diarrhea)*; āa¹ *(crow)*
2.	One central vowel & one semi-vowel (Diphthong)	—	V+V	o̊i³ *(love)*; ái² *(short in height)*
3.	One central vowel & final consonant	—	V+C	ām¹ *(nunnery)*; ūk¹ *(house)*
4.	One initial consonant & one central vowel	C	V	cē¹ *(vehicle)*; fů³ *(trousers)*
5.	One initial consonant & two vowels (Diphthong)	C	V+V	hóu² *(good)*; se̊i³ *(four)*
6.	One initial consonant, one central vowel & final consonant	C	V+C	jāt¹ *(one)*; sẵp⁶ *(ten)*
7.	Nasal consonant (Syllabic nasals)	C	—	m̀⁴ *(not)*; ňg⁵ *(five)*

* I = initial; F = final; V = vowel; C = consonant

There is a complete online course on Cantonese pronunciation, CantoSounds, designed by the Chinese Language Centre of the University of Hong Kong for Cantonese learners. In this online course, you can learn about Cantonese romanization and individual Cantonese sounds, with plenty of recordings, videos, exercises and games. Please feel free to visit it at http://cantonese.hku.hk/cantosounds/ If you register or log in, you can challenge yourself through the Quiz and the game "CantoRocks" to become an expert in Jyutping.

 **Initials**

We shall start with the initials of Cantonese syllables. There are 19 distinctive initials and they can be divided into five groups as seen in the summary table below:

1. Non-aspirated Voiceless		2. Aspirated Voiceless		3. Voiced Nasal		4. Fricative & Continuant		5. Semi-vowel	
b [p]	(b̲o)	p [pʰ]	(p̲o)	m [m]	(m̲o)	f [f]	(f̲o)		
d [t]	(d̲aa)	t [tʰ]	(t̲aa)	n [n]	(n̲aa)	l [l]	(l̲aa)		
g [k]	(g̲aa)	k [kʰ]	(k̲aa)	ng [ŋ]	(ng̲aa)	h [h]	(h̲aa)		
gw [kʷ]	(gw̲o)	kw [kʷʰ]	(kw̲o)					w [w]	(w̲o)
z [ts]	(z̲e)	c [tsʰ]	(c̲e)			s [s]	(s̲i)	j [j]	(j̲i)

Note: The International Phonetic Alphabet (IPA) is shown in brackets [ ] for sounding reference.

Group 1: Non-aspirated Voiceless

There is no puff of air associated with the non-aspirated sound. In English these non-aspirated consonants are normally found in the middle of words and are produced in a non-aspirated manner. Note that in Cantonese the consonants "b", "d", "g", "gw" and "z" are *voiceless* – that the vocal chords *do not vibrate* in producing these consonants.

	Jyutping	*IPA*	*Pronounced similarly as in the English word*	*Cantonese example*	*Meaning in Cantonese*
1)	**b**	[p]	*s**p**y*	**b̲ēng**⁶ 病	*sick*
2)	**d**	[t]	*s**t**y*	**d̲āai**⁶ 大	*big*
3)	**g**	[k]	*s**k**y*	**g̲ūi**⁶ 攰	*tired*
4)	**gw**	[kʷ]	*s**qu**ad*	**gw̲åi**³ 貴	*expensive*
5)	**z**	[ts]	*bi**ds** (very similar but voiceless)*	**z̲óu**² 早	*early*

Group 2:   Aspirated Voiceless

This group is all aspirated. This means that the production of the sound is very similar to Group 1 but there is a puff of air released after the sound. It is said that the aspiration in Cantonese is generally stronger than in that of English.

	Jyutping	IPA	Pronounced similarly as in the English word	Cantonese example	Meaning in Cantonese
1)	p	[pʰ]	*p*an	pèng⁴ 平	*cheap*
2)	t	[tʰ]	*t*an	tǔng³ 痛	*painful*
3)	k	[kʰ]	*k*it	kǎn⁵ 近	*near, close*
4)	kw	[kʷʰ]	*qu*iet	kwāi¹ 虧	*deficient (easy to get sick)*
5)	c	[tsʰ]	*bits*	cì⁴ 遲	*late*

Group 3:   Voiced Nasals

This group of nasals is similar to those found in English and other languages and therefore should be easy to reproduce. The only exception may be "ng" as an initial. To pronounce the initial "ng", make sure that the back of the tongue is against the soft palate. It is said that the initial "ng" is similar to the "*gn*" in the English "*gnaw*", e.g. "ngǒ⁵ *(I; me)*" sounds very much like "gnaw".

	Jyutping	IPA	Pronounced similarly as in the English word	Cantonese example	Meaning in Cantonese
1)	m	[m]	*my*	mūn⁶ 悶	*boring*
2)	n	[n]	*n*o	nàan⁴ 難	*difficult*
3)	ng	[ŋ]	*hang; singer*	ngǒ⁵ 我	*I; me*

Notes:

1. Some Cantonese speakers sound "l" for "n" for words with initial n, e.g. "něi⁵ *(you)*" is pronounced as "lěi⁵". Generally speaking, both pronunciations are understood by people.

2. Some Cantonese speakers do not have "ng" as initial sound. Missing "ng" as initial sound in the pronunciation is considered as "lazy sounding", e.g. "ngǒ⁵ *(I; me)*" is pronounced as "ǒ⁵" instead of "ngǒ⁵".

3. The above mis-sounding should not be encouraged. It would become harder for these people to learn other languages if they had less sounding repertoire in their native language. Unfortunately, many Hong Kong native speakers are found to have these "lazy sound" problem.

Group 4: Fricative and Continuants

Fricatives are consonants produced by forcing air through a narrow channel made by placing two articulators close together (Wikipedia 2020). A continuant is a sound produced with an incomplete closure of the vocal tract (Crystal 1991). The following initials are very likely to be similar to sounds in English. If these sounds do not appear in your language, make sure you pay special attention to their pronunciation here.

	Jyutping	IPA	Pronounced similarly as in the English word	Cantonese example	Meaning in Cantonese
1)	f	[f]	_f_or	fåai³ 快	fast
2)	l	[l]	_l_ine	lĕng³ 靚	beautiful
3)	h	[h]	_h_all	hóu² 好	good
4)	s	[s]	_s_ee	såi³ 細	small

Group 5: Semi-vowels as supplementary initials

This final group of initials is again likely to be very similar to sounds in English. Listen to them carefully to see if there are any slight differences.

	Jyutping	IPA	Pronounced similarly as in the English word	Cantonese example	Meaning in Cantonese
1)	j	[j]	_y_es	jī̆⁶ 易	easy
2)	w	[w]	_w_est	wăai⁶ 壞	bad

2 Finals

This is the term commonly used to describe the remaining part of the Cantonese syllable after the initial. A "final" consists of a central vowel combined with an optional semi-vowel or consonant at the end of the syllable. There are nine main transcriptions for the central vowel sounds, namely "aa, a~, e, i, o, u, oe, eo~" and "yu". It is important to note that a number of vowels have both long and short versions, and it is essential that learners not only distinguish them but also practice and master the six special highlighted short vowels. Please refer to the *Table of 51 Common Finals* below for reference.

Table of 51 Common Finals

	long	short	long	short	long	short	long	short	long	short	long	short	long
Central vowel / Final endings	aa [aː]	(a~) [ɐ]	e [ɛː]		i [iː]		o [ɔː]		u [uː]		oe [œː]	(eo~) [θ]	yu [yː]
~i [j]	aai [aːi]	ai [ɐi]		ei [ei]			oi [ɔːi]		ui [uːi]			eoi [θy]	
~u [w]	aau [aːu]	au [ɐu]			iu [iːu]			ou [ou]					
~m [m]	aam [aːm]	am [ɐm]			im [iːm]								
~n [n]	aan [aːn]	an [ɐn]			in [iːn]		on [ɔːn]		un [uːn]			eon [θn]	yun [yːn]
~ng [ŋ]	aang [aːŋ]	ang [ɐŋ]	eng [ɛːŋ]			ing [ɪŋ]	ong [ɔːŋ]			ung [ʊŋ]	oeng [œːŋ]		
~p [p]	aap [aːp˺]	ap [ɐp˺]			ip [iːp˺]								
~t [t]	aat [aːt˺]	at [ɐt˺]			it [iːt˺]		ot [ɔːt˺]		ut [uːt˺]			eot [θt˺]	yut [yːt˺]
~k [k]	aak [aːk˺]	ak [ɐk˺]	ek [ɛːk˺]			ik [ɪk˺]	ok [ɔːk˺]			uk [ʊk˺]	oek [œːk˺]		

The 51 finals can be divided into four groups as follows:

Group 1: Nine main vowels

Cantonese vowels have been noted for the emphatic movement of the lips and facial muscles and may need extra practice to properly imitate the sounds accurately. You may wish to slightly exaggerate your imitation of the vowels in the following vowel drills. Note that "a~" and "eo~" are always followed by a semi-vowel or consonant, while "u" and "yu" always begin with "w~" and "j~" respectively when there is no other initials appears.

	Jyutping	IPA	Pronounced similarly as in the English word	Cantonese example	Meaning in Cantonese
1)	**aa**	[aː]	*f<u>a</u>ther*	fāa¹ 花 sāan¹ 山	*flower* *mountain*
2)	**a~**	[ɐ]	*b<u>u</u>t*	sān¹ 新	*new*
3)	**e**	[ɛː]	*ch<u>e</u>rry*	cē¹ 車	*a car*
4)	**i**	[iː]	*s<u>ee</u>*	cī¹ 黐	*sticky*
5)	**o**	[ɔː]	*l<u>aw</u>*	dō¹ 多	*many; a lot*
6)	**u**	[uː]	*m<u>oo</u>d*	fů³ 褲	*trousers*
7)	**oe***	[œː]	*h<u>er</u> (French: n<u>eu</u>f)*	hōe¹ 靴	*boot*
8)	**eo~***	[ɵ]	*(French: <u>œ</u>il)*	zéoi² 嘴	*mouth, beak*
9)	**yu***	[yː]	*(French: dess<u>u</u>s)*	sȳu¹ 書	*book*

* "oe","eo~" and "yu" are considered as independent vowels (not diphthongs) pronounced as [œː], [ɵ] and [yː] with rounded lips (known as labialization).

Group 2: Ten diphthongs

Diphthongs are sounds consisting of a combination of two vowels. They are commonly found in many other languages. The ten diphthongs in Cantonese are made up of a central vowel sound as the first element and a semi-vowel either an "**i**" or a "**u**" at the end:

Central vowel + **i** (semi-vowel)
Central vowel + **u** (semi-vowel)

Please note that "aai" has a long "aa" and a weak "i", while "ai" has a short "a" and a strong "i". When first learning to separate these two diphthongs, the shorter "ai" should be pronounced with a tendency to close the mouth, while the longer "aai" should be pronounced with the mouth open for longer. It would be advised to exaggerate these two diphthongs when learning so as to make a clearer distinction.

Please also pay careful attention to the highlighted finals.

	Jyutping	*IPA*	*Pronounced similarly as in the English word*	*Cantonese example*	*Meaning in Cantonese*
1)	**aai**	[aːi]	*<u>ai</u>sle*	fåai³ 快	*fast*
2)	**ai**	[ɐi]	*f<u>i</u>ght*	såi³ 細	*small*
3)	**ei**	[ei]	*d<u>ay</u>*	něi⁵ 你	*you*
4)	**oi**	[ɔːi]	*b<u>oy</u>*	ồi³ 愛	*love*
5)	**ui**	[uːi]	*r<u>ui</u>n*	gūi⁶ 攰	*tired*
6)	**eoi**	[ɵy]	*(French: d<u>eui</u>l)*	kěoi⁵ 佢	*he, she, him, her*
7)	**aau**	[aːu]	*n<u>ow</u>*	māau¹ 貓	*cat*
8)	**au**	[ɐu]	*sh<u>ou</u>t*	gáu² 狗	*dog*
9)	**iu**	[iːu]	*f<u>ew</u>*	síu² 少	*few; a little*
10)	**ou**	[ou]	*g<u>o</u>*	hóu² 好	*good*

Group 3: Seventeen finals ending in nasal consonant

The following nasal endings are commonly found in English and other languages, but for Mandarin speakers they may have difficulty with the "**m**" ending sound since this sound does not exist in their native language. The more important distinction within this group is between the final "**n**" and the similar sounding "**ng**". Note also that some native Cantonese speakers may also wrongly pronounce the final "**~ng**" as "**~n**". Again, some exaggeration of pronouncing at the beginning of the learning stage will aid your mastering of these sounds.

Central vowel + **m**
Central vowel + **n**
Central vowel + **ng**

	Jyutping	*IPA*	*Pronounced similarly as in the English word*	*Cantonese example*	*Meaning in Cantonese*
1)	**aam**	[aːm]	*a**rm***	sāam¹ 三	*three*
2)	**am**	[ɐm]	*s**um***	sām¹ 心	*heart*
3)	**im**	[iːm]	*s**eem***	dím² 點	*how; o'clock*
4)	**aan**	[aːn]	*a**un**t*	dāan¹ 單	*a bill; singular*
5)	**an**	[ɐn]	*s**un***	sān¹ 新	*new*
6)	**in**	[iːn]	*s**een***	gin³ 見	*meet; see*
7)	**on**	[ɔːn]	*l**awn***	gōn¹ 乾	*dry*
8)	**un**	[uːn]	*s**oon***	wún² 碗	*a bowl*
9)	**eon**	[ɵn]	*L**on**don*	sèon³ 信	*a letter*
10)	**yun**	[yːn]	*(French: **une**)*	sȳun¹ 酸	*sour*
11)	**aang**	[aːŋ]	*no equivalent ("aan" + "ng")*	sāang¹ 生	*raw, uncooked*
12)	**ang**	[ɐŋ]	*r**ung***	dáng² 等	*to wait (for)*
13)	**eng**	[ɛːŋ]	*l**eng**th*	léng³ 靚	*beautiful*
14)	**ing**	[ɪŋ]	*s**ing***	sing³ 姓	*surname*
15)	**ong**	[ɔːŋ]	*l**ong***	góng² 港	*harbour*
16)	**ung**	[ʊŋ]	*(German: acht**ung**)*	dúng³ 凍	*cold*
17)	**oeng**	[œːŋ]	*no equivalent (somewhat like "**learning**")*	hōeng¹ 香	*fragrant*

Group 4: Seventeen finals with unreleased stops "p, t, k"

This is an essential final sounding group that many learners of Cantonese find it difficult to pronounce and it is worth spending some time here to master these distinctive ending sounds. Many Cantonese syllables include the consonants "p", "t" or "k" at the end but they are different from many other languages in that they are unreleased, so there is no puff of air at the end of the syllable. This sometimes leads to the three different final consonants sounding similar if pronounced incorrectly so make sure you thoroughly practice these three ending sounds.

Central vowel + **p**
Central vowel + **t**
Central vowel + **k**

	Jyutping	IPA	Pronounced similarly as in the English word	Cantonese example		Meaning in Cantonese
1)	**aap**	[aːp˺]	sh*ar*per	dåap³	搭	to ride
2)	**ap**	[ɐp˺]	s*up*per	sӑp⁶	十	ten
3)	**ip**	[iːp˺]	d*ee*per	díp²	碟	a plate
4)	**aat**	[aːt˺]	st*ar*ter	båat³	八	eight
5)	**at**	[ɐt˺]	b*ut*ter	cāt¹	七	seven
6)	**it**	[iːt˺]	*ea*ter	jӣt⁶	熱	hot
7)	**ot**	[ɔːt˺]	s*or*ter	hǒt³	渴	thirsty
8)	**ut**	[uːt˺]	f*oo*ter	fǔt³	闊	wide
9)	**eot**	[ɵt˺]	no equivalent (p*ut* (but short))	cēot¹	出	to go out
10)	**yut**	[yːt˺]	(French: ch*ute*)	jÿut⁶	月	moon; month
11)	**aak**	[aːk˺]	m*ar*ker	båak³	百	hundred
12)	**ak**	[ɐk˺]	tr*uck*er	dāk¹	得	alright
13)	**ek**	[ɛːk˺]	ch*eck*er	lēk¹	叻	smart; capable
14)	**ik**	[ɪk˺]	th*ick*er	sӣk¹	識	to know
15)	**ok**	[ɔːk˺]	l*ock*er	lōk⁶	落	to descend
16)	**uk**	[ʊk˺]	c*ook*er	lūk⁶	六	six
17)	**oek**	[œːk˺]	j*er*k	gǒek³	腳	a leg; foot

Note that the **~p**, **~t**, **~k** group of finals are, in fact, similar to the previous corresponding **~m**, **~n**, **~ng** group of finals because the tongue and lips are in the same positions for these final sounds, i.e. the lips for "m" & "p" in "sām¹ 心 *(heart)*" and "sāp¹ 濕 *(wet)*", the tongue tip for "n" & "t" in "jān¹ 因 *(reason)*" and "jāt¹ 一 *(one)*", and the back of tongue for "ng" & "k" in "lūng¹ 窿 *(hole)*" and "lūk¹ 轆 *(wheel)*", are the same.

"**~p**": for example "sāp⁶ 十 *(ten)*", you need to close the lips to make the "p" sound, but do not open them again that can cause a puff of air to be released.

"**~t**": for example "jāt¹ 一 *(one)*", make sure you form a regular "t" sound (which you do normally just above the upper teeth) and do not produce a puff of air after stopping the air stream.

"**~k**": for example "lūk⁶ 六 *(six)*", again just form a "k" consonant in the normal way but remember not to aspirate the ending.

3 Syllabic consonants "m" and "ng"

In Cantonese, the sounds "m" and "ng" can form a syllable of their own.

	Jyutping	*IPA*	*Pronounced similarly as in the English word*	*Cantonese example*	*Meaning in Cantonese*
1)	**m**	[m̩]	*sounds just like "__mmh__"*	m̀⁴ 唔	*no; not*
2)	**ng**	[ŋ̍]	*ha__ng__*	ńg⁵ 五	*five*

The syllabic consonant "**m**" is always used in the lowest tone (low falling tone) indicating the negation of verbs or adjectives. The tone mark is marked above the "m". And "**ng**" is always used in low tones such as "ǹg⁴ 吳 *(a Chinese surname)*", "ńg⁵ 五 *(five)*" and "ǹg⁶ 誤 *(mistaken)*". The tone mark is marked above the "g".

Note: The "**ng**" syllabic is often mispronounced as "**m**" by Hong Kong native speakers.

4 Six Tones

The characteristic that distinguishes Cantonese from most Western languages is that it is tonal. Cantonese is a tonal language – each syllable has a specific tone associated with it. A tone is a distinctive relative pitch, high, middle or low, or a distinctive pitch contour, rising or falling in the range of one's voice. There are six different tones in Cantonese. The syllabic tone in Cantonese is an essential element of the language because the meaning of the word can change with a different tone. Here is an example of this feature with the syllable "si" shown here with different tones and meanings. Note the difference in meaning from the change in tone.

Tone	Pitch	Example	
1	High level tone	sī¹	絲 *silk*; 詩 *poem*; 屍 *corpse*; 師 *master*
2	High rising tone	sí²	屎 *feces*; 史 *history*
3	Mid level tone	si̊³	試 *try*; 弒 *kill*
4	Low falling tone	sì⁴	匙 *key*; 時 *time*
5	Low rising tone	sǐ⁵	市 *city; market*
6	Low level tone	sī⁶	事 *matter*; 視 *vision*

As you can see, if you use the wrong tone, you are probably saying a completely different word. It will seem odd at first that in order to speak the language correctly you have to maintain, raise or lower the relative pitch of your voice to produce the correct tone (it's a bit like singing), but after a little practice and finding a comfortable tone range, you will discover it to become progressively easier to do.

- **Tone Numbers** (for ordering of the same sound in a dictionary and typing with keyboard):

  Like in most Cantonese dictionaries or other romanization systems, Jyutping also uses numeral numbers 1 – 6 to indicate from high to low tones. It is recommended that you remember the traditional tone order, and therefore be able to use 1 – 6 to indicate Cantonese tone in typing or in consulting a Cantonese dictionary. In this book, the tone numbers 1 – 6 will be written in superscript in order to make the tone marks clearly recognizable.

- **Tone Mnemonics** (diacritics and hand signals for teaching and learning):

  In order to remind you of the different tones, the author has designed a hand signal system to represent each of the six tones. In addition to the tone numbers 1 – 6, this book uses diacritics – iconic notations on top of first vowels or syllabic nasals – to help visualize the tone for each Cantonese syllable. You may choose to use tone numbers or diacritics to mark down tones. The Jyutping Converter on http://cantonese.hku.hk/goodies/lshk/ can be used to type Jyutping using both tone numbers and diacritics.

The following is an example of this modified system with the sketch illustrating the relative pitch curve of the six tones and the Cantonese syllable "si" in all six tones with diacritics and hand signals.

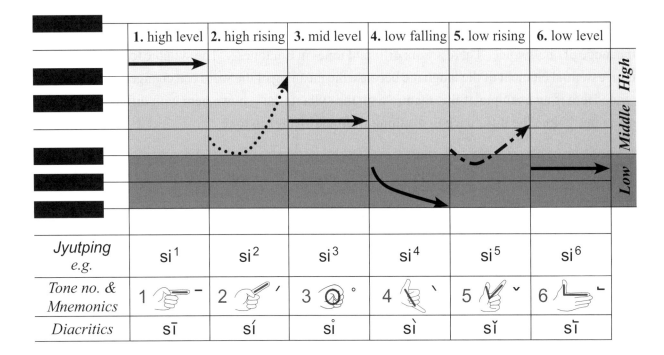

	1. high level	2. high rising	3. mid level	4. low falling	5. low rising	6. low level
Jyutping e.g.	si¹	si²	si³	si⁴	si⁵	si⁶
Tone no. & *Mnemonics*	1 ☞ ‾	2 ☞ ′	3 ⊚ °	4 ✎ `	5 ✔ ˇ	6 👍 ‾
Diacritics	sī	sí	si̊	sì	sǐ	sī

Note: The keyboard-like column on above left gives learners an idea about the range of relative pitch in Cantonese.

Let us describe each of the tones, its hand signals and how its diacritics and tone numbers are written in the following:

The 1ˢᵗ tone is the **high level tone**. If you start your voice high-pitched and let it stay more or less at the same high pitch throughout, that's the high level tone. Hold your left fist and stretch your index finger then keep it in the horizontal level (☞). It is marked with a macron (‾) above the first vowel or the number "1" at the end of the syllable, e.g. sī¹ 絲 *(silk)*, fān¹ 分 *(minute)*.

The 2ⁿᵈ tone is the **high rising tone**. It starts at a fairly low pitch and normally rises above the pitch of the 1ˢᵗ tone. Hold your left fist and stretch your index finger then keep it up in 45 degrees (☞). It is marked with an acute accent (′) above the first vowel or the number "2" at the end of the syllable, e.g. sí² 屎 *(feces)*, fán² 粉 *(powder)*.

The 3ʳᵈ tone is the **mid level tone**. It is a steady pitch around the middle tone of a person's voice and is considered as a comfortable tone of one's voice. Just hold your left fist and no need to use any finger (⊚). It is marked with a small circle (°) above the first vowel or the number "3" at the end of the syllable, e.g. si̊³ 試 *(try)*, fån³ 瞓 *(sleep)*.

The **4th** tone is the **low falling tone**. This is the lowest tone among the six tones in Cantonese. It starts from lower than the medium pitch and falls to a fairly low pitch. Hold your left thumb up indicating the lower tone and show your little finger down representing the falling pitch ( ). It is marked with a grave accent (`) above the first vowel or the number "4" at the end of the syllable, e.g. sì⁴ 匙 *(key)*, fàn⁴ 墳 *(tomb)*.

The **5th** tone is the **low rising tone**. It starts slightly lower than the starting point of the 2nd tone but only rises to about the mid level tone. Also hold your left thumb up indicating the lower tone and stretch your index finger then keep it up in 45 degrees showing it is a rising pitch ( ). It is marked with a hacek (ˇ) above the first vowel or the number "5" at the end of the syllable, e.g. sǐ⁵ 市 *(city)*, fǎn⁵ 奮 *(work vigorously)*.

The **6th** tone is a **low level tone**. It stays at a constant low pitch for its duration of the syllable. Also hold your left thumb up indicating the lower tone and stretch the other four fingers out in the horizontal level. It shows a letter "L" reminding you that it is a low level tone (   ). It is marked with a flattened capital letter "L" (‾) above the first vowel or the number "6" at the end of the syllable, e.g. sī̄⁶ 事 *(matter)*, fān̄⁶ 份 *(portion)*.

Note that in the Syllabic Nasals "m" and "ng", which has no vowel letters, the tone mark is written above the "m" and "g", e.g. m̀⁴ 唔 *(not)* and ňg⁵ 五 *(five)*.

Here are the numerals 0-10 in six tones for you to practice:

Zero	**One**	**Two**	**Three**	**Four**	**Five**	**Six**	**Seven**	**Eight**	**Nine**	**Ten**
0	1	2	3	4	5	6	7	8	9	10
lìng⁴	jāt¹	jī̄⁶	sāam¹	sēi³	ňg⁵	lūk⁶	cāt¹	bāat³	gáu²	sāp⁶

Remember these six numbers in order to help you get used to the six tones:

high level	high rising	mid level	low falling	low rising	low level
3	9	4	0	5	2
sāam¹	gáu²	sēi³	lìng⁴	ňg⁵	jī̄⁶

The sounds of high and low tones depend on individuals and will be different from people to people with higher or lower pitched voices. If the high tone is too high it will not only sound silly but also uncomfortable to say. The low falling tone is quite distinctive in how low it is. If it is too low it will be difficult to reproduce and if not low enough it cannot be easily distinguished by Cantonese speakers. Therefore it is important to first find your own highest tone (the 1ˢᵗ tone) and lowest tone (the 4ᵗʰ tone), e.g. sāam¹ 三 (three) – lìng⁴ 零 (zero), fūn¹ jìng⁴ 歡迎 (welcome), cīu¹ jàn⁴ 超人 (superman). Starting from the 1ˢᵗ tone, establish the 2ⁿᵈ and 3ʳᵈ tones, e.g. sāam¹ 三 (three) – gáu² 九 (nine) – sẻi³ 四 (four), cī¹ zó² sin³ 黐咗線 (got crazy). After that, work on the 5ᵗʰ and 6ᵗʰ tones beginning with your 4ᵗʰ tone, e.g. lìng⁴ 零 (zero) – ňg⁵ 五 (five) – jī⁶ 二 (two), làu⁴ ngǎan⁵ lēoi⁶ 流眼淚 (tears fall from eyes). Establishing and being aware of your tones is a crucial part of the Cantonese language learning so make sure you are able to distinguish and reproduce all six tones well.

Now let's try to practice the following six tones one after another:

	1. high level	2. high rising	3. mid level	4. low falling	5. low rising	6. low level
1)	fū¹	fú²	fủ³	fù⁴	fǔ⁵	fū⁶
2)	bāai¹	báai²	bảai³	bàai⁴	bǎai⁵	bāai⁶
3)	sām¹	sám²	sảm³	sàm⁴	sǎm⁵	sām⁶
4)	dāng¹	dáng²	dảng³	dàng⁴	dǎng⁵	dāng⁶
5)	lūk¹	lúk²	lủk³	lùk⁴	lǔk⁵	lūk⁶
6)	sāam¹ 衫	móu² 帽	fủ³ 褲	hàai⁴ 鞋	jǔu⁵ 與	māt⁶ 襪
	(clothes, hats, trousers, shoes and socks)					
7)	sāam¹ 三	dím² 點	bủn³ 半	lèi⁴ 嚟	ngǒ⁵ 我	dōu⁶ 度
	(Come to my place at half-past three.)					
8)	fūn¹ 歡	héi² 喜	dỏu³ 到	làu⁴ 流	ngǎan⁵ 眼	lēoi⁶ 淚
	(I am so happy that tears fall from my eyes.)					
9)	jāt¹ 一	wún² 碗	sỏi³ 細	ngàu⁴ 牛	nǎam⁵ 腩	mīn⁶ 麵
	(One small bowl of noodles with beef brisket.)					
10)	cīng¹ 清	có² 楚	sảai³ 晒	m̀⁴ 唔	wǔi⁵ 會	mān⁶ 問
	(It is so clear, nobody would ask.)					

3. Immediately Useful Expressions

Here are some very useful expressions for you to try out and this section will also let you get used to the Jyutping. As a beginner, all you need to know is that each Chinese character will have a monosyllabic sound and tone. You will need to get a native Cantonese speaker to say them aloud or listen to the recording and mimic them properly.

1. Basic greetings

	Cantonese	English Equivalent
1.	něi⁵ hóu². *(slightly formal)* 你/ 好/ 。 you/ good/	*Hello!* *Good day.*
2.	něi⁵ hóu². *(1ˢᵗ time meeting)* 你/ 好/ 。 you/ good/	*How do you do!* *Hello!*
3.	*Q:* něi⁵ hóu² måa³? 你/ 好/ 嗎/ ? you/ good/ PT/	*How are you?*
4.	*A₁:* géi² hóu². jǎu⁵ sām¹. 幾/ 好/ ，有/ 心/ 。 quite/ good/ have/ heart/	*Quite good, thanks for asking.*
5.	*A₂:* hóu² hóu². 好/ 好/ 。 very/ good/	*(I'm) fine.*
6.	*A₃:* màa⁴ máa² déi². 麻 麻 哋/ 。 so-so/	*Just so-so.*
7.	*A₄:* m̀⁴ hāi⁶ géi² hóu². 唔/ 係/ 幾/ 好/ 。 not/ be/ quite/ good/	*Not so good.*
8.	*A₅:* m̀⁴ hóu². 唔/ 好/ 。 not/ good/	*Not good.*
9.	wåi³! *(between closer acquaintances)* 喂/ ！ hey/	*Hey!* *Hi!*
10.	hāa¹ lóu²! *(informal)* 哈 佬/ ！ [sound transcription from English]	*Hello!*

2. Everyday greetings

	Cantonese	English Equivalent
Morning	**zóu² sàn⁴.** 早/　晨/。 early/ morning/	*Good morning.*
Night	**zóu² táu².** 早/　抖/。 early/ rest/	*Good night.* *Sleep well.*

3. Greetings around mealtimes

	Cantonese	English Equivalent
Afternoon *(around* *mealtimes)*	*Q:* **sīk⁶ zó² fāan⁶ mēi⁶ åa³?** 食/ 咗/ 飯/　未/ 呀/？ eat/ done/ rice/ yet/ PT/	*Have you eaten yet?* *(How's it going?)*
	A₁: **sīk⁶ zó² låa³.** 食/ 咗/ 喇/。 eat/ done/ PT/	*Yes, I've eaten.*
	A₂: **mēi⁶ åa³.** 未/　呀/。 not yet/ PT/	*No, not yet.*
Evening *(around* *mealtimes)*	*Q:* **sīk⁶ zó² fāan⁶ mēi⁶ åa³?** 食/ 咗/ 飯/　未/ 呀/？ eat/ done/ rice/ yet/ PT/	*Have you eaten yet?* *(How's it going?)*

4. Saying goodbye

	Cantonese	English Equivalent
Leaving	**zòi³ gin³.** *(slightly formal)* 再/　見/。 again/ see/	*Goodbye.* *See you!* *Until next time, goodbye.*
	bāai¹ bāai¹. 拜　　拜/。 [*sound transcription from English*]	*Bye-bye.*
	tīng¹ jāt⁶ gin³. 聽　 日/　見/。 tomorrow/ see/	*See you tomorrow.*
	jāt¹ zān⁶ gin³. 一　 陣/　見/。 one moment/ see/	*See you in a moment.* *See you in a while.* *See you later.*
	māan⁶ máan² hàang⁴. 慢　　　慢/　行/。 slowly/ walk/	*Mind how you go!* *Mind your step.* *Take care!*

5. Useful expressions

	Cantonese	English Equivalent
1.	**fūn¹ jìng⁴!** 歡／迎／！ happy/ welcome/	*Welcome!*
2.	**m̀⁴ gōi¹.** 唔／該／。 not/ ought to/	*Thank you (for a service).* *Excuse me, … (attracting attention, esp. when asking somebody for assistance, etc.)* *Please… (to make a request more politely)*
3.	**dō¹ zē⁶.** 多／謝／。 many/ thanks/	*Thank you.* *(for a gift, an invitation or a compliment, etc.)*
4.	**m̀⁴ sái² håak³ hěi³.** 唔／使／客 氣／。 no/ need/ polite/	*Don't mention it.* *You're welcome.* *Please don't bother.* *Please make yourself at home.*
5.	**děoi³ m̀⁴ zȳu⁶.** 對 唔 住／。 sorry/	*(I'm) sorry! (quite serious)* *Excuse me!*
6.	**m̀⁴ hóu² jǐ³ sī¹.** 唔／好／意 思／。 not/ good/ meaning/	*Sorry! (not so serious)* *It's embarrassing.* *(also pronounced as "m̀⁴ hóu² jǐ³ sǐ³")*
7.	**m̀⁴ gán² jiu³.** 唔／緊 要／。 not/ important/	*Never mind.* *It's all right.* *Forget it.* *Don't worry.*
8.	**mǒu⁵ mǎn⁶ tài⁴.** 冇／ 問 題／。 have not/ problem/	*No problem.* *No question.*
9.	**màai⁴ dāan¹!** 埋／ 單／！ sum-up/ bill/	*The bill!* *The check!*
10.	**jǎu⁵ lōk⁶!** 有／ 落／！ have/ descend/	*I want to get off (from a vehicle).* *(as used in public light buses - minibuses)*
11.	**nī¹ dōu⁶ tìng⁴ (cē¹).** 呢 度／ 停／ （車）。 here/ stop/ car/	*Stop (the car) here!*
12.	**m̀⁴ gōi¹ dáng² dáng².** 唔 該／ 等 等／。 please/ wait a little/	*Please wait (a moment).* *(also "m̀⁴ gōi¹ dáng² jāt¹ zǎn⁶")*

13.	m̀⁴ gōi¹ zě³ zě³. 唔　該／　借 借／　。 please/　lend a little/	*Excuse me. (I want to get through.)* *Please let me go through.*
14.	m̀⁴ gōi¹ fåai³ dī¹. 唔　該／　快／　啲／　。 please/　fast/　~er/	*Faster, please.* *Be quick, please.*
15.	måi⁵ jūk¹, béi² cín² ngǒ⁵! 咪／　郁／，　俾／　錢／　我／！ don't/ move/, give/ money/ me/	*Freeze (Don't move)! Give me the money!* *(*You'd better understand these instructions if you encounter a robbery - if you don't, you might get hurt!)*
16.	gåu³ mēng⁶ åa³! 救／　命／　呀／！ save/　life/　PT/	*Help!!* *(asking for help in a critical situation)*
17.	m̀⁴ gōi¹ dáa² gáu² gáu² gáu²! 唔　該／　打／　九／　九／　九／！ please/　hit/　nine/　nine/　nine/	*Please dial 999! (for the police in Hong Kong)* *Please call the police.*
18.	ngǒ⁵ m̀⁴ zī¹. 我／　唔／　知／　。 I/　not/ know/	*I don't know.*

6. Classroom expressions

	Cantonese	English Equivalent
1.	něi⁵ jǎu⁵ mǒu⁵ mān⁶ tài⁴ åa³? 你／　有／　冇／　問　題／呀／？ you/ have/ have not/ question / PT/	*Do you have any questions?*
2.	ngǒ⁵ jǎu⁵ mān⁶ tài⁴. 我／　有／　問　題／　。 I/　have/　question/	*I have a question.*
3.	ngǒ⁵ mǒu⁵ mān⁶ tài⁴ 我／　冇／　問　題／　。 I/　have not/　question/	*I have no questions.*
4.	něi⁵ mìng⁴ m̀⁴ mìng⁴ åa³? 你／　明／　唔／　明／　呀／？ you/　clear/ not/ clear / PT/	*Do you understand?*
5.	ngǒ⁵ m̀⁴ mìng⁴. 我／　唔／　明／　。 I/　not/　clear/	*I don't understand.*
6.	ngǒ⁵ mìng⁴. 我／　明／　。 I/　clear/	*I understand.*

7.	dāk¹ m̀⁴ dāk¹ åa³? 得／ 唔／ 得／ 呀／？ okay／ not／ okay／ PT／	*Is that okay?*
8.	dāk¹, mǒu⁵ mān⁶ tài⁴. 得／， 冇／ 問 題／。 okay／ have not／ question／	*Okay, no problem.*
9.	mèi⁶ dāk¹ åa³. 未／ 得／ 呀／！ not yet／ okay／ PT／	*Not yet (okay).*
10.	m̀⁴ gōi¹ zǒi³ góng² jāt¹ cì³ āa¹. 唔 該／ 再／ 講／ 一 次／吖／。 please／ again／ say／ once PT／	*Please say it once more.*
11.	m̀⁴ gōi¹ góng² dāai⁶ sēng¹ dī¹. 唔 該／ 講／ 大 聲／ 啲／。 please／ say／ loud／ ~er／	*Please speak louder.*
12.	m̀⁴ gōi¹ góng² māan⁶ dī¹. 唔 該／ 講／ 慢／ 啲／。 please／ say／ slow／ ~er／	*Please speak slower.*
13.	m̀⁴ gōi¹ góng² fåai³ dī¹. 唔 該／ 講／ 快／ 啲／。 please／ say／ fast／ ~er／	*Please speak faster.*
14.	m̀⁴ gōi¹ gān¹ ngǒ⁵ góng². 唔 該／ 跟／ 我／ 講／。 please／ follow／ me／ say／	*Please repeat after me.*
15.	jāt¹ cài⁴ góng². 一 齊／ 講／。 together／ say／	*Say it together.*
16.	hóu² hóu². 好／ 好／。 very／ good／	*Very good.*
17.	hāa⁶ cì³ zǒi³ gìn³. 下／ 次／ 再／ 見／。 below／ time／ again／ see／	*See you next time.*

It is particularly important to seek advice and feedback on how well you are doing at reproducing the correct tones in Cantonese. After some practice, try to find a native Cantonese to try out your newly acquired tones. If they seem to understand what you say then you are doing well. But if they do not seem to understand, then it could either be a tone problem or the inaccuracy of the pronunciation. In this case, you will need to pinpoint the problem and further practice to overcome it.

UNIT TWO
Numerals

1. Cardinal Numbers

2. Ordinal Numbers

3. Traditional Signs for Numbers

4. Money

5. Date

6. Clock Time

7. Counting Things with Measure Words

Unit 2 Numerals

In order to survive in Hong Kong, knowledge of numbers, the number system and how numbers are used in Cantonese are very important. We will tackle all these aspects in the following sections.

Remember, this is also a good opportunity to practice Cantonese sounds and tones you have just learned, so try to pay attention to the accuracy of your pronunciation. Also, the following sections include some fundamental concepts that may be different from your own language, like the concept of measure words or how numbers are built up in Cantonese. Try to spend some time understanding these sections and you will find learning much easier later on in the course.

1. Cardinal Numerals (0 – 1,000,000)

1. Single digit numbers (0 – 9)

0	1	2	3	4	5	6	7	8	9
lìng⁴	jāt¹	jī̄⁶	sāam¹	se̊i³	ng̊⁵	lūk⁶	cāt¹	b̊aat³	gáu²
零	一	二	三	四	五	六	七	八	九

PRACTICE   **My telephone number is….**
For example 2659-4713:

<u>ng̊⁵ ge̊³ dīn⁶ wáa² h̊ai⁶</u> jī̄⁶, lūk⁶, ng̊⁵, gáu², se̊i³, cāt¹, jāt¹, sāam¹.

a) 9534-2095;	b) 2859-1010;
c) 8971-2507;	d) 9500-2468;

2. Building up numbers from 10 to 19

s̊ap⁶	十	10	*Ten*
s̊ap⁶ jāt¹	十一	10 + 1	*Eleven*
s̊ap⁶ jī̄⁶	十二	10 + 2	*Twelve*
s̊ap⁶ sāam¹	十三	10 + 3	*Thirteen*
s̊ap⁶ se̊i³	十四	10 + 4	*Fourteen*
s̊ap⁶ ng̊⁵	十五	10 + 5	*Fifteen*
s̊ap⁶ lūk⁶	十六	10 + 6	*Sixteen*
s̊ap⁶ cāt¹	十七	10 + 7	*Seventeen*
s̊ap⁶ b̊aat³	十八	10 + 8	*Eighteen*
s̊ap⁶ gáu²	十九	10 + 9	*Nineteen*

3. Building up numbers from 20 to 99

20 is "two ten", i.e. jī⁶ sặp⁶ 二十 in Cantonese, therefore 21 is "two ten one", jī⁶ sặp⁶ jāt¹ 二十一, 22 is "two ten two", jī⁶ sặp⁶ jī⁶ 二十二, 30 is "three ten", sāam¹ sặp⁶ 三十, and so on.

4. Abbreviations of "~ sặp⁶~"

a) The two-digit numbers are abbreviated in informal speech, especially in quoting prices. "jī⁶ sặp⁶ + *Numeral*" (*twenty* + something) are often contracted to "jặa⁶ + *Numeral*" or "jě⁶ + *Numeral*":

22	jī⁶ sặp⁶ jī⁶	⟹	jặa⁶ jī⁶; jě⁶ jī⁶
24	jī⁶ sặp⁶ sẻi³	⟹	jặa⁶ sẻi³; jě⁶ sẻi³

b) "sāam¹ sặp⁶ + *Numeral*" (*thirty* + something) are often contracted to "sặa¹ ặa⁶ + *Numeral*":

35	sāam¹ sặp⁶ nǧ⁵	⟹	sặa¹ ặa⁶ nǧ⁵
38	sāam¹ sặp⁶ bặat³	⟹	sặa¹ ặa⁶ bặat³

c) Similarly, in numbers from 40 onwards, the word "sặp⁶" (*ten*) is reduced to "ặa⁶":

46	sẻi³ sặp⁶ lūk⁶	⟹	sẻi³ ặa⁶ lūk⁶
59	nǧ⁵ sặp⁶ gáu²	⟹	nǧ⁵ ặa⁶ gáu²
83	bặat³ sặp⁶ sāam¹	⟹	bặat³ ặa⁶ sāam¹

5. Numerals indicating hundreds "bặak³ 百"

jāt¹ bặak³	1 × 100	*one hundred*
jī⁶ bặak³	2 × 100	*two hundred*
sāam¹ bặak³	3 × 100	*three hundred*
sẻi³ bặak³	4 × 100	*four hundred*
nǧ⁵ bặak³	5 × 100	*five hundred*
lūk⁶ bặak³	6 × 100	*six hundred*
cāt¹ bặak³	7 × 100	*seven hundred*
bặat³ bặak³	8 × 100	*eight hundred*
gáu² bặak³	9 × 100	*nine hundred*

6. Building up numbers from 101 to 999

jāt¹ bǎak³ lìng⁴ jāt¹	1 × 100 + 0 +1	*101*
jī⁶ bǎak³ jī⁶ sǎp⁶ jī⁶	2 × 100 + 20 + 2	*222*
ngˇ⁵ bǎak³ lūk⁶ sǎp⁶ cāt¹	5 × 100 + 60 + 7	*567*
cāt¹ bǎak³ sāam¹ sǎp⁶	7 × 100 + 30	*730*
bǎat³ bǎak³ bǎat³ sǎp⁶ bǎat³	8 × 100 + 80 + 8	*888*
gáu² bǎak³ gáu² sǎp⁶ gáu²	9 × 100 + 90 + 9	*999*

7. Counting thousands and above

In Chinese, "**cīn¹** 千" is used to indicate thousands and there is an additional unit "**māan⁶** 萬" to indicate ten thousands.

Here is a chart to show the Chinese counting system:

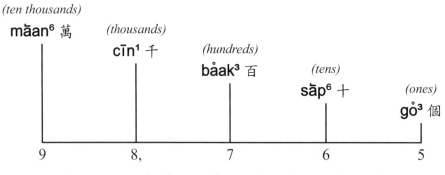

(= Ninety-eight thousand seven hundred and sixty-five)

Above "**māan⁶** 萬" (10,000), the Chinese system counts up to ten "**māan⁶** 萬" (100,000), hundred "**māan⁶** 萬" (1,000,000), and a thousand "**māan⁶** 萬" (10,000,000). The next higher count, a "**māan⁶** 萬" "**māan⁶** 萬" is denoted by a new unit "**jīk¹** 億" (100,000,000). See chart below:

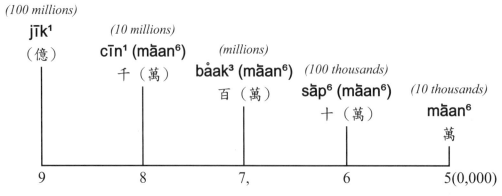

(= Nine hundred eighty-seven million and six hundred & fifty thousand)

8. Numbers with special meaning, lucky and taboo numbers:

To the Chinese, many numbers are endowed with positive or negative (or both) connotations. Here are some numbers that rhyme with special meaning:

Numbers		Associated words	Meaning
0	lìng⁴	nìn⁴ 年	*year*
1	jāt¹	jāt⁶ 日	*day*
2	jī̀⁶	jī̀⁶ 易	*easy*
3	sāam¹	sāang¹ 生	*alive, born*
4	se̊i³	séi² 死	*die, death*
5	ńǧ⁵	m̄⁴ 唔	*not, no*
6	lṻk⁶	lōu⁶ 路	*road, way*
7	cāt¹	sāt¹ 失	*to lose; to die*
8	båat³	fåat³ 發	*prosper, make money*
9	gáu²	còeng⁴ gáu² 長久	*long lasting, long life*
10	sāp⁶	sāp⁶ cỳun⁴ sāp⁶ měi⁵ 十全十美	*perfect*
		sāt⁶ 實	*definitely; certainly*

Lucky numbers for the vehicle license number plate:

18	sāt⁶ fåat³	*surely prosper*		
28	jī̀⁶ fåat³	*easy to prosper*		
118	jāt⁶ jāt⁶ fåat³	*make money every day*		
168	jāt¹ lōu⁶ fåat³	*prosper all the way*		
328	sāang¹ jì³ fåat³	*a business makes money*		
9888	gáu² fåat³ fåat³ fåat³	*long & endless prosperity*		

Taboo numbers:

4	séi²	*to die*		
14	sāt⁶ séi²	*surely die*		
24	jī̀⁶ séi²	*easy to die*		
164	jāt¹ lōu⁶ séi²	*die all the way*		
5354	m̄⁴ sāam¹ m̄⁴ se̊i³	*neither one thing nor the other; (not solid, bad or messy)*		
5354	m̄⁴ sāang¹ m̄⁴ séi²	*not even dead nor alive*		
9394	gáau² sāam¹ gáau² se̊i³	*a man having an affair; to make trouble*		

Choose an auspicious registration number for your car and explain why it is a good choice for you.

2. Ordinal Numbers

When a cardinal number is preceded by "dǎi⁶ 第", it becomes an ordinal.

$$\text{dǎi}^6 \text{ 第 } + \textbf{Number}$$

dǎi⁶ jāt¹	第一	*the first*
dǎi⁶ jī⁶	第二	*the second*
dǎi⁶ sāam¹	第三	*the third*
dǎi⁶ géi²?	第幾？	*which (what) rank*

These ordinal numbers can be placed before a measure word (MW) and noun (N) as a modifier.

$$\text{dǎi}^6 \text{ 第 } + \textbf{Number} + \textbf{MW} + \textbf{N}$$

dǎi⁶ jāt¹ go̊³ (jàn⁴)	第一個（人）	*the first one (person)*
dǎi⁶ jī⁶ gåa³ (cē¹)	第二架（車）	*the second one (vehicle)*
dǎi⁶ sāam¹ gāan¹ (fóng²)	第三間（房）	*the third one (room)*
dǎi⁶ géi² + MW ?	第幾＋ **MW** ？	*what rank?*

PRACTICE

Read out the following ordinal numbers in Cantonese.

e.g. 12ᵗʰ = dǎi⁶ sǎp⁶ jī⁶

3ʳᵈ _____   8ᵗʰ _____   2ⁿᵈ _____   4ᵗʰ _____

10ᵗʰ _____   1ˢᵗ _____   50ᵗʰ _____   *which rank?* _____

Listen to your teacher and write down the ordinal numbers.

e.g. ____5ᵗʰ____ (dǎi⁶ nǧ⁵)   _____ (   )

_____ (   )   _____ (   )

_____ (   )   _____ (   )

3. Traditional Signs for Numbers

These signs are usually used for showing prices in markets, Hong Kong style cafés or sometimes minibuses.

Traditional signs	〇	〡 (一)	〢 (二)	〣 (三)	〤	〥	〦	〧	〨	〩	十
Chinese characters	零	一	二	三	四	五	六	七	八	九	十
	0	1	2	3	4	5	6	7	8	9	10

In written Chinese, we write the digits and the units of money as follows:

千 cīn¹	百 baak³	十 sap⁶	元 jyun⁴	角 gok³/ 毫 hou⁴	分 fan¹
thousands	*hundreds*	*tens*	*dollars*	*ten cents*	*one cent*

Writing and Reading Order: from left to right, top to bottom.

top row for numbers:	1st	3rd	5th
bottom row for digits & units:	2nd	4th	6th

E.g.

a) 〢三 元 ($2.30)	b) 〣一 元 ($3.10)	c) 〤〥 元 ($4.50)
d) 〥〦 十元 ($56.00)	e) 〧〤 十元 ($74.00)	f) 〩〥 十元 ($95.00)
g) 〨〇〣 百十元 ($803.00)	h) 〦〩〤 百十元 ($694.00)	i) 三〥〇〧 千百十元 ($3,507.00)

Note that the small units of money like "ten cents" or "one cent" are omitted.

4. Money

The currency in Hong Kong is the Hong Kong dollar (HK$), which is pegged to the US dollar at a rate of about 7.8 HKD to 1 USD. The bank notes in circulation are in the following denominations: $1,000, $500, $100, $50, $20 and $10. Coins can be found in units of $10, $5, $2, $1, 50¢, 20¢ and 10¢. Several local banks have the authority to issue bank notes so there are more than one design for each denomination. The Hong Kong Monetary Authority issues the HK$10 note, while all the other notes are issued either by HSBC, Bank of China or Standard Chartered Bank. (also see p.83)

1. Dollars

In Hong Kong currency, the basic unit of money "**cín²** 錢" is "**mān¹** 蚊 *(dollars)*". This unit is also used as a measure word, so when you want to say an amount of money, just include "**mān¹** 蚊" after the numerical value.

numerical value + **mān¹** 蚊

For example:

1)	jāt¹ **mān¹**	$1
2)	**lŏeng⁵** mān¹ ①	$2
3)	sāp⁶ **mān¹**	$10
4)	sāp⁶ jī⁶ **mān¹**	$12
5)	jāt¹ bǎak³ **mān¹**	$100
6)	jāt¹ cīn¹ **mān¹**	$1,000
7)	jāt¹ mǎan⁶ **mān¹**	$10,000
8)	sāp⁶ mǎan⁶ **mān¹**	$100,000
9)	jāt¹ bǎak³ mǎan⁶ **mān¹**	$1,000,000

 Read out the amounts of money given below.
For example: $350 = sāam¹ bǎak³ nǧ⁵ sāp⁶ mān¹

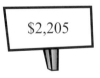 $2,205

 $1,489

 $37,961

 $75,888

---

① In Cantonese, there are two distinct words: "**jī⁶**" and "**lŏeng⁵**" meaning "two". "**jī⁶**" is used in counting and in compound numbers such as "**jī⁶ sāp⁶** (twenty)" and "**jī⁶ bǎak³** (two hundred)", etc. while "**lŏeng⁵**" is used to quantify nouns such as "**lŏeng⁵ mān¹** (two dollars)" and "**lŏeng⁵ gŏ³ jàn⁴** (two persons)", etc. (also see p.47)

2. Ten-cent units

In Hong Kong currency, a smaller unit of money than the dollar (**mān¹** 蚊) is "**hòu⁴ zí²** 毫子", which is a ten-cent unit (similar to the US "dime"). **One "mān¹ 蚊" is equal to ten "hòu⁴ zí² 毫子"**. In colloquial speech, the shorter form "**hòu⁴** 毫" is commonly used. This unit is also a measure word by itself.

$$1 - 9 \ + \ \text{hòu⁴ 毫}$$

For example:

1)	jāt¹ hòu⁴ (zí²)	*ten cents* 10¢
2)	lŏeng⁵ hòu⁴ (zí²)	*twenty cents* 20¢
3)	nŏ⁵ hòu⁴ (zí²)	*fifty cents* 50¢
4)	gáu² hòu⁴ (zí²)	*ninety cents* 90¢

3. Dollars & ten-cent units

a) Using "go̊³ 個" instead of "mān¹ 蚊"

When a figure involves both dollars and ten-cent units, "**go̊³** 個" is used instead of "**mān¹** 蚊" for dollars and "**hòu⁴** 毫" may be omitted in speech. Also, "**jī⁶** 二" is used for 2 ten-cent units and "**bǔn³** 半 *(half)*" is used for 5 ten-cent (i.e. half dollar) units in such cases.

$$\text{figure of dollars} \ + \ \text{go̊³ 個} \ + \ \text{figure of ten-cent unit}$$

For example:

1)	sāam¹ go̊³ sêi³ hòu⁴ (zí²)	$3.40
2)	sǎp⁶ jī⁶ go̊³ sāam¹ hòu⁴ (zí²)	$12.30
3)	gáu² āa⁶ gáu² go̊³ gáu² hòu⁴ (zí²)	$99.90
4)	sêi³ go̊³ bǔn³ ②	$4.50
5)	lŏeng⁵ go̊³ jī⁶	$2.20

b) Omission of "jāt¹" in one dollar and something

Usually, a local speaker will drop the "**jāt¹**" in the case of a single dollar amount followed by multiple ten-cent units.

$$\text{jāt¹} \ + \ \text{go̊³ 個} \ + \ \text{figure of ten-cent unit}$$

For example:

1)	jāt¹ go̊³ cāt¹	$1.70
2)	jāt¹ go̊³ jī⁶	$1.20
3)	jāt¹ go̊³ bǔn³	$1.50

---

② The word "**bǔn³** 半" (half) is used for half a dollar (50 cents) in a multi-unit monetary expression.

4. Asking for the price

Q:	géi² (dō¹) cín² åa³? géi² cín² åa³? 幾　（多）　錢／　呀？ how much　money/　PT = *How much is it?*　　　　　　　　(*Answer: a price*)
Q:	dím² māai⁶ åa³? 點／　賣／　呀？ how/　to sell/　PT = *How much is it?*　(*Answer: a unit or measurement and a price*)

5. To state the price for a quantity of things

In Cantonese, no verb-to-be is required in a positive statement telling the price except when the speaker wants to emphasize the price.

Things	+	[*Nu.* + *MW.*] + ***Price $*** / ***Price $*** + [*Nu.* + *MW.*]
Nu. + *MW.* + Things	+	***Price $***

E.g.

$5.0 ea.

hōeng¹ zīu¹ jāt¹ tìu⁴ ńǧ⁵ mān¹
香　　蕉　一　條　五　蚊

jāt¹ tìu⁴ hōeng¹ zīu¹ ńǧ⁵ mān¹
一　條　香　蕉　五　蚊

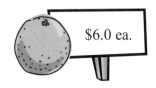

$6.0 ea.

cáang² lūk⁶ mān¹ (jāt¹)* go̊³
橙　　六　蚊　一　　個

jāt¹ go̊³ cáang² lūk⁶ mān¹
一　個　橙　六　蚊

PRACTICE　Practice with your teacher or classmates with the following prices.

1.	2.	3.
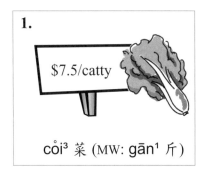	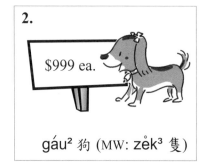	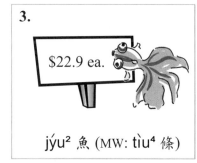
$7.5/catty	$999 ea.	$22.9 ea.
cồi³ 菜 (MW: gān¹ 斤)	gáu² 狗 (MW: ze̊k³ 隻)	jýu² 魚 (MW: tìu⁴ 條)

5. Date

To be able to say and understand the day, date, month and year in Cantonese is a useful skill to acquire. For example "What day are you free for lunch?" or "What year were you born?" are very common questions that you may be asked. In this section you will learn the order of how to say the date in Cantonese, as well as how to ask some useful questions.

1. **Year:** To state a certain year, read off the year number digit by digit and put "**nìn⁴** 年 *(year)*" at the end.

? ? ? ? + **nìn⁴** 年

jāt¹ lūk⁶ lìng⁴ lìng⁴ **nìn⁴**	一六〇〇年	*the year 1600*
jāt¹ gáu² sėi³ jāt¹ **nìn⁴**	一九四一年	*the year 1941*
jāt¹ gáu² gáu² cāt¹ **nìn⁴**	一九九七年	*the year 1997*
jī⁶ lìng⁴ lìng⁴ bảat³ **nìn⁴**	二〇〇八年	*the year 2008*

To ask for the year:

E.g.   1) gām¹ nìn⁴ hāi⁶ géi² dō¹ nìn⁴ ảa³? 今年係幾多年呀？
(What year is it now?)

2) něi⁵ bīn¹ nìn⁴ lèi⁴ Hōeng¹ Góng² gảa³? 你邊年嚟香港㗎？
(Which year did you come to Hong Kong?)

2. **Month:** Naming months is easy in Cantonese: the twelve months are referred to by their ordinal numbers, followed by the word "**jȳut⁶** 月 *(month)*".

1 – 12 + **jȳut⁶** 月

jāt¹ jȳut⁶	一月	*January*	cāt¹ jȳut⁶	七月	*July*
jī⁶ jȳut⁶	二月	*February*	bảat³ jȳut⁶	八月	*August*
sāam¹ jȳut⁶	三月	*March*	gáu² jȳut⁶	九月	*September*
sėi³ jȳut⁶	四月	*April*	sāp⁶ jȳut⁶	十月	*October*
ngǔ⁵ jȳut⁶	五月	*May*	sāp⁶ jāt¹ jȳut⁶	十一月	*November*
lūk⁶ jȳut⁶	六月	*June*	sāp⁶ jī⁶ jȳut⁶	十二月	*December*

To ask for the month:

E.g. 1) jì⁴ gāa¹ hǎi⁶ géi² dō¹ jyut⁶ åa³? 而家係幾多月呀？
      jì⁴ gāa¹ hǎi⁶ géi² jyut⁶ åa³? 而家係幾月呀？
      (What month is this?)

   2) něi⁵ géi² jyut⁶ sāang¹ jāt⁶ gåa³? 你幾月生日㗎？
      něi⁵ bīn¹ gǒ³ jyut⁶ sāang¹ jāt⁶ gåa³? 你邊個月生日㗎？
      (Which month is your birthday?)

3. Days of the month:

When referring to a day in a month, either "**hǒu⁶** 號 *(number)*" or "**jāt⁶** 日 *(day)*" is used as an indicator, and placed after the appropriate number (date: 1-31). "**hǒu⁶** 號" is more often used in the spoken language than "**jāt⁶** 日".

$$1 - 31 \; + \; \text{hǒu⁶ 號 / jāt⁶ 日}$$

jāt¹ hǒu⁶	一號	*1ˢᵗ day of the month*
jī⁶ hǒu⁶	二號	*2ⁿᵈ day of the month*
sāam¹ hǒu⁶	三號	*3ʳᵈ day of the month*
jī⁶ sǎp⁶ gáu² hǒu⁶	二十九號	*29ᵗʰ day of the month*
sāam¹ sǎp⁶ hǒu⁶	三十號	*30ᵗʰ day of the month*
sāam¹ sǎp⁶ jāt¹ hǒu⁶	三十一號	*31ˢᵗ day of the month*

To ask for the date:

E.g. 1) gām¹ jāt⁶ hǎi⁶ géi² dō¹ hǒu⁶ åa³? 今日係幾多號呀？
      gām¹ jāt⁶ hǎi⁶ géi² hǒu⁶ åa³? 今日係幾號呀？
      (What day of the month is it today?)

   2) něi⁵ géi² hǒu⁶ sāang¹ jāt⁶ gåa³? 你幾號生日㗎？
      něi⁵ bīn¹ jāt⁶ sāang¹ jāt⁶ gåa³? 你邊日生日㗎？
      (Which day of the month is your birthday?)

4. Days of the week:

In Chinese, a week begins on Monday and ends on Sunday. The days of the week from Monday to Saturday are expressed by "**sīng¹ kèi⁴** 星期" *(week)* or "**lǎi⁵ båai³** 禮拜" *(week; religious service)* followed by the numbers one to six. Sunday is suffixed with the word "**jāt⁶** 日" *(day; sun)*. Be careful of the similar pronunciations of Sunday and Monday in Cantonese which are distinguished by only a tone difference.

sīng¹ kèi⁴ 星期 + 1 ~ 6					
lǎi⁵ bǎai³ 禮拜 + 1 ~ 6					

sīng¹ kèi⁴ jāt¹	星期一	lǎi⁵ bǎai³ jāt¹	禮拜一	*Monday*
sīng¹ kèi⁴ jī̅⁶	星期二	lǎi⁵ bǎai³ jī̅⁶	禮拜二	*Tuesday*
sīng¹ kèi⁴ sāam¹	星期三	lǎi⁵ bǎai³ sāam¹	禮拜三	*Wednesday*
sīng¹ kèi⁴ sêi³	星期四	lǎi⁵ bǎai³ sêi³	禮拜四	*Thursday*
sīng¹ kèi⁴ nǧ⁵	星期五	lǎi⁵ bǎai³ nǧ⁵	禮拜五	*Friday*
sīng¹ kèi⁴ lūk⁶	星期六	lǎi⁵ bǎai³ lūk⁶	禮拜六	*Saturday*
sīng¹ kèi⁴ jāt⁶	星期日	lǎi⁵ bǎai³ jāt⁶	禮拜日	*Sunday*

To ask for the day of the week:

E.g. 1) gām¹ jāt⁶ hāi⁶ sīng¹ kèi⁴ <u>géi²</u> åa³? 今日係星期幾呀？
gām¹ jāt⁶ hāi⁶ lǎi⁵ bǎai³ <u>géi²</u> åa³? 今日係禮拜幾呀？
(Which day of the week is it today?)

2) něi⁵ <u>bīn¹ gồ³</u> sīng¹ kèi⁴ fồng³ gåa³ åa³? 你邊個星期放假呀？
něi⁵ <u>bīn¹ gồ³</u> lǎi⁵ bǎai³ fồng³ gåa³ åa³? 你邊個禮拜放假呀？
(Which week are you on holiday?)

5. Word order of date indicators:

In Cantonese, the order of dates is the reverse of the English format, beginning with the year and ending with the day. The specification of a date follows the general principle: **the larger unit comes before the smaller unit.**

nìn⁴ –	jyut⁶ –	hồu⁶ / jāt⁶ –	sīng¹ kèi⁴ / lǎi⁵ bǎai³
year	month	date	day of the week

For example: *Friday, 31ˢᵗ October 2008*

jī̅⁶ lìng⁴ lìng⁴ bǎat³ **nìn⁴** sāp⁶ **jyut⁶** sāam¹ sāp⁶ jāt¹ hồu⁶ **sīng¹ kèi⁴** nǧ⁵
二 〇 〇 八 年 十 月 三 十 一 號 星 期 五

 **PRACTICE**   Say the following dates in Cantonese.

16ᵗʰ January
25ᵗʰ December
Sunday, 1ˢᵗ April

Monday, 9ᵗʰ June
Wednesday, 8ᵗʰ March, 2006
Saturday, 26ᵗʰ August, 2101

6. How to ask for specific dates:

1)	gām¹ nìn⁴ hāi⁶ géi² (dō¹) nìn⁴ åa³? 今　年／係／　幾　（多）年／　呀？ this year/　　is/　　what year/　　PT = *What year is it now?*
2)	jì⁴ gāa¹ hāi⁶ géi² (dō¹) jyut⁶ åa³? 而　家／係／　幾　（多）月／　呀？ now/　　is/　　what month/　　PT = *What month is this?*
3)	gām¹ jāt⁶ hāi⁶ géi² (dō¹) hōu⁶ åa³? 今　日／係／　幾　（多）號／　呀？ today/　　is/　　what number/　　PT = *What day of the month is it today?*
4)	gām¹ jāt⁶ hāi⁶ sīng¹ kèi⁴ géi² åa³? 今　日／係／　星　期／　幾／　呀？ today/　　is/　　week/　how many/PT = *What day of the week is it today?*
5)	gām¹ jāt⁶ hāi⁶ géi² jyut⁶ géi² hōu⁶ åa³? 今　日／係／　幾　月／　幾　號／　呀？ today/　　is/ what month/　what number/ PT = *What is today's date?*
6)	gām¹ jāt⁶ hāi⁶ géi² jyut⁶ géi² hōu⁶ sīng¹ kèi⁴ géi² åa³? 今　日／係／　幾　月／　幾　號／　星　期　幾／　呀？ today/　　is/ what month/ what number/ what day of the week/ PT = *What is the day and date today?*

 PRACTICE

Use the calendar of this year to ask and answer the following questions in Cantonese.

1. What day of the month is it today?

2. What day of the week is it today?

3. What is today's date?

4. What is the date of *next* (hāa⁶ jāt¹ gỏ³ 下一個) Sunday?

5. What day of the week is your birthday this year?

6. What day of the week is *Christmas* (sìng³ dåan³ zit³ 聖誕節) this year?

7. What day of the week is next *New Year* (sān¹ nìn⁴ 新年)?

8. What year is it *next year* (cēot¹ nìn⁴ 出年)?

6. Clock Time

The pace in Hong Kong is fast and everybody seems busy. Hong Kong people make the most of their time and they both work and play hard. Offices normally open at 9 a.m. and close at 5 or 5:30 p.m., but many people work late into the evening. After work, some spend their leisure time playing mahjong, sports or singing karaoke, but many go on with continuing education like learning foreign languages or musical instruments. With so many people on a busy schedule, it is useful to know how to say the time of the day in Cantonese.

1. Hour

To say the time in hours, read off the number of the hour hand and put "**dím² 點** *(dot)*" at the end. Note that a more complete way of saying the time is "**dím² zūng¹ 點鐘** *(o'clock: basic time unit)*" but the shorter version "**dím² 點**" is the one you are more likely to hear.

 $1 - 12 \ + \ $ **dím² zūng¹ 點鐘**

For example:

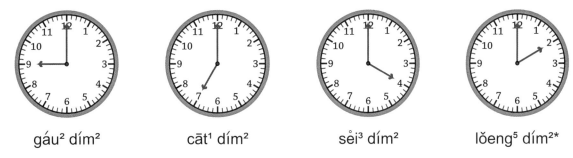

gáu² dím²   cāt¹ dím²   sẻi³ dím²   lŏeng⁵ dím²*

* Note that for "two o'clock", the numeral is always "**lŏeng⁵ 兩**" and **never** "jī⁶ 二".

PRACTICE

Write and read out the following times in Cantonese, e.g. 10 o'clock = sȁp⁶ dím².

2. Exact minute

The Cantonese for minute is "**fān¹** 分". The format is straightforward: after saying the hour, say the number of minutes followed by "**fān¹** 分":

$$1 - 12 \text{ dím}^2 \text{ 點} \quad : \quad 0 - 59 \text{ fān}^1 \text{ 分}$$

E.g.

sōeng⁶ nǧ⁵ (/sōeng⁶ zǎu³) sǎp⁶ dím² lìng⁴ gáu² fān¹

Here are some more examples of minute times:

:01 lìng⁴ jāt¹ fān¹	:02 lìng⁴ jī⁶* fān¹	:03 lìng⁴ sāam¹ fān¹
:04 lìng⁴ sẻi³ fān¹	:05 lìng⁴ nǧ⁵ fān¹	:06 lìng⁴ lūk⁶ fān¹
:07 lìng⁴ cāt¹ fān¹	:08 lìng⁴ bāat³ fān¹	:09 lìng⁴ gáu² fān¹
:10 sǎp⁶ fān¹	:20 jī⁶ sǎp⁶ fān¹	:30 sāam¹ sǎp⁶ fān¹
:40 sẻi³ sǎp⁶ fān¹	:50 nǧ⁵ sǎp⁶ fān¹	:59 nǧ⁵ sǎp⁶ gáu² fān¹

* Note that for "𝒴 o'clock and **two** minutes," it is always "𝒴 dím² lìng⁴ jī⁶ fān¹", and never "𝒴 dím² lìng⁴ lǒeng⁵ fān¹".

 PRACTICE

Read out the following times in hours and exact minutes in Cantonese.

E.g. 10:15 = sǎp⁶ dím² sǎp⁶ nǧ⁵ fān¹

3. Hour & 5-minute unit

A convenient and commonly used way to say the time is to use the 5-minute units on a clock face. After saying the hour, just follow it with numbers 1-5 or 7-11 where the minute hand is pointing to. The exception is 6 and 12. 12 is not used since it is o'clock time. When the minute hand strikes 6, the word "bǔn³ 半", which means "half" of the o'clock, is used.

$$1 - 12 \text{ dím}^2 \text{ 點} : \begin{cases} 1 - 5 \\ \cancel{6} \text{ bǔn}^3 \text{ 半} \\ 7 - 11 \end{cases}$$

E.g.

ng̊⁵ dím² sẻi³   båat³ dím² jāt¹   såp⁶ jāt¹ dím² jī⁶   cāt¹ dím² bǔn³

 Read out the following times in hours and 5-minute units in Cantonese.

E.g. 8:15 = båat³ dím² sāam¹

2:40 = _____   7:30 = _____   5:55 = _____

11:00 = _____   1:05 = _____   3:37 = _____

4. Clock time & the time of the day

Sometimes people want to be more specific about the time of the day, so they put a specific term "sõeng⁶ zẙu³ 上晝 (for A.M.)" or "hãa⁶ zẙu³ 下晝 (for P.M.)" before (not after) the clock time. Here are some more examples:

A.M.	sõeng⁶ zẙu³ 上晝 / sõeng⁶ ng̊⁵ 上午	(1-11 + dím² 點)
Noon	zūng¹ ng̊⁵ 中午	(12 + dím² 點)
P.M.	hãa⁶ zẙu³ 下晝 / hãa⁶ ng̊⁵ 下午	(1-11 + dím² 點)
Midnight	ng̊⁵ jẽ⁶ 午夜	(12 + dím² 點)

zīu¹ tàu⁴ zóu²
朝　頭　早
(in the morning)

åan³ zẙu³
晏　晝
(in the afternoon)

jẽ⁶ mǎan⁵
夜　晚
(in the evening)

 **PRACTICE**   Read out the time of the day in Cantonese:

2:15 in the afternoon = åan³ zåu³ lŏeng⁵ dím² sāam¹

6:12 in the morning = _____

8:30 in the evening = _____

4:00 in the afternoon = _____

10:20 a.m. = _____

9:45 p.m. = _____

5. How to ask and tell the current time

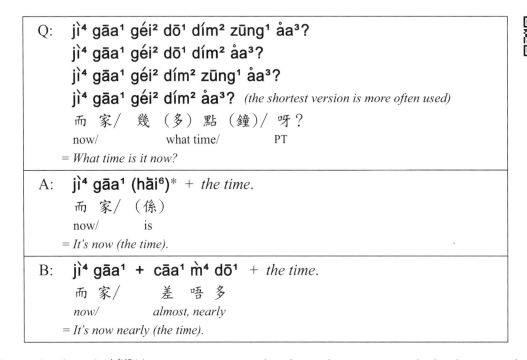

Q:	jì⁴ gāa¹ géi² dō¹ dím² zūng¹ åa³?
	jì⁴ gāa¹ géi² dō¹ dím² åa³?
	jì⁴ gāa¹ géi² dím² zūng¹ åa³?
	jì⁴ gāa¹ géi² dím² åa³? *(the shortest version is more often used)*
	而 家／　幾 （多）點 （鐘）／ 呀？
	now/　　　what time/　　PT
	= *What time is it now?*
A:	jì⁴ gāa¹ (hǎi⁶)* + *the time.*
	而 家／ （係）
	now/　　　is
	= *It's now (the time).*
B:	jì⁴ gāa¹ + cāa¹ m̀⁴ dō¹ + *the time.*
	而 家／　差 唔 多
	now/　　　almost, nearly
	= *It's now nearly (the time).*

* Note that the verb "hǎi⁶" is unnecessary except when the speaker wants to emphasize the current time.

 **PRACTICE**   Practice with your teacher or classmates with the following times.

åan³ zåu³ sāam¹ dím² såp⁶ = 3:50 p.m. _____

zīu¹ tàu⁴ zóu² gáu² dím² sāam¹ såp⁶ sāam¹ fān¹ = _____

jĕ⁶ mǎan⁵ båat³ dím² bǔn³ = _____

hāa⁶ zåu³ ńǧ⁵ dím² såp⁶ jāt¹ = _____

sōeng⁶ zåu³ sėi³ dím² cāt¹ = _____

jĕ⁶ mǎan⁵ såp⁶ dím² jī⁶ såp⁶ båat³ fān¹ = _____

zūng¹ ńǧ⁵ såp⁶ jī⁶ dím² bǔn³ = _____

ńǧ⁵ jĕ⁶ såp⁶ jī⁶ dím² lìng⁴ ńǧ⁵ fān¹ = _____

7. Counting Things with Measure Words

In Cantonese, when nouns are counted or its quantity is made specific, a **Measure Word** must be included. Different types of nouns usually have different measure words. This concept may be new to some foreigners and can present some difficulties to them at the beginning, but it is wise to spend some time to grasp this fundamental concept of Chinese early on.

Note: In English, some of the nouns have measure words similar to Cantonese, e.g. a <u>bunch</u> of grapes, a <u>piece</u> of string, a <u>sheet</u> of paper, a <u>bowl</u> of sugar, a <u>cup</u> of tea, etc.

1. Measure words/Classifiers

Measure words are words that express a unit of things or actions. They serve to sort nouns into **semantic classes of objects** (indicating meanings), and are also known as '**classifiers**'.

Measure words are based on distinctive features of shape, size, nature or function. They may also demonstrate some kind of properties that accounts for its use with certain types of objects. Every noun in Cantonese has its own specific measure word, which should be learned together with the word. Sometimes there are two or more alternative measure words for the same noun.

Here are some common measure words:

1)	go̊³	個	*for persons; round objects; abstract things, such as questions or ideas*
2)	gåa³	架	*for vehicles; machines, e.g. cars, airplanes.*
3)	gīn⁶	件	*for upper body items of clothing, e.g. shirts, coats.*
4)	gāan¹	間	*for buildings; houses; rooms*
5)	bún²	本	*for books; magazines*
6)	ze̊k³	隻	*for most animals; ships; one of a pair*
7)	de̊oi³	對	*for a pair of objects, such as shoes, hands, chopsticks*
8)	tìu⁴	條	*for streets or things that are long and narrow*
9)	zōeng¹	張	*for paper; cards; objects with a flat surface, such as chairs, tables, etc.*
10)	zī¹	枝	*for objects that are cylindrical, rigid, long and thin, e.g. pens, cigarettes*
11)	būi¹	杯	*literally a "cup", for the quantity of something that a cup will hold*
12)	wún²	碗	*literally a "bowl", for the quantity of something that a bowl will hold*
13)	dīp⁶	碟	*literally a "plate", for the quantity of something that a plate will hold*
14)	gůn³	罐	*literally a "can", for the quantity of something that a can will hold*
15)	fān⁶	份	*for objects in a set, such as documents, newspapers; a sandwich or a job*

2. Number of objects

A measure word (MW) helps describe the quantity and quality (such as distinctive features of shape, natural kind and function) of a noun in counting. A number alone usually cannot function enough as an attributive and must be combined with a measure word inserted between the cardinal number and the noun it modifies.

> **Numeral + <u>Measure Word</u> + Noun/Nominal phrase**

For example:

jāt¹ gǒ³ jàn⁴	一個人	*one person*
jāt¹ gǎa³ cē¹	一架車	*one vehicle*
jāt¹ gǐn⁶ sāam¹	一件衫	*one item (piece) of clothing*
jāt¹ gāan¹ fóng²	一間房	*one room*
jāt¹ bún² sȳu¹	一本書	*one book*
jāt¹ zěk³ gáu²	一隻狗	*one dog*
jāt¹ děoi³ hàai⁴	一對鞋	*one pair of shoes*
jāt¹ tìu⁴ fǔ³	一條褲	*one (pair of) trousers*
jāt¹ zōeng¹ zí²	一張紙	*one sheet of paper*
jāt¹ zī¹ bāt¹	一枝筆	*one pen*
jāt¹ būi¹ záu²	一杯酒	*one glass (cup) of wine*
jāt¹ wún² fāan⁶	一碗飯	*one bowl of rice*
jāt¹ dǐp⁶ cǒi³	一碟菜	*one plate of vegetables*
jāt¹ gǔn³ hó² lōk⁶	一罐可樂	*one can of coke*
jāt¹ fàn⁶ sāam¹ màn⁴ zī⁶	一份三文治	*one sandwich*

The measure word "**gǒ³** 個" is the commonest and most neutral in Cantonese. It is used with all noun words denoting people as well as individual items which do not call for a specific measure word. Thus abstract nouns, which refer to non-concrete entities lacking physical features, generally take "**gǒ³** 個" as their measure word. If there is any doubt about what specific measure word to use for a noun, it is usually safe to use "**gǒ³** 個" (you may be corrected if you are obviously wrong).

3. Counting things in twos

Both "jī⁶ 二" and "lǒeng⁵ 兩" mean "*two*". When the number "two" is used before a measure word (or before a noun), "lǒeng⁵ 兩" is normally used instead of "jī⁶ 二", as in "lǒeng⁵ gǒ³ jàn⁴ 兩個人" *(two persons)*. But with numbers larger than ten (12, 20, 22, 32 etc.), "jī⁶ 二" is used always, as in "sāp⁶ jī⁶ gǒ³ jàn⁴ 十二個人" *(twelve persons)*.

Try to figure out what measure words should be used for the following items and count them with the given numbers.

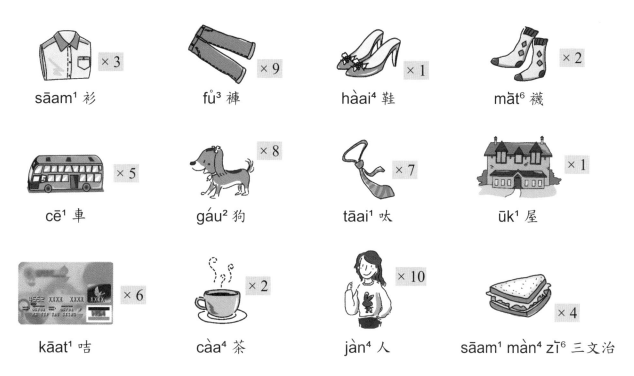

sāam¹ 衫 × 3

fu³ 褲 × 9

hàai⁴ 鞋 × 1

māt⁶ 襪 × 2

cē¹ 車 × 5

gáu² 狗 × 8

tāai¹ 呔 × 7

ūk¹ 屋 × 1

kāat¹ 咭 × 6

càa⁴ 茶 × 2

jàn⁴ 人 × 10

sāam¹ màn⁴ zī⁶ 三文治 × 4

UNIT THREE

Arrival

Lesson 1. Greeting at the airport

Lesson 2. You are here

Lesson 3. Accommodation & check-in

Lesson 4. Money exchange

Main Characters in the Conversation

Zing-Zing Wong, 王晶晶 ,
Hong Kong people,
a university student, the one
assigned to look after *Amy* in HK

Amy Smith, American,
an exchange student from the U.S.,
a newcomer to HK,
a friend of *Siu-Ping Chan*

Tony Lee,
British of Chinese descent,
a lawyer, a friend of *Siu-Ping Chan*

Siu-Ping Chan, 陳小平 ,
Chinese, *Amy*'s friend,
a doctor of Chinese medicine

Other characters:

a taxi driver,
a receptionist,
a cashier,
a salesperson,
a passer-by

wūi⁶ wáa² jàn⁴ mát² 會話人物

Zing-Zing Wong, 王晶晶 ,
Wòng⁴ Zīng¹ Zīng¹,
Hōeng¹ Góng² jàn⁴,
dāai⁶ hŏk⁶ sāang¹,
fū⁶ zăak³ zĭp³ dŏi⁶ *Amy*

Amy Smith,
Měi⁵ Gwŏk³ jàn⁴,
Měi⁵ Gwŏk³ sān¹ lèi⁴ gĕ³
gāau¹ wŭn⁶ hŏk⁶ sāang¹,
Síu² Pìng⁴ gĕ³ pàng⁴ jău⁵

Tony Lee,
Wàa⁴ jēoi⁶ Jīng¹ Gwŏk³ jàn⁴,
lēot⁶ sī¹,
Síu² Pìng⁴ gĕ³ pàng⁴ jău⁵

Siu-Ping Chan, 陳小平 ,
Càn⁴ Síu² Pìng⁴,
Zūng¹ Gwŏk³ jàn⁴, zūng¹ jī¹,
Amy gĕ³ pàng⁴ jău⁵

kèi⁴ tāa¹ jàn⁴ mát² 其他人物

dīk¹ sí² sī¹ gēi¹ 的士司機
zĭp³ dŏi⁶ jỳun⁴ 接待員
sāu¹ ngán² jỳun⁴ 收銀員
sāu⁶ fŏ³ jỳun⁴ 售貨員
lōu⁶ jàn⁴ 路人

Lesson 1 | Greeting at the airport

Learning Objectives

1. To say "Hello" & "Welcome"
2. To indicate possession with "gě³"
3. To address people with title
4. To introduce oneself or someone using the verb "hǎi⁶"
5. To give one's name using the verb "gĭu³"
6. To suggest how you prefer to be addressed

Dialogue

Amy, an exchange student from the U.S., greets Zing-Zing, her "buddy" ① *from the University of Hong Kong, at the airport.*

Amy: nĕi⁵ hóu², ngŏ⁵ hǎi⁶ *Amy Smith.*
您　好，我　係　*Amy Smith*。
(Hello, I am Amy Smith.)

Zing-Zing: nĕi⁵ hóu². ngŏ⁵ hǎi⁶ Hōeng¹ Góng² Dǎai⁶ Hŏk⁶ gě³ hŏk⁶ sāang¹.
您　好。我　係　香　港　大　學　嘅　學　生。
(Hello! I am a student of the University of Hong Kong.)

ngŏ⁵ gĭu³ Wòng⁴ Zīng¹ Zīng¹.
我　叫　王　晶　晶。
(My name is Zing-Zing Wong.)

fūn¹ jìng⁴ nĕi⁵, *Smith* síu² zé².
歡　迎　您，*Smith* 小　姐。
(Welcome, Miss Smith.)

Amy: Wòng⁴ síu² zé², gĭu³ ngŏ⁵ *Amy* lāa¹.
王　小　姐，叫　我　*Amy* 啦。
(Miss Wong, just call me "Amy"!)

Zing-Zing: gám², nĕi⁵ gĭu³ ngŏ⁵ Zīng¹ Zīng¹ lāa¹!
噉，你　叫　我　晶　晶　啦！
(Well, then, you can call me "Zing-Zing"!)

---

① The one assigned to look after someone new to the place.

1.	ngǒ⁵ 我	Pn:	I; me *[Note that there is no case distinction for personal pronouns in Cantonese.]*
2.	něi⁵ 你／您	Pn:	you (singular) *[Note that some people in Hong Kong will say "lěi⁵" instead of "něi⁵".]*
3.	kěoi⁵ 佢	Pn:	he; him; she; her; it *[There is no gender distinction between he, she or it in Cantonese.]* *[Note that some HK people will say "hěoi⁵" instead of "kěoi⁵"]*
4.	hóu² 好	Adj:	good; well; fine; okay
5.	něi⁵ hóu² 你好	SE:	(lit. you good) Hello, Hi, Good day. *[Note that no verb-to-be is needed in a general adjectival predicate sentence.]*
6.	hǎi⁶ 係 (*N₁* + hǎi⁶ + *N₂*)	V:	be (is, am, are; was, were) *[used for all cases, numbers, tenses, etc.]* *[Note that there is no conjugation for verbs in Cantonese.]*
7.	Hōeng¹ Góng² Dǎai⁶ Hōk⁶ 香港大學	PN:	The University of Hong Kong ② ("Góng² Dǎai⁶" is used for the abbreviation.)
8.	gě³ 嘅 (*N₁* + gě³ + *N₂*)	Part:	*[a structural particle used to indicate possession, similar to 's in English]*
9.	hōk⁶ sāang¹ 學生	N:	student(s)
10.	giu³ 叫 (*N₁* + giu³ + *N₂*)	V:	to be called, named; known as; to call (also "giu³ zōu⁶ 叫做")
11.	Wòng⁴ Zīng¹ Zīng¹ 王晶晶	PN:	*[a female Chinese name]* "Wòng⁴" is the surname and "Zīng¹ Zīng¹" is the given name *[Note that Chinese surnames always come before Chinese given names.]*
12.	fūn¹ jìng⁴ 歡迎	V:	welcome *[can be used repeatedly for showing courtesy to customers or visitors]*
13.	síu² zé² 小姐	N:	Miss; young lady
14.	lāa¹ 啦 (*Sentence* + lāa¹)	Part:	*[a modal particle used at the end of a sentence with the sense of request, suggestion or invitation.]*
15.	gám² 噉	Intj:	so, well… *[precedes a sentence and serves to fill a pause or transition]*

---

② Names of other universities in Hong Kong can be found in the Glossaries.

1. **To say "Hello" & "Welcome"**

   a) **To greet someone**

   e.g. <u>něi⁵ hóu².</u>

   (Hello. Good day!)

Personal pronoun + hóu².

   Personal pronouns:

ngǒ⁵	*I; me*
něi⁵	*you*
kěoi⁵	*she; her*
	he; him

> *Your greetings:*
>
> *1.* **něi⁵ hóu².**
>   *(Hello. Good day!)*
>
> *2.* **něi⁵ děi⁶ hóu².**
>   *(Hello everybody.)*

   b) **To welcome someone**

   e.g. <u>fūn¹ jìng⁴ něi⁵.</u>

   (Welcome (you) !)

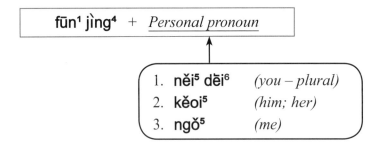

fūn¹ jìng⁴ + *Personal pronoun*

1. **něi⁵ děi⁶**   *(you – plural)*
2. **kěoi⁵**   *(him; her)*
3. **ngǒ⁵**   *(me)*

2. **To indicate possession with "gě³"**

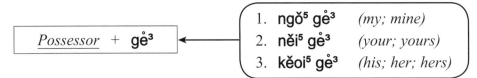

Possessor + gě³

1. **ngǒ⁵ gě³**   *(my; mine)*
2. **něi⁵ gě³**   *(your; yours)*
3. **kěoi⁵ gě³**   *(his; her; hers)*

   e.g. **Hōeng¹ Góng² Dāai⁶ Hǒk⁶ <u>gě³</u> hǒk⁶ sāang¹**

   (Student <u>of</u> the University of Hong Kong)

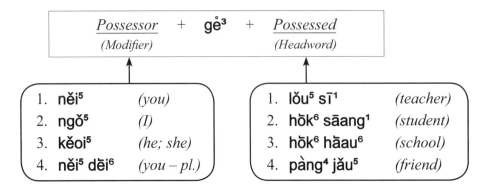

Possessor + gě³ + *Possessed*
(Modifier) *(Headword)*

1. **něi⁵** *(you)*	1. **lǒu⁵ sī¹** *(teacher)*
2. **ngǒ⁵** *(I)*	2. **hǒk⁶ sāang¹** *(student)*
3. **kěoi⁵** *(he; she)*	3. **hǒk⁶ hāau⁶** *(school)*
4. **něi⁵ děi⁶** *(you – pl.)*	4. **pàng⁴ jǎu⁵** *(friend)*

3. To address people with title

e.g. **Wòng⁴ síu² zé²**

(Miss Wong)

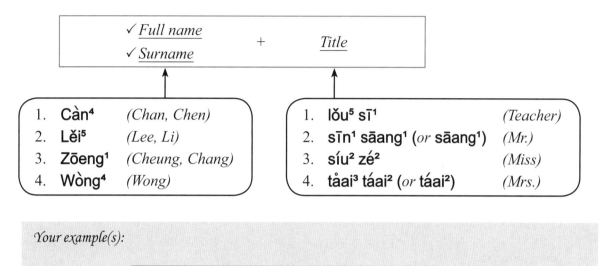

| ✓ Full name | + | Title |
| ✓ Surname | | |

1. Càn⁴	(Chan, Chen)
2. Lěi⁵	(Lee, Li)
3. Zōeng¹	(Cheung, Chang)
4. Wòng⁴	(Wong)

1. lǒu⁵ sī¹	(Teacher)
2. sīn¹ sāang¹ (or sāang¹)	(Mr.)
3. síu² zé²	(Miss)
4. tẚai³ táai² (or táai²)	(Mrs.)

Your example(s):

_____

4. To introduce oneself or someone using the verb "hȁi⁶"

| Noun ₁ | hȁi⁶ (to be) | Noun ₂ |

e.g. 1. **ngǒ⁵ hȁi⁶ *Amy Smith*.**

(I am Amy Smith.)

e.g. 2. **ngǒ⁵ hȁi⁶ Hōeng¹ Góng² Dȁai⁶ Hǒk⁶ gẻ³ hǒk⁶ sāang¹.**

(I am a student of the University of Hong Kong.)

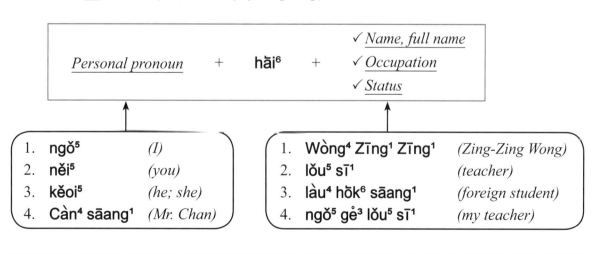

Personal pronoun	+	hȁi⁶	+	✓ Name, full name
				✓ Occupation
				✓ Status

1. ngǒ⁵	(I)
2. něi⁵	(you)
3. kěoi⁵	(he; she)
4. Càn⁴ sāang¹	(Mr. Chan)

1. Wòng⁴ Zīng¹ Zīng¹	(Zing-Zing Wong)
2. lǒu⁵ sī¹	(teacher)
3. làu⁴ hǒk⁶ sāang¹	(foreign student)
4. ngǒ⁵ gẻ³ lǒu⁵ sī¹	(my teacher)

Your example(s):

ngǒ⁵ hȁi⁶ _____ *(full name).*

_____ **hȁi⁶ ngǒ⁵ gẻ³ lǒu⁵ sī¹.**

(your teacher's name)

5. **To give one's name using "g̊iu³"**

e.g.   ngǒ⁵ g̊iu³ Wòng⁴ Zīng¹ Zīng¹.

   (I'm <u>called</u> Zing-Zing.) (My name is Zing-Zing.)

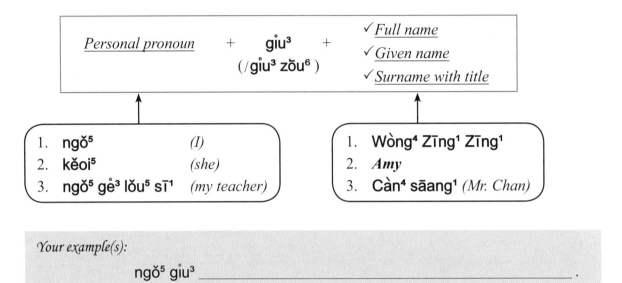

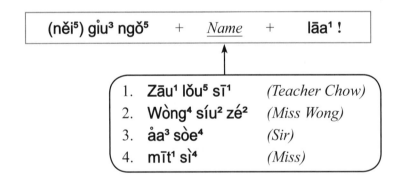

6. **To suggest how you prefer to be addressed**

e.g.   1.   Wòng⁴ síu² zé², g̊iu³ ngǒ⁵ *Amy* lāa¹!

   (Miss Wong, just <u>call me</u> "Amy"!)

e.g.   2.   něi⁵ g̊iu³ ngǒ⁵ Zīng¹ Zīng¹ lāa¹!

   (You can <u>call me</u> "Zing-Zing"!)

(něi⁵) g̊iu³ ngǒ⁵   +   *Name*   +   lāa¹ !

1.   Zāu¹ lǒu⁵ sī¹   *(Teacher Chow)*
2.   Wòng⁴ síu² zé²   *(Miss Wong)*
3.   åa³ sòe⁴   *(Sir)*
4.   mīt¹ sì⁴   *(Miss)*

Your example(s):

   (něi⁵) g̊iu³ ngǒ⁵ _____ lāa¹!

   (a name you prefer to be addressed)

Hong Kong means many different things to many people. To help you make the most of your trip or stay, you can check out the following websites to meet your needs: www.hongkongairport.com; www.hkta.org

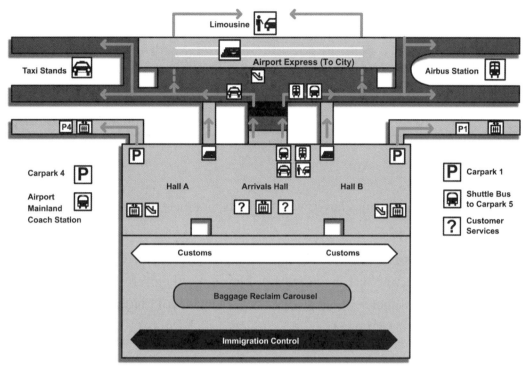

Transportation modes at Arrivals Hall (Level 5) at Terminal 1

FYI – 2. Naming in Chinese

1) Chinese family name first

A personal name in Chinese consists of two parts, the surname "sing³ 姓" and the given name "mìng⁴ 名". The surname comes first, followed by the given name.

Family name *(1-2 syllables)*	Given name *(usually 1-2 syllables, any meaningful combination of Chinese characters)*
Dāng⁶ 鄧	Síu² Pìng⁴ 小平 *(Deng Xiaoping③)*
Lěi⁵ 李	Síu² Lùng⁴ 小龍 *(Bruce Lee④)*

---

③ Deng Xiaoping (1904-1997)
Deng Xiaoping (Chinese: 鄧小平) was the leader of the People's Republic of China (PRC) from 1977 to increase the PRC's economic ties with the West while keeping distant relations with the Soviet Union. Under former leader Mao Zedong (1893-1976), the PRC had operated in political and economic isolation; under Deng, the communist nation began to participate in international markets. (Source: Encyclopedia.com, 2020)

④ Bruce Lee (1940-1973)
Lee Jun-fan (Chinese: 李振藩), known professionally as Bruce Lee (Chinese: 李小龍), was a Hong Kong American actor, director, martial artist, martial arts instructor, and philosopher. Lee is considered by commentators, critics, media, and other martial artists to be the most influential martial artist of all time and a pop culture icon of the 20th century, who bridged the gap between the East and the West. He is often credited with helping to change the way Asians were presented in American films. (Source: wikipedia, the free encyclopedia, 2020)

2) One-syllable & two-syllable family names

Most Chinese surnames have one character (but there are also some surnames with two characters or more). Examples:

1.	Càn⁴ 陳	Chan, Chen	6.	Zāu¹ 周 / 鄒	Chau, Chow
2.	Lěi⁵ 李	Lee, Li	7.	Ǹg⁴ 吳	Ng, Wu
3.	Zōeng¹ 張	Cheung, Chang	8.	Mǎa⁵ 馬	Ma
4.	Wòng⁴ 黃 / 王	Wong	9.	Sī¹ Tòu⁴ 司徒	Szeto
5.	Hò⁴ 何	Ho	10.	Āu¹ Jòeng⁴ 歐陽	Au Yeung

3) Given name

a) Most Chinese given names have two characters, but there are also some given names with a single character or more.

b) Some Chinese like to use English names in addition to their Chinese names nowadays. They can be given at birth by parents or chosen by themselves when older. e.g. Carrie Lam Cheng Yuet-ngor⑤ (林鄭月娥 Làm⁴ Zěng⁶ Jyut⁶ Ngò⁴, 1957 ~) *(A Hong Kong politician serving as the 4ᵗʰ Chief Executive of Hong Kong since 2017)*

4) English translation of Chinese names

a) In mainland China, generally people use Hanyu Pinyin to represent their name, e.g. Dang Xiaoping (鄧小平 Dāng⁶ Síu² Pìng⁴).

b) In Hong Kong, a non-standard transcription of Cantonese is used and is now widely accepted, e.g. the first Chief Executive of HKSAR, Mr. Tung Chee Hwa (董建華 Dúng² Gin³ Wàa⁴).

c) Overseas Chinese also use a non-standard transcription of Chinese, sometimes based on their resident country's language or dialect. That's why sometimes you will see some Chinese people who have the same surname in Chinese character, but different in English transcription. Examples:

Surname	English
Lěi⁵ 李	Lee, Lei, Li
Zāu¹ 周 / 鄒	Chau, Chou, Chow, Zhou
Cèoi⁴ 徐	Chui, Tsui, Zee, Xu

---

⑤ This is a Hong Kong name; Cheng is the maiden name and Lam is the married name. Some married Chinese women like to add husband's surname before the maiden name.

1. **Translate the following into Cantonese.** $(10 \times 8\% = 80\%)$

   1) student   _____

   2) The University of Hong Kong (HKU) _____

   3) student of HKU   _____

   4) I am a student of HKU.   _____

   5) good   _____

   6) Hello   _____

   7) to be called (+ *name*)   _____

   8) I'm called Amy. (My name is Amy) _____

   9) Welcome!   _____

   10) Call me Amy!   _____

2. **Complete the following dialogue.** $(4 \times 5\% = 20\%)$

   Teacher: ngǒi⁵ hāi⁶ Gwóng² Dūng¹ Wáa² fǒ³ cìng⁴ *(course)* gě³ lǒu⁵ sī¹.

   You: ngǒi⁵ hāi⁶ Gwóng² Dūng¹ Wáa² fǒ³ cìng⁴ gě³ _____

   Teacher: něi⁵ hóu². ngǒi⁵ hāi⁶ Zāu¹ lǒu⁵ sī¹.

   You: _____ , něi⁵ hóu².

        ngǒi⁵ hāi⁶ _____ *(full name)*.

   Teacher: fūn¹ jìng⁴ něi⁵. něi⁵ giu³ ngǒi⁵ "Zāu¹ sòe⁴" lāa¹!

   You: Zāu¹ sòe⁴. gám², něi⁵ giu³ ngǒi⁵ _____ lāa¹!

歡 迎 光 臨
fūn¹ jìng⁴ gwōng¹ làm⁴
(*Welcome for coming.*)

Learning Objectives

1. To form plural personal pronouns with "**děi⁶**"
2. To indicate "here", "there" and "where"
3. To ask and tell where one goes using the verb "**hěoi³**"
4. To ask and tell whereabouts using the verb "**hái²**"

Dialogue

Zing-Zing takes Amy to the University by taxi.

Driver: hěoi³ bīn¹ dōu⁶ åa³?
去　邊　度　呀？
(Where do you want to go?) ①

Zing-Zing: m̀⁴ gōi¹, hěoi³ Hōeng¹ Góng² Dāai⁶ Hōk⁶.
(to driver) 唔　該，去　香　港　大　學。
(The University of Hong Kong, please.)

Amy: Zīng¹ Zīng¹, Hōeng¹ Góng² Dāai⁶ Hōk⁶ hái² bīn¹ dōu⁶ åa³?
(to ZZ) 晶　晶，香　港　大　學　喺　邊　度　呀？
(Zing-Zing, where is the University of Hong Kong?)

Zing-Zing: hái² Hōeng¹ Góng² Dóu².
(pointing at 喺　香　港　島。
the map) *(It's in Hong Kong Island.)*

nī¹ dōu⁶ hāi⁶ Hōeng¹ Góng² Gwŏk³ Zåi³ Gēi¹ Còeng⁴,
呢　度　係　香　港　國　際　機　場，
(Here is the Hong Kong International Airport.)

nī¹ dōu⁶ hāi⁶ Gáu² Lùng⁴, nī¹ dōu⁶ hāi⁶ Hōeng¹ Góng² Dóu²,
呢　度　係　九　龍，呢　度　係　香　港　島，
(This is Kowloon and this is Hong Kong Island.)

gó² dōu⁶ hāi⁶ Zūng¹ Gwŏk³ dāai⁶ lūk⁶.
嗰　度　係　中　國　大　陸。
(Over there is mainland China.)

Amy: ngǒ⁵ děi⁶ jì⁴ gāa¹ hái² bīn¹ dōu⁶ åa³?
我　哋　而　家　喺　邊　度　呀？
(Where are we now?)

Zing-Zing: ngǒ⁵ děi⁶ jì⁴ gāa¹ hái² nī¹ dōu⁶.
(pointing at 我　哋　而　家　喺　呢　度。
the map) *(We are here now.)*

---

① This is the intended meaning in this situation. The literal meaning is "Where are you going?"

Map of the Hong Kong Special Administrative Region

Hōeng¹ Góng² Dāk⁶ Bīt⁶ Hàng⁴ Zǐng³ Kēoi¹ děi⁶ tòu⁴

香 港 特 別 行 政 區 地 圖

Mainland China Zūng¹ Gwǒk³ dǎai⁶ lūk⁶ 中國大陸

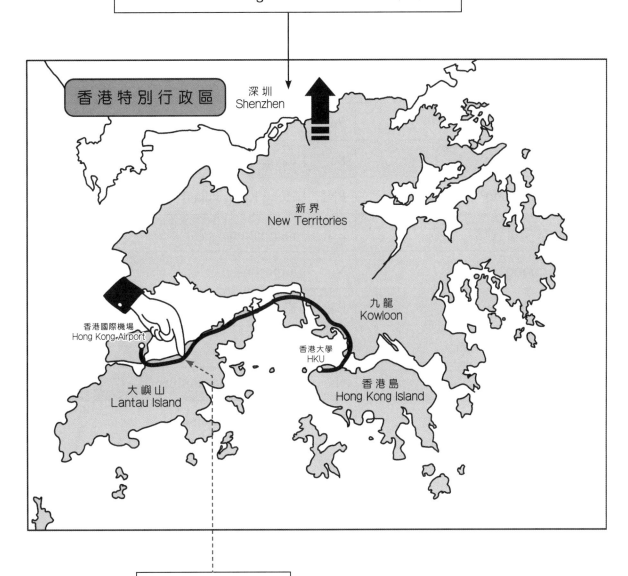

香港特別行政區

深圳
Shenzhen

新界
New Territories

九龍
Kowloon

香港國際機場
Hong Kong Airport

香港大學
HKU

大嶼山
Lantau Island

香港島
Hong Kong Island

You are here!

něi⁵ hái² nī¹ dōu⁶!
你 喺 呢 度!

1.	hẻoi³ 去 (+ *Place / Purpose*)	V:	to go
2.	bīn¹ dōu⁶ 邊度	QW:	where
3.	åa³? 呀？(*Question* + åa³?*)	Part:	*[an interrogative particle commonly used at the end of a question to express an inquiry]*
4.	m̀⁴ gōi¹ 唔該	SE:	(in L.2) please *[to request sb. to do sth.]*
5.	hái² 喺 (+ *Place*)	V:	to be at/in/on *(a place)*
6.	nī¹ dōu⁶ 呢度	Pn:	here
7.	gó² dōu⁶ 嗰度	Pn:	there; over there
8.	Hōeng¹ Góng² Dóu² 香港島	PN:	Hong Kong Island
9.	Gwók³ Zẚi³ 國際	PN:	international
10.	gēi¹ còeng⁴ 機場	N:	airport
11.	Gáu² Lùng⁴ 九龍	PN:	Kowloon
12.	Zūng¹ Gwók³ 中國	PN:	China
13.	dãai⁶ lũk⁶ 大陸	N:	mainland; the continent
14.	Zūng¹ Gwók³ dãai⁶ lũk⁶ 中國大陸	PN:	the Chinese mainland; mainland China
15.	ngǒ⁵ dēi⁶ 我哋	Pn:	we, us
16.	jì⁴ gāa¹ 而家	N:	now

1. To form plural personal pronouns

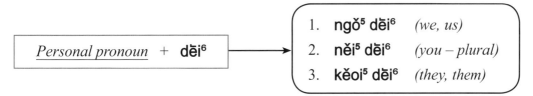

e.g. 1. <u>ngǒ⁵ dĕi⁶</u> jì⁴ gāa¹ hái² bīn¹ dõu⁶ åa³?
(Where are <u>we</u> now?)

e.g. 2. <u>nĕi⁵ dĕi⁶</u> hẻoi³ bīn¹ dõu⁶ åa³?
(Where are <u>you</u> going?)

e.g. 3. <u>kĕoi⁵ dĕi⁶</u> hăi⁶ ngǒ⁵ gẻ³ pàng⁴ jǎu⁵.
(<u>They</u> are my friends.)

2. To indicate "here", "there" & "where"

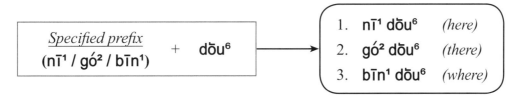

e.g. 1. <u>nī¹ dõu⁶</u> hăi⁶ Gáu² Lùng⁴.
(<u>Here</u> is Kowloon.)

e.g. 2. <u>gó² dõu⁶</u> hăi⁶ Zūng¹ Gwỏk dāai⁶ lŭk⁶.
(<u>There</u> is mainland China.)

e.g. 3. ngǒ⁵ dĕi⁶ jì⁴ gāa¹ hái² <u>bīn¹ dõu⁶</u> åa³?
(<u>Where</u> are we now?)

Your example(s):

nī¹ dõu⁶ hăi⁶ _____

gó² dõu⁶ hăi⁶ _____

ngǒ⁵ dĕi⁶ jì⁴ gāa¹ hái² bīn¹ dõu⁶ åa³?

3. **To ask and tell where one goes – Taking a taxi**

   a) **Ask where to go**

   e.g. hẻoi³ bīn¹ dõu⁶ åa³?
   (Where do you want to go?)

(něi⁵)	+	hẻoi³	+	bīn¹ dõu⁶ *(Question word)*	+	åa³?

   b) **Tell destination**

   e.g. m̀⁴ gōi¹, hẻoi³ Hōeng¹ Góng² Dāai⁶ Hŏk⁶.
   (Please go to the University of Hong Kong.)

   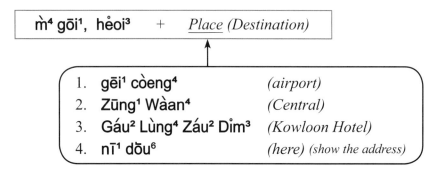

m̀⁴ gōi¹, hẻoi³	+	*Place* (Destination)

   1. gēi¹ còeng⁴   *(airport)*
   2. Zūng¹ Wàan⁴   *(Central)*
   3. Gáu² Lùng⁴ Záu² Dìm³ *(Kowloon Hotel)*
   4. nī¹ dõu⁶   *(here) (show the address)*

   Your example(s):
   m̀⁴ gōi¹, hẻoi³ _____

4. **To ask and tell whereabouts**

   a) **Ask whereabouts**

   e.g. Hōeng¹ Góng² Dāai⁶ Hŏk⁶ hái² bīn¹ dõu⁶ åa³?
   (Where is the University of Hong Kong?)

   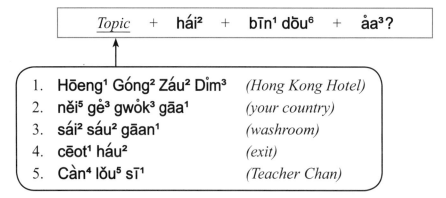

Topic	+	hái²	+	bīn¹ dõu⁶	+	åa³?

   1. Hōeng¹ Góng² Záu² Dìm³ *(Hong Kong Hotel)*
   2. něi⁵ gẻ³ gwŏk³ gāa¹   *(your country)*
   3. sái² sáu² gāan¹   *(washroom)*
   4. cēot¹ háu²   *(exit)*
   5. Càn⁴ lŏu⁵ sī¹   *(Teacher Chan)*

   Your example(s):
   _____ hái² bīn¹ dõu⁶ åa³?

b) Tell whereabouts

e.g. (Hōeng¹ Góng² Dāai⁶ Hŏk⁶) hái² Hōeng¹ Góng² Dóu².

(HKU is in Hong Kong Island.)

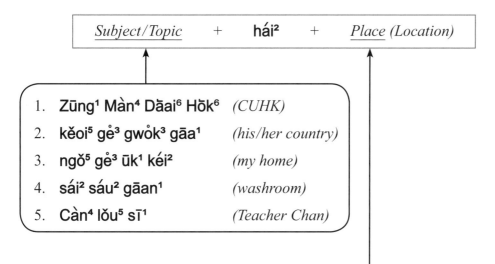

| Subject/Topic | + | **hái²** | + | Place (Location) |

1. Zūng¹ Màn⁴ Dāai⁶ Hŏk⁶ *(CUHK)*
2. kĕoi⁵ gẻ³ gwỏk³ gāa¹ *(his/her country)*
3. ngŏ⁵ gẻ³ ūk¹ kéi² *(my home)*
4. sái² sáu² gāan¹ *(washroom)*
5. Càn⁴ lŏu⁵ sī¹ *(Teacher Chan)*

1. Sān¹ Gảai³ *(New Territories)*
2. Åa³ Zāu¹ *(Asia)*
3. Zīm¹ Sāa¹ Zéoi² *(Tsim Sha Tsui)*
4. gó² dōu⁶ *(there)*
5. nī¹ dōu⁶ *(here)*

Your example(s):

ngŏ⁵ gẻ³ gwỏk³ gāa¹ hái² _____

ngŏ⁵ gẻ³ dāai⁶ hŏk⁶ hái² _____

ngŏ⁵ gẻ³ ūk¹ kéi² hái² _____

Q: _____ hái² bīn¹ dōu⁶ åa³?

1. gēi¹ còeng⁴ fåai³ sin³ 機場快線
   (Airport Express)

2. cȳun¹ sō¹ bāa¹ sí² 穿梭巴士
   (shuttle bus)

3. gēi¹ còeng⁴ bāa¹ sí² 機場巴士
   (airport bus)

4. dīk sí 的士
   (taxi)

---

② For more information about to and from the HK Airport, please go to <http://www.hongkongairport.com>.

1.	Sōeng⁶ Wàan⁴ 上環	*Sheung Wan*
2.	Zūng¹ Wàan⁴ 中環	*Central*
3.	Gām¹ Zūng¹ 金鐘	*Admiralty*
4.	Wāan¹ Zái² 灣仔	*Wan Chai*
5.	Tùng⁴ Lò⁴ Wāan¹ / Tùng⁴ Lò⁴ Wàan⁴ 銅鑼灣	*Causeway Bay*
6.	Zīm¹ Sāa¹ Zéoi² 尖沙咀	*Tsim Sha Tsui*
7.	Zīm¹ Dūng¹ 尖東	*Tsim Sha Tsui East*
8.	Hùng⁴ Hǎm³ 紅磡	*Hung Hom*
9.	Jàu⁴ Màa⁴ Déi² 油麻地	*Yau Ma Tei*
10.	Wōng⁶ Gǒk³ 旺角	*Mong Kok*

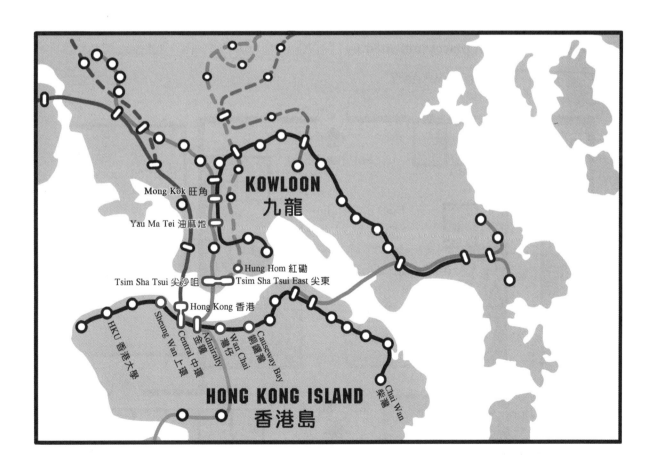

1. **Answer the question and point out your answer.** (1 × 2% = 2%)

   Q: něi⁵ gė³ gwȯk³ gāa¹ *(country)* hái² bīn¹ dȯu⁶ åa³?

   A: hái² nī¹ dȯu⁶. *(Please point it out.)* ngǒ⁵ gė³ gwȯk³ gāa¹ hái² _____.

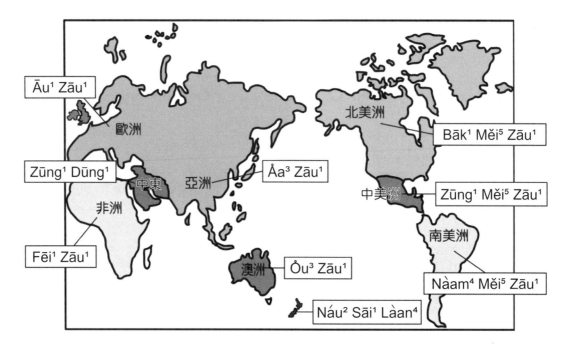

2. **Ask whereabouts of places indicated by** ①②③④⑤⑥⑦⑧**.** (8 × 1.5% = 12%)

   Q: *Place* + hái² bīn¹ dȯu⁶ åa³?

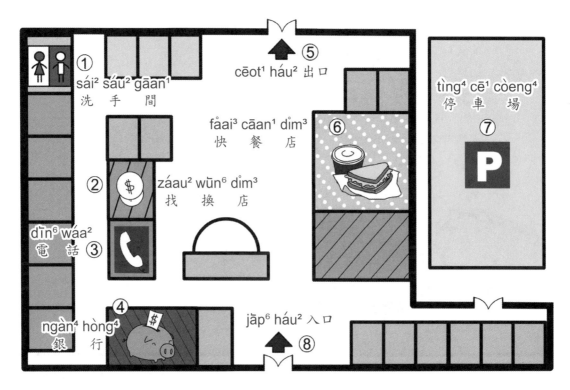

3. Translate the following into Cantonese. $(10 \times 5\% = 50\%)$

1) here _____

2) there _____

3) where _____

4) Where is HKU? _____

5) Where are you going? _____

6) Please go to the airport. _____

7) Here is Hong Kong. _____

8) There is mainland China. _____

9) Kowloon _____

10) New Territories _____

4. Match the Cantonese with the English. $(12 \times 3\% = 36\%)$

1) ngǒ⁵ děi⁶   (c)   a. you

2) něi⁵ děi⁶   ( )   b. they

3) kěoi⁵ děi⁶   ( )   c. we

4) jì⁴ gāa¹   ( )   d. Kowloon

5) dāai⁶ hǒk⁶   ( )   e. Hong Kong Island

6) gwǒk³ zǎi³   ( )   f. New Territories

7) Hōeng¹ Góng² Dóu²   ( )   g. now

8) Gáu² Lùng⁴   ( )   h. to be

9) Sān¹ Gǎai³   ( )   i. go

10) hěoi³   ( )   j. to be at

11) hái²   ( )   k. international

12) hǎi⁶   ( )   l. university

Learning Objectives

1. To ask about numbers *(refer to Unit 2 Section 1)*
2. To ask and tell where one lives
3. To tell where an event takes place
4. To use an adjective as a comment (Adjectival Predicate)
5. To tell what one wants using "**sóeng² jiu³**"
6. To form an imperative sentence of suggestion with "**lāa¹**"

Dialogue

Room 321.

Zing-Zing takes Amy to check in at the hostel for foreign students.

Zing-Zing: Amy, něi⁵ zẙu⁶ hái² bīn¹ dōu⁶ åa³?
你 住 喺 邊 度 呀？
(Amy, where do you live?)

Amy: ngǒ⁵ zẙu⁶ hái² làu⁴ hŏk⁶ sāang¹ sūk¹ sẻ³.
我 住 喺 留 學 生 宿 舍。
(I live in the hostel for foreign students.)

Zing-Zing: sī¹ gēi¹, m̀⁴ gōi¹ něi⁵ hái² cìn⁴ mīn⁶ tìng⁴ cē¹ lāa¹!
司 機，唔 該 你 喺 前 面 停 車 啦！
(Driver, please stop ahead.)

nī¹ dōu⁶ hǎi⁶ làu⁴ hŏk⁶ sāang¹ sūk¹ sẻ³ låa³.
Amy，呢 度 係 留 學 生 宿 舍 喇。
(Amy, here is the hostel for foreign students.)

Amy: *(exclaims when seeing the hostel's reception area)* nī¹ dōu⁶ hóu² lẻng³ åa³! *(then speaks to hostel's receptionist)*
呢 度 好 靚 呀！
(It's very nice here!)

m̀⁴ gōi¹, ngǒ⁵ hǎi⁶ sān¹ lèi⁴ gẻ³ làu⁴ hŏk⁶ sāang¹.
唔 該，我 係 新 嚟 嘅 留 學 生。
(Excuse me. I'm a newly arrived foreign student.)

ngǒ⁵ giu³ Amy Smith. ngǒ⁵ sóeng² jiu³ ngǒ⁵ gẻ³ fóng² gẻ³ só² sì⁴.
我 叫 Amy Smith。我 想 要 我 嘅 房 嘅 鎖 匙。
(I am Amy Smith. I'd like to have the key to my room.)

Receptionist: něi⁵ gẻ³ fóng² géi² dō¹ hōu⁶ åa³?
你 嘅 房 幾 多 號 呀？
(What number is your room?)

Amy: sāam¹ jī⁶ jāt¹ hōu⁶.
三 二 一 號。
(Number 321.)

Receptionist: hóu² åak³. něi⁵ hái² nī¹ dōu⁶ cīm¹ méng² lāa¹!
好 呃。你 喺 呢 度 簽 名 啦！
(Okay, please sign here.)

Vocabulary

1.	zŷu⁶ 住	V:	to live
2.	hái² 喺 (+ *Place* + *Verb*)	Prep:	(in L.3) at; in; on (a place)
3.	làu⁴ hŏk⁶ sāang¹ 留學生	N:	foreign student
4.	sūk¹ se̊³ 宿舍	N:	hostel; dormitory; living quarters (also pronounced as "sūk¹ se̊⁵")
5.	sī¹ gēi¹ 司機	N:	driver; vehicle operator (by profession)
6.	cìn⁴ mīn⁶ 前面	N:	in front; ahead
7.	tìng⁴ cē¹ 停車	Ph:	to stop (a car, a train)
8.	låa³ 喇	Part:	*[a modal particle used to emphasize a point of current relevance.] (It implies that sth. is now what it was not before.)*
9.	hóu² 好 (+ *Adjective*) (e.g. hóu² hóu²: very good)	Adv:	very
10.	le̊ng³ 靚	Adj:	beautiful; good-looking; good quality
11.	åa³ 呀 (*Statement* + åa³.)	Part:	*[a modal particle used to soften the tone of confirmation in a statement]*
12.	m̀⁴ gōi¹ 唔該	SE:	(in L.3) excuse me *[to draw sb's attention usually when one inquires sth.]*
13.	sān¹ 新	Adj:	new
14.	lèi⁴ 嚟	V:	to come (also pronounced as "lài⁴")
15.	sān¹ lèi⁴ ge̊³ 新嚟嘅	Ph:	*(lit. newly come)* just arrived; newcomer
16.	sóeng² 想 (+ *Verbal phrase*)	AV:	to want to; would like to (do something)
17.	ji̊u³ 要 (+ *Noun*)	V:	(in L.3) to want, would like (something)
18.	sóeng² ji̊u³ 想要 (+ *Noun*)	Ph:	to want to have (something)
19.	fóng² 房	N:	room
20.	só² sì⁴ 鎖匙	N:	key
21.	hŏu⁶ 號 (*Nu.* + hŏu⁶)	M:	*[used after a numeral]* number
22.	géi² dō¹ 幾多	QW:	what; how many; how much
23.	géi² dō¹ hŏu⁶ 幾多號	QW:	what number
24.	hóu² åak³ 好呃	SE:	fine; okay
25.	cīm¹ méng² 簽名	V/N:	to sign; signature

1. **To ask about numbers** *(refer to Unit 2 Section 1)*

    e.g.   někˇⁱ⁵ gě³ fóng² géi² dō¹ hǒu⁶ åa³?

    (What number is your room?)

Topic + (hǎi⁶) + géi² dō¹ hǒu⁶ + åa³?

    1. někˇⁱ⁵ gě³ bǎan⁶ gūng¹ sāt¹   *(your office)*
    2. někˇⁱ⁵ gě³ dīn⁶ wáa² hǒu⁶ mǎa⁵   *(your telephone number)*
    3. někˇⁱ⁵ gě³ sān¹ fán² zǐng³   *(your ID card)*

    Your example(s):

    ngǒ⁵ gě³ fóng² hǎi⁶ _____ hǒu⁶.

    ngǒ⁵ gě³ dīn⁶ wáa² hǒu⁶ mǎa⁵ hǎi⁶ _____

    ngǒ⁵ gě³ sān¹ fán² zǐng³ hǎi⁶ _____

2. **To ask and tell where one lives**

    e.g.   1.   někˇⁱ⁵ zỹu⁶ hái² bīn¹ dǒu⁶ åa³?

    (Where do you live?)

    e.g.   2.   ngǒ⁵ zỹu⁶ hái² làu⁴ hǒk⁶ sāang¹ sūk¹ sě³.

    (I live in the hostel for foreign students.)

Q: Subject + zỹu⁶ + hái² + bīn¹ dǒu⁶ + åa³?

A: Subject + zỹu⁶ + [hái² + Place].

    1. ngǒ⁵ gě³ pàng⁴ jǎu⁵   *(my friend)*
    2. Càn⁴ lǒu⁵ sī¹   *(Teacher Chan)*
    3. kěoi⁵   *(he; she)*

    1. dǎai⁶ hǒk⁶ sūk¹ sě³   *(university's hostel)*
    2. Zūng¹ Wàan⁴   *(Central)*
    3. Hōeng¹ Góng² Záu² Dǐm³   *(Hong Kong Hotel)*

    Your example(s):

    ngǒ⁵ zỹu⁶ hái² _____ .

3. **To tell where an event takes place**

e.g. 1. m̀⁴ gōi¹ něi⁵ hái² cìn⁴ mīn⁶ tìng⁴ cē¹ lāa¹!
(Please stop ahead.)

e.g. 2. něi⁵ hái² nī¹ dŏu⁶ cīm¹ méng² lāa¹!
(Please sign here.)

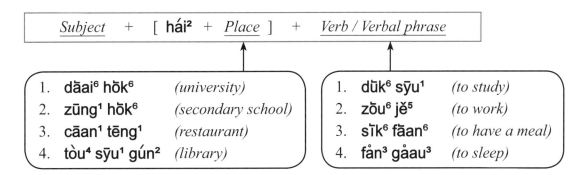

Subject + [hái² + *Place*] + *Verb / Verbal phrase*

1. dāai⁶ hŏk⁶	*(university)*	1. dūk⁶ sȳu¹	*(to study)*
2. zūng¹ hŏk⁶	*(secondary school)*	2. zŏu⁶ jě⁵	*(to work)*
3. cāan¹ tēng¹	*(restaurant)*	3. sīk⁶ fāan⁶	*(to have a meal)*
4. tòu⁴ sȳu¹ gún²	*(library)*	4. fǎn³ gåau³	*(to sleep)*

Your example(s):

ngŏ⁵ hái² _____ dūk⁶ sȳu¹.

ngŏ⁵ hái² _____ zŏu⁶ jě⁵.

ngŏ⁵ hái² _____ sīk⁶ fāan⁶.

ngŏ⁵ hái² tòu⁴ sȳu¹ gún² _____ .

4. **To use an adjective as a comment** *(Descriptive sentence with no verb)*

e.g. nī¹ dŏu⁶ hóu² lěng³ åa³!
(It's very nice here!)

Subject/Topic + hóu²* + *Adjective* (+ åa³).
(Adverb of degree) *(Predicate)*
An adjectival predicate without any adverb in front of it usually conveys a relative sense.

1. Zūng¹ Gwŏk³	*(China)*	1. dāai⁶	*(big)*
2. Hōeng¹ Góng²	*(Hong Kong)*	2. såi³	*(small)*
3. làu⁴ hŏk⁶ sāang¹ sūk¹ sě³	*(hostel for foreign students)*	3. gāu⁶	*(old)*
4. něi⁵ gě³ fóng²	*(your room)*	4. sān¹	*(new)*
5. ngŏ⁵ gě³ lŏu⁵ sī¹	*(my teacher)*	5. hóu²	*(good)*

Your example(s):

_____ hóu² _____ .
(Topic) *(Adjectival predicate) (refer to p.157)*

5. To tell what one wants using "sóeng² jǐu³"

e.g. ngǒ⁵ sóeng² jǐu³ ngǒ⁵ gẻ³ fóng² gẻ³ só² sì⁴.
   (I'd like to have the key to my room.)

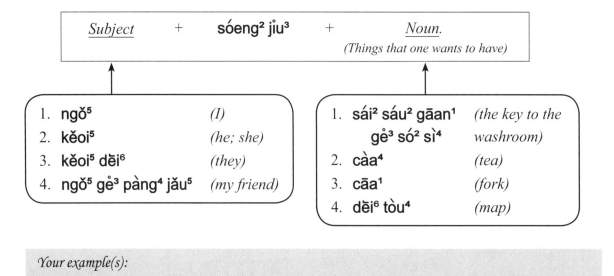

Subject	+	sóeng² jǐu³	+	Noun.
				(Things that one wants to have)

1. ngǒ⁵   *(I)*
2. kěoi⁵   *(he; she)*
3. kěoi⁵ děi⁶   *(they)*
4. ngǒ⁵ gẻ³ pàng⁴ jǎu⁵   *(my friend)*

1. sái² sáu² gāan¹ gẻ³ só² sì⁴   *(the key to the washroom)*
2. càa⁴   *(tea)*
3. cāa¹   *(fork)*
4. děi⁶ tòu⁴   *(map)*

Your example(s):

ngǒ⁵ sóeng² jǐu³ _____ . (something that you want to drink or eat.)
   (refer to p.148, 156, 168 & 169)

6. To form an imperative sentence of suggestion with "lāa¹"

e.g. 1. m̀⁴ gōi¹ něi⁵ hái² cìn⁴ mīn⁶ tìng⁴ cē¹ lāa¹!
       (Please stop ahead.)

e.g. 2. něi⁵ hái² nī¹ dǒu⁶ cīm¹ méng² lāa¹!
       (Please sign here.)

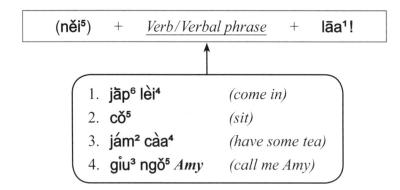

(něi⁵)	+	*Verb/Verbal phrase*	+	lāa¹!

1. jǎp⁶ lèi⁴   *(come in)*
2. cǒ⁵   *(sit)*
3. jám² càa⁴   *(have some tea)*
4. gǐu³ ngǒ⁵ *Amy*   *(call me Amy)*

Your example(s):

m̀⁴ gōi¹ něi⁵ _____ lāa¹.

Q: nĕi⁵ zy̆u⁶ hái² bīn¹ dōu⁶ åa³?

A: ngŏ⁵ zy̆u⁶ hái² _____ .

1. **záu² dĭm³** 酒店
    (hotel)

2. **lĕoi⁵ dĭm³** 旅店
    / **lĕoi⁵ sĕ³** 旅舍
    (hostel)

3. **bān¹ gún²** 賓館
    (guesthouse)

4. **cīng¹ nìn⁴ lĕoi⁵ sĕ³**
    青　年　旅　舍
    (youth hostels)

5. **dōu⁶ gåa³ ūk¹** 度假屋
    (holiday flats)

6. **còng⁴ wái²** 牀位
    (bedspace apartments)

---

① Please check out this website www.hadla.gov.hk to meet your needs.

1.	*bathroom*	jūk⁶ sāt¹ 浴室； cūng¹ lòeng⁴ fóng² 沖涼房
2.	*washroom; toilet*	sái² sáu² gāan¹ 洗手間； cI³ só² 廁所
3.	*kitchen*	cyù⁴ fóng²；cèoi⁴ fóng² 廚房
4.	*living room*	håak³ tēng¹ 客廳
5.	*dining room*	fāan⁶ tēng¹ 飯廳
6.	*bedroom*	sēoi⁶ fóng² 睡房
7.	*double room; room for two*	sōeng¹ jàn⁴ fóng² 雙人房
8.	*single room*	dāan¹ jàn⁴ fóng² 單人房
9.	*study room*	sȳu¹ fóng² 書房； jýut⁶ dūk⁶ sāt¹ 閱讀室
10.	*storeroom*	zāap⁶ māt⁶ fóng² 雜物房
11.	*window ledge*	cōeng¹ tòi⁴ 窗台
12.	*balcony*	lōu⁶ tòi⁴ 露台； kè⁴ láu² 騎樓
13.	*corridor*	záu² lóng² 走廊
14.	*front door*	cìn⁴ mún² 前門
15.	*back door*	hāu⁶ mún² 後門
16.	*lift, elevator*	sīng¹ gǒng³ gēi¹ 升降機；līp¹ 軠； dīn⁶ tāi¹ 電梯 *(also means escalator)*
17.	*staircase*	làu⁴ tāi¹ 樓梯
18.	*garbage room*	lāap⁶ såap³ fòng⁴ 垃圾房
19.	*laundry room*	sái² jī¹ fòng⁴ 洗衣房
20.	*garage*	cē¹ fòng⁴ 車房

Exercise

1. **Translate the following into Cantonese.** $(8 \times 10\% = 80\%)$

   1) Where do you live?

   _____

   2) What number is your room?

   _____

   3) I'd like to have the key to the washroom.

   _____

   4) Please sign here!

   _____

   5) I want to have your signature.

   _____

   6) Please stop here!

   _____

   7) I'm a newly arrived foreign student.

   _____

   8) I live in the Hong Kong International Hotel. $(+ 2\%)$

   _____

2. **Match the Cantonese with the pictures.** $(6 \times 3\% = 18\%)$

   1) làu⁴ hŏk⁶ sāang¹ (   )

   2) záu² dǐm³ (   )

   3) cīm¹ méng² (   )

   4) sūk¹ sè³ (   )

   5) só² sì⁴ (   )

   6) sī¹ gēi¹ (   )

   a)

   b)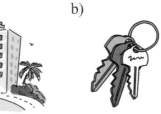

   c)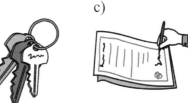

   d)

   e)

   f)

Lesson 4 | Money exchange

Learning Objectives

1. To indicate possession with the verb "**jǎu⁵**" & "**mǒu⁵**"
2. To connect two items with "**tùng⁴** (and)"
3. To express one's wish or desire to do something using "**sóeng²**"
4. To do money exchange *(refer to Unit 2 Section 4)*
5. To ask "how much" or "how many"

Dialogue

Zing-Zing and Amy chat in the room.

Zing-Zing: Amy, něi⁵ jǎu⁵ mǒu⁵ Góng² Bǎi⁶ åa³?
Amy, 你 有 冇 港 幣 呀?
(Amy, have you got any Hong Kong dollars?)

Amy: mǒu⁵ åa³. ngǒ⁵ mǒu⁵ Góng² Bǎi⁶.
冇 呀。 我 冇 港 幣。
(No, I haven't got any Hong Kong dollars.)

ngǒ⁵ zīng⁶ hǎi⁶ jǎu⁵ Měi⁵ Gām¹ tùng⁴ sěon³ jūng⁶ kāat¹.
我 淨 係 有 美 金 同 信 用 咭。
(I only have US dollars and a credit card.)

ngǒ⁵ sóeng² wǔn⁶ jāt¹ dī¹ Góng² Bǎi⁶.
我 想 換 一 啲 港 幣。
(I would like to change for some Hong Kong dollars.)

Zing-Zing: něi⁵ sóeng² wǔn⁶ géi² dō¹ cín² åa³?
你 想 換 幾 多 錢 呀?
(How much would you like to change?)

Amy: jāt¹ bǎak³ mān¹ Měi⁵ Gām¹.
一 百 蚊 美 金。
(One hundred US dollars.)

Zing-Zing: mǒu⁵ mān⁶ tài⁴. ngǒ⁵ jǎu⁵.
冇 問 題。 我 有。
(No problem. I have it.)

nàa⁴, nī¹ dǒu⁶ cāt¹ bǎak³ bǎat³ sāp⁶ mān¹ Góng² Bǎi⁶.
嗱, 呢 度 七 百 八 十 蚊 港 幣。
(Here's seven hundred and eighty Hong Kong dollars.①)

Amy: m̀⁴ gōi¹.
唔 該。
(Thank you.)

---

① The Hong Kong dollar is pegged to the US dollar at about 7.8 HKD to 1 USD.

Vocabulary

1.	jǎu⁵ 有	V:	to have, to possess
2.	mǒu⁵ 冇	V:	not to have, have not (the negation of "**jǎu⁵**")
3.	jǎu⁵ mǒu⁵ (+ *Object*) åa³? 有冇…呀？	QW:	Have you got...? Do you have…?
4.	Góng² Bāi⁶ 港幣	PN:	Hong Kong dollars; Hong Kong currency (also "**Góng² Jỳun⁴** 港元")
5.	zīng⁶ hāi⁶ 淨係 (+ *Verb*)	Adv:	only
6.	Mĕi⁵ Gām¹ 美金	PN:	U.S. dollars (also "**Měi⁵ Jỳun⁴** 美元")
7.	tùng⁴ 同 (*N₁* + tùng⁴ + *N₂*)	Conj:	and (the shortened form of "**tùng⁴ màai⁴** 同埋"
8.	sěon³ jūng⁶ kāat¹ 信用咭	N:	credit card
9.	wūn⁶ 換	V:	to change; exchange; convert (currency)
10.	jāt¹ dī¹ 一啲	Nu:	some, small quantities (can be shortened as "**dī¹**")
11.	cín² 錢	N:	money
12.	géi² dō¹ cín² 幾多錢	Pn:	how much (money) (can be shortened as "**géi² cín²**")
13.	bǎak³ 百	Nu:	hundred
14.	mān¹ 蚊 (*Nu.* + man¹)	M:	dollars *[a measure unit for money]*
15.	mān⁶ tài⁴ 問題	N:	question; problem; trouble
16.	mǒu⁵ mān⁶ tài⁴ 冇問題	SE:	no problem
17.	nàa⁴ 嗱	Intj:	(in L.4) Here it is! *[an indicator of things within a close proximity]*
18.	m̀⁴ gōi¹ 唔該	SE:	(in L.4) thank you *[for a small favor]*

1. To indicate possession with the verb "jǎu⁵" & "mǒu⁵"

  a) To possess

  e.g. ngǒ⁵ zīng⁶ hǎi⁶ jǎu⁵ Měi⁵ Gām¹.

  (I only have US dollars.)

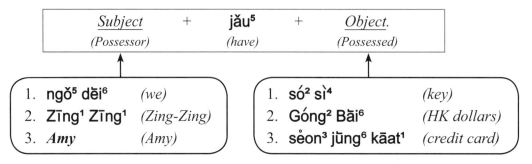

Subject	+	**jǎu⁵**	+	*Object.*
(Possessor)		*(have)*		*(Possessed)*

1. ngǒ⁵ děi⁶   *(we)*
2. Zīng¹ Zīng¹   *(Zing-Zing)*
3. *Amy*   *(Amy)*

1. só² sì⁴   *(key)*
2. Góng² Bǎi⁶   *(HK dollars)*
3. sẻon³ jǔng⁶ kāat¹   *(credit card)*

  b) Negation of "jǎu⁵" (not have – "mǒu⁵")

  e.g. ngǒ⁵ mǒu⁵ Góng² Bǎi⁶.

  (I haven't got any Hong Kong dollars.)

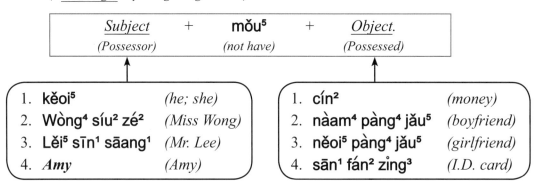

Subject	+	**mǒu⁵**	+	*Object.*
(Possessor)		*(not have)*		*(Possessed)*

1. kěoi⁵   *(he; she)*
2. Wòng⁴ síu² zé²   *(Miss Wong)*
3. Lěi⁵ sīn¹ sāang¹   *(Mr. Lee)*
4. *Amy*   *(Amy)*

1. cín²   *(money)*
2. nàam⁴ pàng⁴ jǎu⁵   *(boyfriend)*
3. něoi⁵ pàng⁴ jǎu⁵   *(girlfriend)*
4. sān¹ fán² zǐng³   *(I.D. card)*

  c) To ask "Have you got...?" or "Do you have......?"

  e.g. něi⁵ jǎu⁵ mǒu⁵ Góng² Bǎi⁶ ǎa³?

  (Have you got any Hong Kong dollars?)

Subject	+	**jǎu⁵ mǒu⁵**	+	*Object*	+	**ǎa³ ?**
		(have not have)				

1. něi⁵   *(you)*
2. kěoi⁵   *(he; she)*
3. kěoi⁵ děi⁶ *(they)*

1. sān¹ fán² zǐng³   *(I.D. card)*
2. pàng⁴ jǎu⁵   *(friend)*
3. sáu² tài⁴ dīn⁶ wáa²   *(mobile phone)*

Your example(s):

  ngǒ⁵ jǎu⁵ _____

  ngǒ⁵ mǒu⁵ _____

2. To connect two items "A and B"

e.g. ngǒ⁵ zīng⁶ hǎi⁶ jǎu⁵ Měi⁵ Gām¹ <u>tùng⁴</u> sěon³ jūng⁶ kāat¹.

(I only have US dollars <u>and</u> a credit card.)

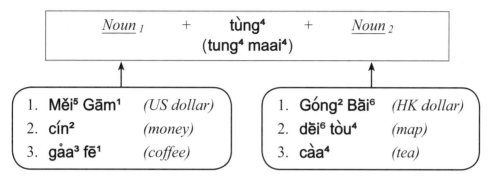

Noun₁	+	tùng⁴	+	Noun₂
		(tung⁴ maai⁴)		

1. Měi⁵ Gām¹	(US dollar)	1. Góng² Bǎi⁶	(HK dollar)
2. cín²	(money)	2. děi⁶ tòu⁴	(map)
3. gåa³ fē¹	(coffee)	3. càa⁴	(tea)

Your example(s):

ngǒ⁵ jǎu⁵ _____ tùng⁴ _____ .

3. To express one's wish or desire to do something

e.g. 1. ngǒ⁵ <u>sóeng²</u> wūn⁶ jāt¹ dī¹ Góng² Bǎi⁶.

(I <u>would like to</u> change for some Hong Kong dollars.)

e.g. 2. ngǒ⁵ <u>sóeng²</u> jǐu³ ngǒ⁵ gě³ fóng² gě³ só² sì⁴.

(I <u>want to</u> have the key to my room.)

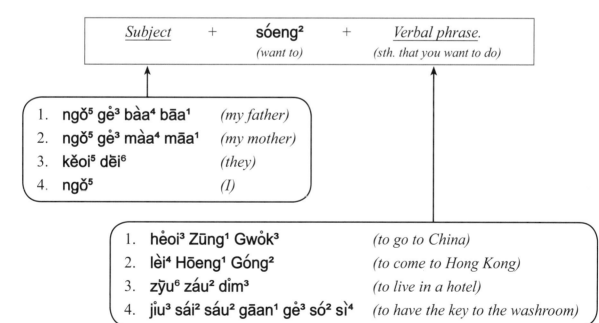

Subject	+	sóeng²	+	Verbal phrase.
		(want to)		(sth. that you want to do)

1. ngǒ⁵ gě³ bàa⁴ bāa¹	(my father)
2. ngǒ⁵ gě³ màa⁴ māa¹	(my mother)
3. kěoi⁵ děi⁶	(they)
4. ngǒ⁵	(I)

1. hěoi³ Zūng¹ Gwǒk³	(to go to China)
2. lèi⁴ Hōeng¹ Góng²	(to come to Hong Kong)
3. zẙu⁶ záu² dǐm³	(to live in a hotel)
4. jǐu³ sái² sáu² gāan¹ gě³ só² sì⁴	(to have the key to the washroom)

Your example(s):

ngǒ⁵ sóeng² _____ .

4. To do money exchange

e.g. ngǒ⁵ sóeng² wǔn⁶ jāt¹ dī¹ Góng² Bǎi⁶.

(I would like to change for some Hong Kong dollars.)

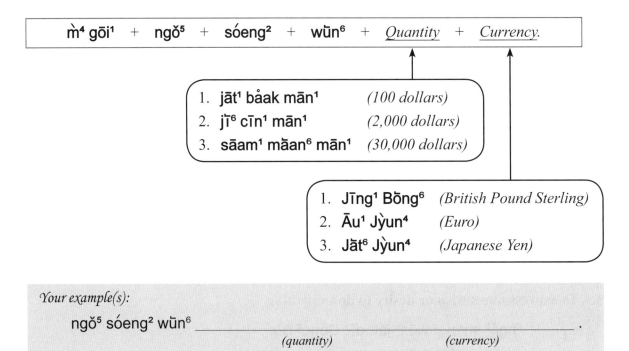

m̀⁴ gōi¹ + ngǒ⁵ + sóeng² + wǔn⁶ + *Quantity* + *Currency.*

1. jāt¹ bǎak mān¹   *(100 dollars)*
2. jī⁶ cīn¹ mān¹   *(2,000 dollars)*
3. sāam¹ mǎan⁶ mān¹   *(30,000 dollars)*

1. Jīng¹ Bǒng⁶   *(British Pound Sterling)*
2. Āu¹ Jỳun⁴   *(Euro)*
3. Jāt⁶ Jỳun⁴   *(Japanese Yen)*

Your example(s):

ngǒ⁵ sóeng² wǔn⁶ _____ .
　　　　　　　　　　　(quantity)　　　　　　　　　*(currency)*

5. To ask "how much" or "how many"

e.g. 1. něi⁵ sóeng² wǔn⁶ géi² dō¹ cín² ǎa³?

(How much would you like to change?)

géi² dō¹ + *Noun* + ǎa³?   →

1. géi² dō¹ cín² ǎa³?   *(How much (money)?)*
2. géi² dō¹ jàn⁴ ǎa³?   *(How many people?)*
3. géi² dō¹ sěoi³ ǎa³? *(How many years old?)*

e.g. 2. něi⁵ jǎu⁵ géi² dō¹ cín² ǎa³?

(How much money do you have?)

e.g. 3. Hōeng¹ Góng² jǎu⁵ géi² dō¹ jàn⁴ ǎa³?

(How many people are there in Hong Kong?)

e.g. 4. Wòng⁴ Zīng¹ Zīng¹ géi² dō¹ sěoi³ ǎa³?

(How old is Zing-Zing Wong?)

Your example(s):

něi⁵ zy̌u⁶ hái² _____ fóng² ǎa³?
　　　　　　　　　　　(what number?)

1) **Hong Kong Currency** *(refer to Unit 2 Section 4 on p.34-36)*

The legal tender is the Hong Kong dollar (HK$). 1 dollar is worth 100 cents. Coins, issued by the government, are bronze-coloured for 10 cents, 20 cents and 50 cents, silver-coloured for $1, $2 and $5, nickel and bronze for $10. Banknotes issued by HSBC and Standard Chartered Bank have denominations of $10, $20, $50, $100, $500 and $1000. The Bank of China issues the same denominations with the exception of $10, while the Government only issues the denomination of $10. These notes vary in design and colour according to denomination and issuer. (Source: Hong Kong Tourism Board, 2020)

Find out more about Hong Kong's coins and banknotes at https://www.hkma.gov.hk

a) **Coins in circulation** (coins: sáan² ngán² 散銀; ngāang⁶ bãi⁶ 硬幣)

(coins not shown to scale)

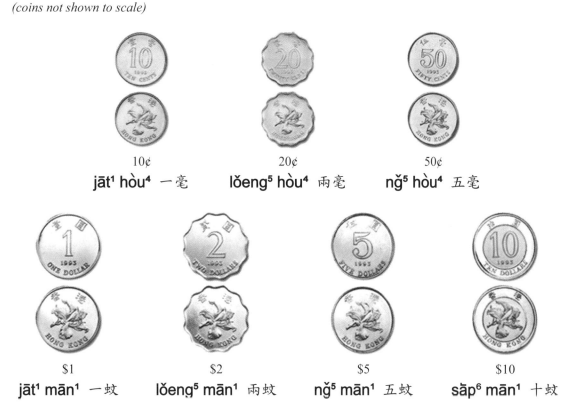

| 10¢ | 20¢ | 50¢ |
| jāt¹ hòu⁴ 一毫 | lŏeng⁵ hòu⁴ 兩毫 | nğ⁵ hòu⁴ 五毫 |

| $1 | $2 | $5 | $10 |
| jāt¹ mān¹ 一蚊 | lŏeng⁵ mān¹ 兩蚊 | nğ⁵ mān¹ 五蚊 | sāp⁶ mān¹ 十蚊 |

b) **Banknotes in circulation** (banknotes: zí² bãi⁶ 紙幣)

$10 = sāp⁶ mān¹ 十蚊
$20 = jī⁶ sāp⁶ mān¹ 二十蚊
$50 = nğ⁵ sāp⁶ mān¹ 五十蚊
$100 = jāt¹ bảak³ mān¹ 一百蚊
$500 = nğ⁵ bảak³ mān¹ 五百蚊
$1000 = jāt¹ cīn¹ mān¹ 一千蚊

2) Other currencies

1.	**Měi⁵ Gām¹** 美金 / **Měi⁵ Jỳun⁴** 美元	*United States Dollars*	**(USD) US$**
2.	**Gāa¹ Jỳun⁴** 加元	*Canadian Dollars*	**(CAD) Can$**
3.	**Āu¹ Lò⁴** 歐羅 / **Āu¹ Jỳun⁴** 歐元	*Euros*	**(EUR) €**
4.	**Jīng¹ Bōng⁶** / **Jīng¹ Bóng²** 英鎊	*British Pounds Sterling*	**(GBP) £**
5.	**Sēoi⁶ Sī̌⁶ Fåat³ Lòng⁴** 瑞士法郎	*Swiss Francs*	**(CHF) SwF**
6.	**Ǒu³ Jỳun⁴** 澳元	*Australian Dollars*	**(AUD) A$**
7.	**Náu² Jỳun⁴** 紐元	*New Zealand Dollars*	**(NZD) NZ$**
8.	**Jāt⁶ Jỳun⁴** 日元	*Japanese Yen*	**(JPY) ¥**
9.	**Nàam⁴ Hòn⁴ Jỳun⁴** / **Wàan⁴** 南韓元/圜	*South Korean Won*	**(WON) ₩**
10.	**Sān¹ Gåa³ Bō¹ Jỳun⁴** 新加坡元	*Singapore Dollars*	**(SGD) S$**
11.	**Tǎai³ Zȳu¹** 泰銖	*Thai Baht*	**(THB) Bht or Bt**
12.	**Jàn⁴ Màn⁴ Bāi⁶** 人民幣	*Chinese Yuan/Renminbi*	**(CNY)(RMB) ¥**
13.	**Sān¹ Tòi⁴ Bāi⁶** 新台幣	*Taiwan Dollars*	**(TWD) NT$**

FYI – 2. Necessities   *Q:* **něi⁵ jǎu⁵ mǒu⁵** _____ **åa³?**

wǔ⁶ ziu³ 護照
(passport)

cīm¹ zǐng³ 簽證
(visa)

sėon³ jǔng⁶ kāat¹ 信用咭
(credit card)

sȯu³ gėoi³ sīm¹ kāat¹ 數據 SIM 卡
(Data SIM card)

sáu² tài⁴ dīn⁶ wáa² 手提電話
(mobile phone)

Hōeng¹ Góng² sān¹ fán² zǐng³
香港身份證 *(HKID card)*

bȧat³ dāat⁶ tūng¹ kāat¹
八達通咭 *(Octopus card)*

cín² 錢
(money)

Exercise

1. **Write the following prices in Arabic numerals.** $(8 \times 2\% = 16\%)$

    e.g. jāt¹ bảak³ mān¹ _____ $100 _____

    1) săp⁶ bảat³ mān¹ _____

    2) jī⁶ săp⁶ jī⁶ mān¹ _____

    3) nǧ⁵ săp⁶ nǧ⁵ mān¹ _____

    4) jī⁶ bảak³ cāt¹ săp⁶ mān¹ _____

    5) sẻi³ bảak³ nǧ⁵ săp⁶ lūk⁶ mān¹ _____

    6) bảat³ bảak³ gáu² săp⁶ lūk⁶ mān¹ _____

    7) nǧ⁵ hòu⁴ _____

    8) lŏeng⁵ mān¹ _____

2. **Use the given words and "jǎu⁵ mǒu⁵" to form a question first and then give a positive and negative answer to each question.** $(12 \times 2\% = 24\%)$

    e.g. **Góng² Bāi⁶**

    Q: nẻi⁵ jǎu⁵ mǒu⁵ Góng² Bāi⁶ ảa³? _____

    A (yes): jǎu⁵, ngǒ⁵ jǎu⁵ Góng² Bāi⁶. _____

    A (no):   mǒu⁵, ngǒ⁵ mǒu⁵ Góng² Bāi⁶. _____

    1) cín²

       Q: _____

       A (yes): _____

       A (no): _____

    2) sẻon³ jūng⁶ kāat¹

       Q: _____

       A (yes): _____

       A (no): _____

    3) sān¹ fán² zỉng³

       Q: _____

       A (yes): _____

       A (no): _____

    4) mān⁶ tài⁴

       Q: _____

       A (yes): _____

       A (no): _____

3. **Translate the following into Cantonese.** $(8 \times 7.5\% = 60\%)$

1) Do you have a boyfriend?

   _____

2) I only have one hundred Hong Kong dollars.

   _____

3) He would like to have a Hong Kong ID card.

   _____

4) How much US dollars would you like to change?

   _____

5) Here're two hundred and fifty dollars.

   _____

6) Mr. Chan and Miss Wong are my teachers.

   _____

7) My father would like to have some tea.

   _____

8) My friend wants to come to Hong Kong.

   _____

Unit Four

Personal Information

Lesson 5 | Self-introduction

1. To talk about one's family (Intimate possession)
2. To know how to use Measure Words *(refer to Unit 2 Section 7)*
3. To tell one's nationality
4. To tell one's age (Nominal Predicate)
5. To tell one's major/subject of study
6. To tell one's hobbies
7. To ask "what" or "what kind of" using "**māt¹ jě⁵**"

Short Speech

Amy introduces herself at a welcome party.

dāai⁶ gāa¹ hóu², ngǒ⁵ giu³ *Amy*. ngǒ⁵ hāi⁶ Měi⁵ Gwok³ jàn⁴.
大　家　好，我　叫　*Amy*。我　係　美　國　人。
(Hello, I am Amy. I am American.)

ngǒ⁵ gām¹ nìn⁴ jī⁶ sǎp⁶ sėoi³. ngǒ⁵ jǎu⁵ lǒeng⁵ go³ hīng¹ dāi⁶ zí² mūi⁶.
我　今　年　二　十　歲。我　有　兩　個　兄　弟　姊　妹。
(I am twenty years old this year. I have two siblings.)

ngǒ⁵ gò⁴ gō¹ hái² Náu² Jȯek³ zȯu⁶ jě⁵. ngǒ⁵ zė⁴ zē¹ hái² Bāa¹ Lài⁴ dūk⁶ sȳu¹.
我　哥　哥　喺　紐　約　做　嘢。我　姐　姐　喺　巴　黎　讀　書。
(My elder brother is working in New York. My elder sister is studying in Paris.)

ngǒ⁵ jì⁴ gāa¹ hāi⁶ Hōeng¹ Góng² Dāai⁶ Hȯk⁶ gė³ gāau¹ wǔn⁶ hȯk⁶ sāang¹.
我　而　家　係　香　港　大　學　嘅　交　換　學　生。
(I am an exchange student in the University of Hong Kong now.)

ngǒ⁵ hái² dāai⁶ hȯk⁶ dūk⁶ gåau³ jūk⁶.
我　喺　大　學　讀　教　育。
(My major at university is education.)

ngǒ⁵ zȳu⁶ hái² Gwȯk³ Zȧi³ làu⁴ hȯk⁶ sāang¹ sūk¹ sė³.
我　住　喺　國　際　留　學　生　宿　舍。
(I live in the hostel for international foreign students.)

ngǒ⁵ gė³ hıng³ cėoi³ hāi⁶ lěoi⁵ hàng⁴ tùng⁴ tēng¹ jām¹ ngȯk⁶.
我　嘅　興　趣　係　旅　行　同　聽　音　樂。
(My hobbies are traveling and listening to music.)

dō¹ zē⁶.
多　謝。
(Thank you.)

Vocabulary

1.	dãai⁶ gāa¹ 大家	Pn:	all, everybody
2.	Měi⁵ Gwȯk³ 美國	PN:	United States of America
3.	jàn⁴ 人	N:	people; person
4.	Měi⁵ Gwȯk³ jàn⁴ 美國人	PN:	American(s)
5.	gām¹ nìn⁴ 今年	N:	this year (also pronounced as "**gām¹ nín²**")
6.	sėoi³ 歲 (*Nu.* + sėoi³)	M:	years old; age
7.	gȯ³ 個 (e.g. jāt¹ gȯ³ jàn⁴)	MW:	*[a general measure word for round objects or abstract things, such as questions or ideas; (in L.5) a measure word for people]*
8.	lǒeng⁵ 兩 (+ *MW* + *N*)	Nu:	two *[used instead of "jī⁶" when counting things in twos]*
9.	hīng¹ dãi⁶ zí² mūi⁶ 兄弟姊妹 (*Nu.* + gȯ³ + hīng¹ dãi⁶ zí² mūi⁶)	Ph:	brothers and sisters; siblings
10.	gȯ⁴ gō¹ 哥哥	N:	elder brother (younger brother is "**dài⁴ dái²** 弟弟")
11.	zė⁴ zē¹ 姐姐	N:	elder sister (younger sister is "**mùi⁴ múi²** 妹妹")
12.	Náu² Jȯek³ 紐約	PN:	New York
13.	Bāa¹ Lài⁴ 巴黎	PN:	Paris
14.	zȯu⁶ jě⁵ 做嘢	VO:	to work
15.	dūk⁶ sÿu¹ 讀書	VO:	to study in school; to read (a book)
16.	gāau¹ wȯn⁰ 交換	V:	to exchange
17.	dūk⁶ 讀 (+ *Object*)	V:	to study (+ *major/subject*); go to school
18.	gȧau³ jŪk⁶ 教育	N:	education
19.	hǐng³ cėoi³ 興趣	N:	a hobby; an interest
20.	lěoi⁵ hàng⁴ 旅行	V/N:	to travel
21.	tēng¹ 聽	V:	to hear; to listen
22.	jām¹ ngȯk⁶ 音樂	N:	music
23.	dō¹ zē⁶ 多謝	SE:	thank you, many thanks *(express one's gratitude)*

1. **To talk about one's family (Intimate possession)**

e.g. ngǒ⁵ gò⁴ gō¹ hái² Náu² Jȯek³ zōu⁶ jě⁵.

(My elder brother is working in New York.)

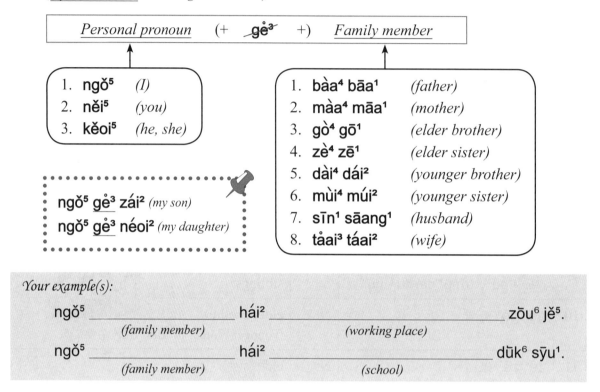

| *Personal pronoun* | (+ _gė³_ +) | *Family member* |

1. ngǒ⁵	*(I)*
2. něi⁵	*(you)*
3. kěoi⁵	*(he, she)*

1. bàa⁴ bāa¹	*(father)*
2. màa⁴ māa¹	*(mother)*
3. gò⁴ gō¹	*(elder brother)*
4. zè⁴ zē¹	*(elder sister)*
5. dài⁴ dái²	*(younger brother)*
6. mùi⁴ múi²	*(younger sister)*
7. sīn¹ sāang¹	*(husband)*
8. tȧai³ táai²	*(wife)*

ngǒ⁵ gė³ zái² *(my son)*
ngǒ⁵ gė³ néoi² *(my daughter)*

Your example(s):

ngǒ⁵ _____ hái² _____ zōu⁶ jě⁵.
    (family member)   *(working place)*

ngǒ⁵ _____ hái² _____ dūk⁶ sȳu¹.
    (family member)   *(school)*

2. **To know how to use Measure Words** *(refer to Unit 2 Section 7, p.45-47)*

e.g. ngǒ⁵ jǎu⁵ lȯeng⁵ gȯ³ hīng¹ dài⁶ zí² mūi⁶.

(I have two siblings.)

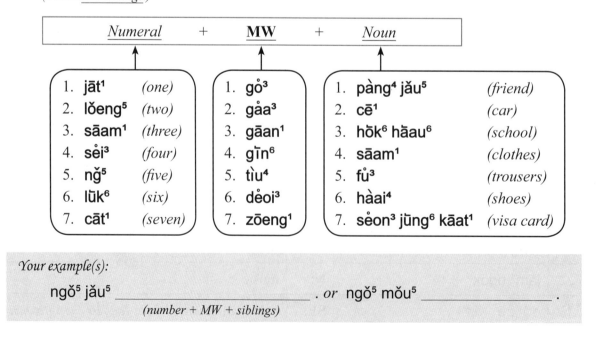

| *Numeral* | + | **MW** | + | *Noun* |

1. jāt¹	*(one)*
2. lȯeng⁵	*(two)*
3. sāam¹	*(three)*
4. sėi³	*(four)*
5. ńǧ⁵	*(five)*
6. lūk⁶	*(six)*
7. cāt¹	*(seven)*

| 1. gȯ³ |
| 2. gȧa³ |
| 3. gāan¹ |
| 4. gīn⁶ |
| 5. tìu⁴ |
| 6. dėoi³ |
| 7. zōeng¹ |

1. pàng⁴ jǎu⁵	*(friend)*
2. cē¹	*(car)*
3. hȯk⁶ hȧau⁶	*(school)*
4. sāam¹	*(clothes)*
5. fȕ³	*(trousers)*
6. hàai⁴	*(shoes)*
7. sėon³ jūng⁶ kāat¹	*(visa card)*

Your example(s):

ngǒ⁵ jǎu⁵ _____ . *or* ngǒ⁵ mǒu⁵ _____ .
    (number + MW + siblings)

3. **To tell one's nationality**

   e.g.   **ngǒ⁵ hāi⁶ Měi⁵ Gwǒk³ jàn⁴.**

       (I am an American <u>citizen</u>.)

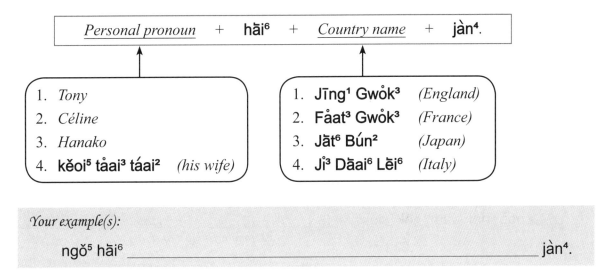

| _Personal pronoun_ | + | **hāi⁶** | + | _Country name_ | + | **jàn⁴**. |

Box 1:
1. *Tony*
2. *Céline*
3. *Hanako*
4. **kěoi⁵ tåai³ táai²** *(his wife)*

Box 2:
1. **Jīng¹ Gwǒk³** *(England)*
2. **Fåat³ Gwǒk³** *(France)*
3. **Jāt⁶ Bún²** *(Japan)*
4. **Jì³ Dāai⁶ Lēi⁶** *(Italy)*

Your example(s):

   ngǒ⁵ hāi⁶ _____ **jàn⁴**.

4. **To tell one's age** *(Nominal Predicate with no verb)*

   e.g.   **ngǒ⁵ gām¹ nìn⁴ jī⁶ sǎp⁶ sèoi³.**

       (I am twenty <u>years old</u> this year.)

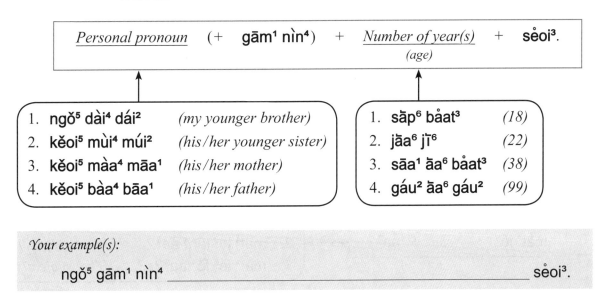

| _Personal pronoun_ | (+ | **gām¹ nìn⁴**) | + | _Number of year(s)_ | + | **sèoi³**. |
| | | | | *(age)* | | |

Box 1:
1. **ngǒ⁵ dài⁴ dái²** *(my younger brother)*
2. **kěoi⁵ mùi⁴ múi²** *(his/her younger sister)*
3. **kěoi⁵ màa⁴ māa¹** *(his/her mother)*
4. **kěoi⁵ bàa⁴ bāa¹** *(his/her father)*

Box 2:
1. **sǎp⁶ båat³** *(18)*
2. **jāa⁶ jī⁶** *(22)*
3. **sāa¹ āa⁶ båat³** *(38)*
4. **gáu² āa⁶ gáu²** *(99)*

Your example(s):

   ngǒ⁵ gām¹ nìn⁴ _____ **sèoi³**.

5. To tell one's major/subject of study (in university)

e.g. ngŏ⁵ hái² dāai⁶ hŏk⁶ dūk⁶ gåau³ jūk⁶.

  (My major at university is education.)

Personal pronoun	+	hái² dāai⁶ hŏk⁶	+	dūk⁶	+	Major/Subject.
				(/zýu² sāu¹)		

1. ngŏ⁵ gò⁴ gō¹   *(my elder brother)*
2. kĕoi⁵ zè⁴ zē¹   *(his/her elder sister)*
3. ngŏ⁵ sīn¹ sāang¹   *(my husband)*
4. kĕoi⁵ tåai³ táai²   *(his wife)*

1. fåat lēot⁶   *(law)*
2. jām¹ ngŏk⁶   *(music)*
3. gīng¹ zåi³   *(economics)*
4. gūng¹ cìng⁴   *(engineering)*

Your example(s):

  ngŏ⁵ hái² dāai⁶ hŏk⁶ dūk⁶ _____ .

  (major/subject of study)

6. To tell one's hobbies

e.g. ngŏ⁵ gė³ hǐng³ cěoi³ hāi⁶ lĕoi⁵ hàng⁴ tùng⁴ tēng¹ jām¹ ngŏk⁶.

  (My hobbies are traveling and listening to music.)

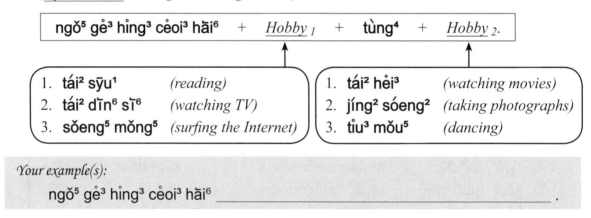

ngŏ⁵ gė³ hǐng³ cěoi³ hāi⁶	+	*Hobby ₁*	+	tùng⁴	+	*Hobby ₂.*

1. tái² sȳu¹   *(reading)*
2. tái² dīn⁶ sī̆⁶   *(watching TV)*
3. sŏeng⁵ mŏng⁵   *(surfing the Internet)*

1. tái² hĕi³   *(watching movies)*
2. jíng² sóeng²   *(taking photographs)*
3. tǐu³ mŏu⁵   *(dancing)*

Your example(s):

  ngŏ⁵ gė³ hǐng³ cěoi³ hāi⁶ _____ .

7. To ask "what" or "what kind of"

māt¹ jĕ⁵ + *Noun* + åa³ ?

1. māt¹ jĕ⁵ méng² åa³ ?   *(What name?)*
2. māt¹ jĕ⁵ jàn⁴ åa³ ?   *(What people?)*
3. māt¹ jĕ⁵ fō¹ åa³ ?   *(What subject?)*

e.g. 1. nĕi⁵ gǐu³ māt¹ jĕ⁵ méng² åa³ ?
      (What's your name?)

e.g. 2. nĕi⁵ hāi⁶ māt¹ jĕ⁵ jàn⁴ åa³ ?
      (lit. what kind of person are you? Re: nationality) (Where are you from?)

e.g. 3. nĕi⁵ hái² dāai⁶ hŏk⁶ dūk⁶ māt¹ jĕ⁵ fō¹ åa³ ?
      (What is your major/subject of study in university?)

e.g. 4. nĕi⁵ gė³ hǐng³ cěoi³ hāi⁶ māt¹ jĕ⁵ åa³ ?
      (What are your hobbies?)

1) **Names of countries** [①]

Names of foreign countries are translated into Chinese using several different methods. Some of them are based on the Chinese pronunciation (normally Putonghua) i.e. phonetic equivalents, e.g.

English	Cantonese
Canada (Ca-na-da)	Gāa¹ Nàa⁴ Dāai⁶ 加拿大
Philippines (Phi-lip-pines)	Fēi¹ Lēot⁶ Bān¹ 菲律賓
Scotland (S-cot-land)	Sōu¹ Gȧak³ Làan⁴ 蘇格蘭
Italy (I-ta-ly)	Ji̊³ Dāai⁶ Lēi⁶ 意大利

Others are combined with "**gwȯk³** 國 *(country)*" as an ending, e.g.

English	Cantonese
America	Měi⁵ Gwȯk³ 美國
United Kingdom (**Eng**land)	Jīng¹ Gwȯk³ 英國
France	Fȧat³ Gwȯk³ 法國
Thailand	Tȧai³ Gwȯk³ 泰國

2) **People:** *Country Name +* **jàn⁴**

To refer to the people who live in that country / city, the word "**jàn⁴** 人 *(person/people)*" is added to the country / city names.   **ngǒ⁵ hāi⁶ _____ jàn⁴**.

English	Cantonese
Chinese	Zūng¹ Gwȯk³ jàn⁴ 中國人
Japanese	Jāt⁶ Bún² jàn⁴ 日本人
Australian	Ȯu³ Zāu¹ jàn⁴ 澳洲人
Hong Kong people	Hōeng¹ Góng² jàn⁴ 香港人

For practice, read out the names of countries again and add the word "**jàn⁴** 人" to the name of the country.

[①] You can find more names of countries in the Glossary.

3) Nationalities

When you want to ask about one's nationality or the question 'where are you from?' you can say:

Question	Answer
1) něi⁵ hāi⁶ **māt¹ jě⁵** (gwők³) jàn⁴ åa³? 你 係 乜 嘢 （國） 人 呀？ *(lit. you/ are/ what/ (country)/ people/ ?)*	a) ngǒ⁵ hāi⁶ + *Place* + jàn⁴. 我 係 + *Place* + 人。
2) něi⁵ hāi⁶ **bīn¹ gwők³** jàn⁴ åa³? 你 係 邊 國 人 呀？ *(lit. you/ are/ which/ country/ people/ ?)*	
3) něi⁵ hāi⁶ **bīn¹ dŏu⁶** jàn⁴ åa³? 你 係 邊 度 人 呀？ *(lit. you/ are/ where/ people/ ?)*	b) ngǒ⁵ hái² + *Place* + lèi⁴ gě³. 我 喺 + *Place* + 嚟 嘅。
4) něi⁵ hái² **bīn¹ dŏu⁶ lèi⁴** gåa³? 你 喺 邊 度 嚟 㗎？ *(lit. you/ at/ where/ come/ ?)*	c) ngǒ⁵ jàu⁴ + *Place* + lèi⁴ gě³. 我 由 + *Place* + 嚟 嘅。
5) něi⁵ jàu⁴ **bīn¹ dŏu⁶ lèi⁴** gåa³? 你 由 邊 度 嚟 㗎？ *(lit. you/ from/ where/ come/ ?)*	

Actually the nationality as described above generally refers to one's current citizenship or nationality but not his/her "native" origin. The word "zīk⁶ 籍" is used to indicate one's current nationality if followed by a distinguishing indication of his/her native origin. E.g.

American nationality	Měi⁵ zīk⁶ 美籍
Japanese nationality	Jāt⁶ zīk⁶ 日籍
British Indian	Jīng¹ zīk⁶ Jǎn³ Dŏu⁶ jàn⁴ 英籍印度人
French Turk	Fåat³ zīk⁶ Tóu² Jǐ⁵ Kèi⁴ jàn⁴ 法籍土耳其人

On the other hand, the word "jēoi⁶ 裔" has added indication of one's ancestral origin or descendance from a specific ethnic[2] group. E.g.

Chinese descent / Chinese origin	Wàa⁴ jēoi⁶ 裔 (Wàa⁴ 華 *is a word that indicates 'China' or 'Chinese', e.g.* Wàa⁴ kìu⁴ 華僑: overseas Chinese)
Korean descent	Hòn⁴ jēoi⁶ 韓裔
American of African descent	Fēi¹ jēoi⁶ Měi⁵ Gwők³ jàn⁴ 非裔美國人
Canadian of French descent	Fåat³ jēoi⁶ Gāa¹ Nàa⁴ Dāai⁶ jàn⁴ 法裔加拿大人

---

② Our ethnic background describes how we think of ourselves. This may be based on many things, including, for example, our skin colour, language, culture, ancestry or family history. Ethnic background is NOT the same as nationality or country of birth. (Source: Kent County Council, UK) ngǒ⁵ dūk⁶ (/zýu² sāu¹ 主修) _____.

English	Jīng¹ Màn⁴ 英文
fine arts	ngāi⁶ sēot⁶ 藝術
history	lĭk⁶ sí² 歷史
translation	fāan¹ jīk¹ 翻譯
accountancy	wūi⁶ gǎi³ hŏk⁶ 會計學
marketing	sĭ⁵ còeng⁴ hŏk⁶ 市場學
electronic engineering	dīn⁶ zí² gūng¹ cìng⁴ 電子工程
medicine	jī¹ hŏk⁶ 醫學
biology	sāng¹ māt⁶ 生物
chemistry	fǎa³ hŏk⁶ 化學
architecture	gin³ zūk¹ hŏk⁶ 建築學
psychology	sām̄ lĕi⁵ hŏk⁶ 心理學
economics	gīng¹ zǎi³ 經濟
business management	gūng¹ sōeng¹ gún² lĕi⁵ 工商管理

ngǒ⁵ gě³ hǐng³ cěoi³ hǎi⁶ _____.

dancing	tiu³ mǒu⁵ 跳舞
hiking	hàang¹ sāan¹ 行山
shopping; walking around	hàang⁴ gāai¹ 行街
traveling	lĕoi⁵ hàng⁴ 旅行
listening to music	tēng¹ jām¹ ngŏk⁶ 聽音樂
reading	tái² sȳu¹ 睇書
karaoke	cǒeng³ kāa¹ lāai¹ ōu¹ kēi¹ 唱卡拉ＯＫ
taking photographs	jíng² sóeng² 影相
watching movies	tái² hěi³ 睇戲
playing chess	zūk¹ kéi² 捉棋
stamp collecting	zāap⁶ jàu⁴ 集郵
playing mahjong	dáa² màa⁴ zǒek³ 打麻雀
surfing the Internet	sǒeng⁵ mǒng⁵ 上網

Exercise

1. **Fill in the blanks with the numerals in parentheses and appropriate measure words.**
   (5 × 3% = 15%)

   1) ngǒ⁵ jǎu⁵ _____ ūk¹ kéi² jàn⁴. (9)

   2) ngǒ⁵ jǎu⁵ _____ hīng¹ dāi⁶ zí² mūi⁶. (5)

   3) ngǒ⁵ bàa⁴ bāa¹ jǎu⁵ _____ cē¹. (2)

   4) ngǒ⁵ gě³ gwǒk³ gāa¹ jǎu⁵ _____ dāai⁶ hǒk⁶. (367)

   5) nī¹ dōu⁶ jǎu⁵ _____ hǒk⁶ sāang¹. (24,500)

2. **Make your own speech in Cantonese by answering the following questions.**
   (8 × 7% + 9% = 65%)

   1) něi⁵ gịu³ māt¹ jě⁵ méng² ảa³?

   2) něi⁵ hāi⁶ māt¹ jě⁵ jàn⁴ ảa³?

   3) něi⁵ gām¹ nìn⁴ géi² dō¹ sẻoi³ ảa³?

   4) něi⁵ ūk¹ kéi² jǎu⁵ géi² dō¹ gỏ³ jàn⁴ ảa³?

   5) něi⁵ jǎu⁵ géi² dō¹ gỏ³ hīng¹ dāi⁶ zí² mūi⁶ ảa³?

   6) něi⁵ jì⁴ gāa¹ zỹu⁶ hái² bīn¹ dōu⁶ ảa³?

   7) něi⁵ hái² bīn¹ dōu⁶ dūk⁶ sỹu¹ ảa³?

   8) něi⁵ hái² dāai⁶ hǒk⁶ dūk⁶ māt¹ jě⁵ fō¹ ảa³?

   9) něi⁵ gě³ hỉng³ cẻoi³ hāi⁶ māt¹ jě⁵ ảa³? *(+2% for two hobbies)*

   _____

   _____

   _____

   _____

   _____

   _____

   _____

   _____

   _____

3. Match the following country names with the flags. (10 × 2% = 20%)

1) Hòn⁴ Gwǒk³   • ( )   • a)

2) Dāk¹ Gwǒk³   • ( )   • b)

green/white/red

3) Jīng¹ Gwǒk³   • ( )   • c)

4) Jǐ³ Dāai⁶ Lěi⁶   • ( )   • d)

5) Zūng¹ Gwǒk³   • ( )   • e)

6) Sān¹ Gǎa³ Bō¹   • ( )   • f)

7) Gāa¹ Nàa⁴ Dāai⁶   • ( )   • g)

8) Fǎat³ Gwǒk³   • ( )   • h)

9) Měi⁵ Gwǒk³   • ( )   • i)

10) Jāt⁶ Bún²   • ( )   • j)

blue/white/red

Lesson 6 | Getting to know a new friend

Learning Objectives

1. To ask for someone's name
2. To use "m̀⁴" to indicate negation of a verb or an adjective
3. To ask a yes-no question
4. To ask and tell one's know-how/ability with "sīk¹"
5. To ask and tell where one comes from
6. The elliptical question with "nē¹" at the end
7. To ask and tell the clock time *(refer to Unit 2 Section 6)*
8. To express necessity or obligation to do something using "jíu³"

síu² zé², něi⁵ hóu²,
něi⁵ giu³ māt¹ jě⁵ méng² åa³?

ngǒ⁵ sing³ Sí², giu³ *Amy*.
něi⁵ nē¹?

m̀⁴ hóu² jǐ³ sī¹, ngǒ⁵ jǎu⁵ sī⁶.
ngǒ⁵ jíu³ záu² låa³, bāai¹ båai³.

zǒi³ gin³!

Tony meets Amy at a welcome party.

Tony: síu² zé², něi⁵ hóu², něi⁵ g̊iu³ māt¹ jě⁵ méng² åa³?
小 姐，您 好，你 叫 乜 嘢 名 呀？
(Hello (Miss), what is your name?)

Amy: ngǒ⁵ sịng³ Sí², g̊iu³ *Amy*. něi⁵ gwǎi³ sịng³ åa³?
我 姓 史，叫 *Amy*。你 貴 姓 呀？
(My surname is Si and my name is Amy. What's your surname?)

Tony: ngǒ⁵ sịng³ Lěi⁵. g̊iu³ ngǒ⁵ *Tony* lāa¹!
我 姓 李。叫 我 *Tony* 啦！
(My surname is Lee. Just call me Tony.)

Amy, něi⁵ hāi⁶ m̀⁴ hāi⁶ Hōeng¹ Góng² jàn⁴ åa³?
Amy，你 係 唔 係 香 港 人 呀？
(Amy, are you a Hong Kong citizen?)

Amy: m̀⁴ hāi⁶, ngǒ⁵ hāi⁶ Měi⁵ Gwǒk³ jàn⁴. něi⁵ nē¹?
唔 係，我 係 美 國 人。你 呢？
(No, I am an American. And you?)

něi⁵ jàu⁴ bīn¹ dōu⁶ lèi⁴ g̊åa³?
你 由 邊 度 嚟 㗎？
(Where are you from?)

Tony: ngǒ⁵ jàu⁴ Jīng¹ Gwǒk³ lèi⁴ g̊ě³.
我 由 英 國 嚟 嘅。
(I'm from U. K.)

ngǒ⁵ hāi⁶ Wàa⁴ jēoi⁶ Jīng¹ Gwǒk³ jàn⁴.
我 係 華 裔 英 國 人。
(I'm British of Chinese descent.)

Amy: gám², něi⁵ sīk¹ m̀⁴ sīk¹ Zūng¹ Màn⁴ åa³?
嗽，你 識 唔 識 中 文 呀？
(Well, do you know Chinese?)

Amy: sīk¹ síu² síu² zē¹.
識 少 少 啫。
(Just a little.)

Amy: hāi⁶ nē¹, jì⁴ gāa¹ géi² dím² zūng¹ åa³?
係 呢，而 家 幾 點 鐘 呀？
(By the way, what time is it now?)

Tony: jì⁴ gāa¹ gáu² dím² zūng¹.
而 家 九 點 鐘。
(It's nine now.)

Amy: *Tony*, m̀⁴ hóu² ji³ sī¹, ngǒ⁵ jǎu⁵ sī̄⁶, ngǒ⁵ jiu³ záu² låa³, bāai¹ båai³.
Tony，唔 好 意 思，我 有 事，我 要 走 喇，拜 拜。
(Excuse me, Tony, I have something to do. I have to go. Bye-bye.)

Tony: zǒi³ g̊in³!
再 見！
(See you!)

1.	māt¹ jě⁵ 乜嘢	QW:	what; what kind of (also "mē¹ jě⁵")
2.	māt¹ jě⁵ méng² 乜嘢名	QW:	What name? How is it called? (also "mē¹ jě⁵ méng²")
3.	sing³ 姓	V/N:	be surnamed; surname
4.	Sí² 史	PN:	*[a Chinese surname]* *[(in L.6) a commonly transcribed Chinese surname for "Smith"]*
5.	něi⁵ gwåi³ sing³ åa³? 你貴姓呀？	SE:	What's your surname? *[a polite and formal way to ask someone's surname, "gwåi³" here means "honorable"]*
6.	m̀⁴ 唔 *(+ Verb/Adjective)*	Adv:	not; no *[used before a verb or an adjective indicating negation]*
7.	hāi⁶ m̀⁴ hāi⁶? 係唔係？	Ph:	*[a yes-no question form of the verb 'to be' (hāi⁶)]*
8.	Hōeng¹ Góng² jàn⁴ 香港人	N:	Hong Kong citizen
9.	nē¹ 呢？ *(Noun + nē¹?)*	Part:	*[an interrogative particle used to form an elliptical question which is related to a previous question, statement or context.]*
10.	něi⁵ nē¹? 你呢？	SE:	And you? How about you?
11.	jàu⁴ 由 *(+ Place/Time)*	Prep:	from (a starting point)
12.	gåa³ 㗎？ *(Question + gåa³?)*	Part:	*[an interrogative particle used to ask something that happened in the past or to require an answer straight away]*
13.	gě³ 嘅 *(Statement + gě³)*	Part:	*[a modal particle used at the end of a sentence to answer a question ending with "ga" or to give an explanation]*
14.	Jīng¹ Gwők³ 英國	PN:	England, United Kingdom
15.	Jīng¹ Gwők³ jàn⁴ 英國人	PN:	British

16.	Wàa⁴ jēoi⁶ 華裔	N:	a person of Chinese descent ("Wàa⁴" means China or Chinese)
17.	sīk¹ 識 (+ *Verb/Noun*)	V:	(in L.6) to know how to do sth.; to have the ability to do sth.
18.	Zūng¹ Màn⁴ 中文	N:	Chinese language (also "**Zūng¹ Mán²**")
19.	síu² síu² 少少	Nu:	a few; a little (opp. hóu² dō¹ 好多: a lot; many)
20.	zē¹ 啫	Part:	*[a modal particle used at the end of a sentence meaning 'only' or 'just' to play down the extent or significance of sth.]*
21.	hāi⁶ nē¹ 係呢	Intj:	by the way *[used when the speaker wants to change the topic of the conversation]*
22.	géi² dím² zūng¹ 幾點鐘	QW:	what's the time (also "**géi² dím²**")
23.	dím² zūng¹ 點鐘 (*Nu.* + dím² zūng¹) (e.g. gáu² dím² zūng¹)	Suff:	o'clock (basic time unit) *(also "Nu. 1-12 + dím² 點")*
24.	m̀⁴ hóu² jì³ sī¹ 唔好意思	SE:	(in L.6) excuse me (also "m̀⁴ hóu² jì³ si³")
25.	jǎu⁵ sī⁶ 有事	Ph:	to be occupied (with a matter); to have something to do
26.	jìu³ 要 (+ *Verb*)	AV:	(in L.6) have to; need to *[indicating the need or obligation to do sth.]*
27.	záu² 走	V:	to leave
28.	bāai¹ bàai³ 拜拜	SE:	bye-bye
29.	zòi³ gìn³ 再見	SE:	*(formal & polite)* goodbye; see you (again)

1. To ask for someone's name

1) Surname – *What is your surname? (lit. What is your honorable surname?)*

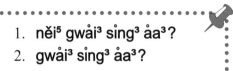

> 1. něi⁵ gwǎi³ sìng³ åa³?
> 2. gwǎi³ sìng³ åa³?

2) Full name or Given name – *What's your name?*

māt¹ jě⁵ =	*1.* mē¹ jě⁵
	2. mē¹
	3. māt¹

> 1. něi⁵ gìu³ <u>māt¹ jě⁵</u> méng² åa³?
> 2. něi⁵ gìu³ <u>mē¹ jě⁵</u> méng² åa³?
> 3. něi⁵ gìu³ <u>mē¹</u> méng² åa³?
> 4. něi⁵ gìu³ <u>māt¹</u> méng² åa³? *(informal)*

Your example(s):

něi⁵ gwǎi³ sìng³ åa³?

něi⁵ gìu³ māt¹ jě⁵ méng² åa³?

2. To use "m̀⁴" to indicate negation

e.g. *Amy* m̀⁴ hǎi⁶ Hōeng¹ Góng² jàn⁴.

(Amy is not a Hong Kong citizen.)

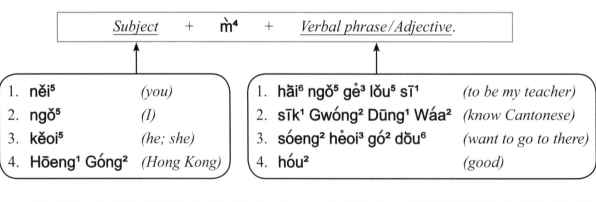

Subject	+	m̀⁴	+	*Verbal phrase/Adjective.*

1. něi⁵ *(you)*	1. hǎi⁶ ngǒ⁵ gě³ lǒu⁵ sī¹ *(to be my teacher)*
2. ngǒ⁵ *(I)*	2. sīk¹ Gwóng² Dūng¹ Wáa² *(know Cantonese)*
3. kěoi⁵ *(he; she)*	3. sóeng² hěoi³ gó² dōu⁶ *(want to go to there)*
4. Hōeng¹ Góng² *(Hong Kong)*	4. hóu² *(good)*

Your example(s):

ngǒ⁵ m̀⁴ _____.

3. To ask a yes-no question

e.g.   něi⁵ hǎi⁶ m̀⁴ hǎi⁶ Hōeng¹ Góng² jàn⁴ åa³?

(Are you a Hong Kong citizen?)

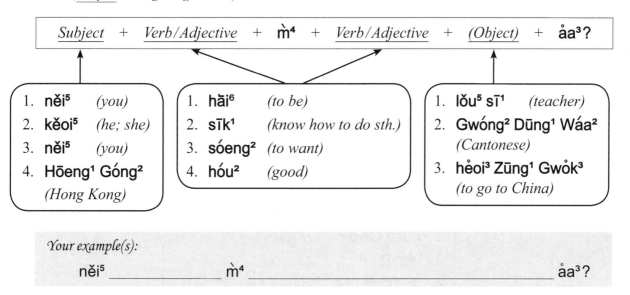

| *Subject* | + | *Verb/Adjective* | + | **m̀⁴** | + | *Verb/Adjective* | + | *(Object)* | + | **åa³?** |

1. něi⁵ *(you)*
2. kěoi⁵ *(he; she)*
3. něi⁵ *(you)*
4. Hōeng¹ Góng² *(Hong Kong)*

1. hǎi⁶ *(to be)*
2. sīk¹ *(know how to do sth.)*
3. sóeng² *(to want)*
4. hóu² *(good)*

1. lǒu⁵ sī¹ *(teacher)*
2. Gwóng² Dūng¹ Wáa² *(Cantonese)*
3. hěoi³ Zūng¹ Gwǒk³ *(to go to China)*

Your example(s):

 něi⁵ _____ m̀⁴ _____ åa³?

4. To ask and tell one's know-how/ability

e.g.   Q: něi⁵ sīk¹ m̀⁴ sīk¹ Zūng¹ Màn⁴ åa³?

(Do you know how to speak Chinese?)

A: (ngǒ⁵) sīk¹ síu² síu² zē¹.

(I only know a little.)

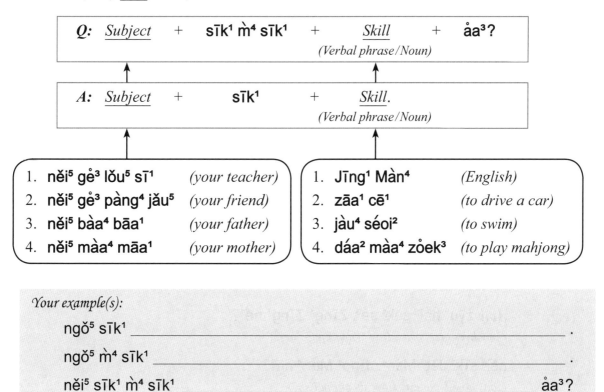

| *Q:* | *Subject* | + | **sīk¹ m̀⁴ sīk¹** | + | *Skill* | + | **åa³?** |
| | | | | | *(Verbal phrase/Noun)* | |

| *A:* | *Subject* | + | **sīk¹** | + | *Skill.* |
| | | | | | *(Verbal phrase/Noun)* |

1. něi⁵ gě³ lǒu⁵ sī¹ *(your teacher)*
2. něi⁵ gě³ pàng⁴ jǎu⁵ *(your friend)*
3. něi⁵ bàa⁴ bāa¹ *(your father)*
4. něi⁵ màa⁴ māa¹ *(your mother)*

1. Jīng¹ Màn⁴ *(English)*
2. zāa¹ cē¹ *(to drive a car)*
3. jàu⁴ séoi² *(to swim)*
4. dáa² màa⁴ zǒek³ *(to play mahjong)*

Your example(s):

ngǒ⁵ sīk¹ _____ .

ngǒ⁵ m̀⁴ sīk¹ _____ .

 něi⁵ sīk¹ m̀⁴ sīk¹ _____ åa³?

5. **To ask or tell where one comes from**

   e.g.   Q: **něi⁵ jàu⁴ bīn¹ dōu⁶ lèi⁴ g̊aa³?**
          (*Where are you from?*)

   A: **ngǒ⁵ jàu⁴ Jīng¹ Gwǒk³ lèi⁴ g̊e³.**
      (*I come from the United Kingdom.*)

Q:	*Subject*	+	**jàu⁴ bīn¹ dōu⁶**	+	**lèi⁴ g̊aa³?**

A:	*Subject*	+	**jàu⁴**	+	*Place*	+	**lèi⁴ g̊e³.**
					(*from somewhere*)		

   1. **Jīng¹ Gwǒk³**   (*the United Kingdom*)
   2. **F̊aat³ Gwǒk³**   (*France*)
   3. **Jāt⁶ Bún²**   (*Japan*)
   4. **J̊i³ Dāai⁶ Lěi⁶**   (*Italy*)

   Your example(s):
   ngǒ⁵ jàu⁴ _____ **lèi⁴ g̊e³.**
   něi⁵ jàu⁴ bīn¹ dōu⁶ lèi⁴ g̊aa³?

6. **The elliptical question with "nē¹" at the end**

   e.g.   1. **ngǒ⁵ hāi⁶ Měi⁵ Gwǒk³ jàn⁴. něi⁵ nē¹?**
             (*I am an American, and you?*)

Topic with information	+	*Noun / Pronoun*	+	**nē¹?**
		(*related to previous context*)		

   1. **něi⁵**   (*you*)
   2. **kěoi⁵**   (*he; she*)

   e.g.   2. **ngǒ⁵ g̊iu³ *Amy*. něi⁵ nē¹?**
             (*My name is Amy. And you?*)

   e.g.   3. ***Amy* zỹu⁶ hái² sūk¹ s̊e³. Zīng¹ Zīng¹ nē¹?**
             (*Amy lives in a hostel. How about Zing-Zing?*)

   e.g.   4. **něi⁵ sīk¹ Jāt⁶ Màn⁴. Jīng¹ Màn⁴ nē¹?**
             (*You know Japanese. How about English?*)

7. **To ask and tell the clock time** *(refer to Unit 1 Section 6)*

e.g. 1. jì⁴ gāa¹ géi² dím² zūng¹ åa³?

  (What time is it now?)

e.g. 2. jì⁴ gāa¹ gáu² dím² zūng¹.

  (It's nine o'clock now.)

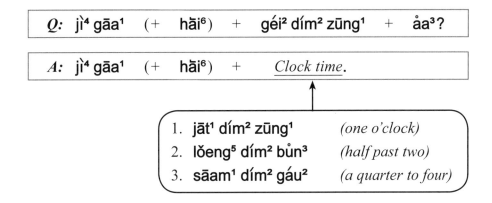

| *Q:* jì⁴ gāa¹ (+ hāi⁶) + géi² dím² zūng¹ + åa³? |

| *A:* jì⁴ gāa¹ (+ hāi⁶) + *Clock time*. |

1. jāt¹ dím² zūng¹ *(one o'clock)*
2. lŏeng⁵ dím² bůn³ *(half past two)*
3. sāam¹ dím² gáu² *(a quarter to four)*

Your example(s):

  jì⁴ gāa¹ (+ hāi⁶) _____ .

8. **To express necessity or obligation to do something**

e.g. ngŏ⁵ jău⁵ sī̊⁶. ngŏ⁵ jĭu³ záu² låa³.

  (I have something to do. I have to go.)

| *Subject* + jĭu³ + *Verb/Verbal phrase.* |
| *(have to, need to)* |

1. dūk⁶ sȳu¹ *(to study)*
2. zŏu⁶ jě⁵ *(to work)*
3. fāan¹ hŏk⁶ *(to go to school)*
4. fāan¹ gūng¹ *(to go to work)*
5. fāan¹ ūk¹ kéi² *(to go home)*

Your example(s):

  m̀⁴ hóu² jĭ³ sī¹. ngŏ⁵ jĭu³ _____ .

Q: něi⁵ sīk¹ (góng²) māt¹ jě⁵(/bīn¹ zúng² *(what kind of)*) jv̌u⁵ jìn⁴ åa³?

A: ngǒ⁵ sīk¹ (góng²) _____ .

1. ~ **Màn⁴** *or* ~ **Mán²** ① 文: stresses the written aspect of the language more

1)	*Chinese*	Zūng¹ Màn⁴; Zūng¹ Mán² 中文
2)	*English*	Jīng¹ Màn⁴; Jīng¹ Mán² 英文
3)	*Latin*	Lāai¹ Dīng¹ Màn⁴; Lāai¹ Dīng¹ Mán² 拉丁文
4)	*Spanish*	Sāi¹ Bāan¹ Ngàa⁴ Màn⁴; Sāi¹ Bāan¹ Ngàa⁴ Mán² 西班牙文
5)	*French*	Fåat³ Màn⁴; Fåat³ Mán² 法文
6)	*German*	Dāk¹ Màn⁴; Dāk¹ Mán² 德文
7)	*Japanese*	Jāt⁶ Màn⁴; Jāt⁶ Mán² 日文
8)	*Korean*	Hòn⁴ Màn⁴; Hòn⁴ Mán² 韓文
9)	*Thai*	Tåai³ Màn⁴; Tåai³ Mán² 泰文

2. ~ **Wáa²** 話: refers to the vernacular speech or spoken form of the language only

1)	*local dialect*	bún² dēi⁶ wáa² 本地話
2)	*foreign language*	ngōi⁶ gwők³ wáa² 外國話
3)	*Cantonese dialect (as opposed to other Chinese dialects)*	Gwóng² Dūng¹ Wáa² 廣東話
4)	*Guangzhou dialect (as opposed to other dialects spoken in Guangdong Province)*	Gwóng² Zāu¹ Wáa² 廣州話
5)	*Shanghaiese dialect*	Sōeng⁶ Hói² Wáa² 上海話
6)	*Spanish*	Sāi¹ Bāan¹ Ngàa⁴ Wáa² 西班牙話
7)	*Filipino*	Fēi¹ Lēot⁶ Bān¹ Wáa² 菲律賓話
8)	*Korean*	Hòn⁴ Gwők³ Wáa² 韓國話
9)	*Japanese*	Jāt⁶ Bún² Wáa² 日本話
10)	*Osaka dialect*	Dāai⁶ Báan² Wáa² 大阪話

---

① The original and formal tone of the Chinese character 文 is 4. Tone 2 reflects the colloquial form of Cantonese. Both are used in spoken Cantonese.

Q: něi⁵ sīk¹ m̀⁴ sīk¹ _____ åa³?

1)	*to drive (a vehicle)*	zāa¹ cē¹ 揸車
2)	*to type*	dáa² zī⁶ 打字
3)	*to play piano*	tàan⁴ kàm⁴ 彈琴
4)	*to play violin*	lāai¹ síu² tài⁴ kàm⁴ 拉小提琴
5)	*to play mahjong*	dáa² màa⁴ zóek³ 打麻雀
6)	*to cook*	zýu² fāan⁶ 煮飯

FYI – 3. Sports (wǎn⁶ dǔng⁶)

Q: něi⁵ zūng¹ jǐ³ zóu⁶ māt¹ jě⁵ wǎn⁶ dǔng⁶ åa³?

A: ngǒ⁵ zūng¹ jǐ³ _____ .

1)	*swimming*	jàu⁴ séoi² 游水
2)	*diving*	cìm⁴ séoi² 潛水
3)	*ice-skating*	làu⁴ bīng¹ 溜冰
4)	*skiing*	wāat⁶ sýut³ 滑雪
5)	*wind-surfing*	wáan² wāat⁶ lōng⁶ fūng¹ fàan⁴ 玩滑浪風帆
6)	*cycling*	jáai² dāan¹ cē¹ 踩單車 (also 'cáai² dāan¹ cē¹')
7)	*kungfu*	dáa² gūng¹ fū¹ 打功夫
8)	*weight lifting*	géoi² cǔng⁵ 舉重
9)	*playing badminton*	dáa² jǔu⁵ mòu⁴ kàu⁴ 打羽毛球
10)	*playing baseball*	dáa² lèoi⁴ kàu⁴ 打壘球
11)	*playing basketball*	dáa² làam⁴ kàu⁴ 打籃球
12)	*playing golf*	dáa² gōu¹ jǐ⁵ fū¹ kàu⁴ 打高爾夫球
13)	*playing table tennis*	dáa² bīng¹ bām¹ bō¹ 打乒乓波
14)	*playing squash*	dáa² bīk¹ kàu⁴ 打壁球
15)	*playing tennis*	dáa² mǒng⁵ kàu⁴ 打網球
16)	*playing volleyball*	dáa² pàai⁴ kàu⁴ 打排球
17)	*playing soccer/football*	těk³ zūk¹ kàu⁴ 踢足球
18)	*running; jogging*	páau² bōu⁶ 跑步

1. **Use the given phrases to form a yes-no question first and then give a positive or negative answer according to your own situation.** (13 × 2% = 26%)

e.g. něi⁵/hāi⁶/dāai⁶ hŏk⁶ sāang¹

    Q: <u>něi⁵ hāi⁶ m̀⁴ hāi⁶ dāai⁶ hŏk⁶ sāang¹ åa³?</u>

    A (yes): <u>hāi⁶, ngŏ⁵ hāi⁶ dāai⁶ hŏk⁶ sāang¹.</u>

    A (no): <u>m̀⁴ hāi⁶, ngŏ⁵ m̀⁴ hāi⁶ dāai⁶ hŏk⁶ sāang¹. ngŏ⁵ hāi⁶ lŏu⁵ sī¹.</u>

1) něi⁵/hāi⁶/gāau¹ wŭn⁶ hŏk⁶ sāang¹

    Q: _____

    A (yes/no): _____

2) nī¹ dōu⁶/hāi⁶/Hōeng¹ Góng² Dóu²

    Q: _____

    A (yes/no): _____

3) něi⁵/sóeng²/wŭn⁶/Góng² Bāi⁶

    Q: _____

    A (yes/no): _____

4) něi⁵/jău⁵/hīng¹ dāi⁶ zí² mūi⁶

    Q: _____

    A (yes/no): _____

5) *Tony*/sīk¹/Gwóng² Dūng¹ Wáa²

    Q: _____

    A (yes/no): _____. něi⁵ nē¹?

    A (yes/no): _____

6) Hōeng¹ Góng²/lěng³

    Q: _____

    A (yes/no): _____

2. **Ask the following questions in Cantonese.** $(10 \times 5\% = 50\%)$

   1) What's your surname?

      _____

   2) What's your name?

      _____

   3) Where are you from?

      _____

   4) How old are you this year?

      _____

   5) Are you a student from the International University?

      _____

   6) Where do you live now?

      _____

   7) What is your major in university?

      _____

   8) How many brothers and sisters do you have?

      _____

   9) Do you know how to speak Chinese?

      _____

   10) What are your hobbies?

      _____

3. **Translate the following into Cantonese.** $(4 \times 6\% = 24\%)$

   1) He doesn't want to have coffee.

      _____

   2) I'm an American of Chinese descent.

      _____

   3) I only know how to speak a little Cantonese.

      _____

   4) Excuse me. I have to go now.

      _____

Learning Objectives

1. To tell one's occupation or working place
2. To use the verb "gåau³ (teach)"
3. To know the function of "dōu¹" in a parallel situation
4. To express one's likes or dislikes
5. To ask a yes-no question with a disyllabic "zūng¹ jǐ³"
6. To use "tùng⁴" to indicate doing something with someone together
7. To indicate how often an action occurs

Zūng¹ Gwŏk³ pàng⁴ jǎu⁵

jāt¹ wái² zūng¹ jī¹

nàam⁴ pàng⁴ jǎu⁵

něoi⁵ pàng⁴ jǎu⁵

Person₁ gåau³ *Person₂* + *Skill/Knowledge*

Person hŏk⁶ + *Skill/Knowledge*

Amy tells Zing-Zing about her Chinese friend, Siu-Ping.

ngǒ⁵ jǎu⁵ jāt¹ gǒ³ Zūng¹ Gwǒk³ pàng⁴ jǎu⁵. kěoi⁵ gǐu³ Càn⁴ Síu² Pìng⁴.
我 有 一 個 中 國 朋 友。佢 叫 陳 小 平。
(I have a Chinese friend. Her name is Siu-Ping Chan.)

ngǒ⁵ gǐu³ kěoi⁵ Åa³ Pìng⁴. kěoi⁵ hāi⁶ Gwóng² Dūng¹ jàn⁴.
我 叫 佢 阿 平。佢 係 廣 東 人。
(I call her "Ah-Ping". She is Cantonese.)

Åa³ Pìng⁴ hāi⁶ jāt¹ wái² zūng¹ jī¹.
阿 平 係 一 位 中 醫。
(Ah-Ping is a doctor of Chinese medicine.)

kěoi⁵ hái² Hōeng¹ Góng² Zūng¹ Jī¹ Hǒk⁶ Jýun² zǒu⁶ jě⁵.
佢 喺 香 港 中 醫 學 院 做 嘢。
(She works in the Hong Kong College of Chinese Medicine.)

kěoi⁵ sīk¹ góng² Póu² Tūng¹ Wáa². kěoi⁵ dōu¹ sīk¹ góng² síu² síu² Jīng¹ Mán².
佢 識 講 普 通 話。佢 都 識 講 少 少 英 文。
(She speaks Mandarin. She also knows how to speak a little English.)

Åa³ Pìng⁴ mǒu⁵ Jīng¹ Mán² lǒu⁵ sī¹,
阿 平 冇 英 文 老 師,
(Ah-Ping does not have an English teacher,)

bāt¹ gwǒ³ Åa³ Pìng⁴ gě³ nàam⁴ pàng⁴ jǎu⁵ hāi⁶ Jīng¹ Gwǒk³ jàn⁴.
不 過 阿 平 嘅 男 朋 友 係 英 國 人。
(but her boyfriend is British.)

kěoi⁵ gǐu³ *Tony*.
佢 叫 *Tony*。
(His name is Tony.)

Tony gǎau³ Åa³ Pìng⁴ Jīng¹ Mán², Åa³ Pìng⁴ gǎau³ *Tony* Gwóng² Dūng¹ Wáa².
Tony 教 阿 平 英 文,阿 平 教 *Tony* 廣 東 話。
(Tony teaches Ah-Ping English and Ah-Ping teaches Tony Cantonese.)

Tony m̀⁴ zūng¹ jǐ³ gǎau³ Jīng¹ Mán²,
Tony 唔 中 意 教 英 文,
(Tony doesn't like to teach English,)

bāt¹ gwǒ³ kěoi⁵ hóu² zūng¹ jǐ³ hǒk⁶ Gwóng² Dūng¹ Wáa².
不 過 佢 好 中 意 學 廣 東 話。
(but he likes to learn Cantonese very much.)

kěoi⁵ sì⁴ sì⁴ tùng⁴ Åa³ Pìng⁴ jāt¹ cài⁴ lìn⁶ zāap⁶ Gwóng² Dūng¹ Wáa².
佢 時 時 同 阿 平 一 齊 練 習 廣 東 話。
(He often practices Cantonese with Ah-Ping together.)

1.	Zūng¹ Gwỏk³ pàng⁴ jǎu⁵ 中國朋友 (*M:* gỏ³ 個)	N:	a Chinese friend ("pàng⁴ jǎu⁵ 朋友": friend)
2.	Càn⁴ Síu² Pìng⁴ 陳小平	PN:	*[a Chinese name]* "Càn" is the surname and "Síu² Pìng⁴" is the given name used by male or female
3.	åa³ 阿 (+ *Name*) (e.g. Åa³ Pìng⁴)	Pref:	*[used as a prefix to names; a friendly form of addressing people]*
4.	Gwóng² Dūng¹ jàn⁴ 廣東人	N:	Cantonese people
5.	wái² 位 (e.g. jāt¹ wái² lǒu⁵ sī¹)	MW:	*[a measure word for a person and a way to show respect]*
6.	zūng¹ jī¹ 中醫	N:	a doctor of Chinese medicine
7.	hȍk⁶ jýun² 學院	N:	college, faculty
8.	góng² 講 (+ *Object*)	V:	to speak; to talk
9.	Pỏu² Tūng¹ Wáa² 普通話	N:	(lit. common speech) Mandarin / Putonghua *[the modern Chinese language]*
10.	dōu¹ 都 (+ *Verb/Adjective*)	Adv:	also, too
11.	Jīng¹ Mán² 英文	N:	English (also "Jīng¹ Màn⁴")
12.	bāt¹ gwỏ³ 不過	Conj:	but, however
13.	nàam⁴ pàng⁴ jǎu⁵ 男朋友	N:	boyfriend (opp. "něoi⁵ pàng⁴ jǎu⁵ 女朋友": girlfriend)
14.	gåau³ 教 (+ *Person* + *Object*)	V:	to teach
15.	hȍk⁶ 學 (+ *Object*)	V:	to learn, to study
16.	zūng¹ jỉ³ 中意／鍾意 (+ *Object*)	V:	to like, be fond of
17.	sì⁴ sì⁴ 時時	Adv:	always; often (also "gīng¹ sòeng⁴ 經常")
18.	tùng⁴ 同 (+ *Person* + *Verb*)	Prep:	with (someone to do something)
19.	jāt¹ cài⁴ 一齊 (+ *Verb*)	Adv:	(do something) together
20.	lȉn⁶ zȁap⁶ 練習	V/N:	to practice; practice

1. To tell one's occupation or working place

e.g. Åa³ Pìng⁴ h̄ăi⁶ jāt¹ wái² zūng¹ jī¹.

(Ah-Ping is a doctor of Chinese medicine.)

kĕoi⁵ hái² Hōeng¹ Góng² Zūng¹ Jī¹ Hŏk⁶ Jýun² zōu⁶ jĕ⁵.

(She works in the Hong Kong College of Chinese Medicine.)

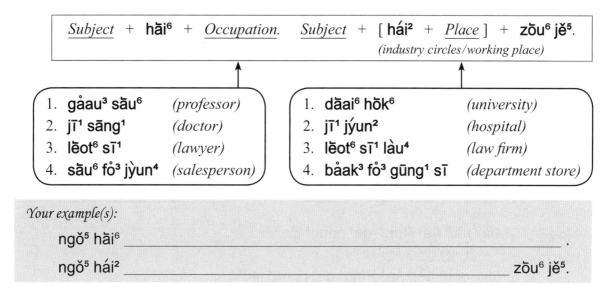

Subject + **h̄ăi⁶** + *Occupation.*	*Subject* + [**hái²** + *Place*] + **zōu⁶ jĕ⁵.**
	(industry circles/working place)

1. gåau³ sāu⁶   *(professor)*
2. jī¹ sāng¹   *(doctor)*
3. lēot⁶ sī¹   *(lawyer)*
4. sāu⁶ fǒ³ jẙun⁴   *(salesperson)*

1. dāai⁶ hŏk⁶   *(university)*
2. jī¹ jýun²   *(hospital)*
3. lēot⁶ sī¹ làu⁴   *(law firm)*
4. båak³ fǒ³ gūng¹ sī   *(department store)*

Your example(s):

ngǒ⁵ h̄ăi⁶ _____ .

ngǒ⁵ hái² _____ zōu⁶ jĕ⁵.

2. To use the verb "teach"

e.g. kĕoi⁵ gåau³ åa³ Pìng⁴ Jīng¹ Mán².

(He teaches Ah-Ping English.)

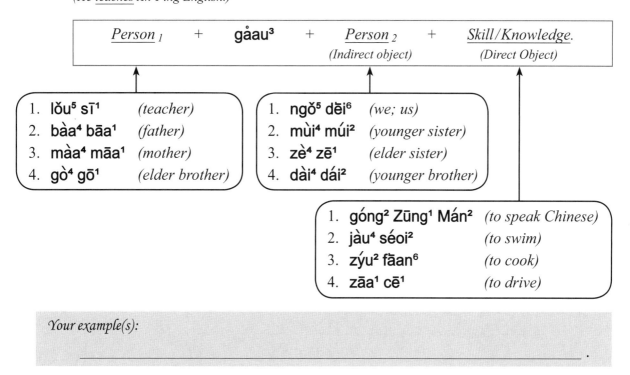

Person ₁ + **gåau³** + *Person ₂* + *Skill/Knowledge.*
(Indirect object)   *(Direct Object)*

1. lǒu⁵ sī¹   *(teacher)*
2. bàa⁴ bāa¹   *(father)*
3. màa⁴ māa¹   *(mother)*
4. gò⁴ gō¹   *(elder brother)*

1. ngǒ⁵ dēi⁶   *(we; us)*
2. mùi⁴ múi²   *(younger sister)*
3. zè⁴ zē¹   *(elder sister)*
4. dài⁴ dái²   *(younger brother)*

1. góng² Zūng¹ Mán²   *(to speak Chinese)*
2. jàu⁴ séoi²   *(to swim)*
3. zýu² fāan⁶   *(to cook)*
4. zāa¹ cē¹   *(to drive)*

Your example(s):

_____ .

3. **The function of "dōu¹" in a parallel situation**

e.g. 1. kěoi⁵ sīk¹ góng² Póu² Tūng¹ Wáa².
   (She knows how to speak Mandarin.)

   kěoi⁵ dōu¹ sīk¹ góng² síu² síu² Jīng¹ Mán².
   (She also knows how to speak English.)

e.g. 2. Åa³ Pìng⁴ hāi⁶ *Tony* gẻ³ něoi⁵ pàng⁴ jǎu⁵.
   (Ah-Ping is Tony's girlfriend.)

   kěoi⁵ dōu¹ hāi⁶ *Tony* gẻ³ Gwóng² Dūng¹ Wáa² lǒu⁵ sī¹.
   (She is also Tony's Cantonese teacher.)

Subject A + **sīk¹ góng²** + *Language ₁.*   *Subject A* + **dōu¹** + **sīk¹ góng²** + *Language ₂.*
(same subject)

---

1. Jāt⁶ Mán²	*(Japanese)*	1. Hòn⁴ Mán²	*(Korean language)*
2. Fåat³ Mán²	*(French)*	2. Dāk¹ Mán²	*(German language)*
3. Sāi¹ Bāan¹ Ngàa⁴ Mán²	*(Spanish)*	3. Tåai³ Mán²	*(Thai language)*

e.g. 3. *Amy* hāi⁶ Åa³ Pìng⁴ gẻ³ pàng⁴ jǎu⁵.
   (Amy is Ah-Ping's friend.)

   Tony dōu¹ hāi⁶ Åa³ Pìng⁴ gẻ³ pàng⁴ jǎu⁵.
   (Tony is also Ah-Ping's friend.)

e.g. 4. Jīng¹ Gwỏk³ jàn⁴ góng² Jīng¹ Mán².
   (The British speak English.)

   Měi⁵ Gwỏk³ jàn⁴ dōu¹ góng² Jīng¹ Mán².
   (Americans also speak English.)

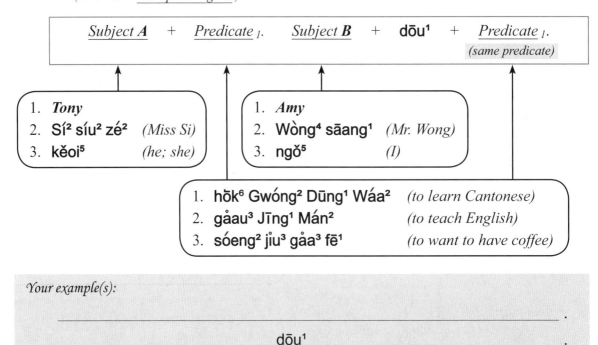

Subject A + *Predicate ₁.*   *Subject B* + **dōu¹** + *Predicate ₁.*
(same predicate)

1. *Tony*		1. *Amy*	
2. Sí² síu² zé²	*(Miss Si)*	2. Wòng⁴ sāang¹	*(Mr. Wong)*
3. kěoi⁵	*(he; she)*	3. ngǒ⁵	*(I)*

1. hȫk⁶ Gwóng² Dūng¹ Wáa²	*(to learn Cantonese)*
2. gåau³ Jīng¹ Mán²	*(to teach English)*
3. sóeng² jiu³ gåa³ fē¹	*(to want to have coffee)*

Your example(s):

_____ .

_____ dōu¹ _____ .

4. **To express one's likes and dislikes**

e.g. *Tony* hóu² zūng¹ jǐ³ hōk⁶ Gwóng² Dūng¹ Wáa².
(Tony likes learning Cantonese very much.)

Tony m̀⁴ zūng¹ jǐ³ gåau³ Jīng¹ Mán².
(Tony doesn't like teaching English.)

Subject	+	(hóu²) zūng¹ jǐ³ m̀⁴ zūng¹ jǐ³	+	Something / Somebody. *(Noun)*

1. Zūng¹ Gwǒk³ jām¹ ngōk⁶   *(Chinese music)*
2. gú² dín² jām¹ ngōk⁶   *(classical music)*
3. ngǒ⁵ gě³ lǒu⁵ báan²   *(my boss)*
4. ngǒ⁵ gě³ tùng⁴ sǐ⁶   *(my colleague)*

Subject	+	(hóu²) zūng¹ jǐ³ m̀⁴ zūng¹ jǐ³	+	to do something. *(Verbal phrase)*

1. tēng¹ jām¹ ngōk⁶   *(listening to music)*
2. cǒeng³ gō¹   *(singing)*
3. hōk⁶ Gwóng² Dūng¹ Wáa²   *(learning Cantonese)*
4. sǒeng⁵ mǒng⁵   *(surfing the Internet)*

Your example(s):

ngǒ⁵ hóu² zūng¹ jǐ³ _____ .

ngǒ⁵ m̀⁴ zūng¹ jǐ³ _____ .

něi⁵ zūng¹ m̀⁴ zūng¹ jǐ³ _____ åa³ ?

5. **To ask a yes-no question with a disyllabic "zūng¹ jǐ³"**

Subject	+	zūng¹ jǐ³	+	m̀⁴ zūng¹ jǐ³	+	Object	+	åa³ ?
						(Noun / Verbal phrase)		

1. Hōeng¹ Góng²   *(Hong Kong)*
2. tái² dǐn⁶ sǐ⁶   *(watching TV)*
3. tái² hěi³   *(watching a movie)*
4. sǒeng⁵ mǒng⁵   *(surfing the Internet)*

6. **To use "tùng⁴" to indicate doing something with someone together**

   e.g. kěoi⁵ sì⁴ sì⁴ tùng⁴ Åa³ Pìng⁴ jāt¹ cài⁴ lìn⁶ zāap⁶ Gwóng² Dūng¹ Wáa².

   (He often practices Cantonese <u>with Ah-Ping together</u>.)

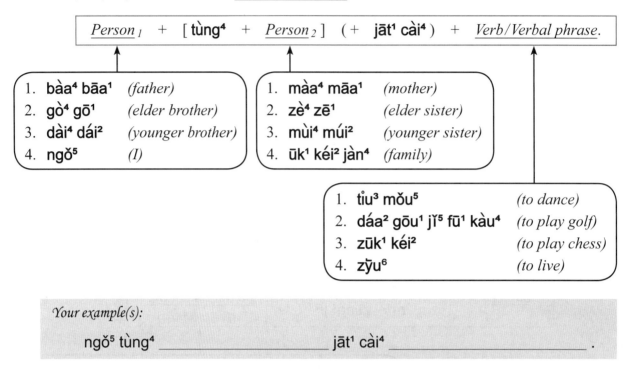

| Person ₁ + [tùng⁴ + Person ₂] (+ jāt¹ cài⁴) + Verb/Verbal phrase. |

1. bàa⁴ bāa¹   *(father)*
2. gò⁴ gō¹   *(elder brother)*
3. dài⁴ dái²   *(younger brother)*
4. ngǒ⁵   *(I)*

1. màa⁴ māa¹   *(mother)*
2. zè⁴ zē¹   *(elder sister)*
3. mùi⁴ múi²   *(younger sister)*
4. ūk¹ kéi² jàn⁴ *(family)*

1. tǐu³ mǒu⁵   *(to dance)*
2. dáa² gōu¹ jǐ⁵ fū¹ kàu⁴ *(to play golf)*
3. zūk¹ kéi²   *(to play chess)*
4. zy̌u⁶   *(to live)*

Your example(s):

ngǒ⁵ tùng⁴ _____ jāt¹ cài⁴ _____ .

7. **To indicate how often an action occurs**

   e.g. kěoi⁵ sì⁴ sì⁴ tùng⁴ Åa³ Pìng⁴ jāt¹ cài¹ lìn⁶ zāap⁶ Gwóng² Dūng¹ Wáa².

   (He <u>often</u> practices Cantonese with Ah-Ping together.)

| Subject + Adverb of Frequency + Verb/Verbal phrase. |

1. jǎu⁵ sì⁴   *(sometimes)*
2. gåan³ zūng¹   *(occasionally)*
3. hóu² síu²   *(rarely; seldom)*
4. cùng⁴ lòi⁴ m̀⁴ *(never)*

1. tái² dīn⁶ sǐ⁶   *(to watch TV)*
2. tái² hěi³   *(to watch a movie)*
3. sǒeng⁵ mǒng⁵   *(to surf the Internet)*
4. sìk⁶ jīn¹   *(to smoke)*

Your example(s):

_____ .

FYI – 1. Occupations (gūng¹ zôk³)

Q: něi⁵ zōeng¹ lòi⁴ *(future)* sóeng² zōu⁶ māt¹ jě⁵ gūng¹ zȯk³ åa³?

A: ngǒ⁵ sóeng² zōu⁶ _____ .

1.	*accountant*	wūi⁶ gåi³ sī¹ 會計師
2.	*civil servant*	gūng¹ mǒu⁶ jỳun⁴ 公務員
3.	*coach; instructor*	gåau³ līn⁶ 教練
4.	*cook; chef*	cèoi⁴ sī¹ 廚師 (also "cỳu⁴ sī¹")
5.	*driver*	sī¹ gēi¹ 司機
6.	*fireman*	sīu¹ fòng⁴ jỳun⁴ 消防員
7.	*lawyer*	lēot⁶ sī¹ 律師
8.	*manager*	gīng¹ lěi⁵ 經理
9.	*medical doctor*	jī¹ sāng¹ 醫生
10.	*nurse*	wū̄⁶ sī̄⁶ 護士
11.	*police*	gíng² cåat³ 警察
12.	*professor*	gåau³ sāu⁶ 教授
13.	*salesperson*	sāu⁶ fo³ jỳun⁴ 售貨員
14.	*social worker*	sě⁵ wúi² gūng¹ zȯk³ zé² 社會工作者
15.	*worker; servant; amah;* *maid; domestic helper*	gūng¹ jàn⁴ 工人
16.	*teller*	ngàn⁴ hòng⁴ cēot¹ nāap⁶ jỳun⁴ 銀行出納員
17.	*waiter; waitress*	sī̄⁶ jing³ sāng¹ 侍應生
18.	*housewife*	gāa¹ tìng⁴ zýu² fǔ⁵ 家庭主婦
19.	*artist; actor; actress*	ngāi⁶ jàn⁴ 藝人；jín² jỳun⁴ 演員
20.	*singer*	gō¹ sáu² 歌手

kĕoi⁵ hái² _____ zŏu⁶ jĕ⁵.

1.	*hotel*	záu² dím³ 酒店
2.	*school*	hŏk⁶ hāau⁶ 學校
3.	*hospital*	jī¹ jýun² 醫院
4.	*clinic*	cán² só² 診所
5.	*bank*	ngàn⁴ hòng⁴ 銀行
6.	*Chinese restaurant*	záu² làu⁴ 酒樓
7.	*restaurant*	cāan¹ tēng¹ 餐廳
8.	*department store*	bǎak³ fŏ³ gūng¹ sī¹ 百貨公司
9.	*insurance company*	bóu² hím² gūng¹ sī¹ 保險公司
10.	*government departments*	zǐng³ fú² bŏu⁶ mùn⁴ 政府部門
11.	*accounting firm*	wūi⁶ gǎi³ sī¹ làu⁴ 會計師樓
12.	*factory*	gūng¹ cóng² 工廠
13.	*company; corporation; firm*	gūng¹ sī¹ 公司
14.	*construction/ architecture company*	gǐn³ zūk¹ gūng¹ sī¹ 建築公司
15.	*real estate company*	dēi⁶ cáan² gūng¹ sī¹ 地產公司
16.	*import/export corporation*	cēot¹ jǎp⁶ háu² gūng¹ sī¹ 出入口公司
17.	*transport/freight corporation*	wān⁶ sȳu¹ gūng¹ sī¹ 運輸公司
18.	*computer firm*	dīn⁶ nŏu⁵ gūng¹ sī¹ 電腦公司
19.	*finance corporation*	gām¹ jùng⁴ gūng¹ sī¹ 金融公司
20.	*airline company*	hòng⁴ hūng¹ gūng¹ sī¹ 航空公司

1. **Rearrange the various parts of the following sentences in their right order.**
   (6 × 10% = 60%)

   1) pàng⁴ jǎu⁵ / jǎu⁵ / ngǒ⁵ / Zūng¹ Gwǒk³ / jāt¹ gǒ³ / . /

   _____

   2) hāi⁶ / Gwóng² Dūng¹ jàn⁴ / kěoi⁵ / . /

   _____

   3) góng² / sīk¹ / Póu² Tūng¹ Wáa² / kěoi⁵ / . /

   _____

   4) gǎau³ / kěoi⁵ / Gwóng² Dūng¹ Wáa² / Åa³ Pìng⁴ / . /

   _____

   5) hāi⁶ / jāt¹ / zūng¹ jī¹ / Åa³ Pìng⁴ / wái² / . /

   _____

   6) Jīng¹ Mán² / síu² síu² / sīk¹ / kěoi⁵ / dōu¹ / góng² / . /

   _____

2. **Add the words in the brackets to the following sentences by placing " ↓ " at the appropriate positions.** (8 × 3% = 24%)

   e.g. ngǒ⁵ hāi⁶ Hōeng¹ Góng² Dāai⁶ hōk⁶ ↓ hōk⁶ sāang¹. (gě³)

   1) Åa³ Pìng⁴ līn⁶ zāap⁶ Jīng¹ Mán². (tùng⁴ *Tony*)
   2) Åa³ Pìng⁴ sīk¹ góng² Póu² Tūng¹ Wáa², kěoi⁵ sīk¹ góng² Jīng¹ Mán². (dōu¹)
   3) *Tony* sīk¹ Póu² Tūng¹ Wáa². (síu² síu²)
   4) Åa³ Pìng⁴ hāi⁶ jāt¹ zūng¹ jī¹. (wái²)
   5) kěoi⁵ hōk⁶ Gwóng² Dūng¹ Wáa². (hái² dāai⁶ hōk⁶)
   6) kěoi⁵ zūng¹ jǐ³ jíng² sóeng². (hóu²)
   7) *Tony* līn⁶ zāap⁶ jàu⁴ séoi². (sì⁴ sì⁴)
   8) Càn⁴ lǒu⁵ sī¹ gǎau³ Gwóng² Dūng¹ Wáa². (ngǒ⁵ dēi⁶)

3. **Make sentences (10 words or above) with the following Cantonese expressions.**
   (8 × 2% = 16%)

   1) … bāt¹ gwǒ³…

   _____

   2) tùng⁴…jāt¹ cài⁴…

   _____

Lesson 8 | Chatting with a friend

Learning Objectives

1. To ask and tell when an event happens *(refer to Unit 2 Section 5)*
2. To inquire about one's occupation or working place
3. To tell if someone is busy or not with adverbs of degree
4. To know the function of "**dōu¹**" expressing all-inclusive or no exception
5. To express that an action/activity is not necessary using "**m̀⁴ sái²**"
6. To ask and tell what one likes to do in one's free time
7. To state a continuous action or activity with "**gán²**"
8. To know how to respond to a compliment

něi⁵ géi² sì⁴ lèi⁴ Hōeng¹ Góng² gǎa³ ?

ngǒ⁵ gām¹ nìn⁴ gáu² jÿut⁶ jāt¹ hǒu⁶ lèi⁴ Hōeng¹ Góng² gě³.

ngǒ⁵ jàu⁴ sīng¹ kèi⁴ jāt¹ zǐ³ sīng¹ kèi⁴ nǧ⁵ dōu¹ hóu² mòng⁴.

Tony is practicing Cantonese with Siu-Ping.

Siu-Ping: Tony, něi⁵ géi² sì⁴ lèi⁴ Hōeng¹ Góng² gǎa³?
Tony，你 幾 時 嚟 香 港 㗎？
(Tony, when did you come to Hong Kong?)

Tony: ngǒ⁵ gām¹ nìn⁴ gáu² jy̌ut⁶ jāt¹ hōu⁶ lèi⁴ Hōeng¹ Góng² gě³.
我 今 年 九 月 一 號 嚟 香 港 嘅。
(I came to Hong Kong this year on the 1ˢᵗ of September.)

Siu-Ping: něi⁵ jì⁴ gāa¹ hái² bīn¹ dōu⁶ zōu⁶ jě⁵ ǎa³？
你 而 家 喺 邊 度 做 嘢 呀？
(Where are you working now?)

Tony: ngǒ⁵ hái² lēot⁶ sī¹ làu⁴ zōu⁶ jě⁵, ngǒ⁵ hāi⁶ lēot⁶ sī¹.
我 喺 律 師 樓 做 嘢，我 係 律 師。
(I work in a law firm. I'm a lawyer.)

Siu-Ping: něi⁵ mòng⁴ m̀⁴ mòng⁴ ǎa³？
你 忙 唔 忙 呀？
(Are you busy?)

Tony: ngǒ⁵ jàu⁴ sīng¹ kèi⁴ jāt¹ zi³ sīng¹ kèi⁴ nǧ⁵ dōu¹ hóu² mòng⁴,
我 由 星 期 一 至 星 期 五 都 好 忙。
(I am very busy from Monday to Friday.)

ngǒ⁵ jǐu³ fāan¹ gūng¹.
我 要 返 工。
(I have to go to work.)

bāt¹ gwǒ³ zāu¹ mūt⁶ m̀⁴ sái² fāan¹ gūng¹, hóu² dāk¹ hàan⁴.
不 過 週 末 唔 使 返 工，好 得 閒。
(But at the weekends I don't need to go to work, I have a lot of free time then.)

Siu-Ping: něi⁵ dāk¹ hàan⁴ zūng¹ jì³ zōu⁶ māt¹ jě⁵ ǎa³？
你 得 閒 中 意 做 乜 嘢 呀？
(What do you like to do in your free time?)

Tony: ngǒ⁵ dāk¹ hàan⁴ zūng¹ jì³ jíng² sóeng²
我 得 閒 中 意 影 相
(I like taking photographs

tùng⁴ līn⁶ zāap⁶ Gwóng² Dūng¹ Wáa².
同 練 習 廣 東 話。
and practicing Cantonese in my free time.)

Siu-Ping: něi⁵ gě³ Gwóng² Dūng¹ Wáa² hóu² lēk¹ wǒ³.
你 嘅 廣 東 話 好 叻 喎。
(Your Cantonese is very good.)

Tony: dō¹ zē⁶! màa⁴ máa² déi² zē¹. ngǒ⁵ jì⁴ gāa¹ hōk⁶ gán² Gwóng² Dūng¹ Wáa².
多 謝！麻 麻 哋 啫。我 而 家 學 緊 廣 東 話。
(Thank you! I speak just so-so. I'm learning Cantonese at the moment.)

1.	géi² sì⁴ 幾時	QW:	when; at what time
2.	jyut⁶ 月 (*Nu. 1-12 + jyut⁶*)	N:	months of the year (January-December) *(See p.37-40)*
3.	hōu⁶ 號 (*Nu.. 1-31 + hōu⁶*)	N:	days of the month (1ˢᵗ day to 31ˢᵗ day)
4.	lēot⁶ sī¹ 律師	N:	lawyer
5.	lēot⁶ sī¹ làu⁴ 律師樓	N:	law firm
6.	mòng⁴ 忙	Adj:	busy
7.	dāk¹ hàan⁴ 得閒	Adj:	have free time, free (in time); not busy
8.	sīng¹ kèi⁴ 星期 (+ *Nu.1-6*)	N:	days of the week (Mon.-Sat.); week (also "lǎi⁵ bǎai³ 禮拜") *(See p.37-40)*
9.	sīng¹ kèi⁴ jāt¹ 星期一	N:	Monday (also "lǎi⁵ bǎai³ jāt¹ 禮拜一")
10.	sīng¹ kèi⁴ ňǧ⁵ 星期五	N:	Friday (also "lǎi⁵ bǎai³ ňǧ⁵ 禮拜五")
11.	zi³ 至 (+ *Place/Time*)	Prep:	until; to (an ending point) (also "dóu³ 到")
12.	dōu¹ 都 (*Subject in plural* + dōu¹)	Adv:	(in L.8) all; all-inclusive *[no exception]*
13.	fāan¹ gūng¹ 返工	VO:	to go to work; go on duty (opp. "fòng³ gūng¹ 放工": to finish work)
14.	zāu¹ mūt⁶ 週末	N:	weekend
15.	m̀⁴ sái² 唔使	SE:	no need *[the negative form of "jiu³ 要"]*
16.	zōu⁶ 做 (+ *Object*)	V:	to do; to work; to engage in
17.	zōu⁶ māt¹ jě⁵ 做乜嘢	SE:	do what? *[a phrase for asking what kind of activity or action is happening]*
18.	jíng² sóeng² 影相	VO:	to take photos
19.	lēk¹ 叻	Adj:	smart; sharp; clever; brilliant
20.	wǒ³ 喎 (*Statement* + wǒ³)	Part:	(in L.8) *[a final particle used to indicate surprise, discovery or realization]*
21.	dō¹ zē⁶ 多謝	SE:	thank you (for a compliment)
22.	màa⁴ máa² déi² 麻麻哋	Adv:	so-so
23.	gán² 緊 (*Verb* + gán² + *Object*) (e.g. hōk⁶ gán² Gwóng² Dūng¹ Wáa²)	Part:	*[an aspectual particle used after a verb, indicating an action in progress]*

1. **To ask and tell when an event happens** *(Refer to Unit 2 Section 5)*

    e.g. Q: *Tony*, něi⁵ géi² sì⁴ lèi⁴ Hōeng¹ Góng² gåa³?
          (Tony, when did you come to Hong Kong?)

    A: ngǒ⁵ gām¹ nìn⁴ gáu² jˇyut⁶ jāt¹ hőu⁶ lèi⁴ Hōeng¹ Góng² gě³.
        (I came to Hong Kong this year on the 1ˢᵗ of September.)

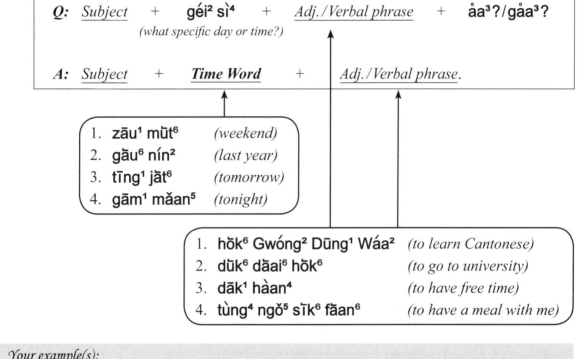

Q: *Subject*	+	**géi² sì⁴** *(what specific day or time?)*	+	*Adj./Verbal phrase*	+	**åa³?/gåa³?**
A: *Subject*	+	***Time Word***	+	*Adj./Verbal phrase*.

1. zāu¹ mūt⁶   *(weekend)*
2. gāu⁶ nín²   *(last year)*
3. tīng¹ jāt⁶   *(tomorrow)*
4. gām¹ mǎan⁵   *(tonight)*

1. hǒk⁶ Gwóng² Dūng¹ Wáa²   *(to learn Cantonese)*
2. dūk⁶ dǎai⁶ hǒk⁶   *(to go to university)*
3. dāk¹ hàan⁴   *(to have free time)*
4. tùng⁴ ngǒ⁵ sȉk⁶ fāan⁶   *(to have a meal with me)*

Your example(s):

ngǒ⁵ _____ hǒk⁶ Gwóng² Dūng¹ Wáa² gě³.
       (time word)

2. **To inquire about one's occupation or working place**

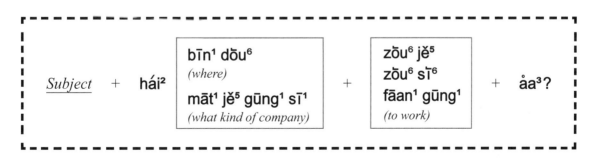

Subject	+	**hái²**	**bīn¹ dőu⁶** *(where)* **māt¹ jě⁵ gūng¹ sī¹** *(what kind of company)*	+	**zőu⁶ jě⁵** **zőu⁶ sȉ⁶** **fāan¹ gūng¹** *(to work)*	+	**åa³?**

Your example(s):

_____.

3. **To tell if someone is busy or not with adverbs of degree**

e.g. ngǒ⁵ jàu⁴ sīng¹ kèi⁴ jāt¹ zǐ³ sīng¹ kèi⁴ ňg⁵ dōu¹ <u>hóu²</u> mòng⁴.

(I am <u>very</u> busy from Monday to Friday.)

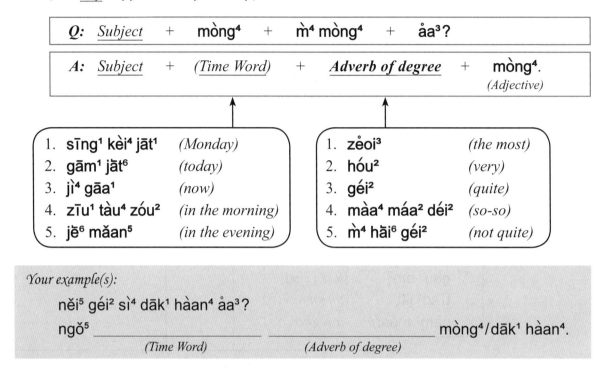

Q:	<u>*Subject*</u>	+	**mòng⁴**	+	**m̀⁴ mòng⁴**	+	**åa³?**

A:	<u>*Subject*</u>	+	*(Time Word)*	+	***Adverb of degree***	+	**mòng⁴.**

(Adjective)

1.	sīng¹ kèi⁴ jāt¹	*(Monday)*
2.	gām¹ jāt⁶	*(today)*
3.	jì⁴ gāa¹	*(now)*
4.	zīu¹ tàu⁴ zóu²	*(in the morning)*
5.	jě⁶ mǎan⁵	*(in the evening)*

1.	zěoi³	*(the most)*
2.	hóu²	*(very)*
3.	géi²	*(quite)*
4.	màa⁴ máa² déi²	*(so-so)*
5.	m̀⁴ hāi⁶ géi²	*(not quite)*

Your example(s):

něi⁵ géi² sì⁴ dāk¹ hàan⁴ åa³?

ngǒ⁵ _____ _____ mòng⁴/dāk¹ hàan⁴.
　　　　　　　(Time Word)　　　　　　　　　*(Adverb of degree)*

4. **To know the function of "dōu¹" expressing all-inclusive or no exception**

e.g. ngǒ⁵ jàu⁴ sīng¹ kèi⁴ jāt¹ zǐ³ sīng¹ kèi⁴ ňg⁵ <u>dōu¹</u> hóu² mòng⁴.

(I am very busy from Monday to Friday.)

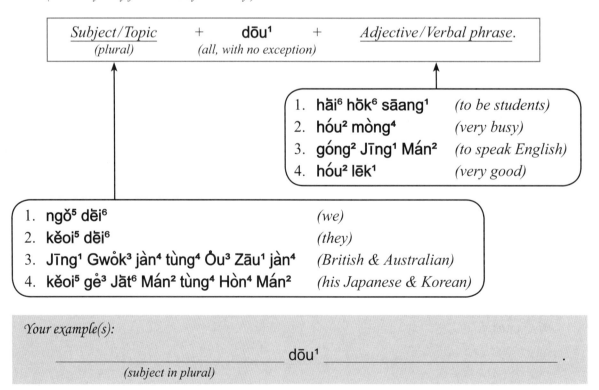

<u>*Subject/Topic*</u>	+	**dōu¹**	+	<u>*Adjective/Verbal phrase.*</u>
(plural)		*(all, with no exception)*		

1.	hāi⁶ hȯk⁶ sāang¹	*(to be students)*
2.	hóu² mòng⁴	*(very busy)*
3.	góng² Jīng¹ Mán²	*(to speak English)*
4.	hóu² lēk¹	*(very good)*

1.	ngǒ⁵ děi⁶	*(we)*
2.	kěoi⁵ děi⁶	*(they)*
3.	Jīng¹ Gwȯk³ jàn⁴ tùng⁴ Óu³ Zāu¹ jàn⁴	*(British & Australian)*
4.	kěoi⁵ gě³ Jāt⁶ Mán² tùng⁴ Hòn⁴ Mán²	*(his Japanese & Korean)*

Your example(s):

_____ dōu¹ _____ .
　　　(subject in plural)

5. **To express an unnecessary action / activity using "m̀⁴ sái²"**

   e.g.   (ngŏ⁵) zāu¹ mūt⁶ m̀⁴ sái² fāan¹ gūng¹.
          (I don't need to go to work at the weekends.)

Subject	+	*(Time Word)*	+	**m̀⁴ sái²**	+	*Verb / Verbal phrase.*
				(no need to)		

   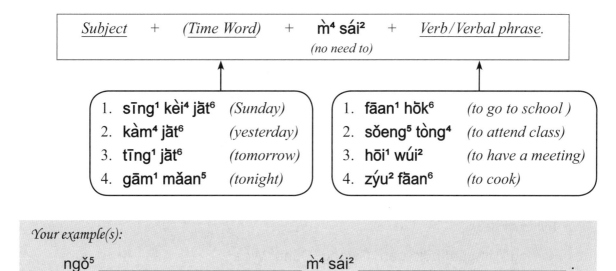

1. sīng¹ kèi⁴ jāt⁶	*(Sunday)*
2. kàm⁴ jāt⁶	*(yesterday)*
3. tīng¹ jāt⁶	*(tomorrow)*
4. gām¹ măan⁵	*(tonight)*

1. fāan¹ hŏk⁶	*(to go to school)*
2. sŏeng⁵ tòng⁴	*(to attend class)*
3. hōi¹ wúi²	*(to have a meeting)*
4. zýu² fāan⁶	*(to cook)*

   Your example(s):

   ngŏ⁵ _____ m̀⁴ sái² _____ .

6. **To ask and tell what one likes to do in one's free time**

   e.g.   Q: něi⁵ dāk¹ hàan⁴ zūng¹ jì³ zŏu⁶ māt¹ jĕ⁵ åa³?
          (What do you like to do in your free time?)

   A: ngŏ⁵ dāk¹ hàan⁴ zūng¹ jì³ jíng² sóeng².
          (I like taking photographs in my free time.)

Q:	*Subject*	+	**dāk¹ hàan⁴**	+	**zūng¹ jì³**	+	**zŏu⁶ māt¹ jĕ⁵**	+	**åa³?**
A:	*Subject*	+	**dāk¹ hàan⁴**	+	**zūng¹ jì³**	+	*Verbal phrase.*		

1. tái² sýu¹	*(to read books)*
2. dáa² gēi¹	*(to play online games)*
3. sŏeng⁵ mŏng⁵	*(to surf the Internet)*
4. tùng⁴ pàng⁴ jău⁵ kīng¹ gái²	*(to chat with friends)*
5. hái² ūk¹ kéi² fån³ gåau³	*(to sleep at home)*

   Your example(s):

   ngŏ⁵ dāk¹ hàan⁴ zūng¹ jì³ _____ ?

   něi⁵ dāk¹ hàan⁴ zūng¹ jì³ zŏu⁶ māt¹ jĕ⁵ åa³?

7. To state a continuous action or activity with "gán²"

e.g. ngǒ⁵ jì⁴ gāa¹ hŏk⁶ <u>gán²</u> Gwóng² Dūng¹ Wáa².

(I'm lear<u>ning</u> Cantonese at the moment.)

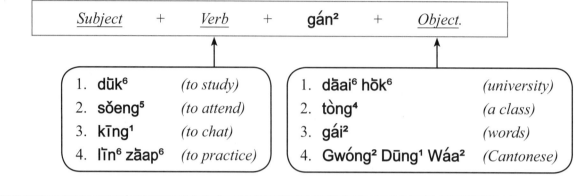

| *Subject* | + | *Verb* | + | **gán²** | + | *Object.* |

1. dūk⁶   *(to study)*
2. sǒeng⁵   *(to attend)*
3. kīng¹   *(to chat)*
4. lìn⁶ zāap⁶ *(to practice)*

1. dāai⁶ hŏk⁶   *(university)*
2. tòng⁴   *(a class)*
3. gái²   *(words)*
4. Gwóng² Dūng¹ Wáa²   *(Cantonese)*

Your example(s):

ngǒ⁵ jì⁴ gāa¹ hŏk⁶ gán² Gwóng² Dūng¹ Wáa².

ngǒ⁵ jì⁴ gāa¹ _____ gán² _____ .

8. To know how to respond to a compliment

X: něi⁵ ge̊³ Gwóng² Dūng¹ Wáa² hóu² lēk¹ wo̊³.

(Your Cantonese is very good.)

Y: 1) dō¹ zē̊⁶!
        (Thank you!)

    2) màa⁴ máa² déi² zē¹.
        (Just so-so.)

    3) něi⁵ gwo̊³ zóeng² lǎa³. *(formal)*
        (Your're flattering me.)

How do you spend your leisure time?

Q: něi⁵ dāk¹ hàan⁴ zūng¹ jǐ³ zǒu⁶ māt¹ jě⁵ åa³?

A: ngǒ⁵ dāk¹ hàan⁴ zūng¹ jǐ³ _____ .

1.	*to chat*	kīng¹ gái² 傾偈	
2.	*to chat on the phone*	kīng¹ dǐn⁶ wáa² 傾電話	
3.	*to dance*	tiu³ mǒu⁵ 跳舞	
4.	*to do physical exercises*	(zǒu⁶) wǎn⁶ dǔng⁶ （做)運動	
5.	*to do shopping; buy something*	mǎai⁵ jě⁵ 買嘢	
6.	*to eat something*	sǐk⁶ jě⁵ 食嘢	
7.	*to take a bath or shower*	cūng¹ lòeng⁴ 沖涼	
8.	*to go shopping; walk around*	hàang⁴ gāai¹ 行街	
9.	*to go to restaurant for dim-sum*	jám² càa⁴ 飲茶	
10.	*to listen to music*	tēng¹ jām¹ ngǒk⁶ 聽音樂	
11.	*to play ball games*	dáa² bō¹ 打波	
12.	*to play online games*	dáa² gēi¹ 打機	
13.	*to play soccer*	tèk³ bō¹ 踢波	
14.	*to read books*	tái² sȳu¹ 睇書	
15.	*to run; to jog*	páau² bǒu⁶ 跑步	
16.	*to sleep*	fàn³ gåau³ 瞓覺	
17.	*to stroll; leisurely walk*	såan³ bǒu⁶ 散步	
18.	*to surf the Internet*	sǒeng⁵ mǒng⁵ 上網	
19.	*to swim*	jàu⁴ séoi² 游水	
20.	*to take photographs*	jíng² sóeng² 影相	
21.	*to visit a friend*	tåam³ pàng⁴ jǎu⁵ 探朋友	
22.	*to watch a film/movie*	tái² hèi³ 睇戲	

When is your birthday?

Q: něi⁵ géi² sì⁴ sāang¹ jāt⁶ åa³/gåa³?

A: ngǒ⁵ _____ sāang¹ jāt⁶ gě³.

	past		*present*	*future*	
year nìn⁴ 年	cìn⁴ nín² /cìn⁴ nìn⁴ 前年 *the year before last*	gāu⁶ nín² /gāu⁶ nìn⁴ 舊年 *last year*	gām¹ nín² /gām¹ nìn⁴ 今年 *this year*	cēot¹ nín² /cēot¹ nìn⁴ 出年 *next year*	hāu⁶ nín² /hāu⁶ nìn⁴ 後年 *the year after next*
month jẙut⁶ 月	zǒi³ sǒeng⁶ gǒ³ jẙut⁶ 再上個月 *the month before last*	sǒeng⁶ gǒ³ jẙut⁶ 上個月 *last month*	gām¹ gǒ³ jẙut⁶ /nī¹ gǒ³ jẙut⁶ 今個月 / 呢個月 *this month*	hāa⁶ gǒ³ jẙut⁶ 下個月 *next month*	zǒi³ hāa⁶ gǒ³ jẙut⁶ 再下個月 *the month after next*
*week** sīng¹ kèi⁴ 星期	zǒi³ sǒeng⁶ gǒ³ sīng¹ kèi⁴ 再上個星期 *the week before last*	sǒeng⁶ gǒ³ sīng¹ kèi⁴ 上個星期 *last week*	gām¹ gǒ³ sīng¹ kèi⁴ /nī¹ gǒ³ sīng¹ kèi⁴ 今個星期 / 呢個星期 *this week*	hāa⁶ gǒ³ sīng¹ kèi⁴ 下個星期 *next week*	zǒi³ hāa⁶ gǒ³ sīng¹ kèi⁴ 再下個星期 *the week after next*
day jāt⁶ 日	cìn⁴ jāt⁶ 前日 *the day before yesterday*	kàm⁴ jāt⁶ /càm⁴ jāt⁶ 琴日 / 噚日 *yesterday*	gām¹ jāt⁶ 今日 *today*	tīng¹ jāt⁶ 聽日 *tomorrow*	hāu⁶ jāt⁶ 後日 *the day after tomorrow*

* Note that "lǎi⁵ bǎai³ 禮拜" is also commonly used for week.

The twelve Months and the days of the week — *(refer to Unit 2 Section 5)*

January	jāt¹ jẙut⁶	一月	*July*	cāt¹ jẙut⁶	七月
February	jī⁶ jẙut⁶	二月	*August*	bǎat³ jẙut⁶	八月
March	sāam¹ jẙut⁶	三月	*September*	gáu² jẙut⁶	九月
April	sěi³ jẙut⁶	四月	*October*	sǎp⁶ jẙut⁶	十月
May	ngǔ⁵ jẙut⁶	五月	*November*	sǎp⁶ jāt¹ jẙut⁶	十一月
June	lūk⁶ jẙut⁶	六月	*December*	sǎp⁶ jī⁶ jẙut⁶	十二月

Monday	sīng¹ kèi⁴ jāt¹	星期一	lǎi⁵ bǎai³ jāt¹	禮拜一
Tuesday	sīng¹ kèi⁴ jī⁶	星期二	lǎi⁵ bǎai³ jī⁶	禮拜二
Wednesday	sīng¹ kèi⁴ sāam¹	星期三	lǎi⁵ bǎai³ sāam¹	禮拜三
Thursday	sīng¹ kèi⁴ sěi³	星期四	lǎi⁵ bǎai³ sěi³	禮拜四
Friday	sīng¹ kèi⁴ ngǔ⁵	星期五	lǎi⁵ bǎai³ ngǔ⁵	禮拜五
Saturday	sīng¹ kèi⁴ lūk⁶	星期六	lǎi⁵ bǎai³ lūk⁶	禮拜六
Sunday	sīng¹ kèi⁴ jāt⁶	星期日	lǎi⁵ bǎai³ jāt⁶	禮拜日

1. **Translate the following questions and answer them in Cantonese.** $(16 \times 3.5\% = 56\%)$

    1) When did you come to Hong Kong?

        Q: _____

        A: _____

    2) What day of the week do you learn Cantonese?

        Q: _____

        A: _____

    3) Where do you learn Cantonese?

        Q: _____

        A: _____

    4) Where does your teacher work?

        Q: _____

        A: _____

    5) What kind of company is Tony working for now?

        Q: _____

        A: _____

    6) What do you like to do in your free time?

        Q: _____

        A: _____

    7) What are you doing right now?

        Q: _____

        A: _____

    8) Do you have free time on Sunday?

        Q: _____

        A: _____

2. Rearrange the various parts of the following sentences in their right order.
(7 × 2% = 14%)

1) *Tony* / zōu⁶ sī⁶ / hái² / lēot⁶ sī¹ làu⁴ / . /

_____

2) kěoi⁵ ge̊³ / hóu² / Gwóng² Dūng¹ Wáa² / wo̊³ / lēk¹ / . /

_____

3) m̀⁴ sái² / kěoi⁵ / fāan¹ hōk⁶ / sīng¹ kèi⁴ lūk⁶ / . /

_____

4) gām¹ nìn⁴ / ngǒ⁵ / sāp⁶ hōu⁶ / lèi⁴ Hōeng¹ Góng² ge̊³ / jāt¹ jẙut⁶ / . /

_____

5) jì⁴ gāa¹ / gán² / lȋn⁶ zāap⁶ / ngǒ⁵ dēi⁶ / Gwóng² Dūng¹ Wáa² / . /

_____

6) kěoi⁵ / dōu¹ / sīng¹ kèi⁴ jāt¹ / sīng¹ kèi⁴ lūk⁶ / jàu⁴ / zi̊³ / ji̊u³ fāan¹ gūng¹ / . /

_____

7) *Tony* / zūng¹ ji̊³ / tùng⁴ / dāk¹ hàan⁴ / jíng² sóeng² / tēng¹ jām¹ ngōk⁶ / . /

_____

3. Add the structural particle "gán²" to the following common activities to indicate the action in progress. (20 × 1.5% = 30%)

1) kīng¹ gái² > kīng¹ <u>gán²</u> gái²	11) te̊k³ bō¹
2) ti̊u³ mǒu⁵	12) tái² sȳu¹
3) zōu⁶ wān⁶ dūng⁶	13) páau² bōu⁶
4) mǎai⁵ je̊⁵	14) fån³ gåau³
5) sīk⁶ je̊⁵	15) såan³ bōu⁶
6) cūng¹ lòeng⁴	16) sǒeng⁵ mǒng⁵
7) hàang⁴ gāai¹	17) jàu⁴ séoi²
8) jám² càa⁴	18) jíng² sóeng²
9) tēng¹ jām¹ ngōk⁶	19) tåam³ pàng⁴ jǎu⁵
10) dáa² bō¹	20) lȋn⁶ zāap⁶ Gwóng² Dūng¹ Wáa²

UNIT FIVE

Essential Basic Conversation

Learning Objectives

1. To tell & ask the purpose of a motion/journey
2. To ask politely with "**céng² mǎn⁶**" before a question
3. To express "There is…" and "There isn't…" using "**jǎu⁵**" and "**mǒu⁵**"
4. To ask the existence of something in a certain place with "**jǎu⁵ mǒu⁵**"
5. To ask where something can be found using "**bīn¹ dõu⁶ jǎu⁵**"
6. To know how to respond after being thanked for

zóu² sàn⁴, hẻoi³ bīn¹ dõu⁶ ảa³?

ngǒ⁵ sóeng² hẻoi³ sīk⁶ zóu² cāan¹.
céng² mǎn⁶ bīn¹ dõu⁶ jǎu⁵ cāan¹ tēng¹ ảa³?

ngǒ⁵ sóeng² hẻoi³ ngàn⁴ hòng⁴ <u>ló² jāt¹ dī¹ cín²</u>.

Amy meets the receptionist of the hostel in the lobby.

Amy:	zóu² sàn⁴. 早　晨　。 *(Good morning.)*
Receptionist:	zóu² sàn⁴, hẻoi³ bīn¹ dōu⁶ åa³? 早　晨　，去　邊　度　呀？ *(Good morning, where are you going?)*
Amy:	ngǒ⁵ sóeng² hẻoi³ sīk⁶ zóu² cāan¹. 我　想　去　食　早　餐　。 *(I would like to go to have breakfast.)* céng² mān⁶ bīn¹ dōu⁶ jǎu⁵ cāan¹ tēng¹ åa³? 請　問　邊　度　有　餐　廳　呀？ *(May I ask where I can find a restaurant?)*
Receptionist:	jī⁶ láu² jǎu⁵ jāt¹ gāan¹ càa⁴ cāan¹ tēng¹. 二　樓　有　一　間　茶　餐　廳　。 *(There is a Hong Kong style café on the second floor.)*
Amy:	gám², nī¹ dōu⁶ jǎu⁵ mǒu⁵ ngàn⁴ hòng⁴ åa³? 噉　，呢　度　有　冇　銀　行　呀？ *(Well, is there a bank around here?)*
Receptionist:	mǒu⁵, nī¹ dōu⁶ mǒu⁵ ngàn⁴ hòng⁴. 冇　，呢　度　冇　銀　行　。 *(No, there is no bank around here.)* něi⁵ hẻoi³ ngàn⁴ hòng⁴ zōu⁶ māt¹ jě⁵ åa³? 你　去　銀　行　做　乜　嘢　呀？ *(What are you going to the bank for?)*
Amy:	ngǒ⁵ sóeng² hẻoi³ ngàn⁴ hòng⁴ ló² jāt¹ dī¹ cín². 我　想　去　銀　行　攞　一　啲　錢　。 *(I want to go to the bank to withdraw some money.)* nī¹ dōu⁶ fū⁶ gān⁶ jǎu⁵ mǒu⁵ ATM åa³? 呢　度　附　近　有　冇　ATM　呀？ *(Is there an ATM nearby?)*
Receptionist:	ngǒ⁵ m̀⁴ zī¹ dỏu³ åa³. bāl¹ ywǒ³ děi⁶ tit³ zāam⁶ lěoi⁵ mīn⁶ 我　唔　知　道　呀　。不　過　地　鐵　站　裏　面 *(I don't know. But I know inside the MTR station* jǎu⁵ ngàn⁴ hòng⁴ tùng⁴ zī⁶ dūng⁶ gwāi⁶ jỳun⁴ gēi¹. 有　銀　行　同　自　動　櫃　員　機　。 *there are a bank and an Automatic Teller Machine.)*
Amy:	hóu² åak³, m̀⁴ gōi¹. bāai¹ bảai³. 好　呃　，唔　該　。拜　拜　。 *(Okay, thank you. Bye-bye.)*
Receptionist:	m̀⁴ sái² m̀⁴ gōi¹, bāai¹ bảai³. 唔　使　唔　該　，拜　拜　。 *(Not at all. Bye-bye.)*

1.	zóu² sàn⁴ 早晨	Ph:	good morning
2.	sīk⁶ 食 (+ *Object*)	V:	to eat
3.	zóu² cāan¹ 早餐 (*M:* cāan¹ 餐 / gò³ 個)	N:	breakfast
4.	céng² màn⁶ 請問	V:	May I ask... (also "cíng² màn⁶")
5.	cāan¹ tēng¹ 餐廳 (*M:* gāan¹ 間)	N:	restaurant
6.	càa⁴ cāan¹ tēng¹ 茶餐廳① (*M:* gāan¹ 間)	N:	Hong Kong style café
7.	gāan¹ 間	M:	*[a measure word for buildings; houses and rooms]*
8.	láu² 樓 (*Nu.* + láu²)	N:	(in L.9) floor
9.	jī⁶ láu² 二樓	Ph:	second floor
10.	ngàn⁴ hòng⁴ 銀行 (*M:* gāan¹ 間)	N:	bank
11.	ló² 攞 (+ *Object*)	V:	to take; to get; to fetch
12.	ló² cín² 攞錢	VO:	withdraw money
13.	zī¹ dòu³ 知道	V:	to know about (also shortened as "zī¹ 知")
14.	fū⁶ gàn⁶ 附近	N:	vicinity; nearby
15.	zī⁶ dūng⁶ 自動	Adj:	automatic
16.	gwāi⁶ jỳun⁴ gēi¹ 櫃員機	N:	teller machine
17.	zī⁶ dūng⁶ gwāi⁶ jỳun⁴ gēi¹ 自動櫃員機	N:	ATM [Automatic Teller Machine]; cash machine
18.	dēi⁶ tit³ 地鐵	N:	MTR [Mass Transit Railway]; underground railway
19.	zāam⁶ 站 (*M:* gò 個)	N:	station; a stop
20.	dēi⁶ tit³ zāam⁶ 地鐵站	N:	MTR station
21.	lěoi⁵ mīn⁶ 裏面	N:	inside; in
22.	m̀⁴ sái² m̀⁴ gōi¹ 唔使唔該	SE:	(lit. no need for thanks) not at all; You're welcome.

---

① **càa⁴ cāan¹ tēng¹** is a typical Hong Kong term. Hong Kong style café is the only place you will find genuine local food such as Cantonese congee, fish ball rice noodle, beef brisket noodles or rice with barbecue pork while you may also order Western style drinks and snacks such as French toast, sandwiches or fried chicken wings, etc.

1. **To tell & ask the purpose of a motion/journey**

    e.g. 1. ngǒ⁵ sóeng² hẻoi³ sīk⁶ zóu² cāan¹.

        (I would like to go to have breakfast.)

    e.g. 2. něi⁵ hẻoi³ ngàn⁴ hòng⁴ zōu⁶ māt¹ jě⁵ ảa³?

        (What are you going to the bank for?)

    e.g. 3. ngǒ⁵ sóeng² hẻoi³ ngàn⁴ hòng⁴ ló² jāt¹ dī¹ cín².

        (I want to go to the bank to withdraw some money.)

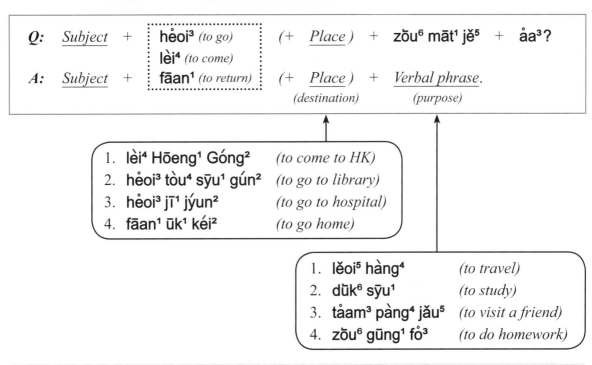

Q:	*Subject*	+	**hẻoi³** *(to go)*	(+ *Place*)	+	**zōu⁶ māt¹ jě⁵**	+	**ảa³?**
			lèi⁴ *(to come)*					
A:	*Subject*	+	**fāan¹** *(to return)*	(+ *Place*)	+	*Verbal phrase.*		
				(destination)		*(purpose)*		

1. lèi⁴ Hōeng¹ Góng²   *(to come to HK)*
2. hẻoi³ tòu⁴ sȳu¹ gún²   *(to go to library)*
3. hẻoi³ jī¹ jýun²   *(to go to hospital)*
4. fāan¹ ūk¹ kéi²   *(to go home)*

1. lěoi⁵ hàng⁴   *(to travel)*
2. dūk⁶ sȳu¹   *(to study)*
3. tẚam³ pàng⁴ jǎu⁵   *(to visit a friend)*
4. zōu⁶ gūng¹ fỏ³   *(to do homework)*

Your example(s):

ngǒ⁵ lèi⁴ Hōeng¹ Góng² _____ .

(purpose)

2. **To ask politely with "céng² mǎn⁶/cíng² mǎn⁶" before a question**

    e.g. céng² mǎn⁶ bīn¹ dōu⁶ jǎu⁵ cāan¹ tēng¹ ảa³?

        (May I ask where I can find a restaurant?)

Q:	**céng² mǎn⁶ / cíng² mǎn⁶**	+	*Question*	?

1. něi⁵ gwẚi³ sỉng³ ảa³?   *(What's your surname?)*
2. něi⁵ hái² bīn¹ dōu⁶ zōu⁶ sī⁶ ảa³?   *(Where are you working?)*
3. sái² sáu² gāan¹ hái² bīn¹ dōu⁶ ảa³?   *(Where is the washroom?)*
4. něi⁵ jǎu⁵ mǒu⁵ sān¹ fán² zỉng³ ảa³?   *(Have you got I.D. card?)*

3. To express "There is..." and "There isn't..." using "jǎu⁵" and "mǒu⁵"

e.g. 1. **jī⁶ láu² jǎu⁵ jāt¹ gāan¹ càa⁴ cāan¹ tēng¹.**

  (There is a Hong Kong style café on the second floor.)

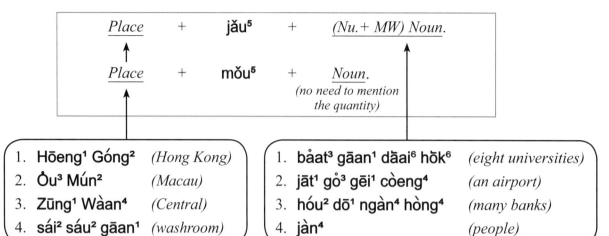

Place	+	**jǎu⁵**	+	*(Nu.+ MW) Noun.*
Place	+	**mǒu⁵**	+	*Noun.* (no need to mention the quantity)

1. **Hōeng¹ Góng²** *(Hong Kong)*
2. **Òu³ Mún²** *(Macau)*
3. **Zūng¹ Wàan⁴** *(Central)*
4. **sái² sáu² gāan¹** *(washroom)*

1. **bǎat³ gāan¹ dāai⁶ hǒk⁶** *(eight universities)*
2. **jāt¹ gǒ³ gēi¹ còeng⁴** *(an airport)*
3. **hóu² dō¹ ngàn⁴ hòng⁴** *(many banks)*
4. **jàn⁴** *(people)*

e.g. 2. **dēi⁶ tǐt³ zāam⁶ lěoi⁵ mīn⁶ jǎu⁵ ngàn⁴ hòng⁴ tùng⁴ *ATM*.**

  (There are a bank and an ATM inside the MTR station.)

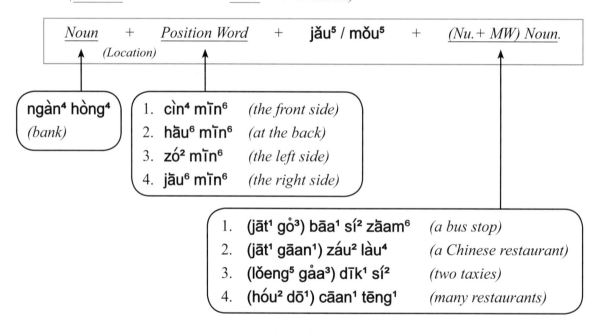

Noun (Location)	+	*Position Word*	+	**jǎu⁵ / mǒu⁵**	+	*(Nu.+ MW) Noun.*

ngàn⁴ hòng⁴
(bank)

1. **cìn⁴ mīn⁶** *(the front side)*
2. **hāu⁶ mīn⁶** *(at the back)*
3. **zó² mīn⁶** *(the left side)*
4. **jāu⁶ mīn⁶** *(the right side)*

1. **(jāt¹ gǒ³) bāa¹ sí² zāam⁶** *(a bus stop)*
2. **(jāt¹ gāan¹) záu² làu⁴** *(a Chinese restaurant)*
3. **(lǒeng⁵ gǎa³) dīk¹ sí²** *(two taxies)*
4. **(hóu² dō¹) cāan¹ tēng¹** *(many restaurants)*

Your example(s):

_____ **jǎu⁵** _____ .
  (Place)   *(Nu. + MW + Noun)*

_____ **mǒu⁵** _____ .

ngǒ⁵ ūk¹ kéi² _____ **jǎu⁵** _____
              (Position Word)

4. **To ask the existence of something in a certain place**

e.g. nī¹ dōu⁶ jǎu⁵ mǒu⁵ ngàn⁴ hòng⁴ ảa³?

(Is there a bank around here?)

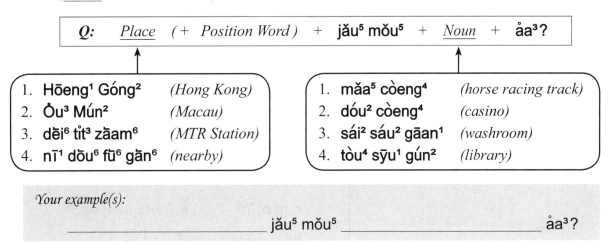

> | **Q:** | *Place* | *(+ Position Word)* | + | **jǎu⁵ mǒu⁵** | + | *Noun* | + | **ảa³?** |

1. **Hōeng¹ Góng²**   *(Hong Kong)*
2. **Ôu³ Mún²**   *(Macau)*
3. **dĕi⁶ tĭt³ zāam⁶**   *(MTR Station)*
4. **nī¹ dōu⁶ fū̆⁶ gān⁶** *(nearby)*

1. **mǎa⁵ còeng⁴**   *(horse racing track)*
2. **dóu² còeng⁴**   *(casino)*
3. **sái² sáu² gāan¹**   *(washroom)*
4. **tòu⁴ sȳu¹ gún²**   *(library)*

> *Your example(s):*
>
> _____ **jǎu⁵ mǒu⁵** _____ **ảa³?**

5. **To ask where something or a place can be found**

e.g. bīn¹ dōu⁶ jǎu⁵ cāan¹ tēng¹ ảa³?

(Where can I find a restaurant?)

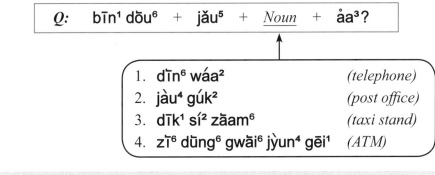

> | **Q:** | **bīn¹ dōu⁶** | + | **jǎu⁵** | + | *Noun* | + | **ảa³?** |

1. **dīn̆⁶ wáa²**   *(telephone)*
2. **jàu⁴ gúk²**   *(post office)*
3. **dīk¹ sí² zāam⁶**   *(taxi stand)*
4. **zī̆⁶ dŭng⁶ gwăi⁶ j̀yun⁴ gēi¹** *(ATM)*

> *Your example(s):*
>
> **bīn¹ dōu⁶ jǎu⁵** _____ **ảa³?**

6. **To know how to respond after being thanked for**

X₁: **m̀⁴ gōi¹.**
   (Thank you.)

Y₁: **m̀⁴ sái² m̀⁴ gōi¹.** *or* **m̀⁴ sái² hảak³ hẻi³.**
   (Not at all.)   *(Don't mention it.)*

X₂: **dō¹ zĕ̆⁶.**
   (Thank you.)

Y₂: **m̀⁴ sái² dō¹ zĕ̆⁶.** *or* **m̀⁴ sái² hảak³ hẻi³.**
   (You're welcome.)   *(Don't mention it.)*

ngŏ⁵ ūk¹ kéi² _____ jău⁵ _____ .

(Position Word)

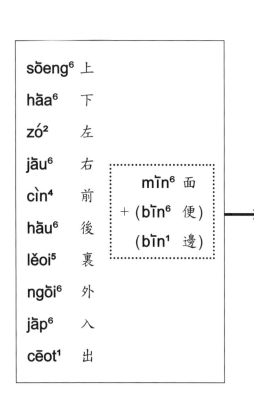

1. sŏeng⁶ mĭn⁶ 上面 *(above; on-top)*
2. hăa⁶ mĭn⁶ 下面 *(below; under)*
3. zó² mĭn⁶ 左面 *(the left side)*
4. jău⁶ mĭn⁶ 右面 *(the right side)*
5. cìn⁴ mĭn⁶ 前面 *(the front side)*
6. hău⁶ mĭn⁶ 後面 *(at the back)*
7. lĕoi⁵ mĭn⁶ 裏面 *(inside)*
8. ngŏi⁶ mĭn⁶ 外面 *(outside)*
9. jăp⁶ mĭn⁶ 入面 *(inside)*
10. cēot¹ mĭn⁶ 出面 *(outside)*
11. dĕoi³ mĭn⁶ 對面 *(opposite (side))*
12. zūng¹ gāan¹ 中間 *(in the middle of; centre)*
13. gåak³ lèi⁴ 隔籬 *(beside; next to)*
14. pòng⁴ bīn¹ 旁邊 *(beside; next to)*
15. zāk¹ bīn¹ 側邊 *(beside; next to)*
16. fŭ⁶ gǎn⁶ 附近 *(vicinity; nearby)*
17. zāu¹ wài⁴ 周圍 *(around; surroundings)*
18. làu⁴ sŏeng⁶ 樓上 *(upstairs)*
19. làu⁴ hăa⁶ 樓下 *(downstairs)*
20. dĕi⁶ háa² 地下 *(ground floor)*
21. dĕi⁶ hăa⁶ 地下 *(underground)*

Q: něi⁵ ūk¹ kéi² fũ⁶ gān⁶ jǎu⁵ mǒu⁵ _____ åa³?

Q: bīn¹ dõu⁶ jǎu⁵ _____ åa³?

1.

5.

9.

13.

2.

6.

10.

14.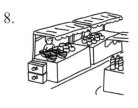

3.

7.

11.

15.

4.

8.

12.

16.

1.	fåai³ cāan¹ dǐm³ 快餐店	*fast food shop*	9.	cīu¹ kāp¹ sǐ⁵ còeng⁴ 超級市場	*supermarket*
2.	bīn⁶ lēi⁶ dǐm³ 便利店	*convenience store*	10.	båak³ fo³ gūng¹ sī¹ 百貨公司	*department store*
3.	záu² dǐm³ 酒店	*hotel*	11.	jàu⁴ gúk² 郵局	*post office*
4.	sȳu¹ dǐm³/sȳu¹ gúk² 書店 / 書局	*bookshop*	12.	gíng² gúk² 警局	*police station*
5.	jī¹ jýun² 醫院	*hospital*	13.	sīu¹ fòng⁴ gúk² 消防局	*fire station*
6.	hěi³ jýun² 戲院	*cinema*	14.	jõek⁶ fòng⁴ 藥房	*pharmacy*
7.	gūng¹ jýun² 公園	*park*	15.	cán² só² 診所	*clinic*
8.	gāai¹ sǐ⁵ 街市	*market*	16.	tòu⁴ sȳu¹ gún² 圖書館	*library*

1. **How should you respond to the following?** $(4 \times 2.5\% = 10\%)$

1) A: něi⁵ hóu²

    B: _____

2) A: zóu² sàn⁴

    B: _____

3) A: m̀⁴ gōi¹

    B: _____

4) A: bāai¹ båai³

    B: _____

2. **Translate the following into Cantonese.** $(8 \times 7.5\% = 60\%)$

1) I live on the thirteen floor of the hostel for foreign students.

    _____

2) I want to go to a restaurant for my breakfast.

    _____

3) Where can I find a student canteen?

    _____

4) There is a Hong Kong style café nearby.

    _____

5) There isn't any ATM inside the bank.

    _____

6) Is there any airport in Hong Kong Island?

    _____

7) What is he going to the airport for?

    _____

8) I don't know.

    _____

3. **Translate the following into English.** $(5 \times 3\% = 15\%)$

1) hěoi³ bīn¹ dõu⁶ åa³?   _____

2) m̀⁴ sái² m̀⁴ gōi¹   _____

3) mǒu⁵ mān⁶ tài⁴.   _____

4) ngǒ⁵ m̀⁴ zī¹ åa³.   _____

5) hóu² åak³.   _____

4. Fill in the blanks. $(5 \times 3\% = 15\%)$

Back

Right

You are here!

Left

Front

1) něi⁵ (gě³) _____ hǎi⁶ hěi³ jýun².

2) sȳu¹ dǐm³ hái² něi⁵ (gě³) _____ .

3) něi⁵ (gě³) _____ jǎu⁵ tìng⁴ cē¹ còeng⁴.

4) něi⁵ (gě³) jāu⁶ mǐn⁶ hǎi⁶ _____ .

5) hěi³ jýun² (gě³) pòng⁴ bīn¹ jǎu⁵ jāt¹ gǒ³ _____ .

Learning Objectives

1. To greet someone according to the situation using "**àa⁴**"
2. To specify "this/these", "that/those" and "which" with "**nī¹**", "**gó²**" & "**bīn¹**"
3. To ask and answer the question "What *is* this?"
4. To call the name of something using "**giu³ zōu⁶**"
5. To express one's feeling or thinking with "**gȯk³ dāk¹**"
6. To express an attempt or trial to do sth. with "**hǎa⁵**"

zóu² sàn⁴, sīk⁶ zóu² cāan¹ àa⁴?

hāi⁶ åa³. zóu² sàn⁴.

nī¹ dī¹ hāi⁶ māt¹ jě⁵ lài⁴ gåa³?

nī¹ dī¹ giu³ zōu⁶ dāan⁶ tāat¹. hóu² hóu² sīk⁶ gåa³. si³ hǎa⁵ lāa¹.

Zing-Zing meets Amy in the student canteen.

Zing-Zing:　Amy, zóu² sàn⁴. sīk⁶ zóu² cāan¹ àa⁴?
　　　　　　Amy，早　晨。食　早　餐　牙？
　　　　　　(Amy, good morning. You're having breakfast, aren't you?)

Amy:　　　hāi⁶ åa³. Zīng¹-Zīng¹. zóu² sàn⁴.
　　　　　　係　呀。晶　晶。早　晨。
　　　　　　(Yes. Zing-Zing, good morning.)

Zing-Zing:　něi⁵ sóeng² sīk⁶ māt¹ jě⁵ åa³?
　　　　　　你　想　食　乜　嘢　呀？
　　　　　　(What do you want to eat?)

Amy:　　　ngǒ⁵ sóeng² sīk⁶ Hōeng¹ Góng² sīk¹ ge³ zóu² cāan¹.
　　　　　　我　想　食　香　港　式　嘅　早　餐。
　　　　　　(I want to have a Hong Kong style breakfast.)

　　　　　　nī¹ dī¹ hāi⁶ māt¹ jě⁵ åa³?
　　　　　　呢　啲　係　乜　嘢　呀？
　　　　　　(What is/are this/these?)

Zing-Zing:　nī¹ dī¹ giu³ zōu⁶ dāan⁶ tāat¹, gó² dī¹ giu³ zōu⁶ bō¹ lò⁴ bāau¹.
　　　　　　呢　啲　叫　做　蛋　撻，嗰　啲　叫　做　菠　蘿　包。
　　　　　　(These are called egg custard tarts, those are called pineapple buns.)

Amy:　　　bīn¹ dī¹ hóu² sīk⁶ åa³?
　　　　　　邊　啲　好　食　呀？
　　　　　　(Which one tastes good?)

Zing-Zing:　dāan⁶ tāat¹ hóu² sīk⁶, bō¹ lò⁴ bāau¹ dōu¹ hóu² hóu² sīk⁶.
　　　　　　蛋　撻　好　食，菠　蘿　包　都　好　好　食。
　　　　　　(Egg custard tarts are good, pineapple buns are also very good.)

Amy:　　　nī¹ dī¹ hāi⁶ māt¹ jě⁵ lài⁴ gåa³?
　　　　　　呢　啲　係　乜　嘢　嚟　㗎？
　　　　　　(What on earth is this?)

Zing-Zing:　nī¹ dī¹ giu³ zōu⁶ zūk¹ ①.
　　　　　　呢　啲　叫　做　粥。
　　　　　　(This is called congee.)

　　　　　　nī¹ wún² hāi⁶ pèi⁴ dáan² såu³ jūk⁶ zūk¹ lài⁴ ge³.
　　　　　　呢　碗　係　皮　蛋　瘦　肉　粥　嚟　嘅。
　　　　　　(This is congee with preserved egg and lean pork.)

　　　　　　bāt¹ gwo³ ngǒ⁵ gǒk³ dāk¹ pèi⁴ dáan² m̀⁴ hóu² sīk⁶.
　　　　　　不　過　我　覺　得　皮　蛋　唔　好　食。
　　　　　　(But I think that preserved egg doesn't taste good.)

Amy:　　　gám², ngǒ⁵ si³ hǎa⁵ dāan⁶ tāat¹ tùng⁴ bō¹ lò⁴ bāau¹ lāa¹.
　　　　　　嗽，我　試　吓　蛋　撻　同　菠　蘿　包　啦。
　　　　　　(Then, I'll try the egg custard tart and pineapple bun.)

---

① "**zūk¹**" is a simple dish made by boiling rice grains in many times its weight of water for several hours. In China, it is eaten as breakfast, often with the addition of crispy deep-fried flour sticks known as "**jàu⁴ zåa³ gwái²**". It is sometimes cooked with lean pork, minced beef, fish, chicken or century egg, etc. Rice congee is easily digestible and is used traditionally in China to nurse the sick back to health or to serve infants and the elderly. Some Cantonese also like to have a bowl of rice congee as a mid-night snack.

1.	àa⁴ 牙? (*Statement + àa⁴?!*)	Part:	*[a modal particle, used at the end of a statement to form a supposition question checking the validity of an assumption about observations of the situation or what has been said]*
2.	Hōeng¹ Góng² sīk¹ 香港式	N:	Hong Kong style (also shortened as "**góng² sīk¹** 港式")
3.	nī¹ dī¹ 呢啲	Pn:	this; these
4.	gó² dī¹ 嗰啲	Pn:	that; those
5.	bīn¹ dī¹ 邊啲	QW:	which
6.	dǎan⁶ tāat¹ ② 蛋撻	N:	(lit. egg tart) egg custard tart
7.	bō¹ lò⁴ bāau¹ ③ 菠蘿包	N:	pineapple(-like) bun
8.	māt¹ jě⁵ lài⁴ gåa³? 乜嘢嚟㗎?	Ph:	what *is* this/that?
9.	lài⁴ gě³ 嚟嘅	Part:	*[a modal particle used at the end of noun predicate sentences to give an explanation]*
10.	hóu² sīk⁶ 好食	Adj:	good to eat; tasty
11.	hóu² hóu² sīk⁶ 好好食	Ph:	delicious; very tasty
12.	gìu³ zōu⁶ 叫做 (*N₁ + gìu³ zōu⁶ + N₂*)	V:	to be called; named; known as (also "**gìu³**" in L.1)
13.	zūk¹ 粥	N:	rice congee, rice porridge
14.	wún² 碗	N/M:	a bowl; a bowl of
15.	pèi⁴ dáan² 皮蛋	N:	century egg: a special type of preserved egg
16.	såu³ jūk⁶ 瘦肉	N:	(lit. thin meat) lean pork; lean meat
17.	pèi⁴ dáan² såu³ jūk⁶ zūk¹ 皮蛋瘦肉粥	Ph:	congee with century egg and lean pork
18.	gǒk³ dāk¹ 覺得	V:	to think; to feel
19.	si³ hǎa⁵ 試吓 (*Verb + hǎa⁵*)	Ph:	have a try *["hǎa⁵" is a structural particle, attached to a verb indicating a sense of trial or tentativeness]*

---

② "**dǎan⁶ tāat¹**" is a baked pastry which consists of a flaky outer crust and sweet egg custard filled in the middle. It is easily found at bakeries, HK style cafés, and dim-sum restaurants in HK, Macau and southern China.

③ "**bō¹ lò⁴ bāau¹**" is a kind of baked bun with a sweet and crunchy checkered top that looks like the skin of a pineapple. It contains no pineapple but a variation known as "**bō¹ lò⁴ jàu⁴**" (buttered pineapple bun) is a pineapple bun with a piece of butter stuffed inside. Both of these are popular in HK.

Sentence Structure

1. **To greet someone according to the situation using "àa⁴"**

e.g. *Amy*, zóu² sàn⁴. sīk⁶ zóu² cāan¹ <u>àa⁴</u>!?

(Amy, good morning. You're having breakfast, <u>aren't you?</u>)

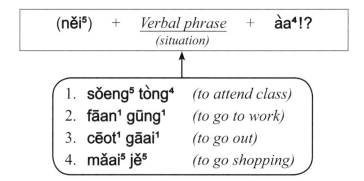

2. **To specify "this/these", "that/those" and "which"**

e.g. 1. <u>nī¹ dī¹</u> hǎi⁶ dāan⁶ tāat¹.
(<u>These</u> are egg custard tarts.)

e.g. 2. <u>gó² dī¹</u> hǎi⁶ bō¹ lò⁴ bāau¹.
(<u>Those</u> are pineapple buns.)

e.g. 3. <u>bīn¹ dī¹</u> hóu² sīk⁶ àa³?
(<u>Which one</u> tastes good?)

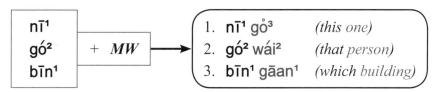

e.g. 4. <u>nī¹ gŏ³</u> hǎi⁶ ngŏ⁵ gě³ něoi⁵ pàng⁴ jǎu⁵.
(<u>This</u> is my girlfriend.)

e.g. 5. <u>gó² wái²</u> hǎi⁶ ngŏ⁵ gě³ Gwóng² Dūng¹ Wáa² lŏu⁵ sī¹.
(<u>That</u> is my Cantonese teacher.)

e.g. 6. něi⁵ hái² <u>bīn¹ gāan¹</u> dāai⁶ hŏk⁶ dūk⁶ sȳu¹ àa³?
(<u>Which</u> university do you study in?)

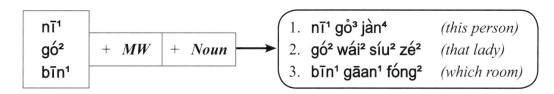

Your example(s): (Refer to Unit 2 Section 7)

Measure Words: _____

3. **To ask and answer the question "What *is* this?"**

   e.g.   Q: nī¹ dī¹ hǎi⁶ māt¹ jě⁵ lài⁴ gǎa³?

               *(What **is** this?)*

          A: nī¹ wún² hǎi⁶ pèi⁴ dáan² sǎu³ jūk⁶ zūk¹ lài⁴ gě³.

               *(This **is** preserved egg and lean pork congee.)*

Q:	nī¹ dī¹	+	hǎi⁶		māt¹ jě⁵	+	lài⁴ gǎa³?
A:	nī¹ dī¹	+	hǎi⁶	+	*Noun*	+	lài⁴ gě³.

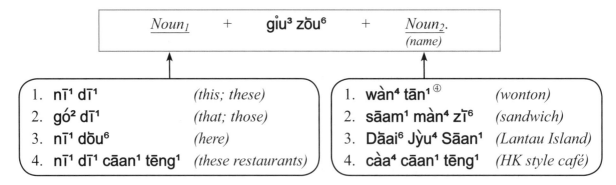

                    1. **zūk¹**   *(congee)*
                    2. **fán²**   *(rice noodles)*
                    3. **mǐn⁶**   *(noodles)*
                    4. **fǎan⁶**   *(cooked rice)*

Your example(s):

   Q: nī¹ dī¹ hǎi⁶ māt¹ jě⁵ lài⁴ gǎa³?   A: nī¹ dī¹ hǎi⁶ _____ lài⁴ gě³.

4. **To call the name of something using "giu³ zōu⁶"**

   e.g.   1. nī¹ dī¹ giu³ zōu⁶ dǎan⁶ tāat¹, gó² dī¹ giu³ zōu⁶ bō¹ lò⁴ bāau¹.

             (These are called egg custard tarts, those are called pineapple buns.)

   e.g.   2. nī¹ dī¹ giu³ zōu⁶ zūk¹.

             (This is called congee.)

Noun₁	+	**giu³ zōu⁶**	+	*Noun₂.* (name)

1. nī¹ dī¹	*(this; these)*		1. wàn⁴ tān¹ ④	*(wonton)*
2. gó² dī¹	*(that; those)*		2. sāam¹ màn⁴ zǐ⁶	*(sandwich)*
3. nī¹ dōu⁶	*(here)*		3. Dǎai⁶ Jỳu⁴ Sāan¹	*(Lantau Island)*
4. nī¹ dī¹ cāan¹ tēng¹	*(these restaurants)*		4. càa⁴ cāan¹ tēng¹	*(HK style café)*

Your example(s):

   nī¹ dī¹ giu³ zōu⁶ _____ .

---

④ Wonton (pronounced as "**wàn⁴ tān¹**" in Cantonese) is one of the many unique Chinese food. It is a kind of filled pasta similar to the Italian ravioli, usually with shrimp and meat inside. Cantonese wonton is usually cooked in soup with or without noodles. The deep fried wonton with sweet and sour sauce is often served as an appetizer or dim-sum in a dim-sum restaurant.

5. To express one's feeling or thinking

e.g. ngŏ⁵ gŏk³ dāk¹ pèi⁴ dáan² m̀⁴ hóu² sīk⁶.

(I think that preserved egg doesn't taste good.)

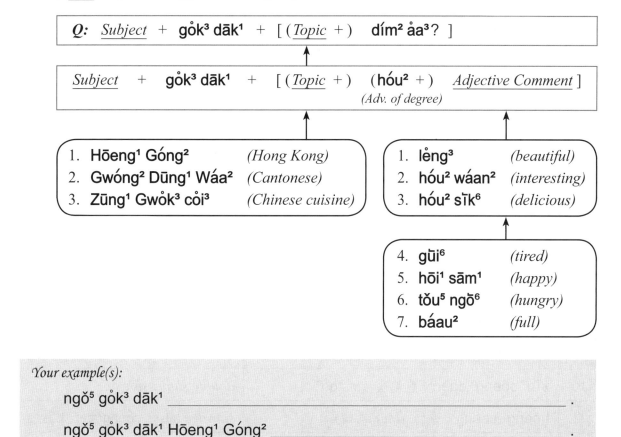

Q: *Subject* + gŏk³ dāk¹ + [(*Topic* +) dím² åa³ ?]

Subject + gŏk³ dāk¹ + [(*Topic* +) (hóu² +) *Adjective Comment*]
(Adv. of degree)

1. Hōeng¹ Góng²　*(Hong Kong)*
2. Gwóng² Dūng¹ Wáa²　*(Cantonese)*
3. Zūng¹ Gwŏk³ cŏi³　*(Chinese cuisine)*

1. lĕng³　*(beautiful)*
2. hóu² wáan²　*(interesting)*
3. hóu² sīk⁶　*(delicious)*

4. gūi⁶　*(tired)*
5. hōi¹ sām¹　*(happy)*
6. tŏu⁵ ngŏ⁶　*(hungry)*
7. báau²　*(full)*

Your example(s):

ngŏ⁵ gŏk³ dāk¹ _____ .

ngŏ⁵ gŏk³ dāk¹ Hōeng¹ Góng² _____ .

6. To express an attempt or trial to do sth. with "hăa⁵"

e.g. ngŏ⁵ si³ hăa⁵ dāan⁶ tāat¹ tùng⁴ bō¹ lò⁴ bāau¹ lāa¹.

(I'll try the egg custard tart and pineapple bun.)

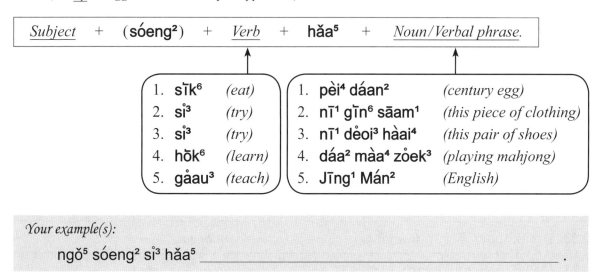

Subject + (sóeng²) + *Verb* + hăa⁵ + *Noun/Verbal phrase.*

1. sīk⁶　*(eat)*
2. si³　*(try)*
3. si³　*(try)*
4. hŏk⁶　*(learn)*
5. gåau³　*(teach)*

1. pèi⁴ dáan²　*(century egg)*
2. nī¹ gīn⁶ sāam¹　*(this piece of clothing)*
3. nī¹ dĕoi³ hàai⁴　*(this pair of shoes)*
4. dáa² màa⁴ zŏek³　*(playing mahjong)*
5. Jīng¹ Mán²　*(English)*

Your example(s):

ngŏ⁵ sóeng² si³ hăa⁵ _____ .

1)	**Chinese style (Zūng¹ sīk¹ 中式):**	
1.	bāak⁶ zūk¹ 白粥 (M: wún² 碗)	*plain rice congee*
2.	jàu⁴ zåa³ gwái² 油炸鬼 (M: tìu⁴ 條)	*deep-fried breadstick* (also "**jàu⁴ tíu² 油條**")
3.	cóeng² fán² 腸粉 (M: dĩp⁶ 碟)	*rice noodle rolls* (also "**zŷu¹ còeng⁴ fán² 豬腸粉**")
4.	dāu⁶ zōeng¹ 豆漿 (M: būi¹ 杯)	*soya bean milk*
5.	cáau² mĩn⁶ 炒麵 (M: dĩp⁶ 碟)	*fried noodle*
6.	zúng² 糭 (M: zẻk³ 隻)	*sticky rice dumpling*
7.	wàn⁴ tān¹ mĩn⁶ 雲吞麵 (M: wún² 碗)	*wonton noodles*
2)	**Western style (Sāi¹ sīk¹ 西式):**	
8.	sāam¹ màn⁴ zĩ⁶ 三文治 (M: fān⁶ 份)	*sandwiches*
9.	cáau² dáan² 炒蛋 (M: zẻk³ 隻/gỏ³ 個)	*scrambled egg*
10.	zīn¹ sōeng¹ dáan² 煎雙蛋 (M: gỏ³ 個)	*double sunny side up*
11.	hōeng¹ cóeng² 香腸 (M: tìu⁴ 條)	*sausage* (also "**cóeng² zái² 腸仔**")
12.	jīn¹ jŭk⁶ 煙肉 (M: fåai³ 塊)	*bacon*
13.	fó² téoi² 火腿 (M: pin³ 片)	*ham*
14.	fó² téoi² tūng¹ fán² 火腿通粉 (M: wún² 碗)	*macaroni in soup with ham*
15.	mĩn⁶ bāau¹ 麵包 (M: gỏ³ 個; fåai³ 塊)	*bread*
16.	gāi¹ měi⁵ bāau¹ 鷄尾包 (M: gỏ³ 個)	*cocktail bun*
17.	bō¹ lò⁴ jàu⁴ 菠蘿油 (M: gỏ³ 個)	*pineapple bun with a slice of butter inserted in it*
18.	dō¹ sí² 多士 (M: fåai³ 塊)	*toast*
19.	sāi¹ dō¹ sí² 西多士 (M: fåai³ 塊)	*French toast*
20.	jàu⁴ zīm¹ dō¹ 油占多 (M: fåai³ 塊)	*butter & jam on toast*
21.	năai⁵ jàu⁴ dō¹ 奶油多 (M: fåai³ 塊)	*butter & condense milk on toast*
22.	māk⁶ pèi⁴ 麥皮 (M: wún² 碗)	*oatmeal*
23.	gūk¹ lēoi⁶ zóu² cāan¹ 穀類早餐	*breakfast cereal*

1. Answer the following questions. $(5 \times 8\% = 40\%)$

1) nī¹ dī¹ hǎi⁶ māt¹ jě⁵ lài⁴ gåa³?　☞

_____

2) gó² dī¹ hǎi⁶ māt¹ jě⁵ lài⁴ gåa³?　☞

_____

3) něi⁵ sóeng² sīk⁶ māt¹ jě⁵ zóu² cāan¹ åa³?

_____

4) něi⁵ gǒk³ dāk¹ hái² Hōeng¹ Góng² māt¹ jě⁵ hóu² sīk⁶ åa³?

_____

5) hái² càa⁴ cāan¹ tēng¹ něi⁵ sóeng² sǐ³ hǎa⁵ māt¹ jě⁵ åa³?

_____

2. Translate the following into Cantonese. $(6 \times 10\% = 60\%)$

1) You're an exchange student, aren't you?

_____

2) What would you like to eat?

_____

3) I would like to try a Hong Kong style milk tea.

_____

4) What *is* this?

_____

5) This is called pineapple bun.

_____

6) I think that lean pork congee is delicious.

_____

Lesson 11 | Ordering food

Learning Objectives

1. To give an explanation of something using "zīk¹ hăi⁶"
2. To state what one wants when ordering food or buying things using the verb "jǐu³"
3. To use an adjective to modify a noun
4. To express the total amount using "jāt¹ gŭng⁶"
5. To give choices to the addressee using "dǐng⁶ hăi⁶" in a question
6. To know topicalization in Cantonese
7. To make a polite request with "céng²"

ngǒ⁵ jǐu³ jāt¹ gǒ³ fó² téoi² dáan² sāam¹ màn⁴ zī⁶,
kěoi⁵ jǐu³ jāt¹ gǒ³ dāan⁶ tāat¹ tùng⁴ jāt¹ gǒ³ bō¹ lò⁴ bāau¹

dō¹ zě⁶.
jāt¹ gŭng⁶ sěi³ sǎp⁶ mān¹.

hái² dōu⁶ sīk⁶ dǐng⁶ hăi⁶ nīng¹ záu² ǎa³?

hái² dōu⁶ sīk⁶, m̀⁴ gōi¹.

Zing-Zing orders the food for Amy and pays at the cashier.

Zing-Zing: Amy, něi⁵ jám² māt¹ jě⁵ åa³?
你 飲 乜 嘢 呀 ？
(Amy, what would you like to drink?)

Amy: ngǒ⁵ sóeng² jám² gåa³ fē¹. ngǒ⁵ dōu¹ sóeng² jám² nǎai⁵ càa⁴.
我 想 飲 咖 啡 。我 都 想 飲 奶 茶 。
(I would like to drink coffee. I also would like to drink milk tea.)

Zing-Zing: gám², sǐ³ hǎa⁵ jīn¹ jōeng¹ lāa¹.
嗷 ， 試 吓 鴛 鴦 啦 ！
(Well, why don't you try "yuanyang"!)

jīn¹ jōeng¹ zīk¹ hǎi⁶ gåa³ fē¹ gāa¹ nǎai⁵ càa⁴.
鴛 鴦 即 係 咖 啡 加 奶 茶 。
("Yuanyang" actually means to add milk tea and coffee together.)

Amy: hóu² åak³. ngǒ⁵ zūng¹ ji³ sǐ³ hǎa⁵ sān¹ jě⁵ ge³.
好 呃 。 我 中 意 試 吓 新 嘢 嘅 。
(Okay! I'd like to try new things.)

Zing-Zing: m̀⁴ gōi¹, lǒeng⁵ būi¹ jīn¹ jōeng¹.
唔 該 ， 兩 杯 鴛 鴦 。
(Excuse me, two cups of "yuanyang", please.)

ngǒ⁵ jiu³ jāt¹ gȯ³ fó² téoi² dáan² sāam¹ màn⁴ zī̄⁶,
我 要 一 個 火 腿 蛋 三 文 治 ，
(I'd like a ham and egg sandwich,

kěoi⁵ jiu³ jāt¹ gȯ³ dāan⁶ tāat¹ tùng⁴ jāt¹ gȯ³ bō¹ lò⁴ bāau¹.
佢 要 一 個 蛋 撻 同 一 個 菠 蘿 包 。
and she'd like an egg custard tart and a pineapple bun.)

Cashier: dō¹ zē⁶. jāt¹ gǔng⁶ sėi³ sāp⁶ mān¹.
多 謝 。 一 共 四 十 蚊 。
(Thank you. Altogether that's $40.)

hái² dȯu⁶ sī̄k⁶ dǐng⁶ hǎi⁶ nīng¹ záu² åa³?
喺 度 食 定 係 拎 走 呀 ？
(Eat in or take away?)

Zing-Zing: hái² dȯu⁶ sī̄k⁶, m̀⁴ gōi¹.
喺 度 食 ， 唔 該 。
(Eat in, please.)

Cashier: jīn¹ jōeng¹ jiu³ jīt⁶ dǐng⁶ důng³ gåa³?
鴛 鴦 要 熱 定 凍 㗎 ？
(Would you like the "yuanyang" hot or cold?)

Zing-Zing: lǒeng⁵ būi¹ dōu¹ jiu³ jīt⁶ ge³.
兩 杯 都 要 熱 嘅 。
(Both of them hot, please.)

Cashier: céng² dáng² jāt¹ zȧn⁶ lāa¹!
請 等 一 陣 啦 ！
(Please wait for a moment!)

1.	jám² 飲 (+ *Object*)	V:	to drink
2.	gåa³ fē¹ 咖啡 (*M:* būi¹ 杯)	N:	coffee
3.	nǎai⁵ càa⁴ 奶茶 (*M:* būi¹ 杯)	N:	milk tea
4.	jīn¹ jōeng¹ 鴛鴦 (*M:* būi¹ 杯)	N:	(in L.11) yuanyang① *[a mixture of HK style milk tea and coffee]*
5.	zīk¹ hāi⁶ 即係	V:	be; mean; namely; it means...; that is...
6.	gāa¹ 加	V:	to add
7.	sān¹ jě⁵ 新野	Ph:	new stuff; new things
8.	būi¹ 杯 (*M:* gǒ³ 個 / zěk³ 隻)	N/M:	glass, cup, mug; a cup of *[a measure of the quantity of something that a cup will hold]*
9.	fó² téoi² 火腿 (*M:* pȉn³ 片)	N:	ham
10.	dáan² 蛋 (*M:* zěk³ 隻 / gǒ³ 個)	N:	egg (also "**gāi¹ dáan²** 雞蛋")
11.	sāam¹ màn⁴ zȉ⁶ 三文治 (*M:* fān⁶ 份 / gǒ³ 個)	N:	sandwich (es)
12.	jāt¹ gūng⁶ 一共 (+ *Quantity*)	Adv:	total, altogether (also "**hām⁶ bāang⁶ lāang⁶** 冚嘭唥")
13.	hái² dōu⁶ sȉk⁶ 喺度食	Ph:	eat here
14.	dȉng⁶ hāi⁶ 定係	Conj:	or *[only used in a question indicating options]* (also shortened as "**dȉng⁶** 定")
15.	nīng¹ záu² 拎走	V:	take away; "to go" (also "**nīk¹ záu²** 擝走")
16.	jȉt⁶ 熱	Adj:	hot (in temperature)
17.	důng³ 凍	Adj:	cold; iced
18.	céng² 請 (céng² + *Verb*)	V:	please (+ *verb*) *[used to show politeness in requests or commands to mean 'be obliging enough (to)']*
19.	dáng² 等	V:	to wait
20.	jāt¹ zān⁶ 一陣	N:	a little while

---

① **Yuanyang** (pronounced as "**jīn¹ jōeng¹**" in Cantonese) is originally a Chinese name of Mandarin Duck. They usually appear in male and female pairs and are referred to as a symbol of conjugal love in Chinese culture. Hong Kong people mix Hong Kong style milk tea and coffee together and call the drink "**jīn¹ jōeng¹**" to make use of the connotation of "pair". This is a popular kind of beverage in HK, the drink **Yuanyang**, is considered as a mixture of Eastern and Western culture as well.

1. To give an explanation of something using "zīk¹ hǎi⁶"

e.g.   jīn¹ jōeng¹ zīk¹ hǎi⁶ gǎa³ fē¹ gāa¹ nǎai⁵ càa⁴.

   ("Yuanyang" <u>actually means</u> to add milk tea and coffee together.)

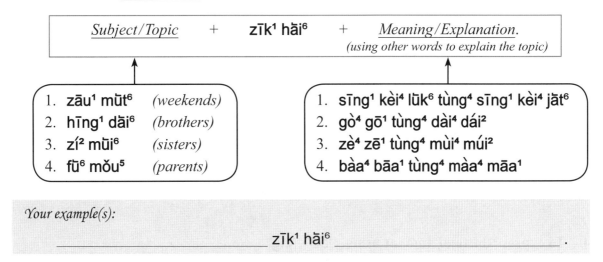

Subject/Topic	+	**zīk¹ hǎi⁶**	+	*Meaning/Explanation.*

(using other words to explain the topic)

1. zāu¹ mǔt⁶   *(weekends)*
2. hīng¹ dǎi⁶   *(brothers)*
3. zí² mūi⁶   *(sisters)*
4. fū⁶ mǒu⁵   *(parents)*

1. sīng¹ kèi⁴ lūk⁶ tùng⁴ sīng¹ kèi⁴ jāt⁶
2. gò⁴ gō¹ tùng⁴ dài⁴ dái²
3. zè⁴ zē¹ tùng⁴ mùi⁴ múi²
4. bàa⁴ bāa¹ tùng⁴ màa⁴ māa¹

Your example(s):

_____ zīk¹ hǎi⁶ _____ .

2. To state what one wants when ordering food or buying things

e.g. 1. m̀⁴ gōi¹, lǒeng⁵ būi¹ jīn¹ jōeng¹.

   (Excuse me, two cups of "yuanyang", please.)

e.g. 2. ngǒ⁵ jǐu³ jāt¹ gǒ³ fó² téoi² dáan² sāam¹ màn⁴ zī⁶.

   (I'd like a ham and egg sandwich.)

e.g. 3. kěoi⁵ jǐu³ jāt¹ gǒ³ dāan⁶ tāat¹ tùng⁴ jāt¹ gǒ³ bō¹ lò⁴ bāau¹.

   (She'd like an egg custard tart and a pineapple bun.)

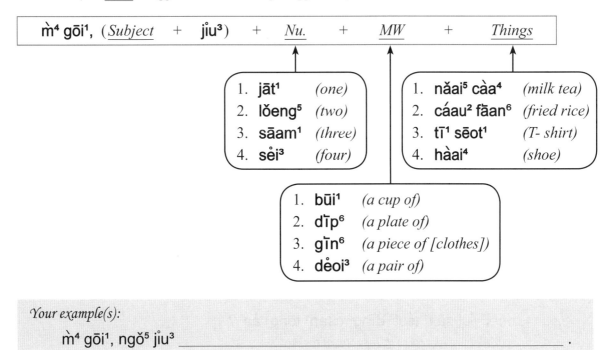

m̀⁴ gōi¹, (*Subject*	+	**jǐu³**)	+	*Nu.*	+	*MW*	+	*Things*

1. jāt¹   *(one)*
2. lǒeng⁵   *(two)*
3. sāam¹   *(three)*
4. sěi³   *(four)*

1. nǎai⁵ càa⁴   *(milk tea)*
2. cáau² fāan⁶   *(fried rice)*
3. tī¹ sēot¹   *(T- shirt)*
4. hàai⁴   *(shoe)*

1. būi¹   *(a cup of)*
2. dīp⁶   *(a plate of)*
3. gīn⁶   *(a piece of [clothes])*
4. děoi³   *(a pair of)*

Your example(s):

m̀⁴ gōi¹, ngǒ⁵ jǐu³ _____ .

3. **To use an adjective to modify a noun**

e.g. ngǒ⁵ zūng¹ jǐ³ sǐ³ hǎa⁵ <u>sān¹</u> jě⁵ gě̊³.

   (I like to try <u>new things</u>.)

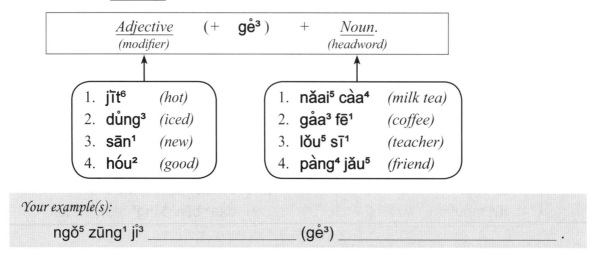

```
         Adjective    (+  ge̊³ )   +    Noun.
         (modifier)                     (headword)
```

1. jīt⁶	(hot)		1. nǎai⁵ càa⁴	(milk tea)
2. dů̊ng³	(iced)		2. gǎa³ fē¹	(coffee)
3. sān¹	(new)		3. lǒu⁵ sī¹	(teacher)
4. hóu²	(good)		4. pàng⁴ jǎu⁵	(friend)

Your example(s):

ngǒ⁵ zūng¹ jǐ³ _____ (ge̊³) _____ .

4. **To express the total amount using "jāt¹ gūng⁶"**

e.g. <u>jāt¹ gūng⁶</u> sě̊i³ sǎp⁶ mān¹.

   (<u>Altogether</u> that's $40.)

```
     jāt¹ gūng⁶   +   Nu.   +   MW   (+   Noun).
                             (total amount)
```

1. jī⁶ bǎak³ lūk⁶ sǎp⁶ mān¹	($260)
2. gáu² cīn¹ gáu² bǎak³ gáu² sǎp⁶ gáu² mān¹	($9,999)
3. sǎp⁶ lūk⁶ gǒ³ jàn⁴	(16 persons)
4. nǧ⁵ būi¹ gǎa³ fē¹	(5 cups of coffee)

5. **To give choices to the addressee using "dīng⁶ hǎi⁶"or "dīng⁶" in a question**

e.g. 1. hái² dōu⁶ sīk⁶ <u>dīng⁶ hǎi⁶</u> nīng¹ záu² å̊a³?

   (Eat in <u>or</u> take away?)

e.g. 2. jīn¹ jōeng¹ jǐu³ jīt⁶ <u>dīng⁶</u> dů̊ng³ å̊a³?

   (Would you like the "yuanyang" hot <u>or</u> cold?)

```
Q:   Alternative A    +   dīng⁶ hǎi⁶/dīng⁶   +   Alternative B   +   å̊a³?
     (Noun₁/Adjective₁/                          (Noun₂/Adjective₂/
     Verbal phrase₁/Clause₁)                     Verbal phrase₂/Clause₂)
```

e.g. 3. něi⁵ jám² māt¹ jě⁵ å̊a³? gǎa³ fē¹ <u>dīng⁶ hǎi⁶</u> càa⁴ å̊a³?

   (What would you like to drink? Coffee <u>or</u> tea?)

e.g. 4. něi⁵ jǐu³ sāa¹ léot² <u>dīng⁶</u> cāan¹ tōng¹ å̊a³?

   (Would you like salad <u>or</u> the soup of the day?)

e.g. 5. gām¹ jāt⁶ hǎi⁶ sīng¹ kèi⁴ jāt⁶ <u>dǐng⁶ hǎi⁶</u> sīng¹ kèi⁴ jāt¹ <u>åa³</u>?
(Today is Sunday <u>or</u> Monday<u>?</u>)

e.g. 6. ngǒ⁵ dēi⁶ hěoi³ <u>dǐng⁶ hǎi⁶</u> m̀⁴ hěoi³ <u>åa³</u>?
(Shall we go <u>or not?</u>)

e.g. 7. něi⁵ gok³ dāk¹ dǎan⁶ tāat¹ hóu² sǐk⁶ <u>dǐng⁶ hǎi⁶</u> m̀⁴ hóu² sǐk⁶ <u>åa³</u>?
(Do you think egg custard tart is tasty <u>or not?</u>)

> *Your example(s):*
>
> _____ dǐng⁶ hǎi⁶ _____ åa³?

6. To know topicalization[2] in Cantonese

e.g. ngǒ⁵ jǐu³ lǒeng⁵ būi¹ jīn¹ jōeng¹. lǒeng⁵ būi¹ dōu¹ jǐu³ jǐt⁶ gě³.
(I'd like two cups of "yuanyang". <u>Both of them</u> hot, please.)

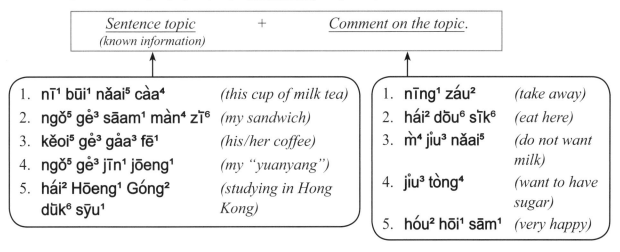

| *Sentence topic* (known information) | + | *Comment on the topic.* |

1. nī¹ būi¹ nǎai⁵ càa⁴ *(this cup of milk tea)*
2. ngǒ⁵ gě³ sāam¹ màn⁴ zǐ⁶ *(my sandwich)*
3. kěoi⁵ gě³ gåa³ fē¹ *(his/her coffee)*
4. ngǒ⁵ gě³ jīn¹ jōeng¹ *(my "yuanyang")*
5. hái² Hōeng¹ Góng² dūk⁶ sȳu¹ *(studying in Hong Kong)*

1. nīng¹ záu² *(take away)*
2. hái² dōu⁶ sǐk⁶ *(eat here)*
3. m̀⁴ jǐu³ nǎai⁵ *(do not want milk)*
4. jǐu³ tòng⁴ *(want to have sugar)*
5. hóu² hōi¹ sām¹ *(very happy)*

7. To make a polite request with "céng²"

e.g. <u>céng²</u> dáng² jāt¹ zǎn⁶ lāa¹!
(Please wait for a moment!)

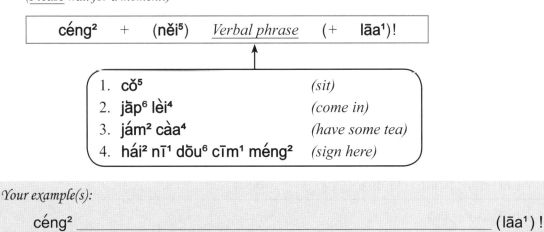

| céng² | + | (něi⁵) | *Verbal phrase* | (+ | lāa¹)! |

1. cǒ⁵ *(sit)*
2. jǎp⁶ lèi⁴ *(come in)*
3. jám² càa⁴ *(have some tea)*
4. hái² nī¹ dōu⁶ cīm¹ méng² *(sign here)*

> *Your example(s):*
>
> céng² _____ (lāa¹)!

---

② **Topicalization** is the promotion of some element of the sentence to the topic position. (Matthews & Yip 1994) Note that the subject of the verb is usually omitted in such sentences.

Q: céng² mān⁶ (něi⁵) jám² māt¹ jě⁵ åa³?

A: m̀⁴ gōi¹, ngǒ⁵ jíu³ _____ .

1.	năai⁵ càa⁴ 奶茶	*milk tea*
2.	gåa³ fē¹ 咖啡	*coffee*
3.	zāai¹ fē¹ 齋啡	*black coffee*
4.	jīn¹ jōeng¹ 鴛鴦	*yuanyang* *(a mixture of HK style milk tea and coffee)*
5.	nìng⁴ mūng¹ càa⁴ 檸檬茶	*lemon tea (also shortened as "níng² càa⁴ 檸茶")*
6.	nìng⁴ mūng¹ séoi² 檸檬水	*lemonade (also shortened as "níng² séoi² 檸水")*
7.	hěi³ séoi² 汽水	*soft drinks*
8.	hó² lōk⁶ 可樂	*Coke*
9.	Cāt¹ Héi² 七喜	*Seven-up*
10.	Sẙut³ Bīk¹ 雪碧	*Sprite*
11.	níng² lōk⁶ 檸樂	*Coke with lemon*
12.	níng² cāt¹ 檸七	*Seven-up with lemon*
13.	níng² māt⁶ 檸蜜	*honey lemonade*
14.	cáang² zāp¹ 橙汁	*orange juice*
15.	sīn¹ năai⁵ 鮮奶	*fresh milk*
16.	ngàu⁴ năai⁵ 牛奶	*milk*
17.	hāng⁶ jàn⁴ sōeng¹ 杏仁霜	*almond drink*
18.	zȳu¹ gū¹ līk¹ 朱古力	*chocolate drink*
19.	Hóu² Lāap⁶ Hāk¹ 好立克	*Horlicks*
20.	Ō¹ Wàa⁴ Tìn⁴ 阿華田	*Ovaltine*
21.	Lēi⁶ Bān¹ Nāap⁶ 利賓納	*Ribena*
22.	bē¹ záu² 啤酒	*beer*
23.	kwǒng³ cẙun⁴ séoi² 礦泉水	*mineral water*

Adjectives are words that describe the nature or state of a person or a thing. Here are some common adjectives for your reference.

No.	English	Cantonese
1.	bad; not up to standard	cāa^1 差 ; séoi^2 pèi^4 水皮
2.	bad; wicked, evil-minded	sēoi^1 衰
3.	bad, out of order	wāai^6 壞
4.	beautiful, pretty	lèng^3 靚
5.	big	dāai^6 大
6.	boring	mūn^6 悶
7.	busy	mòng^4 忙
8.	cheap	pèng^4 平
9.	cold; iced	dǔng^3 凍
10.	comfortable	sÿu^1 fūk^6 舒服
11.	convenient	fōng^1 bīn^6 方便
12.	correct	ngāam^1 啱
13.	crazy	cī^1 sin^3 黐線
14.	dangerous	ngài^4 hím^2 危險
15.	difficult	nàan^4 難
16.	early	zóu^2 早
17.	easy	jùng^4 jī^6 容易
18.	expensive	gwǎi^3 貴
19.	far	jǔun^5 遠
20.	fat	fèi^4 肥
21.	few; a little	síu^2 少
22.	fragrant	hōeng^1 香
23.	free; not busy	dāk^1 hàan^4 得閒
24.	full	báau^2 飽
25.	fun, interesting	hóu^2 wáan^2 好玩
26.	good; obedient	gwāai^1 乖
27.	good; fine; cool	zèng^3 正
28.	great; terrific	hóu^2 好
29.	happy	hōi^1 sām^1 開心
30.	hard, tough	sān^1 fú^2 辛苦
31.	hardworking	kàn^4 lǐk^6 勤力
32.	hot	jīt^6 熱
33.	hungry	tǒu^5 ngǒ^6 肚餓
34.	kind; nice person	hóu^2 jàn^4 好人
35.	late	cì^4 遲
36.	lazy	lǎan^5 懶
37.	long	còeng^4 長
38.	low	dāi^1 低
39.	many, much, a lot	dō^1 多
40.	naughty	jǎi^5 曳
41.	near	kǎn^5/gān^6 近
42.	nervous	gán^2 zōeng^1 緊張
43.	new	sān^1 新
44.	noisy	còu^4 嘈
45.	old (not new)	gāu^6 舊
46.	old (not young)	lǒu^5 老
47.	painful; sore	tùng^3 痛
48.	quick; fast	fǎai^3 快
49.	quiet	zīng^6 靜
50.	safe	ōn^1 cÿun^4 安全
51.	terrific, extreme	sāi^1 lēi^6 犀利
52.	short (in length)	dýun^2 短
53.	short (in height)	ái^2 矮
54.	silly	sò^4 傻
55.	slow	māan^6 慢
56.	small	sǎi^3 細
57.	smart, intelligent	cūng^1 mìng^4 聰明
58.	smelly, stench	cǎu^3 臭
59.	stupid	céon^2 蠢
60.	tall, high	gōu^1 高
61.	tasty (drinks)	hóu^2 jám^2 好飲
62.	tasty (food)	hóu^2 sīk^6 好食 ; hóu^2 mēi^6 好味
63.	thin (in contrast to fat)	sǎu^3 瘦
64.	thirsty	géng^2 hot^3 頸渴
65.	tired	gūi^6 劫
66.	ugly	cáu^2 jóeng^2 醜樣
67.	wrong	cò^3 錯
68.	young	hāu^6 sāang^1 後生

1. **Rearrange the various parts of the following sentences in their right order.**
   (4 × 10% = 40%)

   1) jı̊u³ / ngǒ⁵ / būi¹ / lŏeng⁵ / gåa³ fē¹ / jīt⁶ / . /

   _____

   2) géi² dō¹ cín² / gåa³ fē¹ / tùng⁴ / sāam¹ màn⁴ zī⁶ / jāt¹ gǒ³ / jāt¹ būi¹ / jāt¹ gūng⁶ / åa³ / ? /

   _____

   _____

   3) sóeng² / hái² dōu⁶ / něi⁵ / dı̆ng⁶ hāi⁶ / åa³ / sīk⁶ / nīng¹ záu² / ? /

   _____

   4) tùng⁴ / dāan⁶ tāat¹ / dōu¹ / hóu² hóu² sīk⁶ / bō¹ lò⁴ bāau¹ / . /

   _____

2. **What should you say in the following situations? (in Cantonese)** (5 × 12% = 60%)

   1) You want to know what someone would like to drink.

      You say: _____

   2) You want to explain that "yuanyang" is actually adding milk tea and coffee together.

      You say: _____

   3) You want to ask for someone politely to wait for a moment.

      You say: _____

   4) You want to order one sandwich and two cups of hot coffee.

      You say: _____

      _____

   5) You want to ask which one is tasty, egg custard tart or pineapple bun.

      You say: _____

      _____

Learning Objectives

1. To indicate that something has not yet been done by "**měi⁶**"
2. To indicate that something has been completed by "**zó²**"
3. To ask whether something has occurred or not
4. To suggest doing something together using "**āa¹**" at the end
5. To treat or invite someone to something with "**céng²**"
6. To ask someone's agreement to your suggestion with "**hóu² m̀⁴ hóu² ǎa³?**"
7. To express the sense of "in addition to…" using "**zūng⁶…tīm¹**"
8. To give an alternative in a statement with "**wǎak⁶ zé²**"

sīk⁶ zó² fāan⁶ měi⁶ ǎa³?
jāt¹ cài⁴ hěoi³ jám² càa⁴ āa¹!

hóu² ǎak³. gám², dō¹ zě⁶ sīn¹.

m̀⁴ gōi¹, jāt¹ wù⁴ Póu² Léi²,
jāt¹ wù⁴ gwán² séoi².

m̀⁴ gōi¹, màai⁴ dāan¹ lāa¹!

Tony invites Siu-Ping to have dim-sum for lunch.

Tony:	wǎi³, Síu²-Pìng⁴, sīk⁶ zó² fāan⁶ mềi⁶ åa³?
	喂， 小 平， 食 咗 飯 未 呀？
	(Hi, Siu-Ping, have you eaten yet?)

Siu-Ping:	mềi⁶ åa³. něi⁵ nē¹?
	未 呀。你 呢？
	(Not yet. How about you?)

Tony:	ngǒ⁵ dōu¹ mềi⁶ sīk⁶ åa³. jāt¹ cài⁴ hểoi³ jám² càa⁴ āa¹!
	我 都 未 食 呀。一 齊 去 飲 茶 吖！
	(I haven't eaten either. Let's go to have dim-sum together!)

Siu-Ping:	hóu² åak³.
	好 呃。
	(Good.)

Tony:	něi⁵ sì⁴ sì⁴ gåau³ ngǒ⁵ góng² Gwóng² Dūng¹ Wáa².
	你 時 時 教 我 講 廣 東 話。
	(You often teach me Cantonese.)
	ngǒ⁵ céng² něi⁵ jám² càa⁴ āa¹!
	我 請 你 飲 茶 吖！
	(Let me treat you to a dim-sum!)

Siu-Ping:	gám², dō¹ zẽ⁶ sīn¹. hàang⁴ låa³!
	噉， 多 謝 先。 行 喇！
	(Well, thank you in advance. Let's go.)

At the Chinese restaurant.

Siu-Ping: (to waiter)	m̀⁴ gōi¹, jāt¹ wù⁴ Póu² Léi², jāt¹ wù⁴ gwán² séoi².
	唔 該，一 壺 普 洱，一 壺 滾 水。
	(Excuse me, a pot of Pu'er tea and a pot of boiling water, please.)

Tony:	ngǒ⁵ sóeng² si³ hǎa⁵ hāa¹ gáau², cēon¹ gýun² tùng⁴ cāa¹ sīu¹ bāau¹.
	我 想 試 吓 蝦 餃，春 卷 同 叉 燒 包。
	(I would like to try shrimp dumpling, spring roll and barbecue pork bun.)

Siu-Ping:	hóu² åak³. ngǒ⁵ sóeng² sīk⁶ fāan⁶.
	好 呃。我 想 食 飯。
	(Okay. I'd like to eat rice.)
	ngǒ⁵ dēi⁶ jiu³ jāt¹ gȯ³ cáau² fāan⁶, hóu² m̀⁴ hóu² åa³?
	我 哋 要 一 個 炒 飯，好 唔 好 呀？
	(Shall we have fried rice, okay?)

Tony:	mǒu⁵ mān⁶ tài⁴. ngǒ⁵ zūng⁶ sóeng² jiu³ dī¹ tìm⁴ bán² tīm¹.
	冇 問 題。我 仲 想 要 啲 甜 品 添。
	(No problem. I'd still like to have some dessert.)

Siu-Ping:	si³ hǎa⁵ dāu⁶ fū⁶ fāa¹ wāak⁶ zé² hùng⁴ dáu² sāa¹ lāa¹!
	試 吓 豆 腐 花 或 者 紅 豆 沙 啦！
	(Try tofu pudding or sweet red bean soup!)

After finishing all the food.

Tony:	zān¹ hãi⁶ hóu² sīk⁶ åa³. lǒeng⁵ dím² låa³. ngǒ⁵ jiu³ fāan¹ gūng¹ låa³.
	真 係 好 食 呀。 兩 點 喇。我 要 返 工 喇。
	(It's really tasty. It's two o'clock. I have to go to work now.)

Siu-Ping:	gám², m̀⁴ gōi¹, màai⁴ dāan¹ lāa¹!
	噉， 唔 該， 埋 單 啦！
	(Well, get the bill, please!)

1.	wái³ 喂	Intj:	hello; hey *[to draw sb.'s attention informally]*
2.	fāan⁶ 飯	N:	cooked rice
3.	zó² 咗 (*Verb* + zó² + *Object*) (e.g. sīk⁶ zó² fāan⁶)	Part:	*[a perfective aspect particle used after a verb, indicating completion of an action whether in the past, present or future]*
4.	mēi⁶ 未 (+ *Verb*) (e.g. mēi⁶ sīk⁶ fāan⁶)	Adv:	not yet *[It implies that an action is expected to take place but has not yet taken place]*
5.	jám² càa⁴ 飲茶	VO:	yum-cha① (lit. to drink tea); (in L.12) to have dim-sum② (also "sīk⁶ dím² sām¹ 食點心")
6.	āa¹ 吖	Part:	*[a modal particle used at the end of a sentence, indicating suggestions in a causal mood]*
7.	céng² 請 (*Person₁* + céng² + *Person₂* + *Verb*)	V:	invite, treat, serve or entertain someone to sth. (bear the expense of the entertainment); paying for the expenses; playing host
8.	sīn¹ 先 (*Verb* + sīn¹)	Adv:	first; in advance
9.	dō¹ zē⁶ sīn¹ 多謝先	SE:	Thank you in advance.
10.	hàang⁴ làa³ 行喇	SE:	Let's go.
11.	wù⁴ 壺	N/M:	teapot; a pot of

---

① The Hong Kong word **yum-cha** (Jyutping: jám² càa⁴) literally means "to drink tea", but also commonly refers to the practice of enjoying small dishes known as "dim-sum" while drinking Chinese tea. People in Cantonese-speaking regions or Chinatowns overseas like to yum-cha with family or friends, sharing good conversation over delicious dim-sum.

② **Dim-sum** (Jyutping: dím² sām¹) originally refers to light snacks or refreshments enjoyed between proper meals to satisfy a food craving or an empty stomach. Today, it also popularly refers to a style of Chinese cuisine in which a variety of foods are served in bamboo steamers or on small plates. These small dishes come from a wide spectrum of choices, from the salty to the sweet, and are steamed, baked or fried (See FYI). It also combines different Chinese snacks or cuisines, including cakes and pastries. Dim-sum dishes can be ordered from a menu in some restaurants, while in others, the food is wheeled around on trolleys for diners to choose from.

12.	Póu² Léi² 普洱	PN:	Pu'er tea (also "**Bóu² Léi²**") *[black tea, fully fermented and oxidized tea]*
13.	gwán² séoi² 滾水	Ph:	boiling water
14.	hāa¹ gáau² 蝦餃	N:	shrimp dumpling *[steamed in a small steamer known as "zīng¹ lùng⁴ 蒸籠" usually made of bamboo]*
15.	cēon¹ gýun² 春卷	N:	spring roll *[put on a small plate after deep fried]*
16.	cāa¹ sīu¹ bāau¹ 叉燒包	N:	barbecue pork bun
17.	cáau² fāan⁶ 炒飯	N:	fried rice
18.	hóu² m̀⁴ hóu² åa³? 好唔好呀？	SE:	Is that good? Is it okay? *[attached at the end of a suggestion or request]*
19.	zūng⁶ 仲 (+ *Verb*)	Adv:	(in L.12) (in addition to…) still; also *[implies extra emphasis or surprise]*
20.	tīm¹ 添 (zūng⁶…tīm¹)	Part:	*[a modal particle, accompanying the adverb "**zūng**" to emphasize the idea of 'addition']*
21.	tìm⁴ bán² 甜品	N:	dessert
22.	dāu⁶ fū⁶ fāa¹ 豆腐花	N:	bean curd dessert; tofu pudding
23.	hùng⁴ dáu² sāa¹ 紅豆沙	N:	sweet red bean soup (also "**hùng⁴ dāu⁶ sāa¹**")
24.	wāak⁶ zé² 或者 (A + wāak⁶ zé² + B)	Conj:	or (either one can do) *[used in a statement, not in questions]*
25.	zān¹ hāi⁶ 真係	Adv:	really; indeed
26.	màai⁴ dāan¹ 埋單	VO:	add up the bill; to pay

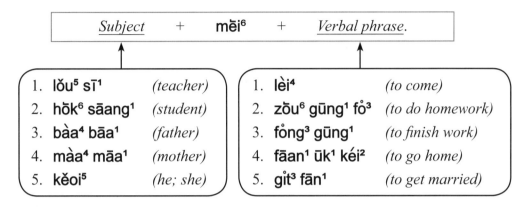

Sentence Structure

1. **To indicate that something has not yet been done by "mĕi⁶"**

   e.g. ngǒ⁵ mĕi⁶ sīk⁶ fāan⁶ åa³.

   (I haven't eaten yet.)

Subject	+	mĕi⁶	+	Verbal phrase.

   1. lǒu⁵ sī¹   *(teacher)*
   2. hǒk⁶ sāang¹   *(student)*
   3. bàa⁴ bāa¹   *(father)*
   4. màa⁴ māa¹   *(mother)*
   5. kěoi⁵   *(he; she)*

   1. lèi⁴   *(to come)*
   2. zǒu⁶ gūng¹ fǒ³   *(to do homework)*
   3. fǒng³ gūng¹   *(to finish work)*
   4. fāan¹ ūk¹ kéi²   *(to go home)*
   5. git³ fān¹   *(to get married)*

   Your example(s):

   _____ mĕi⁶ _____ .

   _____ mĕi⁶ _____ .

2. **To indicate that something has been completed by "zó²"**

   e.g. ngǒ⁵ sīk⁶ zó² fāan⁶ låa³.

   (I have already eaten.)

Subject	+	Verb + zó² (+ Object)	(+ låa³).

   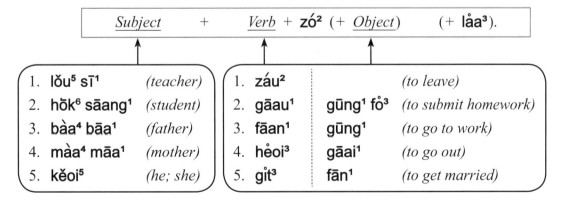

   1. lǒu⁵ sī¹   *(teacher)*
   2. hǒk⁶ sāang¹   *(student)*
   3. bàa⁴ bāa¹   *(father)*
   4. màa⁴ māa¹   *(mother)*
   5. kěoi⁵   *(he; she)*

   1. záu²   *(to leave)*
   2. gāau¹   gūng¹ fǒ³   *(to submit homework)*
   3. fāan¹   gūng¹   *(to go to work)*
   4. hěoi³   gāai¹   *(to go out)*
   5. git³   fān¹   *(to get married)*

   Your example(s):

   _____ zó² _____ .

   _____ zó² _____ .

3. **To ask whether something has occurred or not**

   e.g.   něi⁵ sı̄k⁶ <u>zó²</u> fāan⁶ měi⁶ åa³?

        (Have you eaten yet?)

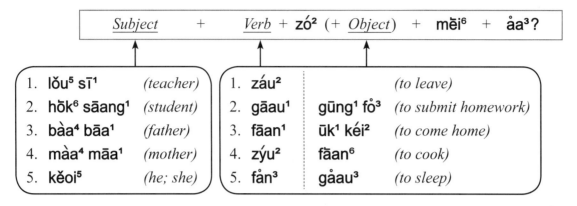

| *Subject* | + | *Verb* + zó² (+ *Object*) | + | měi⁶ | + | åa³? |

1. lǒu⁵ sı̄¹	*(teacher)*	1. záu²		*(to leave)*
2. hǒk⁶ sāang¹	*(student)*	2. gāau¹	gūng¹ fǒ³	*(to submit homework)*
3. bàa⁴ bāa¹	*(father)*	3. fāan¹	ūk¹ kéi²	*(to come home)*
4. màa⁴ māa¹	*(mother)*	4. zýu²	fāan⁶	*(to cook)*
5. kěoi⁵	*(he; she)*	5. fǎn³	gåau³	*(to sleep)*

Your example(s):

_____ zó² měi⁶ åa³?

_____ zó² _____ měi⁶ åa³?

4. **To suggest doing something together**

   e.g.   jāt¹ cài⁴ hǒoi³ jám² càa⁴ āa¹!

        (Let's go to have dim-sum together!)

| (ngǒ⁵ děi⁶) | + | jāt¹ cài⁴ | + | *Verbal phrase* | + | āa¹! |

1. sı̄k⁶ mǎan⁵ fāan⁶	*(to have a dinner)*
2. hǒoi³ tái² hěi³	*(to go watching a movie)*
3. dáa² mǒng⁵ kàu⁴	*(to play tennis)*
4. jíng² sóeng²	*(to take a photo)*
5. lěoi⁵ hàng⁴	*(to go traveling)*

Your example(s):

    ngǒ⁵ děi⁶ jāt¹ cài⁴ _____ āa¹!

    jāt¹ cài⁴ _____ āa¹!

5. To treat or invite someone to something

e.g. ngǒ⁵ céng² něi⁵ jám² càa⁴ lāa¹!

(I will <u>treat</u> you to a dim-sum.)

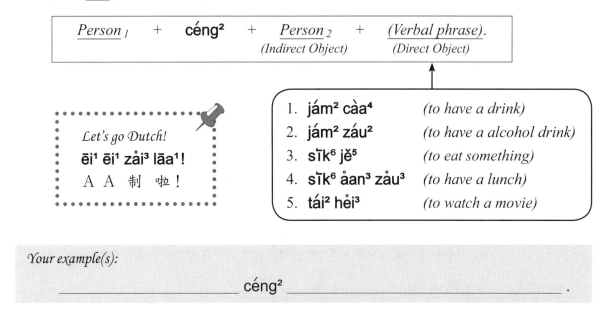

Person ₁	+	**céng²**	+	*Person ₂*	+	*(Verbal phrase).*
				(Indirect Object)		*(Direct Object)*

Let's go Dutch!
ēi¹ ēi¹ zǎi³ lāa¹!
A A 制 啦！

1. jám² càa⁴　　(to have a drink)
2. jám² záu²　　(to have a alcohol drink)
3. sīk⁶ jě⁵　　(to eat something)
4. sīk⁶ åan³ zåu³　　(to have a lunch)
5. tái² hěi³　　(to watch a movie)

Your example(s):

_____ céng² _____ .

6. To ask someone's agreement to your suggestion with "hóu² m̀⁴ hóu² åa³?"

e.g. ngǒ⁵ dēi⁶ jǐu³ jāt¹ gǒ³ cáau² fāan⁶, hóu² m̀⁴ hóu² åa³?

(Shall we have fried rice, <u>okay?</u>)

Suggestion ,	+	**hóu² m̀⁴ hóu² åa³?**
		(do you agree?)

1. (ngǒ⁵ dēi⁶) sīng¹ kèi⁴ jāt⁶ hěoi³ tái² hěi³,
   (We'll go to watch a movie on Sunday.)

2. (ngǒ⁵ dēi⁶) gām¹ mǎan⁵ sīk⁶ Zūng¹ Gwǒk³ cǒi³,
   (We'll eat Chinese cuisine tonight.)

3. (ngǒ⁵ dēi⁶) tīng¹ jāt⁶ hěoi³ hàang⁴ gāai¹,
   (We'll go shopping tomorrow.)

4. (ngǒ⁵ dēi⁶) cēot¹ nín² gǐt³ fān¹,
   (We'll get married next year.)

Your example(s):

(ngǒ⁵ dēi⁶) _____ , hóu² m̀⁴ hóu² åa³ ?

7. **To express the sense of "in addition to…" using "zūng⁶…tīm¹"**

e.g. 1. ngǒ⁵ sóeng² sỉ³ hǎa⁵ hāa¹ gáau², …ngǒ⁵ <u>zūng⁶</u> sóeng² jỉu³ dī¹ tìm⁴ bán² <u>tīm¹</u>.
    (I would like to try shrimp dumpling, … I'd still like to have some dessert.)

Subject + Verb + Object₁, + **zūng⁶** + Verb + Object₂ + **tīm¹**.

$$\underline{Subject\ +\ Verb\ +\ Object_1,}\ +\ \mathbf{z\bar{u}ng^6}\ +\ \underline{Verb\ +\ Object_2}\ +\ \mathbf{t\bar{\imath}m^1}.$$

e.g. 2. kěoi⁵ jǎu⁵ tỏai³ táai², <u>zūng⁶</u> jǎu⁵ jāt¹ gỏ³ zái² tīm¹.
    (He has a wife and also has a son.)

e.g. 3. *Amy* sīk¹ Jīng¹ Mán², <u>zūng⁶</u> sīk¹ Fảat³ Mán² tīm¹.
    (Amy knows English; she also knows French.)

e.g. 4. Åa³-Pìng⁴ gảau³ Gwóng² Dūng¹ Wáa², <u>zūng⁶</u> gảau³ Póu² Tūng¹ Wáa² tīm¹.
    (Ah-Ping teaches Cantonese; she also teaches Mandarin.)

e.g. 5. Tony céng² Åa³-Pìng⁴ jám² càa⁴, <u>zūng⁶</u> céng² kěoi⁵ tái² hẻi³ tīm¹.
    (Tony treated Ah-Ping to have dim-sum, he also treated her to watching a movie.)

Your example(s):

ngǒ⁵ _____ ,

zūng⁶ _____ tīm¹.

8. **To give an alternative in a statement with "wǎak⁶ zé²"**

e.g. 1. sỉ³ hǎa⁵ dāu⁶ fū⁶ fāa¹ <u>wǎak⁶ zé²</u> hùng⁴ dáu² sāa¹ lāa¹!
    (Try tofu pudding or sweet red bean soup!)

A wǎak⁶ zé² *B*

e.g. 2. ngǒ⁵ sóeng² jỉu³ jāt¹ gỏ³ zái² <u>wǎak⁶ zé²</u> jāt¹ gỏ³ néoi².
    (I want to have a son or a daughter.)

e.g. 3. ngǒ⁵ gẻ³ pàng⁴ jǎu⁵ nī¹ gỏ³ sīng¹ kèi⁴ lūk⁶ <u>wǎak⁶ zé²</u> sīng¹ kèi⁴ jāt⁶ lèi⁴ Hōeng¹ Góng².
    (My friend will come to Hong Kong on this Saturday or Sunday.)

e.g. 4. ngǒ⁵ dāk¹ hàan⁴ zūng¹ jỉ³ tái² sȳu¹ <u>wǎak⁶ zé²</u> tēng¹ jām¹ ngōk⁶.
    (I like reading or listening to music in my free time.)

e.g. 5. kěoi⁵ jỉ⁴ gāa¹ hái² ūk¹ kéi² <u>wǎak⁶ zé²</u> bǎan⁶ gūng¹ sāt¹.
    (He is either at home or in the office now.)

Your example(s):

_____

Q: céng² mān⁶ jám² māt¹ jě⁵ càa⁴ åa³?

A: m̀⁴ gōi¹, ngǒ⁵ jíu³ jāt¹ wù⁴ _____ (Tea's name) _____ .

	Category	Name of tea
1.	Lūk⁶ Càa⁴ 綠茶 *(Green tea : non-fermented tea)*	• Lùng⁴ Zéng² 龍井 *(Long-jing tea: best known as King of all green teas)* • Bīk¹ Lò⁴ Cēon¹ 碧螺春 *(Bi-luo-chun tea: best known as Queen of all green teas)*
2.	Wòng⁴ Càa⁴ 黃茶 *(Yellow tea : non-fermented tea with yellow-green appearance)*	• Gwān¹ Sāan¹ Ngàn⁴ Zām¹ 君山銀針 *(Junshan Yinzhen yellow tea; Silver Needle yellow tea)*
3.	Bāak⁶ Càa⁴ 白茶 *(White tea: a light-fermented tea)*	• Ngàn⁴ Zām¹ Bāak⁶ Hòu⁴ 銀針白毫 *(Yinzhen Baihao: widely considered as one of the best grades of white tea)* • Sāu⁶ Méi² 壽眉 *(Shou-mei tea; Long Life Eyebrow tea)*
4.	Cēng¹ Càa⁴ 青茶 / Wū¹ Lúng² Càa⁴ 烏龍茶 *(Oolong tea: a semi-fermented tea)*	• Tǐt³ Gūn¹ Jām¹ 鐵觀音 *(Tie-guan-yin tea: a well-known Oolong tea)* • Tòi⁴ Wāan¹ Wū¹ Lúng² 台灣烏龍 *(Taiwan Oolong tea)* • Séoi² Sīn¹ 水仙 *(Shui-xian tea)*
5.	Hùng⁴ Càa⁴ 紅茶 *(Black tea/red tea: a fully fermented tea)*	• Kèi⁴ Mùn⁴ Hùng⁴ Càa⁴ 祁門紅茶 *(Qimen red tea: the most renowned red tea in the world)*
6.	Hāk¹ Càa⁴ 黑茶 *(Black tea: post-fermented and oxidized tea)*	• Póu² Léi² 普洱 *(also "Bóu² Léi²")* *(Pu'er tea: comes from Yunnan province)* • Lūk⁶ ōn¹ 六安 *(Lu'an black tea)*
7.	Fāa¹ Càa 花茶 *(Scented tea: a mixture of tea leaves and fragrant flowers)*	• Gūk¹ Póu² / Gūk¹ Bóu² 菊普 *(Pu'er tea with dried chrysanthemum)* • Hōeng¹ Pín² 香片 *(Jasmine tea: the most popular scented green tea)* • Gūk¹ Fāa¹ 菊花 *(dried chrysanthemum tea)*

---

① **Tea** was originated in China where tea bushes were first cultivated by the ancient Chinese. Chinese pour hot water onto dried and processed leaves of the tea plant to make a drink. With such a long history of tea drinking in China, it has developed into a custom with a rich culture of its own. As a traditional Chinese custom, tea tasting generates much pleasure in our daily lives. Tea isn't drunk only for the aroma and taste; it's also believed to be for health. It is generally believed that tea drinking can improve our health and enhance our energy in the following aspects: quench thirst, help digest the rich foods, clear saliva, help prevent tooth decay, reduce sleeping time, reduce stress and refreshing, help the urinary tract, purge toxins, help slow ageing, improve eyesight, increase concentration, relax the body and dissolve fat. (Source: University Museum and Art Gallery)

Q: něi⁵ sóeng² sǐ³ hǎa⁵ māt¹ jě⁵ dím² sām¹ åa³?

A: ngǒ⁵ sóeng² sǐ³ hǎa⁵ _____ .

1)	Steamed (zīng¹ 蒸) Dim-Sum:		
1.	hāa¹ gáau² 蝦餃		*shrimp dumplings*
2.	sīu¹ máai² 燒賣		*pork dumplings*
3.	cóeng² fán² 腸粉		*rice noodle rolls*
4.	cāa¹ sīu¹ bāau¹ 叉燒包		*barbecue pork buns*
5.	lìn⁴ jùng⁴ bāau¹ 蓮蓉包		*lotus seed paste buns*
6.	nǎai⁵ wòng⁴ bāau¹ 奶皇包		*sweet egg custard buns*
7.	zān¹ zȳu¹ gāi¹ 珍珠雞 / nǒ⁶ mǎi⁵ gāi¹ 糯米雞		*sticky rice with chicken, wrapped with lotus leaf*
8.	gǔn³ tōng¹ gáau² 灌湯餃		*soup dumplings*
9.	mǎa⁵ lāai¹ gōu¹ 馬拉糕		*sweet sponge cake*
10.	cìu⁴ zāu¹ fán² gwó² 潮洲粉果		*Chiu Chow style dumplings*
11.	sīn¹ zūk¹ gýun² 鮮竹卷		*bean curd rolls*
12.	ngàu⁴ jūk⁶ kàu⁴ 牛肉球		*beef meatballs*
13.	ngàu⁴ påak³ jīp⁶ 牛栢葉		*beef stomach*
14.	gām¹ cìn⁴ tǒu⁵ 金錢肚		*stewed beef tripe*
15.	pàai⁴ gwāt¹ 排骨		*spare ribs*
16.	fūng⁶ záau² 鳳爪		*steamed chicken feet*
17.	lò⁴ bāak⁶ gōu¹ 蘿蔔糕		*Chinese turnip cake*

For vegetarians:

ngǒ⁵ sīk⁶ sóu³ (/zāai¹) gě³.   **ngǒ⁵ m̀ sīk⁶ jūk⁶ gě³.**

(I'm a vegatarian.)   *(I don't eat meat.)*

2) Deep Fried (zåa³ 炸) Dim-Sum:

1.	cēon¹ gýun² 春卷	*spring rolls*
2.	håam⁴ séoi² gȯk³ (/gók²) 咸水角	*sticky rice dumplings with dried shrimp and meat*
3.	wŭ⁶ gȯk³ (/gók²) 芋角	*deep fried taro root dumplings*
4.	hāa¹ gȯk³ (/gók²) 蝦角	*deep fried shrimp dumplings served with salad dressing*
5.	hói² sīn¹ gýun² 海鮮卷	*seafood rolls*
6.	zåa³ wàn⁴ tān¹ 炸雲吞	*deep fried wonton served with sweet and sour sauce*
7.	fŭ⁶ pèi⁴ gýun² 腐皮卷	*bean curd sheet rolls*

3) Baked (gŭk⁶ 焗) Dim-Sum:

1.	cāa¹ sīu¹ sōu¹ 叉燒酥	*barbecue pork pastries*
2.	cāa¹ sīu¹ cāan¹ bāau¹ 叉燒餐包	*oven-baked barbecue pork buns*
3.	dāan⁶ tāat¹ 蛋撻	*egg custard tart*

4) Dessert (tìm⁴ bán² 甜品) :

1.	làu⁴ sāa¹ bāau¹ 流沙包	*steamed salted egg yolk custard buns*
2.	cìu⁴ zāu¹ séoi² zīng¹ bāau¹ 潮洲水晶包	*Chiu Chow style sweet paste buns*
3.	mōng¹ gwó² bȯu³ dīn¹ 芒果布甸	*mango pudding*
4.	lìn⁴ jùng⁴ gŭk⁶ bȯu³ dīn¹ 蓮蓉焗布甸	*baked sago and mashed lotus seed pudding*
5.	hùng⁴ dáu² sāa¹ 紅豆沙	*sweet red bean soup*
6.	lŭk⁶ dáu² sāa¹ 綠豆沙	*sweet mung bean soup*
7.	zī¹ màa⁴ wú² 芝蔴糊	*sweet black sesame soup*
8.	hăng⁶ jàn⁴ lŏu⁶ 杏仁露	*sweet ground almond soup*
9.	hāp⁶ tòu⁴ lŏu⁶ 合桃露	*sweet ground walnut soup*
10.	jòeng⁴ zī¹ gām¹ lŏu 楊枝甘露	*pomelo and sago in mango soup*
11.	sāi¹ mǎi⁵ lŏu⁶ 西米露	*sago in coconut milk*
12.	zāa¹ zàa⁴ 喳咋	*sweet mixed beans soup with taro*
13.	sōeng¹ pèi⁴ năai⁵ 雙皮奶	*double-boiled fresh milk and egg white*
14.	tōng¹ jýun² 湯圓	*sweet dumpling in soup*
15.	dāu⁶ fŭ⁶ fāa¹ 豆腐花	*tofu pudding*

1. **Use words or phrases underlined to construct three separate sentences using the patterns from the box.** (4 × 10% = 40%)

(?)	*Subject* +	*Verb*	+	**zó²**	(+ *Object*)	+	**mèi⁶ åa³?**
(+)	(*Subject* +)	*Verb*	+	**zó²**	(+ *Object*)	+	**låa³.**
(−)	(*Subject* +)	**mèi⁶**	+	*Verb*	(+ *Object*)	(+	**åa³**).

e.g.   ngǒ⁵ dèi⁶ jì⁴ gāa¹ hèoi³ **sīk⁶ zóu² cāan¹**.

Answer: (?) nèi⁵ sīk⁶ **zó²** zóu² cāan¹ **mèi⁶ åa³?** (4%)

(+) sīk⁶ **zó²** låa³. (3%)

(−) **mèi⁶** sīk⁶ åa³. (3%)

1) ngǒ⁵ bàa⁴ bāa¹ cāt¹ dím² zūng¹ **fāan¹ gūng¹** (to go to work).

(?) _____

(+) _____

(−) _____

2) ngǒ⁵ båat³ dím² zūng¹ **héi² sān¹** (to get up).

(?) _____

(+) _____

(−) _____

3) màa⁴ māa¹ sì⁴ sì⁴ sǎp⁶ jāt¹ dím² **fǎn³ gåau³** (to go to bed).

(?) _____

(+) _____

(−) _____

4) gām¹ jǎt⁶ ngǒ⁵ dèi⁶ jiu³ **zǒu⁶** hóu² dō¹ **gūng¹ fò³** (to do homework).

(?) _____

(+) _____

(−) _____

2. What should you say in the following situations? (in Cantonese) (6 × 5% = 30%)

1) You want to invite your friend to have a drink in a Hong Kong style café together.

   You say: _____

2) You want to suggest that your friend try "yuanyang" or HK style milk tea.

   You say: _____

3) You want to ask your friend if it is okay to order some dessert.

   You say: _____

4) You want to ask what tea your friend would like to drink.

   You say: _____

5) You want to get the bill after you finish the food in a dim-sum restaurant.

   You say: _____

6) You want to treat your friends to dim-sum.

   You say: _____

3. Translate the following into English. (10 × 3% = 30%)

1) sīk⁶ zó² fāan⁶ mēi⁶ åa³? _____

2) mēi⁶ åa³. _____

3) jāt¹ cài⁴ hěoi³ lāa¹. _____

4) hàang⁴ låa³. _____

5) hóu² m̀⁴ hóu² åa³? _____

6) mǒu⁵ mān⁶ tài⁴. _____

7) jāt¹ wù⁴ gwán² séoi². _____

8) zān¹ hāi⁶ hóu² sīk⁶ åa³. _____

9) m̀⁴ gōi¹ màai⁴ dāan¹. _____

10) ngǒ⁵ céng² něi⁵ lāa¹. _____

Buying and bargaining

1. To request or invite the addressee to do as he/she pleases
2. To express whether something is worth it or worth doing with "dái²"
3. To express a higher degree than is expected with "tåai³"
4. To state the comparative degree with "dī¹"
5. To seek approval or permission using the tag question "dāk¹ m̀ dāk¹ åa³?"
6. To bargain and ask for discounts
7. To use the verb "béi²" (to pay; to give)
8. To emphasize one's gratitude using "såai³"

fūn¹ jìng⁴, céng² <u>cèoi⁴ bín²</u> tái² lāa¹!

jì⁴ gāa¹ dǎai⁶ gáam² gǎa³, hóu² <u>dái²</u> mǎai⁵ gåa³!

tåai³ gwåi³ låa³. pèng⁴ <u>dī¹</u> lāa¹! jǎu⁵ mǒu⁵ zìt³ åa³?

(After lunch, Tony didn't go to work. He went shopping.) Tony is buying a camera in a camera shop.

Salesperson: fūn¹ jìng⁴, céng² cèoi⁴ bín² tái² lāa¹!
歡 迎 ， 請 隨 便 睇 啦 ！
(Welcome, please feel free to look around!)

Tony: ngǒ⁵ sóeng² mǎai⁵ jāt¹ gȯ³ sóeng² gēi¹.
我 想 買 一 個 相 機。
(I would like to buy a camera.)

Salesperson: nī¹ gȯ³ pàai⁴ zí² jì⁴ gāa¹ dāai⁶ gáam² gȧa³, hóu² dái² mǎai⁵ gȧa³!
呢 個 牌 子 而 家 大 減 價 ， 好 抵 買 㗎 ！
(This brand is currently on sale — it's a great buy!)

Tony: wȧa³! sėi³ cīn¹ mān¹ tȧai³ gwȧi³ lȧa³.
嘩 ！ 四 千 蚊 太 貴 喇。
(Wow! HK$4,000! It's too expensive.)

jǎu⁵ mǒu⁵ pèng⁴ dī¹ gȧa³?
有 冇 平 啲 㗎 ？
(Are there any cheaper ones?)

Salesperson: jǎu⁵, nī¹ gȯ³ sāam¹ cīn¹ mān¹, géi² lėng³ gȧa³, sȋ³ hǎa⁵ lāa¹!
有 ， 呢 個 三 千 蚊 ， 幾 靚 㗎 ， 試 吓 啦 ！
(Yes, this one is HK$3,000. It's good quality. Please have a try.)

Tony: jǎu⁵ mǒu⁵ zȋt³ ȧa³?
有 冇 折 呀 ？
(Is there any discount?)

Salesperson: m̀⁴ hóu² jȋ³ sī¹, nī¹ gȯ³ pàai⁴ zí² mǒu⁵ zȋt³ wȯ³.
唔 好 意 思 ， 呢 個 牌 子 冇 折 喎。
(I'm sorry, there is no discount for this brand.)

Tony: pèng⁴ dī¹ lāa¹! gáu² zȋt³ dāk¹ m̀⁴ dāk¹ ȧa³?
平 啲 啦 ！ 九 折 得 唔 得 呀 ？
(Cheaper, please? Please give me a 10% discount, okay?)

Salesperson: hóu² lāa¹, hóu² lāa¹, jī⁶ cīn¹ cāt¹ bȧak³ mān¹ lāa¹!
好 啦 ， 好 啦 ， 二 千 七 白 蚊 啦 ！
(Okay, okay, HK$2,700 for you.)

Tony: gám², ngǒ⁵ jiu³ jāt¹ gȯ³ hùng⁴ sīk¹ gė³.
噉 ， 我 要 一 個 紅 色 嘅。
(Then I want a red one.)

ngǒ⁵ béi² kāat¹ něi⁵, dāk¹ m̀ dāk¹ ȧa³?
我 俾 咭 你 ， 得 唔 得 呀 ？
(I'll pay you by credit card. Is that okay?)

Salesperson: dāk¹. mǒu⁵ mān⁶ tȧi⁴. dō¹ zḛ⁶ sȧai³!
得。 冇 問 題。 多 謝 晒 ！
(All right. No problem. Thank you very much!)

1.	cèoi² bín² 隨便 (+ *Verb*)	Adv:	do as one pleases
2.	tái² 睇 (+ *Object*)	V:	to see; to look; to watch; to read
3.	sóeng² gēi¹ 相機 (*M:* gờ³ 個)	N:	camera
4.	pàai⁴ zí² 牌子 (*M:* gờ³ 個)	N:	a brand; a brand name; a trademark
5.	dãai⁶ gáam² gåa³ 大減價	SE:	a big sale [*products at reduced prices*]
6.	mǎai⁵ 買 (+ *Object*)	V:	to buy
7.	dái² 抵	Adj:	worthy
8.	dái² mǎai⁵ 抵買	Ph:	worth buying
9.	wåa³ 嘩	Intj:	[*expresses surprise or wonder*] Wow!
10.	cīn¹ 千 (*Nu.* + cīn¹)	Nu:	thousand
11.	tåai³ 太 (+ *Adj.*)	Adv:	too; excessively [*expresses a higher degree than is expected*]
12.	gwåi³ 貴	Adj:	expensive
13.	pèng⁴ 平	Adj:	cheap
14.	dī¹ 啲 (*Adj.* + dī¹)	Part:	a little more… [*a structural particle used after adjectives to denote the comparative degree*]
15.	pèng⁴ dī¹ lāa¹ 平啲啦	SE:	Cheaper, please!
16.	géi² 幾 (+ *Adj.*)	Adv:	quite; fairly
17.	zìt³ 折 (*Nu.* + zìt³)	N:	discount [*the number before indicates the fraction to be paid in tenths*]
18.	gáu² zìt³ 九折	N:	discount of 10 percent [*9/10th of the original price*]
19.	dāk¹ 得	Adj:	all right; okay; fine [*used to express approval or permission*]
20.	dāk¹ m̀⁴ dāk¹ åa³? 得唔得呀？	SE:	Is it okay? [*to seek approval or permission*]
21.	hóu² lāa¹ 好啦	SE:	okay; fine [*used to express agreement*]
22.	hùng⁴ sīk¹ 紅色	N:	red colour
23.	béi² 俾 (+ *sth.* + *sb.*) (e.g. béi² cín² ngǒ⁵)	V:	to give; to pay
24.	kāat¹ 咭 (*M:* zōeng¹ 張)	N:	card; (in L.13) a short form for credit card

1. **To request or invite the addressee to do as he/she pleases**

   e.g.   céng² cèoi⁴ bín² tái² lāa¹!

   (Please feel free to look around!)

(céng²)	+	cèoi⁴ bín²	+	*Verbal phrase*	+	āa¹!
		(as one please)				

   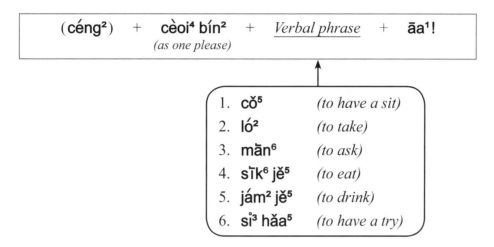

   1. cǒ⁵   *(to have a sit)*
   2. ló²   *(to take)*
   3. mǎn⁶   *(to ask)*
   4. sīk⁶ jě⁵   *(to eat)*
   5. jám² jě⁵   *(to drink)*
   6. sǐ³ hǎa⁵   *(to have a try)*

   Your example(s):

   (céng²) cèoi⁴ bín² _____ āa¹!

2. **To express whether something is worth it or worth doing with "dái²"**

   e.g.   nī¹ gǒ³ pàai⁴ zí² jì⁴ gāa¹ dǎai⁶ gáam² gǎa³, hóu² dái² mǎai⁵ gǎa³!

   (This brand is currently on sale — it's worth buying!)

Sentence Topic	+	(hóu² +)	[dái²	+	*Verb*].
		(Adv. of degree)			

   1. nī¹ gǒ³ sóeng² gēi¹   *(this camera)*
   2. càa⁴ cāan¹ tēng¹ gě³ jě⁵   *(the food in HK style cafés)*
   3. nī¹ dǒu⁶ gě³ gǎa³ fē¹   *(the coffee here)*
   4. Hōeng¹ Góng² gě³ dīk¹ sí²   *(the taxi in Hong Kong)*

   1. mǎai⁵   *(to buy)*
   2. sīk⁶   *(to eat)*
   3. jám²   *(to drink)*
   4. cǒ⁵   *(to ride)*

   Your example(s):

   _____ hóu² dái² _____.

3. **To express a higher degree than is expected with "tåai³"**

e.g. sẻi³ cīn¹ mān¹ tåai³ gwåi³ låa³.

(HK$4,000! It's <u>too</u> expensive.)

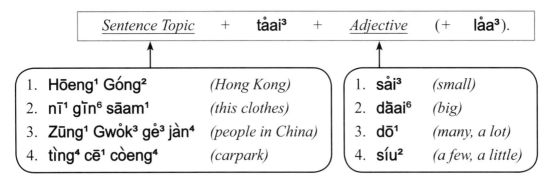

| Sentence Topic | + | tåai³ | + | Adjective | (+ | låa³). |

1. Hōeng¹ Góng²   *(Hong Kong)*
2. nī¹ gĩn⁶ sāam¹   *(this clothes)*
3. Zūng¹ Gwòk³ gẻ³ jàn⁴   *(people in China)*
4. tìng⁴ cē¹ còeng⁴   *(carpark)*

1. sẻi³   *(small)*
2. dãai⁶   *(big)*
3. dō¹   *(many, a lot)*
4. síu²   *(a few, a little)*

Your example(s):

_____ tåai³ _____ .

4. **To state the comparative degree with "dī¹"**

e.g. pèng⁴ dī¹ lāa¹!

(Cheaper, please!)

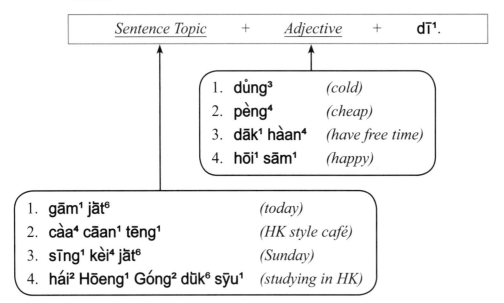

| Sentence Topic | + | Adjective | + | dī¹. |

1. dủng³   *(cold)*
2. pèng⁴   *(cheap)*
3. dāk¹ hàan⁴ *(have free time)*
4. hōi¹ sām¹   *(happy)*

1. gām¹ jāt⁶   *(today)*
2. càa⁴ cāan¹ tēng¹   *(HK style café)*
3. sīng¹ kèi⁴ jāt⁶   *(Sunday)*
4. hái² Hōeng¹ Góng² dūk⁶ sȳu¹   *(studying in HK)*

Your example(s):

_____ dī¹.

5. **To seek approval or permission using the tag question "dāk¹ m̀⁴ dāk¹ åa³?"**

e.g. Q: 1. gáu² zı̆t³ <u>dāk¹ m̀⁴ dāk¹ åa³</u>?
              (Please give me a 10% discount, <u>okay?</u>)

              2. ngŏ⁵ béi² kāat¹ něi⁵, <u>dāk¹ m̀⁴ dāk¹ åa³</u>?
              (I'll pay you by credit card. <u>Is that okay?</u>)

     A: *Yes:* dāk¹. (mŏu⁵ mān⁶ tài⁴.) *(Okay. No problem.)*

         No: m̀⁴ dāk¹. *(No, it's not okay.)*

Q:	*Request,*	+	dāk¹ m̀⁴ dāk¹ åa³?

1. něi⁵ gåau³ ngŏ⁵ Zūng¹ Mán²   *(you teach me Chinese)*
2. něi⁵ céng² ngŏ⁵ jám² gåa³ fē¹   *(you treat me to a coffee)*
3. ngŏ⁵ jì⁴ gāa¹ hĕoi³ sái² sáu² gāan¹   *(I go to the washroom now)*
4. ngŏ⁵ záu² sīn¹   *(I leave first)*

Your example(s):

_____ , dāk¹ m̀⁴ dāk¹ åa³?

6. **To bargain and ask for discounts**

e.g. 1. <u>pèng⁴ dī¹ lāa¹</u>!
        (Cheaper, please!)

e.g. 2. jău⁵ mŏu⁵ zı̆t³ åa³?
        (Is there any discount?)

e.g. 3. jì⁴ gāa¹ jău⁵ mŏu⁵ dāai⁶ gáam² gåa³ åa³?
        (Are there any big sales now?)

e.g. 4. gáu² zı̆t³ dāk¹ m̀⁴ dāk¹ åa³?
        (Please give me a 10% discount, okay?)

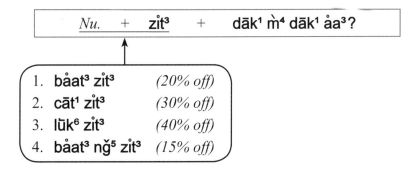

Nu.	+	<u>zı̆t³</u>	+	dāk¹ m̀⁴ dāk¹ åa³?

1. båat³ zı̆t³   *(20% off)*
2. cāt¹ zı̆t³   *(30% off)*
3. lŭk⁶ zı̆t³   *(40% off)*
4. båat³ nğ⁵ zı̆t³   *(15% off)*

Your example(s):

_____ .

7. **To use the verb "béi² " (to pay; to give)**

    e.g.   ngǒ⁵ béi² kāat¹ něi⁵, dāk¹ m̀⁴ dāk¹ åa³?

        (I'll <u>pay</u> you by credit card. Is that okay?)

   a) **To pay**

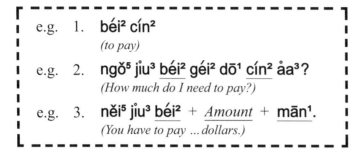

      e.g. 1. **béi² cín²**
                (to pay)

      e.g. 2. **ngǒ⁵ jǐu³ béi² géi² dō¹ cín² åa³?**
                (How much do I need to pay?)

      e.g. 3. **něi⁵ jǐu³ béi²** + *Amount* + **mān¹.**
                (You have to pay ...dollars.)

   b) **To give something to somebody**

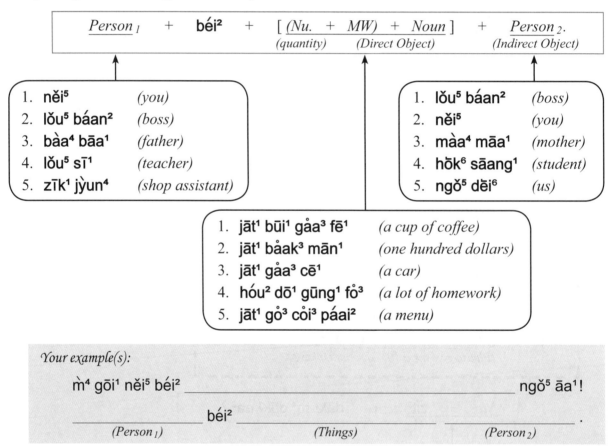

| *Person₁* | + | **béi²** | + | [*(Nu.* + *MW)* + *Noun*] | + | *Person₂.* |

                                 (quantity) *(Direct Object)*   *(Indirect Object)*

1. něi⁵	*(you)*
2. lǒu⁵ báan²	*(boss)*
3. bàa⁴ bāa¹	*(father)*
4. lǒu⁵ sī¹	*(teacher)*
5. zīk¹ j`yun⁴	*(shop assistant)*

1. lǒu⁵ báan²	*(boss)*
2. něi⁵	*(you)*
3. màa⁴ māa¹	*(mother)*
4. hǒk⁶ sāang¹	*(student)*
5. ngǒ⁵ dēi⁶	*(us)*

1. jāt¹ būi¹ gåa³ fē¹	*(a cup of coffee)*
2. jāt¹ båak³ mān¹	*(one hundred dollars)*
3. jāt¹ gåa³ cē¹	*(a car)*
4. hóu² dō¹ gūng¹ fo̊³	*(a lot of homework)*
5. jāt¹ go̊³ cǒi³ páai²	*(a menu)*

Your example(s):

    m̀⁴ gōi¹ něi⁵ béi² _____ ngǒ⁵ āa¹!

_____ béi² _____ _____ .
  (Person₁)   *(Things)*   *(Person₂)*

8. **To emphasize one's gratitude using "såai³ "**

   "såai³ " *expresses the idea of "entirely, completely, all".*

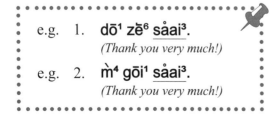

      e.g. 1. **dō¹ zē̆⁶ såai³.**
                (Thank you very much!)

      e.g. 2. **m̀⁴ gōi¹ såai³.**
                (Thank you very much!)

Q: něi⁵ sóeng² mǎai⁵ māt¹ jě⁵ sáu² sẻon³ åa³?

A: ngǒ⁵ sóeng² mǎai⁵ _____ . hái² bīn¹ dōu mǎai⁵ pèng⁴ dī¹ åa³?

1.	*Chinese tea*	càa⁴ jīp⁶ 茶葉
2.	*T shirt*	tī¹ sēot¹ T 裇
3.	*clothes; garment*	sāam¹ 衫
4.	*trousers*	fů³ 褲
5.	*shoes*	hàai⁴ 鞋
6.	*socks*	māt⁶ 襪
7.	*eyeglasses*	ngǎan⁵ géng² 眼鏡
8.	*handbags ; wallets*	sáu² dói² 手袋， ngàn⁴ bāau¹ 銀包
9.	*Chinese clothing*	Zūng¹ sīk¹ fūk⁶ zōng¹ 中式服裝
10.	*Chinese assorted cakes*	Zūng¹ sīk¹ béng² sīk⁶ 中式餅食
11.	*Chinese tableware*	Zūng¹ sīk¹ sīk⁶ gēoi⁶ 中式食具
12.	*handicrafts*	sáu² gūng¹ ngãi⁶ bán² 手工藝品
13.	*embroideries*	cỉ³ sảu³ bán² 刺繡品
14.	*watches*	sáu² bīu¹ 手錶
15.	*jewellery*	sáu² sīk¹ 首飾
16.	*gold jewellery*	gām¹ sīk¹ 金飾
17.	*jade*	jūk⁶ hẻi³ 玉器
18.	*audio & visual gadgets*	jíng² jām¹ hẻi³ còi⁴ 影音器材
19.	*postcards*	mìng⁴ sẻon³ pín² 明信片
20.	*key holders*	só² sì⁴ kảu³ 鎖匙扣

---

① "**sáu² sẻon³**" in Cantonese includes food or things taken, bought or received as a gift after a trip to remind one of a place or an event. For more information about souvenirs and shopping places in HK you can go to <http://www.discoverhongkong.com>

Q: něi⁵ zūng¹ jǐ³ māt¹ jě⁵ ngàan⁴ sīk¹ åa³?

A: ngǒ⁵ zūng¹ jǐ³ _____ sīk¹. něi⁵ jǎu⁵ mǒu⁵ _____ sīk¹ gåa³?

1.	*red*	hùng⁴ sīk¹ 紅色
2.	*orange*	cáang² sīk¹ 橙色
3.	*yellow*	wòng⁴ sīk¹ 黃色
4.	*green*	lǖk⁶ sīk¹ 綠色
5.	*yellowish green*	cēng¹ sīk¹ 青色
6.	*blue*	làam⁴ sīk¹ 藍色
7.	*purple*	zí² sīk¹ 紫色
8.	*black*	hāk¹ sīk¹ 黑色
9.	*white*	bāak⁶ sīk¹ 白色
10.	*grey*	fūi¹ sīk¹ 灰色
11.	*gold*	gām¹ sīk¹ 金色
12.	*silver*	ngàn⁴ sīk¹ 銀色
13.	*brown*	gåa³ fē¹ sīk¹ 咖啡色；fē¹ sīk¹ 啡色

Q: něi⁵ jîu³ māt¹ jě⁵ sāai¹ sí² åa³?　*A:* ngǒ⁵ jîu³ _____ mǎa⁵.

1.	*XL*	gāa¹ dāai⁶ mǎa⁵ 加大碼
2.	*L*	dāai⁶ mǎa⁵ 大碼
3.	*M*	zūng¹ mǎa⁵ 中碼
4.	*S*	såi³ mǎa⁵ 細碼
5.	*XS*	gāa¹ såi³ mǎa⁵ 加細碼
6.	*Free*	jāt¹ gǒ³ mǎa⁵ 一個碼 ；fī¹ sāai¹ sí² *Free* 晒士

1. **Translate the following into Cantonese.** $(6 \times 10\% = 60\%)$

 1) I would like to buy an Octopus card.

 _____

 2) This camera is only $1,000. It's worth it.

 _____

 3) Are there any better ones?

 _____

 4) Can you give me a better price, please?

 _____

 5) I want to have a try. Is that okay?

 _____

 6) Tony is too busy. He has no free time.

 _____

2. **Add the words in the brackets to the following sentences by placing "↓" at appropriate positions.** $(8 \times 5\% = 40\%)$

 e.g. ngŏ⁵ hāi⁶ Gwŏk³ Zåi³ Dāai⁶ hōk⁶ ↓ hōk⁶ sāang¹. (gě³)

 1) céng² sīk⁶ dím² sām¹ lāa¹. (cèoi⁴ bín²)

 2) ngŏ⁵ jǎu⁵ jāt¹ zōeng¹ sěon³ jūng⁶ kāat¹. (sóeny²)

 3) jì⁴ gāa¹ jǎu⁵ dāai⁶ gáam² gåa³, hóu² dái² gåa³. (mǎai⁵)

 4) nī¹ gīn⁶ sāam¹ dāai⁶. (tåai³)

 5) nī¹ gǒ³ sóeng² gēi¹ pèng⁴ gåa³. (géi²)

 6) ngŏ⁵ hóu² zūng¹ jĭ³ nī¹ gǒ³ sóeng² gēi¹, bāt¹ gwŏ³ gwåi³. (dī¹)

 7) ngŏ⁵ sóeng² mǎai⁵ jāt¹ gǒ³ sáu² bīu¹. (hùng⁴ sīk¹ gě³)

 8) lǒu⁵ sī¹ béi² zó² jāt¹ dī¹ gūng¹ fò³. (ngŏ⁵ dēi⁶)

Lesson 14 | Taking public transportation

1. To ask what kind of transportation one should take
2. To ask and tell the method of moving from one place to another
3. To ask "Do you know...?"
4. To tell the route or terminus of transportation
5. To inform the driver where to get off a car

ngǒ⁵ sóeng² hểoi³ Zūng¹ Wàan⁴, dẳap³ géi² dō¹ hồu⁶ síu² bāa¹ ảa³?

dẳap³ bẳat³ hồu⁶ wāak⁶ zé² jī⁶ sẳp⁶ bẳat³ hồu⁶ lāa¹.

m̀⁴ gōi¹ sī¹ gēi¹, Zỉ³ Dēi⁶ Gwóng² Còeng⁴, jǎu⁵ lõk⁶.

Amy asks Zing-Zing how to get to Central.

Amy: Zīng¹-Zīng¹, něi⁵ múi⁵ jāt⁶ dåap³ māt¹ jě⁵ cē¹ fāan¹ hŏk⁶ gåa³?

晶　晶，你　每　日　搭　乜　嘢　車　返　學　㗎？

(Zing-Zing, what transportation do you take to go to school every day?)

Zing-Zing: ngǒ⁵ ūk¹ kéi² hái² dāai⁶ hŏk⁶ fū⁶ gān⁶,

我　屋　企　喺　大　學　附　近，

(My home is near the university,

só² jí⁵ m̀⁴ sái² dåap³ cē¹.

所　以　唔　使　搭　車。

therefore I don't need to take any transportation.)

ngǒ⁵ múi⁵ jāt⁶ hàang⁴ lŏu⁶ fāan¹ hŏk⁶ gě³.

我　每　日　行　路　返　學　嘅。

(I walk to school every day.)

Amy: něi⁵ zī¹ m̀⁴ zī¹ jàu⁴ nī¹ dŏu⁶ hèoi³ Zūng¹ Wàan⁴,

你　知　唔　知　由　呢　度　去　中　環，

dåap³ géi² dō¹ hŏu⁶ síu² bāa¹ åa³?

搭　幾　多　號　小　巴　呀？

(Do you know what no. of minibus I should take to Central from here?)

Zing-Zing: båat³ hŏu⁶ síu² bāa¹ gě³ zúng² zāam⁶ hái⁶ Dāai⁶ Wūi⁶ Tòng⁴①,

八　號　小　巴　嘅　總　站　係　大　會　堂，

(The terminus of No. 8 minibus is (at) the City Hall,

jí⁶ sāp⁶ båat³ hŏu⁶ gīng¹ Zūng¹ Wàan⁴ dēi⁶ tǐt³ zāam⁶

二　十　八　號　經　中　環　地　鐵　站

the No. 28 minibus passes by the Central MTR station

hèoi³ Tùng⁴ Lò⁴ Wāan¹. něi⁵ sóeng² hèoi³ Zūng¹ Wàan⁴ bīn¹ dŏu⁶ åa³?

去　銅　鑼　灣。你　想　去　中　環　邊　度　呀？

and goes to Causeway Bay. Where do you want to go in Central?)

Amy: ngǒ⁵ sóeng² hèoi³ Wūi⁶ Fūng¹ Ngàn⁴ Hòng⁴ zúng² hóng².

我　想　去　匯　豐　銀　行　總　行。

(I want to go to the HSBC headquarters.)

gám², hái² bīn¹ dŏu⁶ lŏk⁶ cē¹ åa³?

噉，喺　邊　度　落　車　呀？

(So where do I get off?)

Zing-Zing: hái² Zǐ³ Dēi⁶ Gwóng² Còeng⁴ lŏk⁶ cē¹ lāa¹.

喺　置　地　廣　場　落　車　啦。

(You should get off at the Landmark.)

něi⁵ wāa⁶：「m̀⁴ gōi¹ sī¹ gēi¹, Zǐ⁶ Dēi⁶ Gwóng² Còeng⁴, jǎu⁵ lŏk⁶.」

你　話：「唔　該　司　機，置　地　廣　場，有　落。」

(You say, "Driver, I want to get off at the Landmark, please."

zāu⁶ dāk¹ låak³.

就　得　嘞。

then that's be fine.)

---

① The terminus of Hong Kong Island Green Minibus No. 8 has been changed to Exchange Square (Gāau¹ Jǐk⁶ Gwóng² Còeng⁴ 交易廣場) Public Light Bus Terminus.

1.	mŭi⁵ jāt⁶ 每日	Pn:	every day
2.	dåap³ 搭 (+ *Transportation*)	V:	to ride (a mode of transportation); (also "cŏ⁵ 坐")
3.	cē¹ 車 (*M*: gåa³ 架)	N:	car [*general term used for any wheeled vehicle*]
4.	dåap³ cē¹ 搭車	VO:	to ride a car; by car (also "cŏ⁵ cē¹ 坐車")
5.	lōk⁶ cē¹ 落車	VO:	to get off a vehicle; alight
6.	māt¹ jě⁵ cē¹ 乜野車	QW:	what mode of transportation; what kind of vehicle
7.	ūk¹ kéi² 屋企	N:	home
8.	só² jĭ⁵ 所以 (+ *Clause*)	Conj:	so; therefore [*used to introduce a consequence clause*]
9.	hàang⁴ lōu⁶ 行路	VO:	(lit: walk road) to walk; on foot
10.	fāan¹ hōk⁶ 返學	VO:	to go to school
11.	něi⁵ zī¹ m̀⁴ zī¹...? 你 知 唔 知...?	Ph:	Do you know...? (also "**něi⁵ zī¹ m̀⁴ zī¹ dŏu³**...? 你知唔知道...?")
12.	síu² bāa¹ 小巴 (*M*: gåa³ 架)	N:	minibus; public light bus
13.	zúng² zāam⁶ 總站	N:	terminus; terminal station
14.	Dāai⁶ Wūi⁶ Tòng⁴ 大會堂	PN:	City Hall ②
15.	gīng¹ 經 (+ *Object*)	V:	to pass by; to pass through; via
16.	Zūng¹ Wàan⁴ 中環	N:	Central [*major district in HK Island*]
17.	Tùng⁴ Lò⁴ Wāan¹ 銅鑼灣	PN:	Causeway Bay [*major district in HK Island*] (also "**Tùng⁴ Lò⁴ Wàan⁴**")

---

② **Hong Kong City Hall** (Jyutping: Hōeng¹ Góng² Dāai⁶ Wūi⁶ Tòng⁴) is a complex located in Central, Hong Kong Island, Hong Kong. Since Hong Kong is a "Special Administrative Region" and not a normal Chinese city, there is no mayor or city council; therefore, the City Hall does not hold the offices of a city government, unlike most city halls around the world. Instead, it is a complex providing municipal services, including performing venues, restaurants and libraries. (Source: https://en.wikipedia.org)

18.	Wūi⁶ Fūng¹ Ngàn⁴ Hòng⁴ 匯豐銀行	PN:	HSBC *[the Hongkong and Shanghai Banking Corporation]*
19.	zúng² hóng² 總行	N:	headquarters
20.	gwóng² còeng⁴ 廣場	N:	square; plaza
21.	Zi³ Dēi⁶ Gwóng² Còeng⁴ 置地廣場	PN:	Landmark *[an office and shopping mall with many prestigious international brands in Central, HK]*
22.	wăa⁶ 話 (+ *Object*)	V:	to say
23.	jău⁵ lōk⁶ 有落	SE:	stop to get off (the vehicle); I want to get off
24.	zāu⁶ 就 (+ *Clause₂*)	Conj:	(in L.14) then *[used in the consequence clause of conditional sentences]*
25.	låak³ 嘞	Part:	*[the emphasis form of "låa³", used to indicate finality or exclamation]*
26.	zāu⁶ dāk¹ låak³ 就得嘞	SE:	then that's be fine

Places of Interest in Hong Kong Central:

1.	Zūng¹ Wàan⁴ Măa⁵ Tàu⁴ 中環碼頭	Central Ferry Piers
2.	Gwŏk³ Zåi³ Gām¹ Jùng⁴ Zūng¹ Sām¹ 國際金融中心	International Finance Centre
3.	Gāau¹ Jĭk⁶ Gwóng² Còeng⁴ 交易廣場	Exchange Square
4.	Lēi⁶ Jỳun⁴ Dūng¹ Sāi¹ Gāai¹ 利源東西街	Li Yuen Street East & West
5.	Làan⁴ Gwåi³ Fōng¹ 蘭桂坊	Lan Kwai Fong
6.	Dāai⁶ Gún² 大館	Tai Kwun
7.	Zūng¹ Sám² Fåat³ Jýun² 終審法院	Court of Final Appeal
8.	Wòng⁴ Hāu⁶ Zōeng⁶ Gwóng² Còeng⁴ 皇后像廣場	Statue Square
9.	Hōeng¹ Góng² Lăi⁵ Bān¹ Fú² 香港禮賓府	Government House
10.	Sìng³ Jŏek³ Hōn⁶ Zō⁶ Tòng⁴ 聖約翰座堂	St. John's Cathedral

Sentence Structure

1. To ask what kind of transportation one should take

e.g. jàu⁴ nī¹ dōu⁶ hěoi³ Zūng¹ Wàan⁴, dảap³ géi² dō¹ hòu⁶ síu² bāa¹ åa³?

(What number of minibus should I take to Central from here?)

Q:	*Subject topic,* *(going to a destination)*	dảap³ *(to ride)* cǒ⁵ *(to sit)*	+	māt¹ jě⁵ cē¹ géi² dō¹ hòu⁶ cē¹	+	åa³?

1. ngǒ⁵ sóeng² hěoi³ Tīn¹ Sīng¹ Mǎa⁵ Tàu⁴   *(I want to go to Star Ferry Pier)*
2. kěoi⁵ sóeng² hěoi³ Zǐ³ Děi⁶ Gwóng² Còeng⁴   *(He/She wants to go to the Landmark)*
3. jàu⁴ nī¹ dōu⁶ hěoi³ Tùng⁴ Lò⁴ Wāan¹   *(to go to Causeway Bay from here)*
4. hěoi³ Gwǒk³ Zǎi³ Gām¹ Jùng⁴ Zūng¹ Sām¹   *(to go to IFC - International Finance Centre)*

Your example(s):

hěoi³ _____ , dảap³ māt¹ jě⁵ cē¹ åa³?

2. To ask and tell the method of moving from one place to another

e.g. Q. něi⁵ mǔi⁵ jåt⁶ dảap³ māt¹ jě⁵ cē¹ fāan¹ hǒk⁶ gåa³?

(What transportation do you take to go to school every day?)

A. ngǒ⁵ mǔi⁵ jåt⁶ hàang⁴ lǒu⁶ fāan¹ hǒk⁶ gě³.

(I walk to school every day.)

Q:	*Subject* + dảap³ māt¹ jě⁵ cē¹	hěoi³ *(to go)* lèi⁴ *(to come)*	+	*Place/Purpose*	+	åa³/gåa³?
A:	*Subject* + *Method of moving* +	fāan¹ *(to return)*	+	*Place/Purpose*	(+	gě³).

1. dảap³ dīk¹ sí²	*(by taxi)*	1. fāan¹ gūng¹	*(to go to work)*
2. dảap³ děi⁶ tit³	*(by MTR)*	2. fāan¹ hǒk⁶	*(to go to school)*
3. dảap³ sỳun⁴	*(by ferry)*	3. hěoi³ Gáu² Lùng⁴	*(to go to Kowloon)*
4. cǒ⁵ fó² cē¹	*(by train)*	4. hěoi³ Sān¹ Gåai³	*(to go to New Territories)*
5. cǒ⁵ fēi¹ gēi¹	*(by aeroplane)*	5. hěoi³ Jåt⁶ Bún²	*(to go to Japan)*

Your example(s):

ngǒ⁵ mǔi⁵ jåt⁶ _____ hěoi³ _____ .
                     (method of movement)   *(destination/purpose)*

3. **To ask "Do you know…?"**

e.g. něki⁵ zī¹ m̀⁴ zī¹ jàu⁴ nī¹ dōu⁶ hěoi³ Zūng¹ Wàan⁴, dåap³ māt¹ jě⁵ cē¹ åa³?
    (Do you know what no. of minibus I should take to Central from here?)

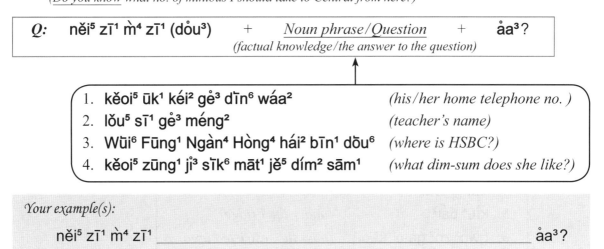

Q: něki⁵ zī¹ m̀⁴ zī¹ (dõu³) + *Noun phrase/Question* + åa³?
        (factual knowledge/the answer to the question)

1. kěoi⁵ ūk¹ kéi² gě³ dīn⁶ wáa²   *(his/her home telephone no.)*
2. lǒu⁵ sī¹ gě³ méng²   *(teacher's name)*
3. Wūi⁶ Fūng¹ Ngàn⁴ Hòng⁴ hái² bīn¹ dōu⁶   *(where is HSBC?)*
4. kěoi⁵ zūng¹ jǐ³ sīk⁶ māt¹ jě⁵ dím² sām¹   *(what dim-sum does she like?)*

Your example(s):

    něki⁵ zī¹ m̀⁴ zī¹ _____ åa³?

4. **To tell the route or terminus of transportation**

e.g. 1. båat³ hōu⁶ síu² bāa¹ gě³ zúng² zāam⁶ hãi⁶ Dāai⁶ Wūi⁶ Tòng⁴.
        (The terminus of No. 8 minibus is the City Hall.)

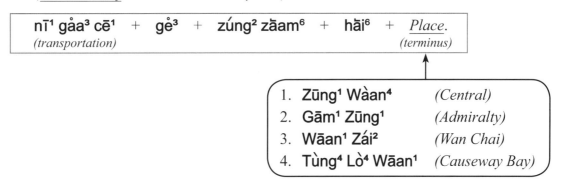

nī¹ gåa³ cē¹ + gě³ + zúng² zāam⁶ + hãi⁶ + *Place.*
(transportation)   *(terminus)*

1. Zūng¹ Wàan⁴   *(Central)*
2. Gām¹ Zūng¹   *(Admiralty)*
3. Wāan¹ Zái²   *(Wan Chai)*
4. Tùng⁴ Lò⁴ Wāan¹   *(Causeway Bay)*

e.g. 2. jī⁶ sǎp⁶ båat hōu⁶ gīng¹ Zūng¹ Wàan⁴ hěoi³ Tùng⁴ Lò⁴ Wāan¹.
        (The No. 28 minibus passes Central and goes to Causeway Bay.)

nī¹ gåa³ cē¹ + gīng¹ + *Place ₁* + hěoi³ + *Place ₂.*
(transportation)   *(midway)*   *(destination)*

1. sēoi⁶ dōu⁶   *(tunnel)*   1. Zīm¹ Sāa¹ Zéoi² *(Tsim Sha Tsui)*
2. Wōng⁶ Gók³   *(Mong Kok)*   2. Hùng⁴ Hǎm³   *(Hung Hom)*
3. Lò⁴ Wù⁴   *(Lo Wu)*   3. Sām¹ Zǎn³   *(Shenzhen)*
4. Bǔn³ Sāan¹   *(Mid-Levels)*   4. Góng² Dāai⁶   *(HKU)*

Your example(s):

    _____ gīng¹ _____ hěoi³ _____ .
    nī¹ gåa³ cē¹ gīng¹ m̀⁴ gīng¹ _____ åa³?

5. To inform the driver where to get off a car

e.g. něi⁵ wāa⁶: 「m̀⁴ gōi¹ sī¹ gēi¹, Zí³ Dĕi⁶ Gwóng² Còeng⁴, jǎu⁵ lŏk⁶.」

(You say, "Driver, I <u>want to get off</u> at the Landmark, please.")

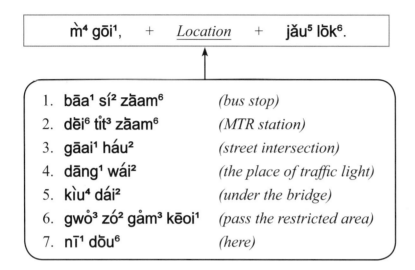

| m̀⁴ gōi¹, | + | *Location* | + | jǎu⁵ lŏk⁶. |

1. bāa¹ sí² zāam⁶   *(bus stop)*
2. dĕi⁶ tit³ zāam⁶   *(MTR station)*
3. gāai¹ háu²   *(street intersection)*
4. dāng¹ wái²   *(the place of traffic light)*
5. kìu⁴ dái²   *(under the bridge)*
6. gwó³ zó² gǎm³ kēoi¹   *(pass the restricted area)*
7. nī¹ dŏu⁶   *(here)*

Your example(s):

     něi⁵ zī¹ m̀⁴ zī¹ _____ åa³?

ngǒ⁵ dåap³ _____ lèi⁴ nī¹ dōu⁶ ge̊³.

1.	*airplane*	fēi¹ gēi¹ 飛機
2.	*bicycle*	dāan¹ cē¹ 單車 (jáai²/cáai² + dāan¹ cē¹)
3.	*bus*	bāa¹ sí² 巴士
4.	*cable car*	lāam⁶ cē¹ 纜車
5.	*ferry*	sỳun⁴ 船 / síu² lèon⁴ 小輪
6.	*motorcycle*	dȉn⁶ dāan¹ cē¹ 電單車 (zāa¹ + dȉn⁶ dāan¹ cē¹)
7.	*public light bus; minibus* (buses with not more than 19 seats)	síu² bāa¹ ③ 小巴
8.	*underground railway; MTR*	dȅi⁶ tit³ 地鐵
9.	*light rail*	hīng¹ tit³ 輕鐵
10.	*peak tram*	sāan¹ déng² lāam⁶ cē¹ 山頂纜車
11.	*taxi*	dīk¹ sí² 的士
12.	*train*	fó² cē¹ 火車
13.	*tram*	dȉn⁶ cē¹ 電車

FYI – 2. A Stop or Terminus

1.	*airport*	gēi¹ còeng⁴ 機場
2.	*bus stop*	bāa¹ sí² zāam⁶ 巴士站
3.	*minibus station*	síu² bāa¹ zāam⁶ 小巴站
4.	*MTR station*	dȅi⁶ tit³ zȁam⁶ 地鐵站
5.	*peak tram station; cable car station*	lāam⁶ cē¹ zāam⁶ 纜車站
6.	*pier*	mǎa⁵ tàu⁴ 碼頭
7.	*railway station*	fó² cē¹ zāam⁶ 火車站
8.	*taxi stand*	dīk¹ sí² zāam⁶ 的士站
9.	*tram station*	dȉn⁶ cē¹ zāam⁶ 電車站

---

③ **síu² bāa¹** : In Hong Kong, green public light buses are operated on scheduled services with fixed routes at fixed fares, while red public light buses on non-scheduled services without control over routes or fares.

港鐵路綫圖 MTR system map

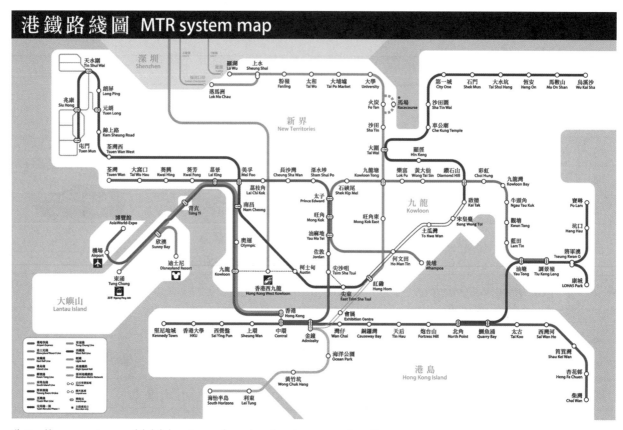

(http://www.mtr.com.hk/ch/customer/services/system_map.html)

1) Island Line (Góng² Dóu² Sin³ 港島綫)

Kennedy Town ⇨ Gīn¹ Nèi⁴ Dēi⁶ Sìng⁴ 堅尼地城	*HKU* ⇨ Hōeng¹ Góng² Dāai⁶ Hōk⁶ 香港大學	*Sai Ying Pun* ⇨ Sāi¹ Jìng⁴ Pùn⁴ 西營盤
Sheung Wan ⇨ Sōeng⁶ Wàan⁴ 上環	*Central* ⇨ Zūng¹ Wàan⁴ 中環	*Admiralty* ⇨ Gām¹ Zūng¹ 金鐘
Wan Chai ⇨ Wāan¹ Zái² 灣仔	*Causeway Bay* ⇨ Tùng⁴ Lò⁴ Wāan¹ 銅鑼灣	*Tin Hau* ⇨ Tīn¹ Hāu⁶ 天后
Fortress Hill ⇨ Pǎau³ Tòi⁴ Sāan¹ 炮台山	*North Point* ⇨ Bāk¹ Gŏk³ 北角	*Quarry Bay* ⇨ Zāk¹ Jy̌u⁴ Cūng¹ 鰂魚涌
Tai Koo ⇨ Tǎai³ Gú² 太古	*Sai Wan Ho* ⇨ Sāi¹ Wāan¹ Hó² 西灣河	*Shau Kei Wan* ⇨ Sāau¹ Gēi¹ Wāan¹ 筲箕灣
Heng Fa Chuen ⇨ Hāng⁶ Fāa¹ Cyūn¹ 杏花邨	*Chai Wan* ⇨ Càai⁴ Wāan¹ 柴灣	

---

④ The MTR (Mass Transit Railway) Corporation has been providing an efficient way to get around Hong Kong since 1979. In December 2007, the Kowloon-Canton Railway Corporation was merged into the MTR Corporation Limited. The Chinese name of the corporation is called "Hōeng¹ Góng² Tit³ Lōu⁶ Gūng¹ Sī¹ 香港鐵路有限公司" ("Góng² Tit³ 港鐵").

2) South Island Line (East) (Nàam⁴ Góng² Dóu² Sin³ 南港島綫)

Admiralty	Ocean Park	Wong Chuk Hang
⇨ Gām¹ Zūng¹ 金鐘	⇨ Hói² Jòeng⁴ Gūng¹ Jýun² 海洋公園	⇨ Wòng⁴ Zūk¹ Hāang¹ 黃竹坑
Lei Tung	South Horizons	
⇨ Lĕi⁶ Dūng¹ 利東	⇨ Hói² Jì⁴ Bǔn³ Dóu² 海怡半島	

3) Tsuen Wan Line (Cỳun⁴ Wāan¹ Sin³ 荃灣綫)

Tsuen Wan	Tai Wo Hau	Kwai Hing
⇨ Cỳun⁴ Wāan¹ 荃灣	⇨ Dāai⁶ Wō¹ Háu² 大窩口	⇨ Kwài⁴ Hīng¹ 葵興
Kwai Fong	Lai King	Mei Foo
⇨ Kwài⁴ Fōng¹ 葵芳	⇨ Lāi⁶ Gíng² 荔景	⇨ Měi⁵ Fū¹ 美孚
Lai Chi Kok	Cheung Sha Wan	Shum Shui Po
⇨ Lāi⁶ Zī¹ Gȯk³ 荔枝角	⇨ Còeng⁴ Sāa¹ Wàan⁴ 長沙灣	⇨ Sām¹ Séoi² Bóu² 深水埗
Prince Edward	Mong Kok	Yau Ma Tei
⇨ Tȧai³ Zí² 太子	⇨ Wōng⁶ Gȯk³ 旺角	⇨ Jàu⁴ Màa⁴ Déi² 油麻地
Jordan	Tsim Sha Tsui	Admiralty
⇨ Zó² Dēon¹ 佐敦	⇨ Zīm¹ Sāa¹ Zéoi² 尖沙咀	⇨ Gām¹ Zūng¹ 金鐘
Central		
⇨ Zūng¹ Wàan⁴ 中環		

4) Kwun Tong Line (Gūn¹ Tòng⁴ Sin³ 觀塘綫)

Whampoa	Ho Man Tin	Yau Ma Tei
⇨ Wòng⁴ Bǒu³ 黃埔	⇨ Hò⁴ Màn⁴ Tìn⁴ 何文田	⇨ Jàu⁴ Màa⁴ Déi² 油麻地
Mong Kok	Prince Edward	Shek Kip Mei
⇨ Wōng⁶ Gȯk³ 旺角	⇨ Tȧai³ Zí² 太子	⇨ Sěk⁶ Gip³ Měi⁵ 石硤尾
Kowloon Tong	Lok Fu	Wong Tai Sin
⇨ Gáu² Lùng⁴ Tòng⁴ 九龍塘	⇨ Lȯk⁶ Fǔ³ 樂富	⇨ Wòng⁴ Dāai⁶ Sīn¹ 黃大仙
Diamond Hill	Choi Hung	Kowloon Bay
⇨ Zẏun³ Sěk⁶ Sāan¹ 鑽石山	⇨ Cói² Hùng⁴ 彩虹	⇨ Gáu² Lùng⁴ Wāan¹ 九龍灣
Ngau Tau Kok	Kwun Tong	Lam Tin
⇨ Ngàu⁴ Tàu⁴ Gȯk³ 牛頭角	⇨ Gūn¹ Tòng⁴ 觀塘	⇨ Làam⁴ Tìn⁴ 藍田
Yau Tong	Tiu Keng Leng	
⇨ Jàu⁴ Tòng⁴ 油塘	⇨ Tìu⁴ Gíng² Lěng⁵ 調景嶺	

5) Tung Chung Line (Dūng¹ Cūng¹ Sin³ 東涌綫)

Hong Kong ⇨ Hōeng¹ Góng² 香港	Kowloon ⇨ Gáu² Lùng⁴ 九龍	Olympic ⇨ Ỏu³ Wān⁶ 奧運
Nam Cheong ⇨ Nàam⁴ Cōeng¹ 南昌	Lai King ⇨ Lāi⁶ Gíng² 荔景	Tsing Yi ⇨ Cīng¹ Jī¹ 青衣
Sunny Bay ⇨ Jān¹ Ỏu³ 欣澳	Tung Chung ⇨ Dūng¹ Cūng¹ 東涌	

6) Tseung Kwan O Line (Zōeng¹ Gwān¹ Ỏu³ Sin³ 將軍澳綫)

Po Lam ⇨ Bóu² Làm⁴ 寶琳	Hang Hau ⇨ Hāang¹ Háu² 坑口	Tseung Kwan O ⇨ Zōeng¹ Gwān¹ Ỏu³ 將軍澳
LOHAS Park ⇨ Hōng¹ Sìng⁴ 康城	Tiu Keng Leng ⇨ Tìu⁴ Gíng² Lěng⁵ 調景嶺	Yau Tong ⇨ Jàu⁴ Tòng⁴ 油塘
Quarry Bay ⇨ Zāk¹ Jỳu⁴ Cūng¹ 鰂魚涌	North Point ⇨ Bāk¹ Gỏk³ 北角	

7) Disneyland Resort Line (Dīk⁶ Sī⁶ Nèi⁴ Sin³ 迪士尼綫)

Sunny Bay ⇨ Jān¹ Ỏu³ 欣澳	Disneyland Resort ⇨ Dīk⁶ Sī⁶ Nèi⁴ 迪士尼

8) Airport Express (Gēi¹ Còeng⁴ Fảai³ Sin³ 機場快綫)

Hong Kong ⇨ Hōeng¹ Góng² 香港	Kowloon ⇨ Gáu² Lùng⁴ 九龍	Tsing Yi ⇨ Cīng¹ Jī¹ 青衣
Airport ⇨ Gēi¹ Còeng⁴ 機場	AsiaWorld-Expo ⇨ Bỏk³ Lăam⁵ Gún² 博覽館	

9) West Rail Line (Sāi¹ Tỉt³ Sin³ 西鐵綫)

Hung Hom ⇨ Hùng⁴ Hảm³ 紅磡	East Tsim Sha Tsui ⇨ Zīm¹ Dūng¹ 尖東	Austin ⇨ Ō¹ Sī⁶ Dīn¹ 柯士甸
Nam Cheong ⇨ Nàam⁴ Cōeng¹ 南昌	Mei Foo ⇨ Měi⁵ Fū¹ 美孚	Tsuen Wan West ⇨ Cỳun⁴ Wāan¹ Sāi¹ 荃灣西
Kam Sheung Road ⇨ Gám² Sōeng⁶ Lōu⁶ 錦上路	Yuen Long ⇨ Jỳun⁴ Lǒng⁵ 元朗	Long Ping ⇨ Lǒng⁵ Pìng⁴ 朗屏
Tin Shui Wai ⇨ Tīn¹ Séoi² Wài⁴ 天水圍	Siu Hong ⇨ Sīu⁶ Hōng¹ 兆康	Tuen Mun ⇨ Tỳun⁴ Mùn⁴ 屯門

10) East Rail Line (Dūng¹ Tit³ Sin³ 東鐵线)

Hung Hom ⇨ Hùng⁴ Hảm³ 紅磡	*Mong Kok East* ⇨ Wōng⁶ Gòk³ Dūng¹ 旺角東	*Kowloon Tong* ⇨ Gáu² Lùng⁴ Tòng⁴ 九龍塘
Tai Wai ⇨ Dāai⁶ Wài⁴ 大圍	*Sha Tin* ⇨ Sāa¹ Tìn⁴ 沙田	*Fo Tan* ⇨ Fó² Tản³ 火炭
Racecourse ⇨ Mǎa⁵ Còeng⁴ 馬場	*University* ⇨ Dāai⁶ Hŏk⁶ 大學	*Tai Po Market* ⇨ Dāai⁶ Bồu³ Hēoi¹ 大埔墟
Tai Wo ⇨ Tảai³ Wò⁴ 太和	*Fanling* ⇨ Fán² Lěng⁵ 粉嶺	*Sheung Shui* ⇨ Sōeng⁶ Séoi² 上水
Lo Wu ⇨ Lò⁴ Wù⁴ 羅湖	*Lok Ma Chau* ⇨ Lŏk⁶ Mǎa⁵ Zāu¹ 落馬洲	

11) Ma On Shan Line (Mǎa⁵ Ōn¹ Sāan¹ Sin³ 馬鞍山綫)

Wu Kai Sha ⇨ Wū¹ Kāi¹ Sāa¹ 烏溪沙	*Ma On Shan* ⇨ Mǎa⁵ Ōn¹ Sāan¹ 馬鞍山	*Heng On* ⇨ Hàng⁴ Ōn¹ 恆安
Tai Shui Hang ⇨ Dāai⁶ Séoi² Hāang¹ 大水坑	*Shek Mun* ⇨ Sēk⁶ Mùn⁴ 石門	*City One* ⇨ Dāi⁶ Jāt¹ Sìng⁴ 第一城
Sha Tin Wai ⇨ Sāa¹ Tìn⁴ Wài⁴ 沙田圍	*Che Kung Temple* ⇨ Cē¹ Gūng¹ Míu² 車公廟	*Tai Wai* ⇨ Dāai⁶ Wài⁴ 大圍

12) Shatin to Central Link (Sāa¹ Tìn⁴ zi³ Zūng¹ Wàan⁴ Sin³ 沙田至中環綫)⑤

Tai Wai ⇨ Dāai⁶ Wài⁴ 大圍	*Hin Keng* ⇨ Hín² Gìng³ 顯徑	*Diamond Hill* ⇨ Zỷun³ Sēk⁶ Sāan¹ 鑽石山
Kai Tak ⇨ Kái² Dāk¹ 啟德	*To Kwa Wan* ⇨ Tóu² Gwāa¹ Wàan⁴ 土瓜灣	*Ma Tau Wai* ⇨ Mǎa⁵ Tàu⁴ Wài⁴ 馬頭圍
Ho Man Tin ⇨ Hồ⁴ Màn⁴ Tìn⁴ 何文田	*Hung Hom* ⇨ Hùng⁴ Hảm³ 紅磡	*Exhibition* ⇨ Wūi⁶ Zín² 會展
Admiralty ⇨ Gām¹ Zūng¹ 金鐘		

---

⑤ Sāa¹ Zūng¹ Sin³ 沙中綫 is the shortened Chinese name for the Shatin to Central Link (SCL). The 17-km SCL will have two sections. The first section, connecting Tai Wai to Hung Hom, is an extension of the existing Ma On Shan Line. The second section, the cross-harbour section, is an extension of the existing East Rail Line, connecting Hung Hom to a new station at Exhibition and terminating at Admiralty. According to a press release from the MTR in May 2020, the opening of the remainder of the first section from Kai Tak to Hong Hom is anticipated to be in 2021, while the second section from Hung Hom to Admiralty is scheduled to open in 2022.

13) Tuen Ma Line (Tỳun⁴ Măa⁵ Sìn³ 屯馬綫) ⑥

Ma On Shan Line (refer to p.193) ⇨ Măa⁵ Ōn¹ Sāan¹ Sìn³ 馬鞍山綫	Tai Wai ⇨ Dāai⁶ Wài⁴ 大圍	Hin Keng ⇨ Hín² Gìng³ 顯徑
Diamond Hill ⇨ Zyun³ Sèk⁶ Sāan¹ 鑽石山	Kai Tak ⇨ Kái² Dāk¹ 啟德	Sung Wong Toi ⇨ Sùng³ Wòng⁴ Tòi⁴ 宋皇臺
To Kwa Wan ⇨ Tó² Gwāa¹ Wàan⁴ 土瓜灣	Ho Man Tin ⇨ Hò⁴ Màn⁴ Tìn⁴ 何文田	Hung Hom ⇨ Hùng⁴ Hảm³ 紅磡
West Rail Line (refer to p.192) ⇨ Sāi¹ Tit³ Sìn³ 西鐵綫		

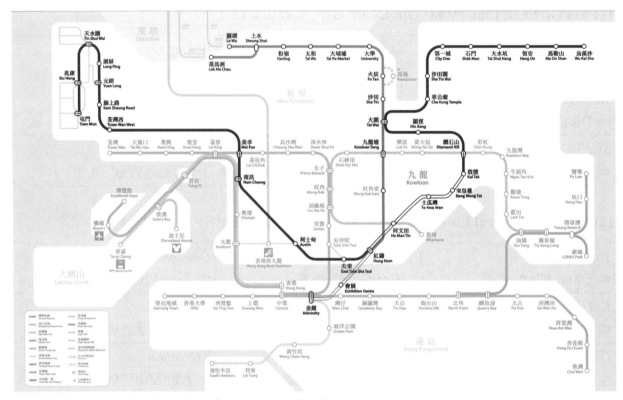

Shatin to Central Link & Tuen Ma Line

14) Light Rail (Hīng¹ Tit³ 輕鐵)

(Please check www.mtr.com.hk for the route map and stations.)

---

⑥ The Tuen Ma Line (TML) will be the longest railway line in Hong Kong, running 56 km with 27 stations and connecting the Ma On Shan Line with the West Rail Line. Phase 1 of the TML (Tỳun⁴ Măa⁵ Sìn³ Jāt¹ Kèi⁴ 屯馬綫一期), connecting Wu Kai Sha station to Kai Tak station, opened on 14 February 2020. The full opening of the TML is anticipated to be in 2021.

1. **Write the answers to the following questions in Cantonese.** $(8 \times 9.5\% = 76\%)$

   (Please search on the Internet.)

   1) něi⁵ mǔi⁵ jāt⁶ dåap³ māt¹ jě⁵ cē¹ fāan¹ hŏk⁶ gåa³?

   _____

   2) jàu⁴ něi⁵ ūk¹ kéi² hěoi³ Zūng¹ Wàan⁴, dåap³ māt¹ jě⁵ cē¹ åa³?

   _____

   3) Hōeng¹ Góng² Dóu² jāt¹ hŏu⁶ bāa¹ sí² ge̊³ zúng² zāam⁶ hǎi⁶ bīn¹ dŏu⁶ åa³?

   _____

   4) cíng² mǎn⁶ géi² dō¹ hŏu⁶ síu² bāa¹ hěoi³ sāan¹ déng² åa³?

   _____

   5) hěoi³ sāan¹ déng² ge̊³ lǎam⁶ cē¹ zāam⁶ hái² māt¹ jě⁵ gāai¹*(street)* åa³?

   _____

   6) géi² dō¹ hŏu⁶ bāa¹ sí² gīng¹ Gām¹ Zūng¹ děi⁶ tit̊³ zāam⁶ åa³?

   _____

   7) ngǒ⁵ sóeng² hěoi³ Cāt¹ Hŏu⁶ Mǎa⁵ Tàu⁴, hái² bīn¹ go̊³ děi⁶ tit̊³ zāam⁶ lŏk⁶ cē¹ åa³?

   _____

   8) hái² Hōeng¹ Góng² dåap³ síu² bāa¹, něi⁵ sóeng² lŏk⁶ cē¹ jiů³ góng² māt¹ jě⁵ åa³?

   _____

2. **Translate the following into Cantonese.** $(6 \times 4\% = 24\%)$

   1) What transportation do you take to go to work?

   _____

   2) Do you know where your teacher lives?

   _____

   3) My friend and I walk to the Central MTR station every day.

   _____

   4) I want to go to the City Hall. What transportation should I take?

   _____

   5) May I ask if this minibus passes by the Landmark?

   _____

   6) Driver, I want to get off at the HSBC headquarters.

   _____

Learning Objectives

1. To ask how to carry out an action using "**dím² jóeng²**"
2. To give instruction to find one's way
3. To coordinate/indicate a sequence of events with "**jìn⁴ hāu⁶**" or "**gān¹ zy̌u⁶**"
4. The ordinal numbers *(refer to Unit 2 Section 2)*
5. To ask how long it takes to do something using "**géi² nõi⁶**"
6. To state the time duration of an event
7. To state the possibility or likelihood that something will happen with "**wǔi⁵**"

nī¹ tìu⁴ hāi⁶ Bāt¹ Dáa² Gāai¹.
cìn⁴ mīn⁶ gó² tìu⁴ gāai¹ hāi⁶ Dāk¹ Fū⁶ Dōu⁶.

céng² mǎn⁶ nī¹ tìu⁴ hāi⁶ māt¹ jě⁵ gāai¹ åa³?

něi⁵ wǔi⁵ gǐn³ dóu² lǒeng⁵ gǒ³ sī¹ zí² zōeng⁶, gó² dōu⁶ zāu⁶ hāi⁶ Wūi⁶ Fūng¹ Ngàn⁴ Hòng⁴ zúng² hóng² låak³.

Amy is asking the way to the HSBC headquarters in Central.

Amy: céng² mān⁶ nī¹ tìu⁴ hāi⁶ māt¹ jě⁵ gāai¹ åa³?
請 問 呢 條 係 乜 嘢 街 呀？
(Excuse me, what street is this?)

Passer-by: nī¹ tìu⁴ hāi⁶ Bāt¹ Dáa² Gāai¹.
呢 條 係 畢 打 街。
(This is Pedder Street.)

Amy: gám², Wūi⁶ Fūng¹ Ngàn⁴ Hòng⁴ zúng² hóng² hái² bīn¹ dōu⁶ åa³?
噉， 匯 豐 銀 行 總 行 喺 邊 度 呀？
(Well, where is the HSBC headquarters?)

Passer-by: Wūi⁶ Fūng¹ Ngàn⁴ Hòng⁴ zúng² hóng² hái² Dāk¹ Fū⁶ Dōu⁶.
匯 豐 銀 行 總 行 喺 德 輔 道。
(The HSBC headquarters is on Des Voeux Road.)

Amy: céng² mān⁶ dím² jóeng² hěoi³ åa³?
請 問 點 樣 去 呀？
(How do I get there, please?)

Passer-by: cìn⁴ mīn⁶ gó² tìu⁴ gāai¹ zāu⁶ hāi⁶ Dāk¹ Fū⁶ Dōu⁶ låak³.
前 面 嗰 條 街 就 係 德 輔 道 嘅。
(That street ahead is Des Voeux Road.)

něi⁵ hǒeng³ bāk¹ zīk⁶ hàang⁴, hái² dāi⁶ jāt¹ gò³ gāai¹ háu² zyun³ jāu⁶,
你 向 北 直 行， 喺 第 一 個 街 口 轉 右，
(Go north straight down the road, turn right at the first junction,

jìn⁴ hāu⁶ hǒeng³ dūng¹ hàang⁴ lāa¹!
然 後 向 東 行 啦！
then go east.)

Amy: jiu³ hàang⁴ géi² nǒi⁶ åa³?
要 行 幾 耐 呀？
(How long does it take to walk there?)

Passer-by: něi⁵ zòi³ hàang⁴ ňg⁵ fān¹ zūng¹,
你 再 行 五 分 鐘，
(You walk 5 minutes more.)

wǔi⁵ gin³ dóu² Wūi⁶ Fūng¹ Ngàn⁴ Hòng⁴ mùn⁴ háu² gě³
會 見 到 匯 豐 銀 行 門 口 嘅
(You'll see two lion statues at the entrance of the HSBC...)

lǒeng⁵ gò³ sī¹ zí² zōeng⁶, gó² dōu⁶ zāu⁶ hāi⁶ låak³.
兩 個 獅 子 像， 嗰 度 就 係 嘅。
(...and that will be it.)

Amy: zān¹ hāi⁶ m̀⁴ gōi¹ såai³ něi⁵ åa³.
真 係 唔 該 晒 你 呀。
(Thank you very much indeed.)

1.	tìu⁴ 條	M:	[a measure word for streets or things with a long shape]
2.	gāai¹ 街 (M: tìu⁴ 條)	N:	street
3.	Bāt¹ Dáa² Gāai¹ 畢打街	PN:	Pedder Street [a major street in Central, Hong Kong Island]
4.	Dāk¹ Fū⁶ Dòu⁶ 德輔道	PN:	Des Voeux Road [a major street in Central, Hong Kong Island]
5.	dím² jóeng² 點樣 (+ Verb)	QW:	how (to do sth.) (also "dím²")
6.	dím² jóeng² hěoi³ àa³? 點樣去呀？	SE:	How to get there?
7.	zāu⁶ 就 (+ Verb)	Adv:	(in L.15) [tells the result and signifies emphatic confirmation]

Map of Central:

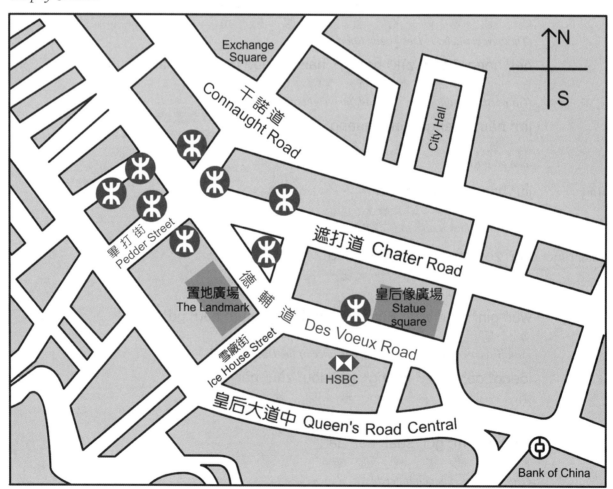

8.	hòeng³ 向 (+ Object)	Prep:	toward; face to
9.	bāk¹ 北	N:	north
10.	dūng¹ 東	N:	east
11.	hàang⁴ 行	V:	to walk
12.	zīk⁶ hàang⁴ 直行	Ph:	walk straight ahead
13.	dāi⁶ jāt¹ 第一 (+ MW + Noun)	Ph:	the first (Refer to Unit 2 Section 2 on p.32)
14.	gāai¹ háu² 街口 (M: gó³ 個)	N:	street intersection; street junction (also "lōu⁶ háu² 路口")
15.	zyun³ 轉 (+ Direction) (e.g. zyun³ jāu⁶: turn right)	V:	to change; to turn (direction)
16.	jāu⁶ 右	N:	(the) right side; the right-hand side
17.	jìn⁴ hāu⁶ 然後 (+ Event)	Conj:	afterwards [used to coordinate a sequence of events] (also "gān¹ zyu⁶ 跟住")
18.	géi² nòi⁶ 幾耐	QW:	how long
19.	zói³ 再 (+ Verb)	Adv:	again, once more, (in L.15) further; then [used to indicate an action that takes place after another action]
20.	fān¹ zūng¹ 分鐘 (Nu + fān¹ zūng¹)	N:	minute (of time duration)
21.	wúi⁵ 會 (+ Verb)	AV:	would; will [stresses the possibility or likelihood of sth. happening]
22.	gin³ dóu² 見到 (Verb + dóu²)	V:	to see ["dóu²" is a structural particle, indicating achieving a desired result through an action]
23.	mùn⁴ háu² 門口	N:	doorway; entrance
24.	sī¹ zí² 獅子 (M: zēk³ 隻)	N:	lion
25.	zōeng⁶ 像 (M: gó³ 個)	N:	statue

1. **To ask how to carry out an action using "dím² jóeng²"**

   e.g. 1. něi⁵ mǔi⁵ jāt⁶ <u>dím² jóeng²</u> fāan¹ gūng¹ gåa³?

   (<u>How</u> do you go to work every day?)

Topic	+	(/Subject)	+	**dím² jóeng²**	+	Verbal phrase	+	**åa³/gåa³?**

   e.g. 2. gām¹ zīu¹ něi⁵ <u>dím² jóeng²</u> fāan¹ hȍk⁶ gåa³?

   (<u>How</u> did you go to school this morning?)

   e.g. 3. něi⁵ gẻ³ méng² <u>dím² jóeng²</u> sé² åa³?

   (<u>How</u> do you write your name?)

   e.g. 4. Jīng¹ Mán² gẻ³ '*Goodbye*', Gwóng² Dūng¹ Wáa² <u>dím² jóeng²</u> góng² åa³?

   (<u>How</u> do you say 'Good-bye' in Cantonese?)

   e.g. 5. (ngǒ⁵) <u>dím² jóeng²</u> cīng¹ fū¹ něi⁵ åa³? [formal way to ask one's name]

   (<u>How</u> may I address you?)

   e.g. 6. <u>dím² jóeng²</u> hẻoi³ něi⁵ ūk¹ kéi² åa³?

   (<u>How</u> do I get to your home?)

   Your example(s):

   _____ **dím² jóeng²** _____ **åa³?**

2. **To give instruction to find one's way**

   e.g. něi⁵ hȍeng³ bāk¹ zīk⁶ hàang⁴, hái² gāai¹ háu² zẙun³ jāu⁶.

   (*Go north straight down the road, turn right at the junction.*)

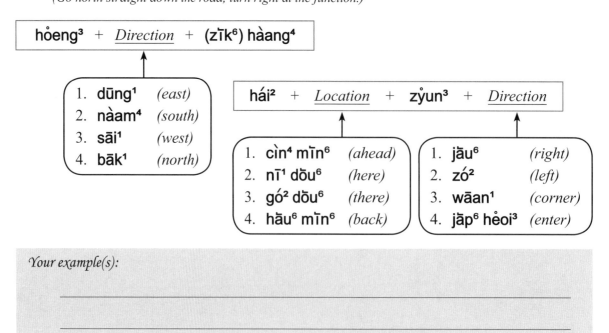

hȍeng³	+	*Direction*	+	(zīk⁶) hàang⁴

   1. dūng¹ *(east)*
   2. nàam⁴ *(south)*
   3. sāi¹ *(west)*
   4. bāk¹ *(north)*

hái²	+	*Location*	+	zẙun³	+	*Direction*

   1. cìn⁴ mīn⁶ *(ahead)*
   2. nī¹ dȍu⁶ *(here)*
   3. gó² dȍu⁶ *(there)*
   4. hȁu⁶ mīn⁶ *(back)*

   1. jāu⁶ *(right)*
   2. zó² *(left)*
   3. wāan¹ *(corner)*
   4. jāp⁶ hẻoi³ *(enter)*

   Your example(s):

   _____

   _____

3. **To coordinate/indicate a sequence of events with "jìn⁴ hău⁶" or "gān¹ zÿu⁶"**

e.g.　hái² gāai¹ háu² zÿun³ jău⁶, jìn⁴ hău⁶ hŏeng³ dūng¹ hàang⁴ lāa¹!
(Turn right at the junction, then go east straight ahead.)

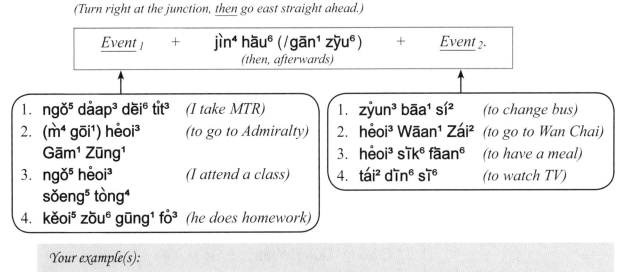

Event ₁	+	jìn⁴ hău⁶ (/gān¹ zÿu⁶)	+	*Event* ₂.
		(then, afterwards)		

1. ngŏ⁵ dǎap³ dĕi⁶ tït³　*(I take MTR)*
2. (m̀⁴ gōi¹) hĕoi³　*(to go to Admiralty)*
   Gām¹ Zūng¹
3. ngŏ⁵ hĕoi³　*(I attend a class)*
   sŏeng⁵ tòng⁴
4. kĕoi⁵ zŏu⁶ gūng¹ fŏ³　*(he does homework)*

1. zÿun³ bāa¹ sí²　*(to change bus)*
2. hĕoi³ Wāan¹ Zái²　*(to go to Wan Chai)*
3. hĕoi³ sïk⁶ fāan⁶　*(to have a meal)*
4. tái² dïn⁶ sï⁶　*(to watch TV)*

Your example(s):

_____ jìn⁴ hău⁶ _____ .

4. **The ordinal number** *(refer to Unit 2 Section 2 on p.32)*

e.g.　hái² dāi⁶ jāt¹ gŏ³ gāai¹ háu² zÿun³ jău⁶, jìn⁴ hău⁶ hŏeng³ dūng¹ hàang⁴ lāa¹!
(Turn right at the first junction, then go east straight ahead.)

dāi⁶	+	*Number*	+	*MW*	+	*Noun*

1. dāi⁶ jāt¹ gŏ³ (jàn⁴)　　*the first one (person)*
2. dāi⁶ jï⁶ gǎa³ (cē¹)　　*the second one (vehicle)*
3. dāi⁶ sāam¹ gāan¹ (fŏng²)　*the third one (room)*
4. dāi⁶ géi² + *MW* ?　　*what rank?*

5. **To ask how long it takes to do something**

e.g.　jĭu³ hàang⁴ géi² nŏi⁶ åa³?
(How long does it take to walk there?)

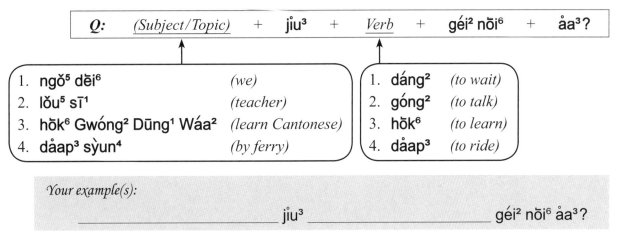

Q:	*(Subject/Topic)*	+	jĭu³	+	*Verb*	+	géi² nŏi⁶	+	åa³?

1. ngŏ⁵ dĕi⁶　　　　　　*(we)*
2. lŏu⁵ sï¹　　　　　　*(teacher)*
3. hŏk⁶ Gwóng² Dūng¹ Wáa²　*(learn Cantonese)*
4. dǎap³ sÿun⁴　　　　*(by ferry)*

1. dáng²　*(to wait)*
2. góng²　*(to talk)*
3. hŏk⁶　*(to learn)*
4. dǎap³　*(to ride)*

Your example(s):

_____ jĭu³ _____ géi² nŏi⁶ åa³?

6. To state the time duration of an event

e.g. **něi⁵ zǒi³ hàang⁴ <u>ng̊⁵ fān¹ zūng¹</u>.**

(You walk <u>5 minutes</u> more.)

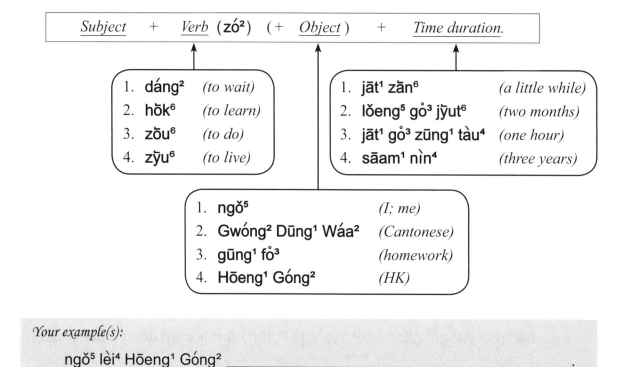

| *Subject* | + | *Verb* (**zó²**) | (+ *Object*) | + | *Time duration.* |

1. **dáng²** *(to wait)*
2. **hŏk⁶** *(to learn)*
3. **zŏu⁶** *(to do)*
4. **zẙu⁶** *(to live)*

1. **jāt¹ zǎn⁶** *(a little while)*
2. **lŏeng⁵ gå³ jẙut⁶** *(two months)*
3. **jāt¹ gå³ zūng¹ tàu⁴** *(one hour)*
4. **sāam¹ nìn⁴** *(three years)*

1. **ngŏ⁵** *(I; me)*
2. **Gwóng² Dūng¹ Wáa²** *(Cantonese)*
3. **gūng¹ få³** *(homework)*
4. **Hōeng¹ Góng²** *(HK)*

Your example(s):

ngŏ⁵ lèi⁴ Hōeng¹ Góng² _____ .

ngŏ⁵ hŏk⁶ zó² Gwóng² Dūng¹ Wáa² _____ .

7. To state the possibility or likelihood that something will happen with "wŭi⁵"

e.g. **něi⁵ wŭi⁵ gin³ dóu² Wūi⁶ Fūng¹ Ngàn⁴ Hòng⁴ mùn⁴ háu² gě³ lŏeng⁵ gå³ sī¹ zí² zōeng⁶.**

(You <u>will</u> see two lion statues at the entrance of the HSBC.)

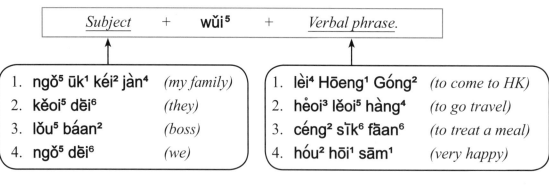

| *Subject* | + | **wŭi⁵** | + | *Verbal phrase.* |

1. **ngŏ⁵ ūk¹ kéi² jàn⁴** *(my family)*
2. **kěoi⁵ dēi⁶** *(they)*
3. **lŏu⁵ báan²** *(boss)*
4. **ngŏ⁵ dēi⁶** *(we)*

1. **lèi⁴ Hōeng¹ Góng²** *(to come to HK)*
2. **hě̊oi³ lěoi⁵ hàng⁴** *(to go travel)*
3. **céng² sīk⁶ fāan⁶** *(to treat a meal)*
4. **hóu² hōi¹ sām¹** *(very happy)*

Your example(s):

zāu¹ mūt⁶ ngŏ⁵ wŭi⁵ _____ .

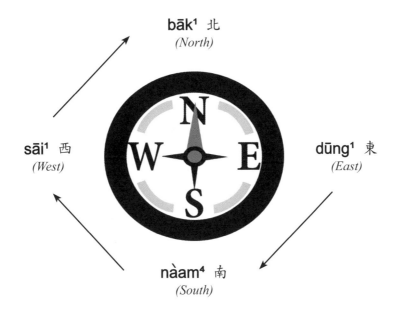

bāk¹ 北
(North)

sāi¹ 西
(West)

dūng¹ 東
(East)

nàam⁴ 南
(South)

FYI – 2. Banks in Hong Kong

1.	Hong Kong and Shanghai Banking Corporation (HSBC)	Wūi⁶ Fūng¹ Ngàn⁴ Hòng⁴ 匯豐銀行
2.	Bank of China (Hong Kong)	Zūng¹ Gwŏk³ Ngàn⁴ Hòng⁴ (Hōeng¹ Góng²) 中國銀行（香港）
3.	Hang Seng Bank	Hàng⁴ Sāng¹ Ngàn⁴ Hòng⁴ 恒生銀行
4.	Standard Chartered Bank	Zāa¹ Dáa² Ngàn⁴ Hòng⁴ 渣打銀行
5.	The Bank of East Asia	Dūng¹ Åa³ Ngàn⁴ Hòng⁴ 東亞銀行
6.	Bank of Communications	Gāau¹ Tūng¹ Ngàn⁴ Hòng⁴ 交通銀行
7.	DBS Bank Limited	Sīng¹ Zín² Ngàn⁴ Hòng⁴ 星展銀行
8.	Dah Sing Bank Limited	Dāai⁶ Sān¹ Ngàn⁴ Hòng⁴ 大新銀行
9.	Citibank (Hong Kong) Limited	Fāa¹ Kèi⁴ Ngàn⁴ Hòng⁴ (Hōeng¹ Góng²) 花旗銀行（香港）
10.	Industrial and Commercial Bank of China (Asia) (ICBC Asia)	Zūng¹ Gwŏk³ Gūng¹ Sōeng¹ Ngàn⁴ Hòng⁴ (Åa³ Zāu¹) 中國工商銀行（亞洲）

Q: něi⁵ lèi⁴ zó² Hōeng¹ Góng² gél² nòi⁶ åa³?

A: ngǒ⁵ lèi⁴ zó² Hōeng¹ Góng² _____ .

1.	*year(s)*	*Nu.* + **nìn⁴** ~ 年*
2.	*month(s)*	*Nu.* + **gǒ³** + **jy̌ut⁶** ~ 個月
3.	*week(s)*	*Nu.* + **gǒ³** + **sīng¹ kèi⁴** ~ 個星期
4.	*day(s)*	*Nu.* + **jāt⁶** ~ 日*
5.	*night(s)*	*Nu.* + **mǎan⁵** ~ 晚*
6.	*hour(s)*	*Nu.* + **gǒ³** + **zūng¹ tàu⁴** ~ 個鐘頭
7.	*minute(s)*	*Nu.* + **fān¹ zūng¹** ~ 分鐘*
8.	*second(s)*	*Nu.* + **mǐu⁵ zūng¹** ~ 秒鐘*
9.	*a little while*	**jāt¹ zān⁶** 一陣
10.	*long time*	**hóu² nòi⁶** 好耐

* Note that "**nìn⁴**", "**jāt⁶**", "**mǎan⁵**", "**fān¹**" & "**mǐu⁵**" can also be measure words by themselves; therefore there is no need to use the measure word "**gǒ³**".

1. **Translate the following into English.** (10 × 5% = 50%)

    1) hái² bīn¹ dōu⁶ åa³ ? _____

    2) dím² jóeng² hěoi³ åa³ ? _____

    3) māt¹ jě⁵ gāai¹ åa³ ? _____

    4) zẙun³ jāu⁶ _____

    5) zẙun³ zó² _____

    6) zīk⁶ hàang⁴ _____

    7) hǒeng³ dūng¹ hàang⁴ _____

    8) jẙu³ géi² nǒi⁶ åa³ ? _____

    9) nǧ⁵ fān¹ zūng¹ _____

    10) gó² dōu³ zāu³ hāi³ lǻak³. _____

2. **What should you say in the following situations? (in Cantonese)** (7 × 7% = 49%)

    1) You want to ask how to say "Happy" in Cantonese.

        You say: _____

    2) You want to ask formally how you should address someone's name.

        You say: _____

    3) You want to tell the taxi driver to go straight and turn right at the street junction.

        You say: _____

    4) You want to tell the taxi driver to go to Wan Chai and then to Causeway Bay.

        You say: _____   _____

    5) You want to ask how long you would have to wait.

        You say: _____

    6) You want to say you have learned Cantonese for two months.

        You say: _____

    7) You want to tell someone that he/she will see two lion statues at the entrance.

        You say: _____

Glossary

1. Cantonese to English
2. English to Cantonese
3. Grammatical Terms

The Cantonese to English list includes:

1. Words which appear in the Introduction (U.1) and Numerals (U.2);
2. Words used in the Dialogue or the Story (L. 1 – 15);
3. Words which are introduced in the FYI (L. 1 – 15);
4. Related words in example sentences in the Sentence Structure (L. 1 – 15);
5. Extra related words, marked by a "*".

All words are listed in alphabetical order. Those words which differ only in tones are given in the traditional tone order with number 1 to 6 representing high level, high rising, mid-level, low falling, low rising and low level, for example, āa¹, áa², åa³, àa⁴, ăa⁵ and āa⁶.

The English to Cantonese contains the same list of words indexed in English. Note that all the Measure Words *(MW)* and Particles *(Part)* in the Cantonese list are under the entries "measure words" and "particles" respectively.

A

āa¹ 鴉 *(N) crow*	U.1
āa¹ 吖 *(Part)* [a modal particle used at the end of a sentence, indicating suggestion]	L.12
åa³ 呀 *(Part)* [an interrogative particle commonly used at the end of a question to express an inquiry]	L.2
åa³ 呀 *(Part)* [a modal particle used to soften the tone of a confirmation in a statement]	L.3
åa³ 阿 *(Pref)* [used as a prefix to names; a polite and friendly form of addressing people]	L.7
Åa³ Gān¹ Tìng⁴ 阿根廷 *(PN) Argentina*	*
åa³ sòe⁴ 阿 Sir *(Pn) Sir*	L.1
Åa³ Zāu¹ 亞洲 *(PN) Asia*	L.2
àa⁴ 牙 *(Part)* [a modal particle, used at the end of a statement to form a supposition question seeking confirmation]	L.10
Āai¹ Kåp⁶ 埃及 *(PN) Egypt*	*
åan³ zåu³ 晏晝 *(N) afternoon*	U.2
ái² 矮 *(Adj) short (in height)*	U.1
ām¹ 庵 *(N) nunnery*	U.1
Āu¹ Lò⁴ 歐羅 *(PN) Euros*	L.4
Āu¹ Jòeng⁴ 歐陽 *(PN)* a Chinese surname: Au Yeung	L.1
Āu¹ Jẙun⁴ 歐元 *(N) Euros*	L.4
Āu¹ Zāu¹ 歐洲 *(PN) Europe*	L.2

B

Bāa¹ Gēi¹ Sī¹ Táan² 巴基斯坦 *(PN) Pakistan*	*
Bāa¹ Lài⁴ 巴黎 *(PN) Paris*	L.5
Bāa¹ Làm⁴ 巴林 *(PN) Bahrain*	*
Bāa¹ Nàa⁴ Măa⁵ 巴拿馬 *(PN) Panama*	*
Bāa¹ Sāi¹ 巴西 *(PN) Brazil*	*
bāa¹ sí² 巴士 *(N) bus*	L.14
bāa¹ sí² zāam⁶ 巴士站 *(N) bus stop*	L.14
bàa⁴ bāa¹ 爸爸 *(N) father*	L.4

bāai¹ båai³ 拜拜 *(SE) bye-bye*	L.6
båak³ 百 *(Nu) hundred*	U.1
båak³ fő³ gūng¹ sī¹ 百貨公司 *(N) department store*	L.7
båak⁶ sīk¹ 白色 *(N) white colour*	L.13
Bāak⁶ Wáa² 白話 *(PN) white/plain speech*	U.1
båak⁶ zūk¹ 白粥 *(N) plain rice congee*	L.10
båan⁶ gūng¹ sāt¹ 辦公室 *(N) office*	L.3
båat³ 八 *(Nu) eight*	U.1
båat³ dāat⁶ tūng¹ kāat¹ 八達通咭 *(PN) Octopus card*	L.4
båat³ jẙut⁶ 八月 *(PN) August*	L.8
båat³ nǧ⁵ zit³ 八五折 *(Ph) 15% off*	L.13
båat³ zit³ 八折 *(Ph) 20% off*	L.13
báau² 飽 *(Adj) full (opp. hungry)*	L.10
bāk¹ 北 *(N) north*	L.15
Bāk¹ Gīk⁶ 北極 *(PN) Arctic*	*
Bāk¹ Gők³ 北角 *(PN)* a MTR station: North Point	L.14
Bāk¹ Hòn⁴ 北韓 *(PN) North Korea*	*
Bāk¹ Měi⁵ Zāu¹ 北美洲 *(PN) North America*	L.2
Bāk¹ Ôi³ Jĭ⁵ Làan⁴ 北愛爾蘭 *(PN) Northern Ireland*	*
bān¹ gún² 賓館 *(N) guesthouse*	L.3
bāt¹ 筆 *(N) pen*	U.2
Bāt¹ Dáa² Gāai¹ 畢打街 *(PN) Pedder Street* [a major street in Central, Hong Kong Island]	L.15
bāt¹ gwő³ 不過 *(Conj) but, however*	L.7
bē¹ záu² 啤酒 *(N) beer*	L.3
béi² 俾 *(V) to give; to pay*	L.13
béi² cín² 俾錢 *(VO) to pay; to give money*	L.13
Béi² Lěi⁶ Sì⁴ 比利時 *(PN) Belgium*	*
běng⁶ 病 *(Adj) sick*	U.1
Bīk¹ Lò⁴ Cēon¹ 碧螺春 *(PN)* Pi-luo-chu tea, best known as Queen of all green teas	L.12
bīn¹ dī¹ 邊啲 *(QW) which*	L.10
bīn¹ dõu⁶ 邊度 *(QW) where*	L.2

bīn¹ gāan¹ 邊間 (QW) which building	L.10
bīn¹ zúng² jǔyu⁵ jìn⁴ 邊種語言 (QW) what kind of language	L.6
bīn⁶ lěi⁶ dim³ 便利店 (N) convenience store	L.9
bō¹ lò⁴ bāau¹ 菠蘿包 (N) pineapple(-like) bun	L.10
bō¹ lò⁴ jàu⁴ 菠蘿油 (N) pineapple(-like) bun with a slice of butter inserted in it	L.10
Bok³ Lǎam⁵ Gún² 博覽館 (PN) a MTR station: AsiaWorld-Expo	L.14
bóu² hím² gūng¹ sī¹ 保險公司 (N) insurance company	L.7
Bóu² Làm⁴ 寶琳 (PN) a MTR station: Po Lam	L.14
Bóu² Léi² 普洱 (PN) (see "Póu² Léi²")	L.12
bòu³ dīn¹ 布甸 (N) pudding	*
bóu³ zí² 報紙 (N) newpapers	L.8
būi¹ 杯 (N) glass, cup, mug	L.11
būi¹ 杯 (M) a cup of [a measure of the quantity of something that a cup will hold]	L.11
bún² 本 (M) [a measure for books; magazines]	U.2
bún² děi⁶ wáa² 本地話 (N) local dialect	L.6
Bùn³ Sāan¹ 半山 (PN) Mid-Level: a district in HK Island	L.14

• *C*

cāa¹ 叉 (N) fork	L.3
cāa¹ 差 (Adj) bad; not up to standard	L.11
cāa¹ m̀⁴ dō¹ 差唔多 (Adv) almost; nearly	U.2
cāa¹ sīu¹ bāau¹ 叉燒包 (N) barbecue pork buns (a popular dim-sum)	L.12
cāa¹ sīu¹ cāan¹ bāau¹ 叉燒餐包 (N) Western style barbecue pork buns	L.12
cāa¹ sīu¹ sōu¹ 叉燒酥 (N) barbecue pork pastries	L.12
càa⁴ cāan¹ tēng¹ 茶餐廳 (N) Hong Kong style café	L.9
càa⁴ jīp⁶ 茶葉 (N) tea leaves	L.13
cáai² dāan¹ cē¹ 踩單車 (VO) cycling	L.6
Càai⁴ Wāan¹ 柴灣 (PN) a MTR station: Chai Wan	L.14
cāan¹ tēng¹ 餐廳 (N) restaurant	L.7

cáang² 橙 (N) orange	U.1
cáang² sīk¹ 橙色 (N) orange	L.13
cáang² zāp¹ 橙汁 (N) orange juice	L.11
cáau² dáan² 炒蛋 (N) scrambled egg	L.10
cáau² fāan⁶ 炒飯 (N) fried rice	L.12
cáau² mīn⁶ 炒麵 (N) fried noodle	L.10
càm⁴ jāt⁶ 噚日 (N) yesterday	L.8
cán² só² 診所 (N) clinic	L.7
Càn⁴ 陳 (PN) a Chinese surname: Chan, Chen	L.1
Càn⁴ Síu² Pìng⁴ 陳小平 (PN) a Chinese name: Siu-Ping Chan	L.7
cāt¹ 七 (Nu) seven	U.1
Cāt¹ Héi² 七喜 (PN) 7 up	L.11
cāt¹ jǔyut⁶ 七月 (PN) July	L.8
cāt¹ zit³ 七折 (N) 30% off	L.13
cáu² 醜 (Adj) ugly	L.11
cáu² jóeng² 醜樣 (Adj) ugly	L.11
càu³ 臭 (Adj) smelly, stench	L.11
cē¹ 車 (N) a car [general term used for any wheeled vehicle]	U.1
cē¹ fòng⁴ 車房 (N) garage	L.3
Cē¹ Gūng¹ Míu² 車公廟 (PN) a MTR station: Che Kung Temple	L.14
cek³ mǎa⁵ 尺碼 (N) size	L.13
Cēng¹ Càa⁴ 青茶 (PN) Oolong tea: a semi-fermented tea (also "Wū¹ Lúng² càa⁴ 烏龍茶")	L.12
cēng¹ sīk¹ 青色 (N) yellowish green	L.13
céng² 請 (V) please (+ verb) [used to show politeness in requests or commands to mean 'be obliging enough (to)']	L.11
céng² 請 (V) invite, treat, serve or entertain someone to sth. (bear the expense of the entertainment); paying for the expenses; playing host	L.12
céng² màn⁶ 請問 (V) may I ask	L.9
céng² sīk⁶ fāan⁶ 請食飯 (VO) treat a meal	L.15
Cèoi⁴ 徐 (PN) a Chinese surname: Chui, Tsui, Zee	L.1
cèoi⁴ bín² 隨便 (Adv) do as one pleases	L.13

cèoi⁴ fóng² 廚房 (N) kitchen		L.3
cèoi⁴ sī¹ 廚師 (N) cook; chef		L.7
cēon¹ gýun² 春卷 (N) spring rolls (a popular dim-sum)		L.12
céon² 蠢 (Adj) stupid		L.11
cēot¹ 出 (V) exit; go/come out from		U.1
cēot¹ gāai¹ 出街 (VO) go out		L.10
cēot¹ háu² 出口 (N) exit		L.2
cēot¹ jăp⁶ háu² gūng¹ sī¹ 出入口公司 (N) import-export corporation		L.7
cēot¹ mĭn⁶ 出面 (N) outside		L.9
cēot¹ nín² 出年 (N) (see "cēot¹ nìn⁴")		L.8
cēot¹ nìn⁴ 出年 (N) next year		U.2; L.8
cī¹ 黐 (Adj) sticky		U.1
cī¹ sin³ 黐線 (Adj) crazy		L.11
cî³ sáu³ bán² 刺繡品 (N) embroideries		L.13
cî³ só² 廁所 (N) washroom; toilet		L.3
cì⁴ 遲 (Adj) late		U.1
cīm¹ méng² 簽名 (V) to sign		L.3
cīm¹ méng² 簽名 (N) signature		L.3
cìm⁴ séoi² 潛水 (VO) dive		L.6
cīm¹ zing³ 簽證 (N) visa		L.4
cīn¹ 千 (Nu) thousand		L.13
cín² 錢 (N) money		L.4
cìn⁴ mĭn⁶ 前面 (N) in front; ahead; the front side		L.3
cìn⁴ mún² 前門 (N) front door		L.3
cìn⁴ nín² 前年 (N) (see "cìn⁴ nìn⁴")		L.8
cìn⁴ nìn⁴ 前年 (N) the year before last		L.8
cìn⁴ jăt⁶ 前日 (N) the day before yesterday		L.8
cīng¹ có² 清楚 (Adj) clear		U.1
cīng¹ fū¹ 稱呼 (V) to address		L.15
Cīng¹ Jī¹ 青衣 (PN) a MTR station: Tsing Yi		L.14
cīng¹ nìn⁴ lěoi⁵ sě³ 青年旅舍 (N) youth hostels		L.3
cīu¹ kāp¹ sĭ⁵ còeng⁴ 超級市場 (N) supermarket		L.9
cìu⁴ zāu¹ fán² gwó² 潮洲粉果 (N) Chiu Chow style dumplings		L.12

cìu⁴ zāu¹ séoi² zīng¹ bāau¹ 潮洲水晶包 (N) Chiu Chow style sweet paste buns		L.12
cǒ³ 錯 (Adj) wrong		L.11
cǒ⁵ 坐 (V) sit		L.3
cǒ⁵ 坐 (V) ride (a mode of transportation)		L.14
cǒ⁵ cē¹ 坐車 (VO) ride a car; by car		L.14
cǒ⁵ fēi¹ gēi¹ 坐飛機 (VO) take an aeroplane; by aeroplane		L.14
cǒ⁵ fó² cē¹ 坐火車 (VO) take a train; by train		L.14
cōeng¹ tòi⁴ 窗台 (N) window-ledge		L.3
cóeng² fán² 腸粉 (N) rice noodle rolls		L.10
cóeng² zái² 腸仔 (N) sausage		L.10
cóeng³ gō¹ 唱歌 (VO) sing		L.5
cóeng³ kāa¹ lāai¹ ōu¹ kēi¹ 唱卡拉 OK (VO) karaoke		L.5
còeng⁴ 長 (Adj) long		L.11
Còeng⁴ Sāa¹ Wàan⁴ 長沙灣 (PN) a MTR station: Cheung Sha Wan		L.14
Cói² Hùng⁴ 彩虹 (PN) a MTR station: Choi Hung		L.14
cói³ 菜 (N) vegetables		U.2
cói³ páai² 菜牌 (N) menu		L.13
còng⁴ wái² 牀位 (N) bedspace apartments		L.3
còu⁴ 嘈 (Adj) noisy		L.11
cūng¹ lòeng⁴ 沖涼 (V) take a bath or shower		L.8
cūng¹ lòeng⁴ fóng² 沖涼房 (N) bathroom		L.3
cūng¹ mìng⁴ 聰明 (Adj) smart, intelligent		L.11
cùng⁴ lòi⁴ m̀⁴ 從來唔 (Adv) never		L.7
cỳu⁴ fóng² 廚房 (N) kitchen		L.3
cỳu⁴ sī¹ 廚師 (N) cook; chef		L.7
cỳun¹ sō¹ bāa¹ sí² 穿梭巴士 (N) shuttle bus		L.2
Cỳun⁴ Wāan¹ 荃灣 (PN) a MTR station: Tsuen Wan		L.14
Cỳun⁴ Wāan¹ Sin³ 荃灣綫 (PN) Tsuen Wan Line		L.14
● *D*		
dáa² bīk¹ kàu⁴ 打壁球 (VO) play squash		L.6
dáa² bīng¹ bām¹ bō¹ 打乒乓波 (VO) play table tennis		L.6

dáa² bō¹ 打波 (VO) play ball games	L.8	
dáa² (dīn⁶ wáa²) 打(電話) (V) dial	U.1	
dáa² gēi¹ 打機 (VO) play online games	L.8	
dáa² gōu¹ jǐ⁵ fū¹ kàu⁴ 打高爾夫球 (VO) play golf	L.6	
dáa² gūng¹ fū¹ 打功夫 (VO) kungfu	L.6	
dáa² jǔu⁵ mòu⁴ kàu⁴ 打羽毛球 (VO) play badminton	L.6	
dáa² làam⁴ kàu⁴ 打籃球 (VO) play basketball	L.6	
dáa² lèoi⁴ kàu⁴ 打壘球 (VO) play baseball	L.6	
dáa² màa⁴ zóek³ 打麻雀 (VO) play mahjong	L.5	
dáa² mǒng⁵ kàu⁴ 打網球 (VO) play tennis	L.6	
dáa² pàai⁴ kàu⁴ 打排球 (VO) play volleyball	L.6	
dáa² zī⁶ 打字 (VO) type	L.6	
dāai⁶ 大 (Adj) big	L.3	
Dāai⁶ Báan² Wáa² 大阪話 (PN) Osaka dialect	L.6	
Dāai⁶ Bóu⁶ Hēoi¹ 大埔墟 (PN) a MTR station: Tai Po Market	L.14	
dāai⁶ gāa¹ 大家 (Pn) all, everybody	L.5	
dāai⁶ gáam² gàa³ 大減價 (SE) a sale [products at reduced prices]	L.13	
Dāai⁶ Gún² 大館 (PN) Tai Kwun	L.14	
dāai⁶ hŏk⁶ 大學 (N) university	L.3	
Dāai⁶ Hŏk⁶ 大學 (PN) a MTR station: University	L.14	
dāai⁶ hŏk⁶ sūk¹ sé³ 大學宿舍 (N) university's hostel	L.3	
Dāai⁶ Jǔu⁴ Sāan¹ 大嶼山 (PN) Lantau Island	L.10	
dāai⁶ lūk⁶ 大陸 (N) mainland; the continent	L.2	
dāai⁶ mǎa⁵ 大碼 (N) large size	L.13	
Dāai⁶ Sān¹ Ngàn⁴ Hòng⁴ 大新銀行 (PN) Dah Sing Bank Limited	L.15	
dāai⁶ sēng¹ 大聲 (Adj) loud	U.2	
Dāai⁶ Séoi² Hāang¹ 大水坑 (PN) a MTR station: Tai Shui Hang	L.14	
Dāai⁶ Wài⁴ 大圍 (PN) a MTR station: Tai Wai	L.14	
Dāai⁶ Wō¹ Háu² 大窩口 (PN) a MTR station: Tai Wo Hau	L.14	
Dāai⁶ Wūi⁶ Tòng⁴ 大會堂 (PN) City Hall	L.14	
dāan¹ 單 (N) a bill; single	U.1	
dāan¹ cē¹ 單車 (N) bicycle	L.14	
dāan¹ jàn⁴ fóng² 單人房 (N) single room	L.3	
Dāan¹ Mǎk⁶ 丹麥 (PN) Denmark	*	
dáan² 蛋 (N) egg	L.11	
dāan⁶ tāat¹ 蛋撻 (N) (lit. egg tart) egg custard tart	L.10	
dåap³ 搭 (V) ride (a mode of transportation)	U.1	
dåap³ cē¹ 搭車 (VO) ride a car; by car	L.14	
dåap³ dēi⁶ tit³ 搭地鐵 (VO) by MTR	L.14	
dåap³ dīk¹ sí² 搭的士 take a taxi; by taxi	L.14	
dåap³ sỳun⁴ 搭船 (VO) by ferry	L.14	
dāi¹ 低 (Adj) low	L.11	
dái² 抵 (Adj) worthy	L.13	
dái² mǎai⁵ 抵買 (SE) worth buying	L.13	
dài⁴ dái² 弟弟 (N) younger brother	L.5	
dāi⁶ jāt¹ 第一 (N) first	L.15	
Dāi⁶ Jāt¹ Sìng⁴ 第一城 (PN) a MTR station: City One	L.14	
dāk¹ 得 (Adj) alright; okay; fine [used to express approval or permission]	U.1	
Dāk¹ Fū⁶ Dōu⁶ 德輔道 (PN) Des Voeux Road [a major street in Central, Hong Kong Island]	L.15	
Dāk¹ Gwǒk³ 德國 (PN) Germany	*	
dāk¹ hàan⁴ 得閒 (Adj) have free time, free (in time); not busy	L.8	
dāk¹ jì³ 得意 (Adj) cute	*	
dāk¹ m̀⁴ dāk¹ åa³? 得唔得呀? (SE) Is it okay?	L.13	
Dāk¹ Mán² 德文 (PN) (see "Dāk¹ Màn⁴")	L.6	
Dāk¹ Màn⁴ 德文 (N) German language	L.6	
dāng¹ wái² 燈位 (Ph) the place of traffic light	L.14	
dáng² 等 (V) wait; wait for	U.1	
dáng² dáng² 等等 (Ph) wait a moment	U.2	
Dāng⁶ Síu² Pìng⁴ 鄧小平 (PN) Deng Xiaoping	L.1	
dāu⁶ fū⁶ fāa¹ 豆腐花 (N) tofu pudding	L.12	
dāu⁶ zōeng¹ 豆漿 (N) soya bean milk	L.10	
dēi⁶ cáan² gūng¹ sī¹ 地產公司 (N) real estate company	L.7	
dēi⁶ háa² 地下 (N) ground floor	L.9	
dēi⁶ hāa⁶ 地下 (N) underground	L.9	

děi⁶ tit³ 地鐵 *(N) underground railway*	L.9
děi⁶ tit³ zǎam⁶ 地鐵站 *(N) MTR station*	L.9
děi⁶ tòu⁴ 地圖 *(N) map*	L.2
dẻoi³ 對 *(M)* *[a measure for a pair of objects, such as shoes, hands, chopsticks]*	U.2
dẻoi³ m̀⁴ zỹu⁶ 對唔住 *(SE) sorry; excuse me*	U.2
dẻoi³ mǐn⁶ 對面 *(N) opposite (side)*	L.9
dī¹ 啲 *(Part) a little more...* *[a structural particle used after adjectives to denote the comparative degree]*	L.13
dīk¹ sí² 的士 *(N) taxi*	L.2
dīk¹ sí² sī¹ gēi¹ 的士司機 *(Ph) taxi driver*	p.51
dīk¹ sí² zǎam⁶ 的士站 *(N) taxi stand*	L.14
Dīk⁶ Sī⁶ Nèi⁴ 迪士尼 *(PN)* *a MTR station: Disneyland Resort*	L.14
Dīk⁶ Sī⁶ Nèi⁴ Sîn³ 迪士尼綫 *(PN)* *Disneyland Resort Line*	L.14
dím² 點 *(M) (short form of "dím² zūng¹")*	U.1
dím² 點 *(QW) (short form of "dím² jóeng²")*	L.15
dím² jóeng² 點樣 *(QW) how (to do sth.)*	L.15
dím² jóeng² cīng¹ fū¹ něi⁵ åa³? 點樣稱呼你呀？*(Q) How may I address you?*	L.15
dím² jóeng² hẻoi³ åa³? 點樣去呀？*(SE) How to get there?*	L.15
dím² sām¹ 點心 *(N) dim-sum*	L.12
dím² sām¹ zí² 點心紙 *(N) dim-sum menu*	L.12
dím² zūng¹ 點鐘 *(M) o'clock*	U.1
dīn⁶ cē¹ 電車 *(N) tram*	L.14
dīn⁶ cē¹ zǎam⁶ 電車站 *(N) tram station*	L.14
dīn⁶ dāan¹ cē¹ 電單車 *(N) motor bike*	L.14
dīn⁶ nǒu⁵ gūng¹ sī¹ 電腦公司 *(N)* *computer firm*	L.7
dīn⁶ tāi¹ 電梯 *(N) escalator; elevator*	L.3
dīn⁶ wáa² 電話 *(N) telephone*	L.2
dīn⁶ wáa² hòu⁶ mǎa⁵ 電話號碼 *(N)* *telephone number*	L.3
dīn⁶ zí² gūng¹ cìng⁴ 電子工程 *(N)* *electronic engineering*	L.5
dīng⁶ 定 *(Conj) or (see "dīng⁶ hǎi⁶")*	L.11
dīng⁶ hǎi⁶ 定係 *(Conj) or* *[only used in a question indicating options]*	L.11

díp² 碟 *(N) a plate*	U.1
dǐp⁶ 碟 *(M) a plate of*	L.11
dō¹ 多 *(Adj) a lot; many; much*	U.1
dō¹ sí² 多士 *(N) toast*	L.10
dō¹ zě⁶ 多謝 *(SE) thank you, many thanks* *[express one's gratitude]*	L.5
dō¹ zě⁶ sīn¹ 多謝先 *(SE) thank you in advance*	L.12
dōu¹ 都 *(Adv) also; too*	L.7
dōu¹ 都 *(Adv) all; all-inclusive [no exception]*	L.8
dóu² còeng⁴ 賭場 *(N) casino*	L.9
dỏu³ 到 *(Prep) until; to*	L.8
dǒu⁶ gåa³ ūk¹ 度假屋 *(N) holiday flats*	L.3
dǔk⁶ 讀 *(V) go to school; study*	L.5
dǔk⁶ dǎai⁶ hŏk⁶ 讀大學 *(VO) go to university*	L.8
dǔk⁶ sȳu¹ 讀書 *(VO)* *study in school; study; read books*	L.5
dūng¹ 東 *(N) east*	L.15
Dūng¹ Aå³ Ngàn⁴ Hòng⁴ 東亞銀行 *(PN)* *The Bank of East Asia*	L.15
Dūng¹ Cūng¹ 東涌 *(PN)* *a MTR station: Tung Chung*	L.14
Dūng¹ Cūng¹ Sîn³ 東涌綫 *(PN)* *Tung Chung Line*	L.14
Dūng¹ Tit³ Sîn³ 東鐵綫 *(N) East Rail Line*	L.14
Dúng² Gin³ Wàa⁴ 董建華 *(PN)* *Tung Chee-Hwa, the first Chief Executive of HKSAR*	L.1
dǔng³ 凍 *(Adj) cold; iced*	U.1
dýun² 短 *(Adj) short (in length)*	L.11
● *E*	
ēi¹ ēi¹ zåi³ AA 制 *(SE) go Dutch*	L.12
● *F*	
fāa¹ 花 *(N) flower*	U.1
fāa¹ càa⁴ 花茶 *(N)* *scented tea: a mixture of tea leaves and fragrant flowers*	L.12
Fāa¹ Kèi⁴ Ngàn⁴ Hòng⁴ (Hōeng¹ Góng²) 花旗銀行（香港）*(PN)* *Citibank (Hong Kong) Limited*	L.15
fåa³ hŏk⁶ 化學 *(N) chemistry*	L.5
fåai³ 快 *(Adj) fast; quick*	U.1

fåai³ cāan¹ dim³ 快餐店 (N) fast food shop	L.2
fāan¹ 返 (V) return; go/come back	L.9
fāan¹ gūng¹ 返工 (VO) go to work; go on duty	L.8
fāan¹ hŏk⁶ 返學 (VO) go to school; attend school	L.6
fāan¹ jĭk⁶ 翻譯 (N) translation	L.5
fāan¹ jĭk⁶ 翻譯 (V) translate	L.5
fāan¹ ūk¹ kéi² 返屋企 (VO) go/come home	L.12
fāan⁶ 飯 (N) cooked rice	L.12
fāan⁶ tēng¹ 飯廳 (N) dining room	L.3
Fåat³ Gwŏk³ 法國 (PN) France	L.5
Fåat³ jĕoi⁶ Gāa¹ Nàa⁴ Dāai⁶ jàn⁴ 法裔加拿大人 (Ph) Canadian of French descent	L.5
Fåat³ Mán² 法文 (PN) (see "Fåat³ Màn⁴")	L.6
Fåat³ Màn⁴ 法文 (PN) French language	L.6
Fåat³ zĭk⁶ Tóu² Jĭ⁵ Kèi⁴ jàn⁴ 法籍土耳其人 (Ph) French Turk	L.5
fān¹ 分 (M) minute	U.2
Fān¹ Làan⁴ 芬蘭 (PN) Finland	*
fān¹ zūng¹ 分鐘 (Suff) minute(s) (of time duration)	L.15
fán² 粉 (N) rice noodles	L.10
Fán² Lĕng⁵ 粉嶺 (PN) a MTR station: Fanling	L.14
fán³ 瞓 (V) sleep	L.15
fán³ gåau³ 瞓覺 (VO) sleep	L.8
fān⁶ 份 (M) [a measure for objects in a set, such as documents, newspapers; a sandwich or a job]	U.2
fē¹ sīk¹ 啡色 (N) brown	L.13
fēi¹ gēi¹ 飛機 (N) airplane	L.14
Fēi¹ jĕoi⁶ Mĕi⁵ Gwŏk³ jàn⁴ 非裔美國人 (Ph) American of African descent	L.5
Fēi¹ Lĕot⁶ Bān¹ 菲律賓 (PN) Philippines	L.5
Fēi¹ Lĕot⁶ Bān¹ Wáa² 菲律賓話 (PN) Filipino language	L.6
fēi¹ Wàa⁴ jĕoi⁶ 非華裔 (Ph) Non-Chinese descent	*
Fēi¹ Zāu¹ 非洲 (PN) Africa	L.2
fèi⁴ 肥 (Adj) fat	L.11

fī¹ sāai¹ sí² Free 晒士 (Ph) free size	L.13
fó² cē¹ 火車 (N) train	L.14
fó² cē¹ zāam⁶ 火車站 (N) railway station	L.14
Fó² Tǎn³ 火炭 (PN) a MTR station: Fo Tan	L.14
fó² téoi² 火腿 (N) ham	L.10
fó² téoi² tūng¹ fán² 火腿通粉 (Ph) macaroni in soup with ham	L.10
fò³ cìng⁴ 課程 (N) course	L.1
fōng¹ bĭn⁶ 方便 (Adj) convenient	L.11
fóng² 房 (N) room	L.3
fŏng³ gūng¹ 放工 (VO) finish work at the end of the day; off duty	L.12 (L.8)
fŭ³ 褲 (N) trousers	U.1
fŭ⁶ găn⁶ 附近 (N) vicinity; nearby	L.9
fŭ⁶ mŏu⁵ 父母 (N) parents	L.11
fūi¹ sīk¹ 灰色 (N) grey	L.13
fūn¹ héi² 歡喜 (Adj) happy	U.1
fūn¹ jìng⁴ 歡迎 (V) to welcome	L.1
fūn¹ jìng⁴ gwōng¹ làm⁴ 歡迎光臨 (SE) welcome for coming	L.1
fūng⁶ záau² 鳳爪 (N) steamed chicken feet	L.12
fŭt³ 闊 (Adj) wide	U.1
● G	
gāa¹ 加 (V) add	L.11
gāa¹ dāai⁶ măa⁵ 加大碼 (Ph) extra-large size	L.13
Gāa¹ Jỳun⁴ 加元 (PN) Canadian Dollars	L.4
Gāa¹ Nàa⁴ Dāai⁶ 加拿大 (PN) Canada	L.5
gāa¹ săi³ măa⁵ 加細碼 (Ph) extra-small size	L.13
gåa³ 架 (M) [a measure word for vehicles; machines; e.g. cars, airplanes]	U.2
gåa³ 㗎 (Part) [an interrogative particle used to ask something that happened in the past or to require an answer straight away]	L.6
gåa³ fē¹ 咖啡 (N) coffee	L.11
gåa³ fē¹ sīk¹ 咖啡色 (N) brown	L.13
gāa¹ tìng⁴ zýu² fŭ⁵ 家庭主婦 (N) housewife	L.7
gāai¹ 街 (N) street	L.15

Term	Ref
gāai¹ háu² 街口 *(N)* *street intersection; street junction*	L.14
gāai¹ sǐ⁵ 街市 *(N) market*	L.9
gåak³ lèi⁴ 隔離 *(N) beside; next to*	L.9
gāan¹ 間 *(M)* *[a measure for buildings; houses and rooms]*	L.9
Gáan² Pòu⁴ Zāai⁶ 柬埔寨 *(PN) Cambodia*	*
gåan³ zūng¹ 間中 *(Adv) occasionally*	L.7
gāau¹ gūng¹ fǒ³ 交功課 *(VO) submit homework*	L.12
Gāau¹ Jǐk⁶ Gwóng² Còeng⁴ 交易廣場 *(PN)* *Exchange Square*	L.14
Gāau¹ Tūng¹ Ngàn⁴ Hòng⁴ 交通銀行 *(PN)* *Bank of Communications*	L.15
gāau¹ wǔn⁶ 交換 *(V) exchange*	L.5
gåau³ 教 *(V) teach*	L.7
gåau³ jǔk⁶ 教育 *(N) education*	L.5
gåau³ lǐn⁶ 教練 *(N) coach; instructor*	L.7
gåau³ sǎu⁶ 教授 *(N) professor*	L.7
gāi¹ dáan² 雞蛋 *(N) egg*	L.11
gāi¹ měi⁵ bāau¹ 雞尾包 *(N) cocktail bun*	L.10
gām¹ cìn⁴ tǒu⁵ 金錢肚 *(N) stewed beef tripe*	L.12
gām¹ gǒ³ sīng¹ kèi⁴ 今個星期 *(N) this week*	L.8
gām¹ gǒ³ jŷut⁶ 今個月 *(N) this month*	L.8
gām¹ jǎt⁶ 今日 *(N) today*	L.8
gām¹ jùng⁴ gūng¹ sī¹ 金融公司 *(N)* *finance corporation*	L.7
gām¹ mǎan⁵ 今晚 *(N) tonight*	L.8
gām¹ nín² 今年 *(N) (see "gām¹ nìn⁴")*	L.8
gām¹ nìn⁴ 今年 *(N) this year*	L.5
gām¹ sīk¹ 金色 *(N) gold colour*	L.13
gām¹ sīk¹ 金飾 *(N) gold jewellery*	L.13
Gām¹ Zūng¹ 金鐘 *(PN) a MTR station: Admiralty*	L.2
gám² 噉 *(Intj) so, well...* *(occurs preceding sentence and serves to fill a pause or transition)*	L.1
Gám² Sōeng⁶ Lōu⁶ 錦上路 *(PN)* *a MTR station: Kam Sheung Road*	L.14
gåm³ kēoi¹ 禁區 *(N) restricted area*	L.14
gān¹ 跟 *(V) follow*	U.2
gān¹ zŷu⁶ 跟住 *(Conj) afterwards; then*	L.15
gán² 緊 *(Part)* *[an aspectual particle used after a verb indicating an action in progress]*	L.8
gán² zōeng¹ 緊張 *(Adj) nervous*	L.11
gáu² 狗 *(N) a dog*	U.1
gáu² 九 *(Nu) nine*	U.1
gáu² gáu² gáu² 九九九 *(Nu)* *(telephone no. for police; emergency call)*	U.2
gáu² jŷut⁶ 九月 *(PN) September*	L.8
Gáu² Lùng⁴ 九龍 *(PN) Kowloon*	L.2
Gáu² Lùng⁴ Tòng⁴ 九龍塘 *(PN)* *a MTR station: Kowloon Tong*	L.14
Gáu² Lùng⁴ Wāan¹ 九龍灣 *(PN)* *a MTR station: Kowloon Bay*	L.14
Gáu² Lùng⁴ Záu² Dim 九龍酒店 *(PN)* *Kowloon Hotel*	L.2
gáu² zǐt³ 九折 *(N) discount of 10 percent* *[9/10ᵗʰ of the original price]*	L.13
gåu³ měng⁶ åa³ 救命呀 *(SE) help!!*	U.2
gāu⁶ 舊 *(Adj) old (not new)*	L.3
gāu⁶ nín² 舊年 *(N) (see "gāu⁶ nìn⁴")*	L.8
gāu⁶ nìn⁴ 舊年 *(N) last year*	L.8
gě³ 嘅 *(Part)* *[a structural particle used to indicate possession, similar to 's in English]*	L.1
gě³ 嘅 *(Part)* *[a modal particle used at the end of a sentence to answer a question ending with "gåa³" or to give an explanation]*	L.6
gēi¹ còeng⁴ 機場 *(N) airport*	L.2
gēi¹ còeng⁴ bāa¹ sí² 機場巴士 *(N)* *airport bus*	L.2
gēi¹ còeng⁴ fåai³ sìn³ 機場快線 *(PN)* *Airport Express*	L.2
géi² 幾 *(Adv) quite; fairly*	L.8
géi² cín² 幾錢 *(QW)* *(short form of "géi² dō¹ cín²")*	L.4
géi² dím² 幾點 *(QW)* *(short form of "géi² dím² zūng¹")*	U.2; L.6
géi² dím² zūng¹ 幾點鐘 *(QW) what time*	U.2; L.6
géi² dō¹ 幾多 *(QW) what; how many; how much*	L.3

géi² dō¹ cín² 幾多錢 (QW) how much (money)	L.4
géi² dō¹ hŏu⁶ 幾多號 (QW) what number	L..3
géi² dō¹ sèoi³ 幾多歲 (QW) how many years old; how old	L.4
géi² dō¹ jàn⁴ 幾多人 (QW) how many people	L.4
géi² hóu² 幾好 (Ph) quite good	U.2
géi² nŏi⁶ 幾耐 (QW) how long	L.15
géi² sì⁴ 幾時 (QW) when; at what time	L.8
géng² hòt³ 頸渴 (Adj) thirsty	L.11
géoi² cŭng⁵ 舉重 (VO) weight lifting	L.6
Gīn¹ Nèi⁴ Dĕi⁶ Sìng⁴ 堅尼地城 (PN) a MTR station: Kennedy Town	L.14
gin³ 見 (V) meet; see	U.1
gin³ dóu² 見到 (Ph) see [indicating achieving a desired result through an action]	L.15
gin³ zūk¹ gūng¹ sī¹ 建築公司 (N) architecture/construction company	L.7
gin³ zūk¹ hŏk⁶ 建築學 (N) architecture	L.5
gìn⁶ 件 (M) [a measure word for items of clothing usually on top, such as shirt, coat, etc.]	U.2
gīng¹ 經 (V) via; to pass by; to pass through	L.14
gīng¹ lĕi⁵ 經理 (N) manager	L.7
gīng¹ sòeng⁴ 經常 (Adv) always; often	L.7
gīng¹ zài³ 經濟 (N) economics	L.5
gíng² càat³ 警察 (N) police	L.7
gíng² gúk² 警局 (N) police station	L.9
git³ fān¹ 結婚 (VO) get married	L.12
giu³ 叫 (V) to be called; named; known as; to call	L.1
giu³ zŏu⁶ 叫做 (V) to be called; named; known as	L.10
Gō¹ Lèon⁴ Béi² Aå³ 哥倫比亞 (PN) Colombia	*
gō¹ sáu² 歌手 (N) singer	L.7
gó² dī¹ 嗰啲 (Pn) that; those	L.10
gó² dòu⁶ 嗰度 (Pn) there; over there	L.2
gó² wái² 嗰個 (Pn) that person	L.10
gŏ³ 個 (M) [a measure word for people; round objects or abstract things, such as questions or ideas]	U.2

gŏ³ jŷut⁶ 個月 (Suff) month(s) [of time duration]	L.15
gŏ³ sīng¹ kèi⁴ 個星期 (Suff) week(s) [of time duration]	L.15
gŏ³ zūng¹ tàu⁴ 個鐘頭 (Suff) hour(s) [of time duration]	L.15
gŏ⁴ gō¹ 哥哥 (N) elder brother	L.5
gòek³ 腳 (N) a leg; foot	U.1
gŏk³ dāk¹ 覺得 (V) to think; to feel	L.10
gōn¹ 乾 (Adj) dry	U.1
góng² 港 (N) harbour	U.1
góng² 講 (V) speak; talk	L.7
Góng² Bāi⁶ 港幣 (PN) Hong Kong dollars; Hong Kong currency	L.4
Góng² Dāai⁶ 港大 (PN) (short form of "Hōeng¹ Góng² Dāai⁶ Hŏk⁶")	L.1
Góng² Dóu² Sin³ 港島綫 (PN) Island Line	L.14
Góng² Jyun⁴ 港元 (N) Hong Kong dollars; Hong Kong currency	L. 4
Góng² sīk¹ 港式 (N) short form of "Hōeng¹ Góng² sīk¹")	L.10
Góng² Tit¹ 港鐵 (PN) MTR [Mass Transit Railway Corporation Limited]	L.14
gōu¹ 高 (Adj) tall; high	L.11
gú² dín² jām¹ ngŏk⁶ 古典音樂 (N) classical music	L.5
gŭi⁶ 攰 (Adj) tired	U.1
Gūk¹ Bóu² 菊普 (PN) Pu'er tea with chrysanthemum	L.12
gūk¹ lēoi⁶ zóu² cāan¹ 穀類早餐 (N) breakfast cereal	L.10
gūk⁶ 焗 (V) baked	L.12
Gūn¹ Tòng⁴ 觀塘 (PN) a MTR station: Kwun Tong	L.14
Gūn¹ Tòng⁴ Sin³ 觀塘綫 (PN) Kwun Tong Line	L.14
gŭn³ 罐 (M) a can of [a measure for the quantity of something that a can will hold]	U.2
gŭn³ tōng¹ gáau² 灌湯餃 (N) soup dumplings	L.12
gūng¹ cóng² 工廠 (N) factory	L.7
gūng¹ jàn⁴ 工人 (N) worker; servant; amah; maid; domestic helper	L.7

gūng¹ jỳun² 公園 (N) park	L.9
gūng¹ mõu⁶ jỳun⁴ 公務員 (N) civil servant	L.7
gūng¹ sōeng¹ gún² lẻi⁵ 工商管理 (N) business managment	L.5
gūng¹ sī¹ 公司 (N) company; corporation; firm	L.7
gūng¹ zòk³ 工作 (N) work; occupations	L.7
gwāai¹ 乖 (Adj) good; obedient	L.11
gwải³ 貴 (Adj) expensive	U.1
gwāi⁶ jỳun⁴ gēi¹ 櫃員機 (N) teller machine	L.9
gwán² séoi² 滾水 (Ph) boiling water	L.12
gwỏ³ zóeng² 過獎 (SE) you flatter me	L.8
gwòk³ gāa¹ 國家 (N) country	L.2
gwòk³ zải³ 國際 (N) international	L.2
Gwōk³ Zải³ Gām¹ Jùng⁴ Zūng¹ Sām¹ 國際金融中心 (PN) IFC [International Finance Centre]	L.14
gwóng² còeng⁴ 廣場 (N) square; plaza	L.14
Gwóng² Dūng¹ jàn⁴ 廣東人 (N) Cantonese people	L.7
Gwóng² Dūng¹ Sáang² 廣東省 (PN) Guangdong Province; Canton	U.1
Gwóng² Dūng¹ Wáa² 廣東話 (PN) Guangdong speech; Cantonese dialect (as opposed to other Chinese dialects)	U.1; L.6
Gwóng² Sāi¹ Sáang² 廣西省 (PN) Guangxi Province	U.1
Gwóng² Zāu¹ 廣州 (PN) Guangzhou City; Canton	U.1
Gwóng² Zāu¹ Wáa² 廣州話 (PN) Guangzhou speech; Guangzhou dialect (as opposed to other dialects spoken in Guangdong Province)	U.1; L.6
● *H*	
hāa¹ gáau² 蝦餃 (N) shrimp dumpling	L.12
hāa¹ gòk³ 蝦角 (N) deep fried shrimp dumplings served with salad dressing	L.12
hāa¹ lóu² 哈佬 (Intj) hello	U.2
hāa⁶ cỉ³ 下次 (N) next time	U.2
hāa⁶ gỏ³ jỳut⁶ 下個月 (N) next month	L.8
hāa⁶ gỏ³ sīng¹ kèi⁴ 下個星期 (N) next week	L.8

hāa⁶ jāt¹ gỏ³ 下一個 (Ph) next one	U.2
hāa⁶ mĩn⁶ 下面 (N) below; under	L.9
hāa⁶ ng̉⁵ 下午 (N) P.M.	U.2
hāa⁶ zảu³ 下晝 (N) P.M.	U.2
hàai⁴ 鞋 (N) shoes	U.1
håak³ tēng¹ 客廳 (N) living room	L.3
hàam⁴ séoi² gòk³ 咸水角 (N) sticky rice dumplings with meat	L.12
Hāang¹ Háu² 坑口 (PN) a MTR station: Hang Hau	L.14
hàang⁴ 行 (V) walk	L.15
hàang⁴ gāai¹ 行街 (VO) shopping; walking around	L.5
hàang⁴ làa³ 行喇 (SE) let's go	L.12
hàang⁴ lòu⁶ 行路 (VO) (lit walk road) walk; on foot	L.14
hàang⁴ sāan¹ 行山 (VO) hike	L.5
hái² 喺 (V) be at/in/on (a place)	L.2
hái² 喺 (Prep) at; in; on (a place)	L.3
hái² dòu⁶ sìk⁶ 喺度食 (Ph) eat here	L.11
hãi⁶ 係 (V) be [is, am, are; was, were]	L.1
hãi⁶ m̀⁴ hãi⁶ 係唔係 (Ph) Is it true?	L.6
hãi⁶ nē¹ 係呢 (Intj) by the way	L.6
Hāk¹ Càa⁴ 黑茶 (PN) Black tea: post-fermented and oxidized tea	L.12
hāk¹ sīk¹ 黑色 (N) black colour	L.13
hàm⁴ bãang⁶ lãang⁶ 冚唪唥 (Pn) all; whole	L.11
Hàng⁴ Ōn¹ 恒安 (PN) a MTR station: Heng On	L.14
Hàng⁴ Sāang¹ Ngàn⁴ Hòng⁴ 恒生銀行 (PN) Hang Seng Bank	L.15
Hãng⁶ Fāa¹ Cȳun¹ 杏花邨 (PN) a MTR station: Heng Fa Chuen	L.14
hãng⁶ jàn⁴ lòu⁶ 杏仁露 (N) sweet ground almond soup	L.12
hãng⁶ jàn⁴ sōeng¹ 杏仁霜 (N) almond drink	L.11
hãp⁶ tòu⁴ lòu⁶ 合桃露 (N) sweet ground walnut soup	L.12
hãu⁶ jāt⁶ 後日 (N) the day after tomorrow	L.8
hãu⁶ mĩn⁶ 後面 (N) at the back	L.9
hãu⁶ mún² 後門 (N) back door	L.3

hāu⁶ nín² 後年 (N) (see "hāu⁶ nìn⁴")	L.8
hāu⁶ nìn⁴ 後年 (N) the year after next	L.8
hāu⁶ sāang¹ 後生 (Adj) young	L.11
Hēi¹ Lāap⁶ 希臘 (PN) Greece	*
héi² sān¹ 起身 (VO) get up	L.8
hẻi³ jýun² 戲院 (N) cinema	L.9
hẻi³ séoi² 汽水 (N) soft drinks	L.11
hẻoi³ 去 (V) go	L.2
hẻoi³ gāai¹ 去街 (VO) go out	L.12
Hín² Gỉng³ 顯徑 (PN) a MTR station: Hin Keng	L.14
hīng¹ dãi⁶ 兄弟 (N) brothers	L.11
hīng¹ dãi⁶ zí² mūi⁶ 兄弟姊妹 (Ph) brothers and sisters; siblings	L.5
hīng¹ tỉt³ 輕鐵 (N) light rail	L.14
hỉng³ cẻoi³ 興趣 (N) a hobby; an interest	L.5
hó² lõk⁶ 可樂 (N) coke	L.11
hó² ỏi³ 可愛 (Adj) cute	*
Hò⁴ 何 (PN) a Chinese surname: Ho	L.1
Hò⁴ Lāan¹ 荷蘭 (PN) Holland; The Netherlands	*
Hò⁴ Màn⁴ Tìn⁴ 何文田 (PN) a MTR station: Ho Man Tin	L.14
hōe¹ 靴 (N) boot	U.1
hōeng¹ 香 (Adj) fragrant	U.1
hōeng¹ cóeng² 香腸 (N) sausage	L.10
Hōeng¹ Góng² 香港 (PN) Hong Kong	L.5
Hōeng¹ Góng² Dãai⁶ Hõk⁶ 香港大學 (PN) The University of Hong Kong	L.1
Hōeng¹ Góng² Dãai⁶ Hõk⁶ 香港大學 (PN) a MTR station: HKU	L.14
Hōeng¹ Góng² Dãk⁶ Bĩt⁶ Hàng⁴ Zỉng³ Kēoi¹ 香港特別行政區 (PN) Special Administrative Region of Hong Kong	U.1
Hōeng¹ Góng² Dóu² 香港島 (PN) Hong Kong Island	L.2
Hōeng¹ Góng² Fō¹ Gẽi⁶ Dãai⁶ Hõk⁶ 香港科技大學 (PN) The Hong Kong University of Science and Technology	*
Hōeng¹ Góng² Gảau³ Jũk⁶ Dãai⁶ Hõk⁶ 香港教育大學 (PN) The Education University of Hong Kong	*
Hōeng¹ Góng² Lẻi⁵ Gūng¹ Dãai⁶ Hõk⁶ 香港理工大學 (PN) The Hong Kong Polytechnic University	*
Hōeng¹ Góng² jàn⁴ 香港人 (N) Hong Kong people; Hong Kong citizen	L.6
Hōeng¹ Góng² Lẻi⁵ Bān¹ Fú² 香港禮賓府 (PN) Government House	L.14
Hōeng¹ Góng² sān¹ fán² zỉng³ 香港身份證 (N) HKID card	L.4
Hōeng¹ Góng² sīk¹ 香港式 (N) Hong Kong style	L.10
Hōeng¹ Góng² Sìng⁴ Sỉ⁵ Dãai⁶ Hõk⁶ 香港城市大學 (PN) City University of Hong Kong	*
Hōeng¹ Góng² Sỹu⁶ Jàn⁴ Dãai⁶ Hõk⁶ 香港樹仁大學 (PN) Hong Kong Shue Yan University	*
Hōeng¹ Góng² Tỉt³ Lõu⁶ Gūng¹ Sī¹ 香港鐵路有限公司 (PN) MTR Corporation Limited	L.14
Hōeng¹ Góng² Wáa² 香港話 (PN) Hong Kong speech; Hong Kong vernacular	U.1
Hōeng¹ Góng² Zãam⁶ 香港站 (PN) Hong Kong Station	L.14
Hōeng¹ Góng² Zảm³ Wúi² Dãai⁶ Hõk⁶ 香港浸會大學 (PN) Hong Kong Baptist University	*
Hōeng¹ Góng² Záu² Dim³ 香港酒店 (PN) Hong Kong Hotel	L.2
Hōeng¹ Góng² Zūng¹ Màn⁴ Dãai³ Hõk⁶ 香港中文大學 (PN) The Chinese University of Hong Kong	*
Hōeng¹ Pín² 香片 (PN) Jasmine tea: the most popular scented green tea	L.12
hōeng¹ zīu¹ 香蕉 (N) banana	U.1
hỏeng³ 向 (Prep) toward; face to	L.15
hōi¹ sām¹ 開心 (Adj) happy	L.11
hōi¹ wúi² 開會 (VO) to attend a meeting	L.6
Hói² Jì⁴ Bủn³ Dóu² 海怡半島 (PN) a MTR station: South Horizons	L.14

Hói² Jòeng⁴ Gūng¹ Jýun² 海洋公園 *(PN)* *a MTR station: Ocean Park*	L.14
hói² sīn¹ gýun² 海鮮卷 *(N) seafood rolls*	L.12
hŏk⁶ 學 *(V) learn; study*	L.7
hŏk⁶ hāau⁶ 學校 *(N) school*	L.1
hŏk⁶ jýun² 學院 *(N) college; faculty*	L.7
hŏk⁶ sāang¹ 學生 *(N) student*	L.1
hŏk⁶ sāang¹ sūk¹ sẻ³ 學生宿舍 *(N)* *student hostel*	L.13
Hòn⁴ Gwŏk³ 韓國 *(PN) Korea*	*
Hòn⁴ Gwŏk³ Wáa² 韓國話 *(PN)* *Korean speech*	L.6
Hòn⁴ jēoi⁶ 韓裔 *(N) Korean descent*	L.5
Hòn⁴ Mán² 韓文 *(N) (see "Hòn⁴ Màn⁴")*	L.6
Hòn⁴ Màn⁴ 韓文 *(N) Korean language*	L.6
Hōng¹ Sìng⁴ 康城 *(PN)* *a MTR station: LOHAS Park*	L.14
hòng⁴ hūng¹ gūng¹ sī¹ 航空公司 *(N)* *airline company*	L.7
hóu² 好 *(Adj) good; well; fine; okay*	U.1; L.3
hóu² 好 *(Adv) very*	L.3
hóu² åak³ 好呃 *(SE) fine, okay*	L.3
hóu² dō¹ 好多 *(Nu) a lot; many; much*	L.13
hóu² hóu² 好好 *(Ph) very good*	U.2
hóu² hóu² sīk⁶ 好好食 *(Ph)* *delicious; very tasty*	L.10
hóu² jám² 好飲 *(Adj)* *good to drink; tasty (for drinks)*	L.11
hóu² jàn⁴ 好人 *(Adj) kind; nice person*	L.11
hóu² lāa¹ 好啦 *(SE) okay; fine* *[used to express agreement]*	L.13
Hóu² Lāap⁶ Hāk¹ 好立克 *(PN) Horlicks*	L.11
hóu² m̀⁴ hóu² åa³? 好唔好呀？ *(SE)* *Is that good? Is it okay?* *[attached at the end of a suggestion or request]*	L.12
hóu² mèi⁶ 好味 *(Adj) tasty*	L.10
hóu² nŏi⁶ 好耐 *(N) long time*	L.15
hóu² sīk⁶ 好食 *(Adj) good to eat; tasty*	L.10
hóu² síu² 好少 *(Adv) rarely; seldom*	L.7

hóu² wáan² 好玩 *(Adj) fun, interesting*	L.11
hŏu⁶ 號 *(M) number [used after a number]*	L.3
hŏu⁶ 號 *(N)* *days of the month (1ˢᵗ day to 31ˢᵗ day)*	L.8
hŏt³ 渴 *(Adj) thirsty*	U.1
Hūng¹ Ngàa⁴ Lĕi⁶ 匈牙利 *(PN) Hungary*	*
hùng⁴ càa⁴ 紅茶 *(N)* *black tea: a fully-fermented tea and its infusion has a bright reddish colour*	L.12
hùng⁴ dáu² sāa¹ 紅豆沙 *(N)* *sweet red bean soup*	L.12
Hùng⁴ Hàm³ 紅磡 *(PN) Hung Hom* *[a major district in Kowloon]*	L.2
Hùng⁴ Hàm³ 紅磡 *(PN)* *a MTR station: Hung Hom*	L.14
hùng⁴ sīk¹ 紅色 *(N) red colour*	L.13
● **J**	
jáai² dāan¹ cē¹ 踩單車 *(VO)* *(see "cáai² dāan¹ cē¹")*	L.6
jǎi⁵ 曳 *(Adj) naughty*	L.11
jām¹ ngŏk⁶ 音樂 *(N) music*	L.5
jám² 飲 *(V) drink*	L.11
jám² càa⁴ 飲茶 *(VO) have some tea*	L.3
jám² càa⁴ 飲茶 *(VO) (lit. to drink tea)* *to go to restaurant for dim-sum; yum-cha*	L.8; L.12
jám² jě⁵ 飲嘢 *(VO) have a drink*	L.12
jám² záu² 飲酒 *(VO) have a alcohol drink*	L.12
Jān¹ Oů³ 欣澳 *(PN) a MTR station: Sunny Bay*	L.14
Jản³ Dĕi⁶ Wáa² 印地話 *(PN) Hindi*	*
Jản³ Dŏu⁶ 印度 *(PN) India*	*
Jản³ Nèi⁴ 印尼 *(PN) Indonesia*	*
Jản³ Nèi⁴ Wáa² 印尼話 *(PN)* *Indonesian language*	*
jàn⁴ 人 *(N) people; person*	L.5
Jàn⁴ Màn⁴ Bāi⁶ 人民幣 *(PN)* *Chinese Yuan; Renminbi*	L.4
jăp⁶ háu² 入口 *(N) entrance*	L.2
jăp⁶ hěoi³ 入去 *(Ph) enter; go inside*	L.15
jăp⁶ lèi⁴ 入嚟 *(Ph) come in*	L.3
jăp⁶ mĭn⁶ 入面 *(N) inside; in*	L.9

jāt¹ 一 *(Nu) one*	U.1
jāt¹ båak³ mān¹ 一百蚊 *(Ph)* one hundred dollars	L.4
jāt¹ cài⁴ 一齊 *(Adv) together*	L.7
jāt¹ ci̊³ 一次 *(Nu) once*	U.2
jāt¹ cīn¹ mān¹ 一千蚊 *(Ph)* one thousand dollars	L.4
jāt¹ dī̊¹ 一啲 *(Nu) some* (can be shortened as "dī̊¹")	L.4
jāt¹ go̊³ zūng¹ tàu⁴ 一個鐘頭 *(Ph) one hour*	L.15
jāt¹ go̊³ mǎa⁵ 一個碼 *(Ph) free size*	L.13
jāt¹ gūng⁶ 一共 *(Adv) total, altogether*	L.11
jāt¹ hòu⁴ 一毫 *(Ph) ten cents*	L.4
jāt¹ jẙut⁶ 一月 *(PN) January*	L.8
jāt¹ mān¹ 一蚊 *(Ph) one dollar*	L.4
jāt¹ zån⁶ 一陣 *(N) a little while*	L.11
jāt¹ zån⁶ gi̊n³ 一陣見 *(SE) see you later*	U.2
jāt⁶ 日 *(N) day; sun*	U.2
Jāt⁶ Bún² 日本 *(PN) Japan*	L.5
Jāt⁶ Bún² Wáa² 日本話 *(PN) Japanese speech*	L.6
Jāt⁶ Jỳun⁴ 日元 *(PN) Japanese Yen*	L.4
Jāt⁶ Mán² 日文 *(PN) (see "Jāt⁶ Màn⁴")*	L.6
Jāt⁶ Màn⁴ 日文 *(PN) Japanese language*	L.6
Jāt⁶ zi̊k⁶ 日籍 *(N) Japanese nationality*	L.5
jàu⁴ 由 *(Prep) from (a starting point)*	L.6
jàu⁴ gúk² 郵局 *(N) post office*	L.9
Jàu⁴ Màa⁴ Déi² 油麻地 *(PN)* a MTR station: Yau Ma Tei	L.2
jàu⁴ séoi² 游水 *(VO) swim*	L.6
Jàu⁴ Tòng⁴ 油塘 *(PN)* a MTR station: Yau Tong	L.14
jàu⁴ tíu² 油條 *(N) deep-fried breadstick*	L.10
jàu⁴ zåa³ gwái² 油炸鬼 *(N)* deep-fried breadstick	L.10
jàu⁴ zīm¹ dō̊¹ 油占多 *(N)* butter and jam on toast	L.10
jǎu⁵ 有 *(V) have; possess*	L.4
jǎu⁵ lŏk⁶ 有落 *(SE)* stop to get off (the vehicle); I want to get off	L.14
jǎu⁵ mǒu⁵ ...åa³? 有冇...呀？*(QW)* Have you got...? Do you have...?	L.4
jǎu⁵ sām¹ 有心 *(SE) thanks for asking*	U.2
jǎu⁵ si̊⁴ 有時 *(Adv) sometimes*	L.7
jǎu⁵ sī̊⁶ 有事 *(Ph) be occupied (with a matter); have something to do*	L.6
jǎu⁶ 右 *(N) the right side; the right-hand side*	L.15
jǎu⁶ mǐn⁶ 右面 *(N) the right side*	L.9
jě⁶ mǎan⁵ 夜晚 *(N) in the evening; night*	U.2
jī̊¹ hŏk⁶ 醫學 *(N) medicine*	L.5
jī̊¹ jýun² 醫院 *(N) hospital*	L.7
Jī̊¹ Lāai¹ Hāk¹ 伊拉克 *(PN) Iraq*	*
Jī̊¹ Lŏng⁵ 伊朗 *(PN) Iran*	*
jī̊¹ sāng¹ 醫生 *(N) medical doctor*	L.7
Ji̊³ Dāai⁶ Lěi⁶ 意大利 *(PN) Italy*	L.5
ji̊⁴ gāa¹ 而家 *(N) now*	L.2
ji̊⁴ màn⁴ gúk² 移民局 *(PN)* Immigration Depatment	*
Jǐ⁵ Sīk¹ Lī̊t⁶ 以色列 *(PN) Israel*	*
jī̊⁶ 二 *(Nu) two*	U.1
jī̊⁶ 易 *(Adj) easy*	U.1
jī̊⁶ jẙut⁶ 二月 *(PN) February*	L.8
jī̊⁶ láu² 二樓 *(Ph) second floor*	L.9
jī̊⁶ såp⁶ mān¹ 二十蚊 *(Ph) twenty dollars*	L.4
jīn¹ jōeng¹ 鴛鴦 *(PN) yuanyang* [a mixture of HK style milk tea and coffee]	L.11
jīn¹ jŭk⁶ 煙肉 *(N) bacon*	L.10
jín² jýun² 演員 *(N) actor; actress*	L.7
jìn⁴ håu⁶ 然後 *(Conj) afterwards*	L.15
Jīng¹ Bŏng⁶ 英鎊 *(PN) British Pounds Sterling*	L.4
Jīng¹ Gåak³ Làan⁴ 英格蘭 *(PN) England*	*
Jīng¹ Gwŏk³ 英國 *(PN) United Kingdom*	L.6
Jīng¹ Gwŏk³ jàn⁴ 英國人 *(PN) British*	L.6
Jīng¹ Mán² 英文 *(PN) (see "Jīng¹ Màn⁴")*	L.6
Jīng¹ Màn⁴ 英文 *(PN) English language*	L.5
Jīng¹ zi̊k⁶ Jǎn³ Dŏu⁶ jàn⁴ 英籍印度人 *(Ph)* British Indian	L.5
jíng² jām¹ hěi³ còi⁴ 影音器材 *(Ph)* audio & visual gadgets	L.13

jíng² sóeng² 影相 (VO) take photographs	L.5
jīt⁶ 熱 (Adj) hot (in temperature)	U.1
jiu³ 要 (AV) have to; need to [indicating the need or obligation to do sth.]	L.6
jiu³ 要 (V) want, would like (something)	L.3
jóek⁶ fòng⁴ 藥房 (N) pharmacy	L.9
jòeng⁴ zī¹ gām¹ lōu⁶ 楊枝甘露 (PN) pomelo and sago in mango soup	L.12
jýu² 魚 (N) fish	U.1
jūk⁶ 肉 (N) meat	L.12
jūk⁶ hẻi³ 玉器 (N) jade	L.13
jūk⁶ sāt¹ 浴室 (N) bathroom	L.3
jùng⁴ jī⁶ 容易 (Adj) easy	L.11
Jỳun⁴ Lóng² 元朗 (PN) Yuen Long	L.14
jỳun⁵ 遠 (Adj) far	L.11
jỳut⁶ 月 (N) moon; months of the year (January-December)	U.1; L.8
jỳut⁶ dūk⁶ sāt¹ 閱讀室 (N) study room	L.3
Jỳut⁶ Jỳu⁵ 粵語 (PN) Yue language	U.1
Jỳut⁶ Nàam⁴ 越南 (PN) Vietnam	*

● 𝒦

kāat¹ 咭 (N) card; a short form for credit card	L.13
Kái² Dāk¹ 啟德 (PN) a MTR station: Kai Tak	L.14
kàm⁴ jāt⁶ 琴日 (N) yesterday	L.8
kàn⁴ līk⁶ 勤力 (Adj) hardworking	L.11
kắn⁵ 近 (Adj) near, close	U.1
kè⁴ láu² 騎樓 (N) balcony	L.3
kẻoi⁵ 佢 (Pn) he, she, him, her	U.1
kẻoi⁵ dẽi⁶ 佢哋 (Pn) they, them	L.1
kẻoi⁵ gẻ³ 佢嘅 (Ph) his, her, hers	L.1
kīng¹ dīn⁶ wáa² 傾電話 (VO) chat on the phone	L.8
kīng¹ gái² 傾偈 (VO) chat	L.8
kìu⁴ dái² 橋底 (Ph) under the bridge	L.14
kwāi¹ 虧 (Adj) deficient [easy to get sick]	U.1
Kwài⁴ Fōng¹ 葵芳 (PN) a MTR station: Kwai Fong	L.14
Kwài⁴ Hīng¹ 葵興 (PN) a MTR station: Kwai Hing	L.14

kwỏng³ cỳun⁴ séoi² 礦泉水 (N) mineral water	L.11

● 𝓛

lāa¹ 啦 (Part) [a modal particle used at the end of sentence with the sense of request, suggestion or invitation]	L.1
lảa³ 喇 (Part) [a modal particle used to emphasize a point of current relevance]	L.3
Lāai¹ Dīng¹ Mán² 拉丁文 (N) (see "Lāai¹ Dīng¹ Màn⁴")	L.6
Lāai¹ Dīng¹ Màn⁴ 拉丁文 (N) Latin language	L.6
lāai¹ síu² tài⁴ kàm⁴ 拉小提琴 (VO) play violin	L.6
lảak³ 嘞 (Part) [the emphasis form of "lảa³", used to indicate finality or exclamation]	L.14
làam⁴ sīk¹ 藍色 (N) blue	L.13
Làam⁴ Tìn⁴ 藍田 (PN) a MTR station: Lam Tin	L.14
lãam⁶ cē¹ 纜車 (N) cable car	L.14
lãam⁶ cē¹ zãam⁶ 纜車站 (N) peak tram station; cable car station	L.14
Làan⁴ Gwải³ Fōng¹ 蘭桂坊 (PN) Lan Kwai Fong	L.14
lắan⁵ 懶 (Adj) lazy	L.11
lãap⁶ sảap³ fòng⁴ 垃圾房 (N) garbage room	L.3
lài⁴ 嚟 (V) come (also pronounced as "lèi⁴")	L.3
lài⁴ gẻ³ 嚟嘅 (Part) [used at the end of noun predicate sentences to give an explanation]	L.10
lắi⁵ bảai³ 禮拜 (N) week; days of the week	L.8
lắi⁵ bảai³ jāt⁶ 禮拜日 (PN) Sunday	L.8
lắi⁵ bảai³ jāt¹ 禮拜一 (PN) Monday	L.8
lắi⁵ bảai³ jī⁶ 禮拜二 (PN) Tuesday	L.8
lắi⁵ bảai³ lūk⁶ 禮拜六 (PN) Saturday	L.8
lắi⁵ bảai³ nğ⁵ 禮拜五 (PN) Friday	L.8
lắi⁵ bảai³ sāam¹ 禮拜三 (PN) Wednesday	L.8
lắi⁵ bảai³ sẻi³ 禮拜四 (PN) Thursday	L.8
Lãi⁶ Gíng² 荔景 (PN) a MTR station: Lai King	L.14
Lãi⁶ Zī¹ Gỏk³ 荔枝角 (PN) a MTR station: Lai Chi Kok	L.14
láu² 樓 (N) floor	L.9
làu⁴ bīng¹ 溜冰 (VO) ice-skating	L.6

làu⁴ hāa⁶ 樓下 *(N) downstairs*	L.9
làu⁴ hōk⁶ sāang¹ 留學生 *(N) foreign student*	L.3
làu⁴ sāa¹ bāau¹ 流沙包 *(N)* steamed salted egg yolk custard buns	L.12
làu⁴ sõeng⁶ 樓上 *(N) upstairs*	L.9
làu⁴ tāi¹ 樓梯 *(N) staircase*	L.3
lèi⁴ 嚟 *(V) (see "lài⁴")*	L.3
lěi⁵ 你/您 *(Pn) (see "něi⁵")*	L.1
Lěi⁵ 李 *(PN) a Chinese surname: Lee, Li*	L.1
Lěi⁵ Dūng¹ 利東 *(PN) a MTR station: Lei Tung*	L.14
Lěi⁵ Jỳun⁴ Dūng¹ Sāi¹ Gāai¹ 利源東西街 *(PN) Li Yuen Street East & West*	L.14
Lěi⁵ Síu² Lùng⁴ 李小龍 *(PN) Bruce Lee*	L.1
Lěi⁶ Bān¹ Nāap⁶ 利賓納 *(PN) Ribena*	L.11
lēk¹ 叻 *(Adj)* smart; sharp; clever; brilliant	U.1
lěng³ 靚 *(Adj)* beautiful; good-looking; good quality	U.1; L.3
lěoi⁵ dim³ 旅店 *(N) hostel*	L.3
lěoi⁵ hàng⁴ 旅行 *(V) travel*	L.5
lěoi⁵ hàng⁴ 旅行 *(N) traveling*	L.5
lěoi⁵ mīn⁶ 裏面 *(N) in; inside*	L.9
lěoi⁵ sě³ 旅舍 *(N) hostel*	L.3
lēot⁶ sī¹ 律師 *(N) lawyer*	L.7
lēot⁶ sī¹ làu⁴ 律師樓 *(N) law firm*	L.8
līk⁶ sí² 歷史 *(N) history*	L.5
lìn⁴ jùng⁴ bāau¹ 蓮蓉包 *(N)* ground lotus seed buns	L.12
lìn⁴ jùng⁴ gūk⁶ bòu³ dīn¹ 蓮蓉焗布甸 *(N)* baked sago and mashed lotus seed pudding	L.12
lïn⁶ zāap⁶ 練習 *(V) to practice*	L.7
lïn⁶ zāap⁶ 練習 *(N) practice*	L.7
lìng⁴ 零 *(Nu) zero*	U.1
Lǐng⁵ Nàam⁴ Dāai⁶ Hōk⁶ 嶺南大學 *(PN)* Lingnan University	*
līp¹ 軑 *(N) lift, elevator*	L.3
Lìu⁴ Gwòk³ 寮國 *(PN) Laos*	*
ló² 攞 *(V) take; get; fetch*	L.9
ló² cín² 攞錢 *(VO) withdraw money*	L.9

Lò⁴ bāak⁶ gōu¹ 蘿蔔糕 *(N) Chinese turnip cake*	L.12
Lò⁴ Wù⁴ 羅湖 *(PN) a MTR station: Lo Wu*	L.14
lŏeng⁵ 兩 *(Nu) two*	U.2; L.5
lŏeng⁵ gò³ jỳut⁶ 兩個月 *(Ph) two months*	L.15
lŏeng⁵ hòu⁴ 兩毫 *(Ph) twenty cents*	L.4
lŏeng⁵ mān¹ 兩蚊 *(Ph) two dollars*	L.4
lōk⁶ 落 *(V) descend; fall*	U.1
lōk⁶ cē¹ 落車 *(VO) to get off a vehicle; alight*	L.14
Lōk⁶ Fù³ 樂富 *(PN) a MTR station: Lok Fu*	L.14
Lōk⁶ Mǎa⁵ Zāu¹ 落馬洲 *(PN) a MTR station: Lok Ma Chau*	L.14
Lŏng⁵ Pìng⁴ 朗屏 *(PN) a MTR station: Long Ping*	L.14
lǒu⁵ 老 *(Adj) old (not young)*	L.11
lǒu⁵ báan² 老闆 *(N) boss*	L.5
lǒu⁵ sī¹ 老師 *(N) teacher*	L.2
lōu⁶ jàn⁴ 路人 *(N) passer-by*	p.51
lōu⁶ tòi⁴ 露台 *(N) balcony*	L.3
lūk⁶ 六 *(Nu) six*	U.1
lūk⁶ càa⁴ 綠茶 *(N) green tea: non-fermented tea*	L.12
lūk⁶ dáu² sāa¹ 綠豆沙 *(N)* sweet mung bean soup	L.12
lūk⁶ jỳut⁶ 六月 *(PN) June*	L.8
lūk⁶ sīk¹ 綠色 *(N) green*	L.13
lūk⁶ zit³ 六折 *(Ph) 40% off*	L.13
Lùng⁴ Zéng² 龍井 *(PN)* Long-jing tea: best known as King of all green teas	L.12

<table>
<tr><td colspan="2" align="center">● M</td></tr>
</table>

m̀⁴ 唔 *(Adv) no; not* [used before a verb or an adjective indicating negation]	U.1
m̀⁴ gán² jiu³ 唔緊要 *(SE) never mind*	U.2
m̀⁴ gōi¹ 唔該 *(SE) please* [to request sb. to do sth.]	L.2
m̀⁴ gōi¹ 唔該 *(SE) excuse me* [to draw sb's attention usually when one inquires sth.]	L.3
m̀⁴ gōi¹ 唔該 *(SE) thank you [for a small favor]*	L.4

m̀⁴ gōi¹ sǎai³ 唔該晒 (SE) thank you very much!	L.13
m̀⁴ hǎi⁶ géi² 唔係幾 (Adv) not quite	L.8
m̀⁴ hóu² jǐ³ sī¹ 唔好意思 (SE) excuse me	L.6
m̀⁴ hóu² jǐ³ sì³ 唔好意思 (SE) (see "m̀⁴ hóu² jǐ³ sī¹")	L.6
m̀⁴ sái² 唔使 (Adv) no need [the negative form of "jǐu³"]	L.8
m̀⁴ sái² dō¹ zē⁶ 唔使多謝 (SE) You're welcome.	L.9
m̀⁴ sái² hǎak³ hěi³ 唔使客氣 (SE) Don't mention it.	L.9
m̀⁴ sái² m̀⁴ gōi¹ 唔使唔該 (SE) (lit. no need for thanks) not at all; you're welcome	L.9
màa⁴ māa¹ 媽媽 (N) mother	L.4
màa⁴ máa² déi² 麻麻哋 (Adv) so-so	L.8
Mǎa⁵ 馬 (PN) a Chinese surname: Ma	L.1
mǎa⁵ còeng⁴ 馬場 (N) horse racing track	L.9
Mǎa⁵ Còeng⁴ 馬場 (PN) a MTR station: Racecourse	L.14
Mǎa⁵ Lāai¹ gōu¹ 馬拉糕 (N) sweet sponge cake	L.12
Mǎa⁵ Lòi⁴ Sāi¹ Aǎ³ 馬來西亞 (PN) Malaysia	*
Mǎa⁵ Ōn¹ Sāan¹ 馬鞍山 (PN) a MTR station: Ma On Shan	L.14
Mǎa⁵ Ōn¹ Sāan¹ Sin³ 馬鞍山綫 (PN) Ma On Shan Line	L.14
mǎa⁵ tàu⁴ 碼頭 (N) pier	L.14
Mǎa⁵ Tàu⁴ Wài⁴ 馬頭圍 (PN) a MTR station: Ma Tau Wai	L.14
màai⁴ dāan¹ 埋單 (VO) add up the bill; pay	L.12
mǎai⁵ 買 (V) (+ Object) buy	L.13
mǎai⁵ jě⁵ 買野 (VO) do shopping; buy something	L.8
mǎan⁵ 晚 (N) night(s)	L.15
mǎan⁵ fāan⁶ 晚飯 (N) dinner	L.12
màan⁶ 慢 (Adj) slow	L.11
màan⁶ máan² hàang⁴ 慢慢行 (SE) mind your step; walk slowly	U.2
Màang⁶ Gāa¹ Lāai¹ 孟加拉 (PN) Bangladesh	*
māau¹ 貓 (N) a cat	U.1
mǎi⁵ jūk¹ 咪郁 (Ph) don't move	U.2
māk⁶ pèi⁴ 麥皮 (N) oatmeal	L.10
Māk⁶ Sāi¹ Gō¹ 墨西哥 (PN) Mexico	*
mān¹ 蚊 (M) dollars [a measure unit for money]	L.4
mān⁶ 問 (V) ask	U.1
mān⁶ tài⁴ 問題 (N) question; problem; trouble	L.4
māt¹ jě⁵ 乜野 (QW) what; what kind of	L.6
māt¹ jě⁵ cē¹ 乜野車 (QW) what mode of transportation; what kind of vehicle	L.14
māt¹ jě⁵ fō¹ 乜野科 (QW) what subject?	L.5
māt¹ jě⁵ gūng¹ sī¹ 乜野公司 (QW) what kind of company	L.8
māt¹ jě⁵ jàn⁴ 乜野人 (QW) what people? what nationality?	L.5
māt¹ jě⁵ lài⁴ gǎa³ 乜野嚟㗎 (Q) what on earth is this/that?	L.10
māt¹ jě⁵ méng² 乜野名 (QW) What name? How is it called?	L.5
māt⁶ 襪 (N) socks	U.1
mē¹ jě⁵ 咩野 (QW) what; what kind of	L.6
mē¹ jě⁵ méng² 咩野名 (QW) What name? How is it called?	L.6
Měi⁵ Fū¹ 美孚 (PN) a MTR station: Mei Foo	L.14
Měi⁵ Gām¹ 美金 (PN) U.S. Dollars	L.4
Měi⁵ Gwòk³ 美國 (PN) United States of America	L.5
Měi⁵ Gwòk³ jàn⁴ 美國人 (PN) Americans	L.5
Měi⁵ Jỳun⁴ 美元 (PN) U.S. Dollars	L.4
Měi⁵ zīk⁶ 美籍 (N) American nationality	L.5
měi⁶ 未 (Adv) not yet	L.12
Mǐn⁵ Dǐn⁶ 緬甸 (PN) Burma	*
mǐn⁶ 麵 (N) noodles	L.10
mǐn⁶ bāau¹ 麵包 (N) bread	L.10
mìng⁴ 明 (V) understand	U.2
mìng⁴ sèon³ pín² 明信片 (N) postcards	L.13
mīt¹ sì⁴ (N) Miss	L.1
mǐu⁵ 秒 (N) second	U.2
mǐu⁵ zūng¹ 秒鐘 (Suff) second(s) [of time duration]	L.15

mōng¹ gwó² bóu³ dīn¹ 芒果布甸 *(N)* mango pudding	L.12
mòng⁴ 忙 *(Adj)* busy	L.8
móu² 帽 *(N)* hats	U.1
móu⁵ 冇 *(V)* have not, not to have [the negation of "jáu⁵"]	L.4
móu⁵ màn⁶ tài⁴ 冇問題 *(SE)* no problem; no questions	L.4
mūn⁶ 悶 *(Adj)* boring; dull	U.1
mùn⁴ háu² 門口 *(N)* doorway; entrance	L.15
mùi⁴ múi² 妹妹 *(N)* younger sister	L.5
múi⁵ jāt⁶ 每日 *(Pn)* every day	L.14

• N

nàa⁴ 嗱 *(Intj)* Here it is! [an indicator of things within a close proximity]	L.4
náai⁵ 奶 *(N)* milk	L.11
náai⁵ càa⁴ 奶茶 *(N)* milk tea	L.11
náai⁵ jàu⁴ dō¹ 奶油多 *(N)* butter & condense milk on toast	L.10
náai⁵ wòng⁴ bāau¹ 奶皇包 *(N)* sweet egg custard buns	L.12
nàam⁴ 南 *(N)* south	L.15
Nàam⁴ Aå³ 南亞 *(PN)* South Asia	*
Nàam⁴ Aå³ jēoi⁶ 南亞裔 *(Ph)* South Asia origin	*
Nàam⁴ Cōeng¹ 南昌 *(PN)* a MTR station: Nam Cheong	L.14
Nàam⁴ Fēi¹ 南非 *(PN)* South Africa	L.4
Nàam⁴ Góng² Dóu² Sin³ (Dūng¹ Dyun⁶) 南港島綫（東段）*(PN)* South Island Line (East)	L.14
Nàam⁴ Gīk⁶ 南極 *(PN)* Antarctic	*
Nàam⁴ Hòn⁴ 南韓 *(PN)* South Korea	L.4
Nàam⁴ Hòn⁴ Jyun⁴ 南韓元 *(PN)* South Korean Won	L.4
Nàam⁴ Hòn⁴ Wàan⁴ 南韓圜 *(PN)* South Korean Won	L.4
Nàam⁴ Měi⁵ Zāu¹ 南美洲 *(PN)* South America	L.2
nàam⁴ pàng⁴ jáu⁵ 男朋友 *(N)* boyfriend	L.7
Nàam⁴ Sī¹ Lāai¹ Fū¹ 南斯拉夫 *(PN)* Yogoslavia	*
nàan⁴ 難 *(Adj)* difficult	U.1
Náu² Joek³ 紐約 *(PN)* New York	L.5

Náu² Jyun⁴ 紐元 *(PN)* New Zealand Dollars	L.4
Náu² Sāi¹ Làan⁴ 紐西蘭 *(PN)* New Zealand	L.5
nē¹ 呢 *(Part)* [an interrogative particle used to form an elliptical question which is related to a previous question, statement or context.]	L.6
Nèi⁴ Jāt⁶ Lēi⁶ Aå³ 尼日利亞 *(PN)* Nigeria	*
Nèi⁴ Bōk⁶ Jí⁵ 尼泊爾 *(PN)* Nepal	*
něi⁵ 你 *(Pn)* you	U.1
něi⁵ děi⁶ 你哋 *(Pn)* you – plural	L.1
něi⁵ ge³ 你嘅 *(Ph)* your, yours	L.1
něi⁵ gwái³ sing³ aå³? 你貴姓呀？*(SE)* What's your surname?	L.6
něi⁵ hóu² 你好 *(SE)* (lit. you good) Hello, Hi, Good day.	L.1
něi⁵ hóu² maå³ 你好嗎 *(Q)* How are you?	U.2
něi⁵ zī¹ m̀⁴ zī¹...? 你知唔知...？*(Ph)* Do you know...?	L.14
néoi² 女 *(N)* daughter	L.12
něoi⁵ pàng⁴ jáu⁵ 女朋友 *(N)* girlfriend	L.4
Ǹg⁴ 吳 *(PN)* a Chinese surname: Ng, Wu	L.1
ńg⁵ 五 *(Nu)* five	U.1
ńg⁵ bảak³ mān¹ 五百蚊 *(Ph)* five hundred dollars	L.4
ńg⁵ hòu⁴ 五毫 *(Ph)* fifty cents	L.4
ńg⁵ jě⁶ 午夜 *(N)* midnight	U.2
ńg⁵ jyut⁶ 五月 *(PN)* May	L.8
ńg⁵ mān¹ 五蚊 *(Ph)* five dollars	L.4
ńg⁵ sǎp⁶ mān¹ 五十蚊 *(Ph)* fifty dollars	L.4
ńg⁵ zit³ 五折 *(Ph)* 50% off	*
ngāam¹ 啱 *(Adj)* correct	L.11
ngàan⁴ sīk¹ 顏色 *(N)* colour	L.13
ngǎan⁵ géng² 眼鏡 *(N)* eyeglasses	L.13
ngǎan⁵ lēoi⁶ 眼淚 *(N)* tears	U.1
ngāang⁶ bǎi⁶ 硬幣 *(N)* coin	L. 4
ngài⁴ hím² 危險 *(Adj)* dangerous	L.11
ngāi⁶ jàn⁴ 藝人 *(N)* artist	L.7
ngāi⁶ sēot⁶ 藝術 *(N)* fine arts	L.5

ngàn⁴ bāau¹ 銀包 (N) wallets	L.13
ngàn⁴ hòng⁴ 銀行 (N) bank	L.2
ngàn⁴ hòng⁴ cēot¹ nǎap⁶ jỳun⁴ 銀行出納員 (N) teller	L.7
ngàn⁴ sīk¹ 銀色 (N) silver	L.13
ngàu⁴ jŭk⁶ 牛肉 (N) beef	*
ngàu⁴ jŭk⁶ kàu⁴ 牛肉球 (N) beef meatballs	L.12
ngàu⁴ nǎam⁵ 牛腩 (N) beef brisket	U.1
ngàu⁴ nǎai⁵ 牛奶 (N) milk	L.11
ngàu⁴ pǎak³ jīp⁶ 牛栢葉 (N) beef stomach	L.12
Ngàu⁴ Tàu⁴ Gȯk³ 牛頭角 (PN) a MTR station: Ngau Tau Kok	L.14
Ngȯ⁴ Lȯ⁴ Sī¹ 俄羅斯 (PN) Russia	L.4
ngǒ⁵ 我 (Pn) I; me	U.1
ngǒ⁵ dĕi⁶ 我哋 (Pn) we, us	L.2
ngǒ⁵ gė³ 我嘅 (Ph) my; mine	L.1
ngǒ⁶ 餓 (Adj) hungry	L.11
ngȯi⁶ gwȯk³ wáa² 外國話 (N) foreign language	L.6
ngȯi⁶ mīn⁶ 外面 (N) outside	L.9
nī¹ dėoi³ hàai⁴ 呢對鞋 (Ph) this pair of shoes	L.10
nī¹ dī¹ 呢啲 (Pn) this; these	L.10
nī¹ dȯu⁶ 呢度 (Pn) here	L.2
nī¹ gȯ³ 呢個 (Pn) this one	L.10
nī¹ gȯ³ jỳut⁶ 呢個月 (N) this month	L.8
nī¹ gȯ³ sīng¹ kèi⁴ 呢個星期 (N) this week	L.8
nī¹ gȉn⁶ sāam¹ 呢件衫 (Ph) this piece of clothing; this clothes	L.10
nīk¹ záu² 搦走 (V) take away; "to go"	L.11
nìn⁴ 年 (N) year; year(s) [of time duration]	L.8
nīng¹ záu² 拎走 (V) take away, "to go"	L.11
níng² càa⁴ 檸茶 (N) lemon tea	L.11
níng² cāt¹ 檸七 (N) 7 up with lemon	L.11
níng² lȯk⁶ 檸樂 (N) Coke with lemon	L.11
níng² mȁt⁶ 檸蜜 (N) honey lemonade	L.11
níng² séoi² 檸水 (N) lemonade	L.11
nìng⁴ mūng¹ càa⁴ 檸檬茶 (N) lemon tea (also "níng² càa⁴")	L.11
nìng⁴ mūng¹ séoi² 檸檬水 (N) lemonade (also "níng² séoi²")	L.11

Nȯ⁴ Wāi¹ 挪威 (PN) Norway	*
nǒ⁶ mǎi⁵ gāi¹ 糯米雞 (N) lotus leaf wrapped sticky rice with chicken	L.12
● 𝒪	
ȍ¹ 屙 (N/V) diarrhea	U.1
Ȏ¹ Sī⁶ Dīn¹ 柯士甸 (PN) a MTR station: Austin	L.14
Ȏ¹ Wàa⁴ Tìn⁴ 阿華田 (PN) Ovaltine	L.11
ȯi³ 愛 (V) love	U.1
Ȍi³ Jī⁵ Làan⁴ 愛爾蘭 (PN) Ireland	*
ōn¹ cỳun⁴ 安全 (Adj) safe	L.11
Ȍu³ Dĕi⁶ Lĕi⁶ 奧地利 (PN) Austria	*
Ȍu³ Jỳun⁴ 澳元 (PN) Australian Dollars	L.4
Ȍu³ Mún² 澳門 (PN) (see "Ȍu³ Mùn⁴")	L.9
Ȍu³ Mùn⁴ 澳門 (PN) Macau	L.9
Ȍu³ Mùn⁴ Dȁk⁶ Bīt⁶ Hàng⁴ Zȉng³ Kēoi¹ 澳門特別行政區 (PN) Special Administrative Region of Macau	U.1
Ȍu³ Wȁn⁶ 奧運 (PN) a MTR station: Olympic	L.14
Ȍu³ Zāu¹ 澳洲 (PN) Australia	L.2
● 𝒫	
pàai⁴ gwāt¹ 排骨 (N) spare ribs	L.12
pàai⁴ zí² 牌子 (N) a brand; a brand name; a trademark	L.13
páau⁴ bȯu⁶ 跑步 (VO) running; jogging	L.6
Pǎau³ Tòi⁴ Sāan¹ 炮台山 (PN) a MTR station: Fortress Hill	L.14
pàng⁴ jǎu⁵ 朋友 (N) friend	L.3; L.7
pèi⁴ dáan² 皮蛋 (N) century egg: a special type of preserved egg	L.10
pèi⁴ dáan² sǎu³ jŭk⁶ zūk¹ 皮蛋瘦肉粥 (Ph) congee with century egg and lean pork	L.10
pèi⁴ gĕoi⁶ 皮具 (N) leather goods	L.13
pèng⁴ 平 (Adj) cheap	U.1
pèng⁴ dī¹ lāa¹ 平啲啦 (SE) Cheaper, please!	L.13
pòng⁴ bīn¹ 旁邊 (N) beside; next to	L.9
Póu² Léi² 普洱 (PN) Pu'er tea: black tea, fully fermented and oxidized tea (also pronounced as "Bóu² Léi²")	L.12

Póu² Tūng¹ Wáa² 普通話 *(PN)* *(lit. common speech) Mandarin/Putonghua [the modern Chinese language]*	U.1
pou³ táu² 鋪頭 *(N) shop*	*
Pòu⁴ Tòu⁴ Ngàa⁴ 葡萄牙 *(PN) Portugal*	L.4

● *S*

Sāa¹ Tìn⁴ 沙田 *(PN) a MTR station: Shatin*	L.14
Sāa¹ Tìn⁴ Wàa⁴ 沙田圍 *(PN)* *a MTR station: Shatin Wai*	L.14
Sāa¹ Zūng¹ Sin³ 沙中綫 *(PN)* *Shatin to Central Link*	L.14
sāai¹ sí² 晒士 *(N) size*	L.13
såai³ 晒 *(Part)* *[comes after a verb to express the idea 'all, completely, entirely']*	L.13
sāam¹ 三 *(Nu) three*	U.1
sāam¹ 衫 *(N) clothes; clothing; garments*	U.1
sāam¹ dím² bun³ 三點半 *(Pn) half-past three*	U.1
sāam¹ jyut⁶ 三月 *(N) March*	L.8
sāam¹ màn⁴ zī⁶ 三文治 *(N) sandwich(es)*	L.10
sāam¹ nìn⁴ 三年 *(Ph) three years*	L.15
sāan¹ 山 *(N) mountain*	U.1
sāan¹ déng² lāam⁶ cē¹ 山頂纜車 *(N)* *peak tram*	L.14
sáan² ngán² 散銀 *(N) coins*	L.4
såan³ bōu⁶ 散步 *(VO) stroll*	L.8
sāang¹ 生 *(Adj) raw, uncooked*	U.1
Sāau¹ Gēi¹ Wāan¹ 筲箕灣 *(PN)* *a MTR station: Shau Kei Wan*	L.14
sāi¹ 西 *(N) west*	L.15
Sāi¹ Bāan¹ Ngàa⁴ 西班牙 *(PN) Spain*	L.4
Sāi¹ Bāan¹ Ngàa⁴ Mán² 西班牙文 *(PN)* *(see "Sāi¹ Bāan¹ Ngàa⁴ Màn⁴")*	L.6
Sāi¹ Bāan¹ Ngàa⁴ Màn⁴ 西班牙文 *(N)* *Spanish language*	L.6
Sāi¹ Bāan¹ Ngàa⁴ Wáa² 西班牙話 *(N)* *Spanish speech*	L.6
sāi¹ dō¹ sí² 西多士 *(N) French toast*	L.10
sāi¹ lēi⁶ 犀利 *(Adj) terrific, extreme*	L.11
sāi¹ mǎi⁵ lōu⁶ 西米露 *(N) sago in coconut milk*	L.12

Sāi¹ Tit³ Sin³ 西鐵綫 *(PN) West Rail Line*	L.14
sāi¹ sīk¹ 西式 *(N) Western style*	L.10
Sāi¹ Wāan¹ Hó² 西灣河 *(PN)* *a MTR station: Sai Wan Ho*	L.14
Sāi¹ Jìng⁴ Pùn⁴ 西營盤 *(PN)* *a MTR station: Sai Ying Pun*	L.14
sái² jī¹ fòng⁴ 洗衣房 *(N) laundry room*	L.3
sái² sáu² gāan¹ 洗手間 *(N) toilet; washroom*	L.2
såi³ 細 *(Adj) small*	U.1; L.3
såi³ mǎa⁵ 細碼 *(N) small size*	L.13
sām¹ 心 *(N) a heart*	U.1
sām¹ lěi⁵ hōk⁶ 心理學 *(N) psychology*	L.5
Sām¹ Séoi² Bóu² 深水埗 *(PN)* *a MTR station: Shum Shui Po*	L.14
Sām¹ Zan³ 深圳 *(PN) Shenzhen*	L.14
sān¹ 新 *(Adj) new*	U.1; L.3
sān¹ fú² 辛苦 *(Adj) hard; tough*	L.11
Sān¹ Gåa³ Bō¹ 新加坡 *(PN) Singapore*	L.4
Sān¹ Gåa³ Bō¹ Jyun⁴ 新加坡元 *(PN)* *Singapore Dollars*	L.4
sān¹ jě⁵ 新嘢 *(Ph) new stuff*	L.11
sān¹ lèi⁴ ge³ 新嚟嘅 *(Ph)* *(lit. newly come) just arrived; newcomer*	L.3
Sān¹ Nìn⁴ 新年 *(PN) New Year*	U.2
Sān¹ Sāi¹ Làan⁴ 新西蘭 *(PN) New Zealand*	L.5
Sān¹ Tòi⁴ Bāi⁶ 新台幣 *(PN) Taiwan Dollars*	L.4
sāng¹ māt⁶ 生物 *(N) biology*	L.5
såp⁶ 十 *(Nu) ten*	U.1
såp⁶ jāt¹ jyut⁶ 十一月 *(PN) November*	L.8
såp⁶ jī⁶ jyut⁶ 十二月 *(PN) December*	L.8
såp⁶ jyut⁶ 十月 *(PN) October*	L.8
såp⁶ mān¹ 十蚊 *(Ph) ten dollars*	L.4
sāu¹ ngán² jyun⁴ 收銀員 *(N) cashier*	p.51
sáu² bīu¹ 手錶 *(N) watches*	L.13
sáu² dói² 手袋 *(N) handbags*	L.13
sáu² gūng¹ ngāi⁶ bán² 手工藝品 *(N)* *handicrafts*	L.13

sáu² sīk¹ 首飾 *(N) jewellery*	L.13
sáu² tài⁴ dīn⁶ wáa² 手提電話 *(N)* mobile phone	L.4
såu³ 瘦 *(Adj) thin (in contrast to fat)*	L.11
såu³ jūk⁶ 瘦肉 *(N) lean pork; lean meat*	L.10
sãu⁶ fò³ jỳun⁴ 售貨員 *(N) salesperson*	p.51
Sãu⁶ Méi² 壽眉 *(PN)* Shou-mei tea: a popular light-fermented tea	L.12
sé² 寫 *(V) write*	L.15
sě⁵ wúi² gūng¹ zòk³ zé² 社會工作者 *(N)* social worker	L.7
sěi³ 四 *(Nu) four*	U.1
sěi³ jỳut⁶ 四月 *(PN) April*	L.8
Sěk⁶ Gip³ Měi⁵ 石硤尾 *(PN)* a MTR station: Shek Kip Mei	L.14
Sěk⁶ Mùn⁴ 石門 *(PN)* a MTR station: Shek Mun	L.14
sēoi¹ 衰 *(Adj) bad; wicked, evil-minded*	L.11
séoi² 水 *(N) water*	*
séoi² pèi⁴ 水皮 *(Adj) not up to standard; bad*	L.11
sěoi³ 歲 *(M) years old*	L.5
Sēoi⁶ Dín² 瑞典 *(PN) Sweden*	L.4
sēoi⁶ dõu⁶ 隧道 *(N) tunnel*	L.14
sēoi⁶ fóng² 睡房 *(N) bedroom*	L.3
Sēoi⁶ Sī⁶ 瑞士 *(PN) Switzerland*	L.4
Sēoi⁶ Sī⁶ Fåat³ Lòng⁴ 瑞士法郎 *(PN)* Swiss Francs	L.4
sěon³ 信 *(N) a letter*	U.1
sěon³ jūng⁶ kāat¹ 信用咭 *(N) credit card*	L.4
sī¹ 屍 *(N) corpse*	U.1
sī¹ 師 *(N) master*	U.1
sī¹ 詩 *(N) poem*	U.1
sī¹ gēi¹ 司機 *(N)* driver; vehicle operator (by profession)	L.3
Sī¹ Lěi⁵ Làan⁴ Kāa¹ 斯里蘭卡 *(PN) Sri Lanka*	*
Sī¹ Tòu⁴ 司徒 *(PN) a Chinese surname: Szeto*	L.1
sī¹ zí² 獅子 *(N) lion*	L.15
sí² 屎 *(N) feces*	U.1
sí² 史 *(N) history*	U.1

Sí² 史 *(PN) a Chinese surname: Si*	L.6
si³ 弒 *(V) kill*	U.1
si³ 試 *(V) try*	U.1
si³ hǎa⁵ 試吓 *(Ph) have a try*	L.10
si⁴ 時 *(N) time*	U.1
si⁴ 匙 *(N) key*	U.1
si⁴ si⁴ 時時 *(Adv) always; often*	L.7
sǐ⁵ 市 *(N) market; city*	U.1
sǐ⁵ còeng⁴ hõk⁶ 市場學 *(N) marketing*	L.5
sī⁶ 事 *(N) matter*	U.1
sī⁶ 視 *(N) vision*	U.1
sī⁶ jǐng³ sāng¹ 侍應生 *(N) waiter; waitress*	L.7
sīk¹ 識 *(V) know; know how to do sth.; have the ability to do sth.*	U.1; L.6
sīk⁶ 食 *(V) eat*	L.9
sīk⁶ åan³ zåu³ 食晏晝 *(VO) have a lunch*	L.12
sīk⁶ dím² sām¹ 食點心 *(VO)* going for dim-sum	L.12
sīk⁶ jě⁵ 食嘢 *(VO) eat something*	L.8
sīk⁶ jīn¹ 食煙 *(VO) smoke*	L.5
sīn¹ 先 *(Adv) first; in advance*	L.12
sīn¹ nǎai⁵ 鮮奶 *(N) fresh milk*	L.11
sīn¹ sāang¹ 先生 *(N) Mr.; sir*	L.1
sīn¹ sāang¹ 先生 *(N) husband*	L.5
sīn¹ sāang¹ 先生 *(N) teacher*	*
sīn¹ zūk¹ gýun² 鮮竹卷 *(N)* steamed bean curd rolls	L.12
sīng¹ góng³ gēi¹ 升降機 *(N) lift, elevator*	L.3
sīng¹ kèi⁴ 星期 *(N)* day of a week (Mon.-Sat.); week	L.8
sīng¹ kèi⁴ jāt¹ 星期一 *(N) Monday*	L.8
sīng¹ kèi⁴ jāt⁶ 星期日 *(N) Sunday*	L.8
sīng¹ kèi⁴ jī⁶ 星期二 *(N) Tuesday*	L.8
sīng¹ kèi⁴ lūk⁶ 星期六 *(N) Saturday*	L.8
sīng¹ kèi⁴ ng̃⁵ 星期五 *(N) Friday*	L.8
sīng¹ kèi⁴ sāam¹ 星期三 *(N) Wednesday*	L.8
sīng¹ kèi⁴ sěi³ 星期四 *(N) Thursday*	L.8
Sīng¹ Zín² Ngàn⁴ Hòng⁴ 星展銀行 *(PN)* DBS Bank Limited	L.15

sìng³ 姓 (N) a surname	U.1
sìng³ 姓 (V) be surnamed	L.6
Sìng³ Dàan³ Zìt³ 聖誕節 (PN) Christmas	U.2
Sìng³ Jòek⁶ Hōn⁶ Zō⁶ Tòng⁴ 聖約翰座堂 (PN) St. John's Cathedral	L.14
sīu¹ fòng⁴ gúk² 消防局 (N) fire station	L.9
sīu¹ fòng⁴ jỳun⁴ 消防員 (N) fireman	L.7
sīu¹ máai² 燒賣 (N) pork dumplings	L.12
síu² 少 (Adj) few; a little	U.1
síu² bāa¹ 小巴 (N) minibus; public light bus	L.14
síu² bāa¹ zāam⁶ 小巴站 (N) minibus station	L.14
síu² lèon⁴ 小輪 (N) ferry	L.14
síu² síu² 少少 (Nu) a few; a little	L.6
síu² zé² 小姐 (N) Miss, young lady	L.1
Sīu⁶ Hōng¹ 兆康 (PN) a MTR station: Siu Hong	L.14
só² jǐ⁵ 所以 (Conj) therefore	L.14
só² sì⁴ 鎖匙 (N) key	L.3
só² sì⁴ kǎu³ 鎖匙扣 (N) key holders	L.13
sò⁴ 傻 (Adj) silly	L.11
sōeng¹ jàn⁴ fóng² 雙人房 (N) double room; room for two	L.3
sōeng¹ pèi⁴ nǎai⁵ 雙皮奶 (N) double-boiled fresh milk and egg white	L.12
sóeng² 想 (AV) to want to; would like to (do something)	L.3
sóeng² gēi¹ 相機 (N) camera	L.13
sóeng² jìu³ 想要 (Ph) to want to have (something)	L.3
sǒeng⁵ mǒng⁵ 上網 (VO) to surf the Internet	L.5
sǒeng⁵ tòng⁴ 上堂 (VO) to attend class	L.8
sōeng⁶ gò³ jỳut⁶ 上個月 (N) last month	L.8
sōeng⁶ gò³ sīng¹ kèi⁴ 上個星期 (N) last week	L.8
Sōeng⁶ Hói² Wáa² 上海話 (PN) Shanghaiese dialect	L.6
sōeng⁶ mìn⁶ 上面 (N) above; on-top	L.9
sōeng⁶ nǧ⁵ 上午 (N) A.M.	U.2
Sōeng⁶ Séoi² 上水 (PN) a MTR station: Sheung Shui	L.14

Sōeng⁶ Wàan⁴ 上環 (PN) a MTR station: Sheung Wan	L.2
sōeng⁶ zàu³ 上晝 (N) A.M.	U.2
Sōu¹ Gåak³ Làan⁴ 蘇格蘭 (PN) Scotland	L.5
sòu³ gěoi³ sīm¹ kāat¹ 數據SIM卡 (N) data SIM card	L.4
sūk¹ sě³ 宿舍 (N) hostel; dormitory; living quarters	L.3
sūk¹ sě⁵ 宿舍 (N) (see "sūk¹ sě³")	L.3
Sǔng³ Wòng⁴ Tòi⁴ 宋皇臺 (PN) a MTR station: Sung Wong Toi	L.14
sȳu¹ 書 (N) book	U.1
sȳu¹ dìm³ 書店 (N) bookshop	L.9
sȳu¹ fóng² 書房 (N) study room	L.3
sȳu¹ fūk⁶ 舒服 (Adj) comfortable	L.11
sȳu¹ gúk² 書局 (N) bookshop	L.9
sȳun¹ 酸 (Adj) sour	U.1
sỳun⁴ 船 (N) ferry	L.14
Sỳut³ Bīk¹ 雪碧 (PN) Sprite	L.11

<table>
<tr><td colspan="2">● 𝒯</td></tr>
<tr><td>tåai³ 太 (Adv) too; excessively</td><td>L.13</td></tr>
<tr><td>Tåai³ Gú² 太古 (PN) a MTR station: Tai Koo</td><td>L.14</td></tr>
<tr><td>Tåai³ Gwòk³ 泰國 (PN) Thailand</td><td>L.5</td></tr>
<tr><td>Tåai³ Mán² 泰文 (PN) (see "Tåai³ Màn⁴")</td><td>L.6</td></tr>
<tr><td>Tåai³ Màn⁴ 泰文 (PN) Thai language</td><td>L.6</td></tr>
<tr><td>tåai³ táai² 太太 (N) Mrs.</td><td>L.1</td></tr>
<tr><td>tåai³ táai² 太太 (N) wife</td><td>L.5</td></tr>
<tr><td>Tåai³ Wò⁴ 太和 (PN) a MTR station: Tai Wo</td><td>L.14</td></tr>
<tr><td>Tåai³ Zí² 太子 (PN) a MTR station: Prince Edward</td><td>L.14</td></tr>
<tr><td>Tåai³ Zȳu¹ 泰銖 (PN) Thai Baht</td><td>L.4</td></tr>
<tr><td>tåam³ pàng⁴ jǎu⁵ 探朋友 (VO) visit a friend</td><td>L.8</td></tr>
<tr><td>tàan⁴ kàm⁴ 彈琴 (VO) play piano</td><td>L.6</td></tr>
<tr><td>tái² 睇 (V) see; look; watch; read</td><td>L.13</td></tr>
<tr><td>tái² bóu³ zí² 睇報紙 (VO) read newspaper</td><td>*</td></tr>
<tr><td>tái² dìn⁶ sī⁶ 睇電視 (VO) watch TV</td><td>L.15</td></tr>
<tr><td>tái² hèi³ 睇戲 (VO) watch movies</td><td>L.5</td></tr>
<tr><td>tái² sȳu¹ 睇書 (VO) read books</td><td>L.5</td></tr>
</table>

těk³ bō¹ 踢波 *(VO) play soccer*	L.8
těk³ zūk¹ kàu⁴ 踢足球 *(VO)* *play soccer/football*	L.6
tēng¹ 聽 *(V) hear; listen*	L.5
tēng¹ jām¹ ngŏk⁶ 聽音樂 *(VO) listen to music*	L.5
tī¹ sēot¹ Ｔ裇 *(N) T shirt*	L.13
tīm¹ 添 *(Part)* *[a sentence particle, accompanying the adverb "zūng⁶" to emphasize the idea of 'addition']*	L.12
tìm⁴ bán² 甜品 *(N) dessert*	L.12
Tīn¹ Hāu⁶ 天后 *(PN) a MTR station: Tin Hau*	L.14
Tīn¹ Séoi² Wài⁴ 天水圍 *(PN)* *a MTR station:Tin Shui Wai*	L.14
Tīn¹ Sīng¹ Mǎa⁵ Tàu⁴ 天星碼頭 *(PN)* *Star Ferry Pier*	L.14
tīng¹ jāt⁶ 聽日 *(N) tomorrow*	L.8
tìng⁴ 停 *(V) stop*	U.2
tìng⁴ cē¹ 停車 *(Ph) to stop (a car, a train)*	L.3
tìng⁴ cē¹ còeng⁴ 停車場 *(N) carpark*	L.2; L.13
Tit³ Gūn¹ Jām¹ 鐵觀音 *(N)* *Tie-guan-yin tea: a type of Oolong tea*	L.12
tiu³ mǒu⁵ 跳舞 *(VO) dance*	L.5
tìu⁴ 條 *(M)* *[a measure word for streets or things with a long shape]*	L.15
Tìu⁴ Gíng² Lěng⁵ 調景嶺 *(PN)* *a MTR station: Tiu Keng Leng*	L.14
Tòi⁴ Wāan¹ 台灣 *(PN) Taiwan*	L.4
tōng¹ jýun² 湯圓 *(N) sweet dumpling in soup*	L.12
tòng⁴ 糖 *(N) sugar*	L.11
Tòng⁴ Wáa² 唐話 *(PN) Tang speech*	U.1
Tóu² Gwāa¹ Wàan⁴ 土瓜灣 *(PN)* *a MTR station: To Kwa Wan*	L.14
Tóu² Jǐ⁵ Kèi⁴ 土耳其 *(PN) Turkey*	*
tòu⁴ sȳu¹ gún² 圖書館 *(N) library*	L.3
tǒu⁵ ngŏ⁶ 肚餓 *(Adj) hungry*	L.10
tǔng³ 痛 *(Adj) painful; sore*	U.1
tùng⁴ 同 *(Conj) and*	L.4
tùng⁴ 同 *(Prep) with*	L.7

Tùng⁴ Lò⁴ Wāan¹ 銅鑼灣 *(PN)* *Causeway Bay [major district in HK Island] (also pronounced as "Tùng⁴ Lò⁴ Wàan⁴")*	L.2
tùng⁴ mǎai⁵ 同埋 *(Conj) and*	L.4
tùng⁴ sī⁶ 同事 *(N) colleague*	L.5
Tỳun⁴ Mǎa⁵ Sìn³ 屯馬綫 *(PN) Tuen Ma Line*	L.14
Tỳun⁴ Mǎa⁵ Sìn³ Jāt¹ Kèi⁴ 屯馬綫一期 *(PN)* *Tuen Ma Line Phrase 1*	L.14
Tỳun⁴ Mùn⁴ 屯門 *(PN)* *a MTR station: Tuen Mun*	L.14
● *U*	
ūk¹ 屋 *(N) house*	U.1
ūk¹ kéi² 屋企 *(N) home*	L.14
ūk¹ kéi² gě³ dīn⁶ wáa² 屋企嘅電話 *(Ph)* *home telephone no.*	L.14
ūk¹ kéi² jàn⁴ 屋企人 *(N) family; family members*	L.3
● *W*	
wǎa³ 嘩 *(Intj)* *[express surprise or wonder] Wow!*	L.13
Wàa⁴ jēoi⁶ 華裔 *(N)* *Chinese descent; Chinese origin*	L.5
Wàa⁴ kìu⁴ 華僑 *(N) overseas Chinese*	L.5
wǎa⁶ 話 *(V) say*	L.14
wǎai⁶ 壞 *(Adj) bad; out of order*	U.1
wǎak⁶ zé² 或者 *(Conj) or (either one can do)* *[used in a statement, not in questions]*	L.12
wāan¹ 彎 *(N) corner*	L.15
Wāan¹ Zái² 灣仔 *(PN)* *Wan Chai: a major district in HK Island*	L.2
wǎat⁶ lòng⁶ fūng¹ fàan⁴ 滑浪風帆 *(VO)* *wind-surfing*	L.6
wǎat⁶ sỳut³ 滑雪 *(VO) ski*	L.6
Wāi¹ Jǐ⁵ Sī¹ 威爾斯 *(PN) Wales*	*
wái² 位 *(M)* *[a measure word for a person and a way to show respect]*	L.7
wǎi³ 喂 *(Intj) hello; hey*	L.12
wàn⁴ tān¹ 雲吞 *(N) wonton*	L.10
wàn⁴ tān¹ mīn⁶ 雲吞麵 *(N) wonton noodles*	L.10
wǎn⁶ dǔng⁶ 運動 *(N) sports*	L.6

wàn⁶ dūng⁶ 運動 *(V) do physical exercises*	L.8
wàn⁶ sȳu¹ gūng¹ sī¹ 運輸公司 *(N)* *transport/freight corporation*	L.7
wó³ 喎 *(Part)* *[a final particle used to indicate surprise, discovery or realization]*	L.8
Wòng⁴ 黃／王 *(PN) a Chinese surname: Wong*	L.1
Wòng⁴ Bóu³ 黃埔 *(PN)* *a MTR station: Whampoa*	L.14
Wòng⁴ Càa⁴ 黃茶 *(PN)* *Yellow tea: non-fermented tea with yellow-green appearance*	L.12
Wòng⁴ Dāai⁶ Sīn¹ 黃大仙 *(PN)* *a MTR station: Wong Tai Sin*	L.14
Wòng⁴ Hāu⁶ Zōeng⁶ Gwóng² Còeng⁴ 皇后像廣場 *(PN) Statue Square*	L.14
Wòng⁴ Zūk¹ Hāang¹ 黃竹坑 *(PN)* *a MTR station: Wong Chuk Hang*	L.14
wòng⁴ sīk¹ 黃色 *(N) yellow*	L.13
Wòng⁴ Zīng¹ Zīng¹ 王晶晶 *(PN)* *a Chinese name: Zing-Zing Wong*	L.1
Wōng⁶ Gȯk³ 旺角 *(PN)* *Mong Kok: a major district in Kowloon*	L.2
Wōng⁶ Gȯk³ Dūng¹ 旺角東 *(PN)* *a MTR station: Mong Kok East*	L.14
Wū¹ Jǐ⁵ Dōu¹ Wáa² 烏爾都話 *(PN) Urdo*	*
Wū¹ Kāi¹ Sāa¹ 烏溪沙 *(PN)* *a MTR station: Wu Kai Sha*	L.14
Wū¹ Lúng² càa⁴ 烏龍茶 *(PN)* *Oolong tea: a semi-fermented tea*	L.12
wȕ⁴ 壺 *(N) teapot; a pot*	L.12
wȕ⁴ 壺 *(M) a pot of*	L.12
wū⁶ gȯk³ 芋角 *(N) taro dumplings*	L.12
wū⁶ sī⁶ 護士 *(N) nurse*	L.7
wū⁶ ziu³ 護照 *(N) passport*	L.4
wúi⁵ 會 *(AV) would; will* *[stresses the possibility or likelihood of such an event]*	L.15
Wūi⁶ Fūng¹ Ngàn⁴ Hòng⁴ 匯豐銀行 *(PN)* *HSBC [the Hongkong and Shanghai Banking Corporation]*	L.14
wūi⁶ gȧi³ hōk⁶ 會計學 *(N) accountancy*	L.5

wūi⁶ gȧi³ sī¹ 會計師 *(N) accountant*	L.7
Wūi⁶ Zín² 會展 *(PN) a MTR station: Exhibition*	L.14
wún² 碗 *(N) a bowl*	U.1
wún² 碗 *(M) a bowl of* *[a measure for the quantity of something that a bowl will hold]*	U.2
wūn⁶ 換 *(V)* *change; exchange; convert (currency)*	L.4

● Z

zāa¹ cē¹ 揸車 *(VO) drive (a vehicle)*	L.6
Zāa¹ Dáa² Ngàn⁴ Hòng⁴ 渣打銀行 *(PN)* *Standard Chartered Bank*	L.15
zāa¹ zàa⁴ 喳咋 *(N)* *sweet mixed beans soup with taro*	L.12
zȧa³ 炸 *(V) deep fry*	L.12
zȧa³ wàn⁴ tān¹ 炸雲吞 *(N)* *deep fried wonton served with sweet and sour sauce*	L.12
zāai¹ 齋 *(N) vegetarian food*	L.12
zāai¹ fē¹ 齋啡 *(N) black coffee*	L.11
zāam⁶ 站 *(N) station; a stop*	L.9
zāap⁶ jàu⁴ 集郵 *(VO) stamp collecting*	L.5
zāap⁶ māt⁶ fóng² 雜物房 *(N) store room*	L.3
záau² wūn⁶ dỉm³ 找換店 *(N)* *money exchange shop*	L.2
zái² 仔 *(N) son*	L.12
zāk¹ bīn¹ 側邊 *(N) beside; next to*	L.9
Zāk¹ J̀yu⁴ Cūng¹ 鰂魚涌 *(PN)* *a MTR station: Quarry Bay*	L.14
zān¹ hāi⁶ 真係 *(Adv) really; indeed*	L.12
zān¹ zȳu¹ gāai¹ 珍珠雞 *(N)* *lotus leaf wrapped sticky rice with chicken*	L.12
Zāng¹ Jȧm³ K̀yun⁴ 曾蔭權 *(PN)* *Donald Yam-Kuen Tsang, the Chief Executive of HKSAR, 2007*	L.1
Zāu¹ 周 *(PN)* *a Chinese surname: Chau, Chow, Chou*	L.1
zāu¹ mūt⁶ 週末 *(N) weekend*	L.8
zāu¹ wài⁴ 周圍 *(N) around; surroundings*	L.9
záu² 走 *(V) leave*	L.6
záu² 酒 *(N) wine; alcoholic beverage*	U.2

záu² dìm³ 酒店 *(N) hotel*	L.3
záu² làu⁴ 酒樓 *(N) Chinese restaurant*	L.7
záu² lóng² 走廊 *(N) corridor*	L.3
záu² sīn¹ 走先 *(Ph) leave first*	L.13
zău⁶ 就 *(Adv)* [tells the result and signifies emphatic confirmation]	L.15
zău⁶ 就 *(Conj) then* [used in a clause to indicate the consequence or result of an action]	L.14
zău⁶ dāk¹ làak³ 就得嘞 *(SE)* then that's be fine	L.14
zē¹ 啫 *(Part)* [a modal particle meaning 'only' or 'just' to play down the extent or significance of sth.]	L.6
zě³ zě³ 借借 *(Ph) let me go through*	U.2
zè⁴ zē¹ 姐姐 *(N) elder sister*	L.5
zěk³ 隻 *(M)* [a general measure word for most animals]	U.2
zěng³ 正 *(Adj) excellent, exact; cool*	L.11
zěoi³ 最 *(Adv) the most*	L.8
zī¹ 枝 *(M)* [a measure word for objects that are cylindrical, rigid, long and thin, e.g. pencils, cigarettes, etc.]	U.2
zī¹ 知 *(V) (short form of "zī¹ dǒu³")*	L.9
zī¹ dǒu³ 知道 *(V) to know about*	L.9
zī¹ màa⁴ wú² 芝蔴糊 *(N)* sweet black sesame soup	L.12
zí² 紙 *(N) paper*	U.2
zí² bǎi⁶ 紙幣 *(N) banknotes*	L.4
zí² mūi⁶ 姐妹 *(N) sisters*	L.11
zí² sīk¹ 紫色 *(N) purple*	L.13
zǐ³ 至 *(Prep) until; to*	L.8
Zǐ³ Děi⁶ Gwóng² Còeng⁴ 置地廣場 *(PN)* Landmark [an office and shopping mall with many prestige international brands in Central, HK]	L.14
Zǐ³ Lěi⁶ 智利 *(PN) Chile*	*
zī⁶ dūng⁶ 自動 *(Adj) automatic*	L.9
zī⁶ dūng⁶ gwǎi⁶ jỳun⁴ gēi¹ 自動櫃員機 *(N)* ATM (Automatic Teller Machine); cash machine	L.9
zīk¹ hǎi⁶ 即係 *(V) be; mean; namely; it means...*	L.11
zīk¹ jỳun⁴ 職員 *(N) shop assistant*	L.13
zīk⁶ hàang⁴ 直行 *(Ph) walk straight ahead*	L.15
Zīm¹ Dūng¹ 尖東 *(PN) Tsim Sha Tsui East* [a major district in Kowloon]	L.2, L.14
Zīm¹ Sāa¹ Zéoi² 尖沙咀 *(PN) Tsim Sha Tsui* [a major district in Kowloon]	L.2
zīn¹ sōeng¹ dáan² 煎雙蛋 *(Ph)* double sunny side up	L.10
zīng¹ 蒸 *(V) steam*	L.12
zīng¹ lùng⁴ 蒸籠 *(N)* food steamer (usually made of bamboo)	L.12
zìng³ fú² bǒu⁶ mùn⁴ 政府部門 *(N)* government departments	L.7
zìng³ ńg⁵ 正午 *(N) noon*	U.2
zīng⁶ 靜 *(Adj) quiet*	L.11
zīng⁶ hǎi⁶ 淨係 *(Adv) only*	L.4
zip³ dǒi⁶ jỳun⁴ 接待員 *(N) receptionist*	p.51
zit³ 折 *(N) discount* [the number before indicates the fraction to be paid in tenths]	L.13
Zit³ Hāk¹ 捷克 *(PN) Czech Republic*	*
zīu¹ tàu⁴ zóu² 朝頭早 *(N) in the morning*	U.2
zó² 咗 *(Part)* [an aspect particle used after a verb, indicating completed action whether in the past, present or future]	L.12
Zó² Dēon¹ 佐敦 *(PN) a MTR station: Jordan*	L.14
zó² mīn⁶ 左面 *(N) the left side*	L.9
Zōeng¹ 張 *(PN)* a Chinese surname: Cheung, Chang	L.1
zōeng¹ 張 *(M)* [a measure word for paper; cards; objects with a flat surface, such as chairs, tables or beds]	U.2
Zōeng¹ Gwān¹ Ôu³ 將軍澳 *(PN)* a MTR station: Tseung Kwan O	L.14
Zōeng¹ Gwān¹ Ôu³ Sin³ 將軍澳綫 *(PN)* Tseung Kwan O Line	L.14
zōeng¹ lòi⁴ 將來 *(N) future*	L.7
zōeng⁶ 像 *(N) statue*	L.15
zòi³ 再 *(Adv) again; once more*	*

zòi³ 再 (Adv) further; then	L.15
zòi³ gin³ 再見 (SE) goodbye; see you (again)	L.6
zòi³ hāa⁶ gò³ jỹut⁶ 再下個月 (N) the month after next	L.8
zòi³ hāa⁶ gò³ sīng¹ kèi⁴ 再下個星期 (Ph) the week after next	L.8
zòi³ sōeng⁶ gò³ jỹut⁶ 再上個月 (Ph) the month before last	L.8
zòi³ sōeng⁶ gò³ sīng¹ kèi⁴ 再上個星期 (Ph) the week before last	L.8
zóu² 早 (Adj) early	U.1
zóu² cāan¹ 早餐 (N) breakfast	L.9
zóu² sàn⁴ 早晨 (SE) good morning	L.9
zóu² táu² 早抖 (SE) good night	U.2
zòu⁶ 做 (V) do; work; engage in	L.8
zòu⁶ gūng¹ fò³ 做功課 (VO) do homework	L.9
zòu⁶ jě⁵ 做嘢 (VO) work	L.5
zòu⁶ māt¹ jě⁵ 做乜嘢 (SE) do what? [a phrase for asking what kind of activity or action is happening]	L.8
zòu⁶ sī⁶ 做事 (VO) work	L.8
zòu⁶ wàn⁶ dūng⁶ 做運動 (VO) do physical exercises	L.8
zūk¹ 粥 (N) rice congee; rice porridge	L.10
zūk¹ kéi² 捉棋 (VO) play chess	L.5
Zūng¹ Dūng¹ 中東 (PN) Middle East	L.2
zūng¹ gāan¹ 中間 (N) in the middle of; centre	L.9
Zūng¹ Gwòk³ còi³ 中國菜 (N) Chinese cuisine	L.12
Zūng¹ Gwòk³ 中國 (PN) China	L.2
Zūng¹ Gwòk³ dāai⁶ lūk⁶ 中國大陸 (PN) the Chinese mainland; mainland China	L.2
Zūng¹ Gwòk³ jām¹ ngòk⁶ 中國音樂 (N) Chinese music	L.5
Zūng¹ Gwòk³ Gūng¹ Sōeng¹ Ngàn⁴ Hòng⁴ (Åa³ Zāu¹) 中國工商銀行（亞洲）(PN) Industrial and Commercial Bank of China (Asia) (ICBC Asia)	L.15
Zūng¹ Gwòk³ Ngàn⁴ Hòng⁴ (Hōeng¹ Góng²) 中國銀行（香港）(PN) Bank of China (Hong Kong)	L.15

Zūng¹ Gwòk³ pàng⁴ jǎu⁵ 中國朋友 (N) a Chinese friend	L.7
zūng¹ hòk⁶ 中學 (N) secondary school	L.3
zūng¹ jī¹ 中醫 (N) a doctor of Chinese medicine	L.7
zūng¹ jì³ 中意／鍾意 (V) to like, be fond of	L.7
zūng¹ mǎa⁵ 中碼 (N) medium size	L.13
Zūng¹ Mán² 中文 (N) (see "Zūng¹ Màn⁴")	L.6
Zūng¹ Màn⁴ 中文 (N) Chinese language	L.6
Zūng¹ Měi⁵ Zāu¹ 中美洲 (PN) Middle America	L.2
zūng¹ nǧ⁵ 中午 (N) noon	U.2
Zūng¹ sīk¹ 中式 (N) Chinese style	L.10
Zūng¹ Sám² Fåat³ Jýun² 終審法院 (PN) Court of Final Appeal	L.14
Zūng¹ sīk¹ béng² sīk⁶ 中式餅食 (N) Chinese assorted cakes	L.13
Zūng¹ sīk¹ fūk⁶ zōng¹ 中式服裝 (N) Chinese clothing	L.13
Zūng¹ sīk¹ sīk⁶ gěoi⁶ 中式食具 (N) Chinese tableware	L.13
Zūng¹ Wàan⁴ 中環 (PN) Central [a major district in HK Island]	L.2
Zūng¹ Wàan⁴ Mǎa⁵ Tàu⁴ 中環碼頭 (PN) Central Ferry Piers	L.14
zúng² 糉 (N) glutinous rice dumpling	L.10
zúng² hóng² 總行 (N) headquarters	L.14
zúng² zāam⁶ 總站 (N) terminus; terminal station	L.14
zūng⁶ 仲 (Adv) (in addition to…) still; also [implies extra emphasis or surprise]	L.12
zȳu¹ jūk⁶ 豬肉 (N) pork	*
zȳu¹ còeng⁴ fán² 豬腸粉 (N) rice noodle rolls	L.10
zȳu¹ gū¹ līk¹ 朱古力 (N) chocolate; chocolate drink	L.11
zýu² fāan⁶ 煮飯 (VO) cook	L.6
zȳu⁶ 住 (V) live	L.3
zýun³ 轉 (V) to change; to turn (direction)	L.15
Zýun³ Sěk⁶ Sāan¹ 鑽石山 (PN) a MTR station: Diamond Hill	L.14

A	
above (N) sōeng⁶ mīn⁶ 上面	L.9
accountancy (N) wūi⁶ gåi³ hōk⁶ 會計學	L.5; L.7
accountant (N) wūi⁶ gåi³ sī¹ 會計師	L.7
actor; actress (N) jín² jýun⁴ 演員	L.7
add (V) gāa¹ 加	L.11
add up the bill; pay (VO) màai⁴ dāan¹ 埋單	L.12
address (V) cīng¹ fū¹ 稱呼	L.15
Admiralty (PN) a MTR station: Gām¹ Zūng¹ 金鐘	L.2
Africa (PN) Fēi¹ Zāu¹ 非洲	L.2
afternoon (N) åan³ zåu³ 晏晝	U.2
afterwards (Conj) jìn⁴ hāu⁶ 然後;gān¹ zy̌u⁶ 跟住	L.15
again (Adv) zói³ 再	L.15
age (N) ~ sẻoi³ 歲;nìn⁴ géi² 年紀	L.5
ahead (N) cìn⁴ mīn⁶ 前面	L.3
airline company (N) hòng⁴ hūng¹ gūng¹ sī¹ 航空公司	L.7
airplane (N) fēi¹ gēi¹ 飛機	L.14
airport (N) gēi¹ còeng⁴ 機場	L.2
airport bus (N) gēi¹ còeng⁴ bāa¹ sí² 機場巴士	L.2
Airport Express (PN) gēi¹ còeng⁴ fảai³ sin³ 機場快線	L.2
alcoholic beverage (N) záu² 酒	U.2
alight (VO) lōk⁶ cē¹ 落車	L.14
all (all-inclusive) (Adv) dōu¹ 都	L.8
all (everybody) (Pn) dāai⁶ gāa¹ 大家	L.5
almond drink (N) hāng⁶ jàn⁴ sōeng¹ 杏仁霜	L.11
almost (Adv) cāa¹ m̀² dō¹ 差唔多	U.2
alright; okay; fine (Adj) dāk¹ 得	U.1
also (Adv) dōu¹ 都	L.7
altogether (Adv) jāt¹ gūng⁶ 一共	L.11
always (Adv) sì⁴ sì⁴ 時時;gīng¹ sòeng⁴ 經常	L.7
A.M. (N) sōeng⁶ zåu³ 上晝;sōeng⁶ nǧ⁵ 上午	U.2
amah (N) gūng¹ jàn⁴ 工人	L.7
Americans (PN) Měi⁵ Gwỏk³ jàn⁴ 美國人	L.5

American nationality (N) Měi⁵ zīk⁶ 美籍	L.5
American of African descent (Ph) Fēi¹ jēoi⁶ Měi⁵ Gwỏk³ jàn⁴ 非裔美國人	L.5
and (Conj) tùng⁴ 同;tùng⁴ màai⁴ 同埋	L.4
And you? (SE) něi⁵ nē¹? 你呢?	L.6
Antarctic (PN) Nàam⁴ Gīk⁶ 南極	*
April (PN) sẻi³ jýut⁶ 四月	L.8
architecture (N) gin³ zūk¹ hōk⁶ 建築學	L.5
Arctic (PN) Bāk¹ Gīk⁶ 北極	*
Argentina (PN) Åa³ Gān¹ Tìng⁴ 阿根廷	*
around (N) zāu¹ wài⁴ 周圍	L.9
artist (N) ngāi⁶ jàn⁴ 藝人	L.7
Asia (PN) Åa³ Zāu¹ 亞洲	L.2
AsiaWorld-Expo (PN) a MTR station: Bỏk³ Lǎam⁵ Gún² 博覽館	L.14
ask (V) màn⁶ 問	U.1
at (a place) (Prep) hái² 喺	L.3
at (a place) (V) hái² 喺	L.2
at the back (N) hāu⁶ mīn⁶ 後面	L.9
at what time (QW) géi² sì⁴ 幾時	L.8
ATM (N) zī⁶ dūng⁶ gwāi⁶ jýun⁴ gēi¹ 自動櫃員機	L.9
attend a meeting (VO) hōi¹ wúi² 開會	L.6
attend class (VO) sōeng⁵ tòng⁴ 上堂	L.8
attend school (VO) fāan¹ hōk⁶ 返學	L.6
Au Yeung (Chinese surname) (PN) Āu¹ Jòeng⁴ 歐陽	L.1
audio & visual gadgets (Ph) jíng² jām¹ hēi³ còi⁴ 影音器材	L.13
August (PN) båat³ jýut⁶ 八月	L.8
Austin (PN) a MTR station: Ō¹ Sī⁶ Dīn¹ 柯士甸	L.14
Australia (PN) Où³ Zāu¹ 澳洲	L.2
Australian Dollars (PN) Où³ Jýun⁴ 澳元	L.4
Austria (PN) Où³ Dēi³ Lēi¹ 奧地利	*
automatic (Adj) zī⁶ dūng⁶ 自動	L.9
Automatic Teller Machine (N) zī⁶ dūng⁶ gwāi⁶ jýun⁴ gēi¹ 自動櫃員機	L.9

back door (N) hāu⁶ mún² 後門	L.3
bacon (N) jīn¹ jūk⁶ 煙肉	L.10
bad (Adj) wāai⁶ 壞	U.1
bad (not up to standard) (Adj) cāa¹ 差；séoi² pèi⁴ 水皮	L.11
bad (wicked, evil-minded) (Adj) sēoi¹ 衰	L.11
Bahrain (PN) Bāa¹ Làm⁴ 巴林	*
baked (V) gūk⁶ 焗	L.12
baked sago and mashed lotus seed pudding (N) lìn⁴ jùng⁴ gūk⁶ bòu³ dīn¹ 蓮蓉焗布甸	L.12
balcony (N) kè⁴ láu² 騎樓；lòu⁶ tòi⁴ 露台	L.3
Bangladesh (PN) Māang⁶ Gāa¹ Lāai¹ 孟加拉	*
bank (N) ngàn⁴ hòng⁴ 銀行	L.2
Bank of China (PN) Zūng¹ Gwók³ Ngàn⁴ Hòng⁴ 中國銀行	L.15
Bank of Communications (PN) Gāau¹ Tūng¹ Ngàn⁴ Hòng⁴ 交通銀行	L.15
Bank of East Asia (PN) Dūng¹ Aả³ Ngàn⁴ Hòng⁴ 東亞銀行	L.15
banknotes (N) zí² bāi⁶ 紙幣	L.4
banana (N) hōeng¹ zīu¹ 香蕉	U.1
barbecue pork buns (N) cāa¹ sīu¹ bāau¹ 叉燒包	L.12
barbecue pork pastries (N) cāa¹ sīu¹ sōu¹ 叉燒酥	L.12
bath (V) cūng¹ lòeng⁴ 沖涼	L.3
bathroom (N) cūng¹ lòeng⁴ fóng² 沖涼房；jūk⁶ sāt¹ 浴室	L.3
be (is, am, are; was, were) (V) hāi⁶ 係	L.1
be (namely) (V) zīk¹ hāi⁶ 即係	L.11
be called (known as) (V) giu³ zōu⁶ 叫做；giu³ 叫	L.10
be fond of (V) zūng¹ jì³ 中意/鍾意	L.7
be occupied (with a matter) (Ph) jǎu⁵ sī⁶ 有事	L.6
be surnamed (V) sing³ 姓	L.6
beautiful (Adj) lěng³ 靚	U.1; L.3
bedroom (N) sēoi⁶ fóng² 睡房	L.3
bedspace apartments (N) còng⁴ wái² 牀位	L.3
beef (N) ngàu⁴ jūk⁶ 牛肉	*
beef brisket (N) ngàu⁴ nǎam⁵ 牛腩	U.1
beef meatballs (N) ngàu⁴ jūk⁶ kàu⁴ 牛肉球	L.12
beef stomach (N) ngàu⁴ pǎak³ jīp⁶ 牛栢葉	L.12
beer (N) bē¹ záu² 啤酒	L.3
Belgium (PN) Béi² Lēi⁶ Sì⁴ 比利時	*
below (N) hǎa⁶ mīn⁶ 下面	L.9
beside (N) gảak³ lèi⁴ 隔籬；zāk¹ bīn¹ 側邊；pòng⁴ bīn¹ 旁邊	L.9
bicycle (N) dāan¹ cē¹ 單車	L.14
big (Adj) dāai⁶ 大	U.1; L.3
bill (N) dāan¹ 單	U.1
biology (N) sāng¹ māt⁶ 生物	L.5
black (N) hāk¹ sīk¹ 黑色	L.13
black coffee (N) zāai¹ fē¹ 齋啡	L.11
black tea (N) hùng⁴ càa⁴ 紅茶；Hāk¹ Càa⁴ 黑茶	L.12
blue (N) làam⁴ sīk¹ 藍色	L.13
boiling water (Ph) gwán² séoi² 滾水	L.12
book (N) sȳu¹ 書	U.1
bookshop (N) sȳu¹ dìm³ 書店；sȳu¹ gúk² 書局	L.9
boot (N) hōe¹ 靴	U.1
boring (Adj) mūn⁶ 悶	U.1
boss (N) lǒu⁵ báan² 老闆	L.5
bowl (N/M) wún² 碗	L.10
boyfriend (N) nàam⁴ pàng⁴ jǎu⁵ 男朋友	L.7
brand (brand name) (N) pàai⁴ zí² 牌子	L.13
Brazil (PN) Bāa¹ Sāi¹ 巴西	*
bread (N) mīn⁶ bāau¹ 麵包	L.10
breakfast (N) zóu² cāan¹ 早餐	L.9
breakfast cereal (N) gūk¹ lēoi⁶ zóu² cāan¹ 穀類早餐	L.10
British (PN) Jīng¹ Gwók³ jàn⁴ 英國人	L.6
British Indian (Ph) Jīng¹ zīk⁶ Jản³ Dōu⁶ jàn⁴ 英籍印度人	L.5
British Pounds Sterling (PN) Jīng¹ Bòng⁶ 英鎊；Jīng¹ Bóng² 英鎊	L.4
brothers (N) hīng¹ dāi⁶ 兄弟	L.11
brothers and sisters (Ph) hīng¹ dāi⁶ zí² mūi⁶ 兄弟姊妹	L.5

brown (N) gåa³ fē¹ sīk¹ 咖啡色；fē¹ sīk¹ 啡色	L.13
Bruce Lee (PN) Lěi⁵ Síu² Lùng⁴ 李小龍	L.1
Burma (PN) Mǐn⁵ Dīn⁶ 緬甸	*
bus (N) bāa¹ sí² 巴士	L.14
bus stop (N) bāa¹ sí² zāam⁶ 巴士站	L.14
business management (N) gūng¹ sōeng¹ gún² lěi⁵ 工商管理	L.5
busy (Adj) mòng⁴ 忙	L.8
but (Conj) bāt¹ gwỏ³ 不過	L.7
butter & jam on toast (N) jàu⁴ zīm¹ dō¹ 油占多	L.10
butter & condense milk on toast (N) nǎai⁵ jàu⁴ dō¹ 奶油多	L.10
buy (V) mǎai⁵ 買	L.13
by ferry (VO) dåap³ sỳun⁴ 搭船	L.14
by MTR (VO) dåap³ dēi⁶ tit³ 搭地鐵	L.14
by the way (Intj) hǎi⁶ nē¹ 係呢	L.6
by the side of (N) zåk¹ bīn¹ 側邊；pòng⁴ bīn¹ 旁邊	*
bye-bye (SE) bāai¹ båai³ 拜拜	L.6

● C

cable car (N) lāam⁶ cē¹ 纜車	L.14
cable car station (N) lāam⁶ cē¹ zāam⁶ 纜車站	L.14
call; ***be called*** (V) giu³ 叫	L.1
Cambodia (PN) Gáan² Pòu⁴ Zāai⁶ 柬埔寨	*
camera (N) sóeng² gēi¹ 相機	L.13
Canada (PN) Gāa¹ Nàa⁴ Dāai⁶ 加拿大	L.5
Canadian Dollars (PN) Gāa¹ Jỳun⁴ 加元	L.4
Canadian of French descent (Ph) Fåat³ jēoi⁶ Gāa¹ Nàa⁴ Dāai⁶ jàn⁴ 法裔加拿大人	L.5
Canton (PN) Gwóng² Dūng¹ Sáang² 廣東省；Gwóng² Zāu¹ 廣州	U.1
Cantonese dialect (PN) Gwóng² Dūng¹ Wáa² 廣東話	U.1
Cantonese people (N) Gwóng² Dūng¹ jàn⁴ 廣東人	L.7
capable (clever; brilliant) (Adj) lēk¹ 叻	U.1
car (N) cē¹ 車	U.1

card (N) kāat¹ 咭／卡	L.13
carpark (N) tìng⁴ cē¹ còeng⁴ 停車場	L.2; L.13
cash machine (N) zī⁶ dūng⁶ gwāi⁶ jỳun⁴ gēi¹ 自動櫃員機	L.9
cashier (N) sāu¹ ngán² jỳun⁴ 收銀員	p.50
casino (N) dóu² còeng⁴ 賭場	L.8
cat (N) māau¹ 貓	U.1
Causeway Bay (PN) a MTR station: Tùng⁴ Lò⁴ Wāan¹ 銅鑼灣；Tùng⁴ Lò⁴ Wàan⁴ 銅鑼灣	L.2
Central (PN) a MTR station: Zūng¹ Wàan⁴ 中環	L.2
century egg (N) pèi⁴ dáan² 皮蛋	L.10
Central Ferry Piers (PN) Zūng¹ Wàan⁴ Mǎa⁵ Tàu⁴ 中環碼頭	L.14
Chai Wan (PN) a MTR station: Càai⁴ Wāan¹ 柴灣	L.14
Chan (Chinese surname) (PN) Càn⁴ 陳	L.1
Chang (Chinese surname) (PN) Zōeng¹ 張	L.1
change (direction) (V) zýun³ 轉	L.15
chat (VO) kīng¹ gái² 傾偈	L.8
chat on the phone (VO) kīng¹ dīn⁶ wáa² 傾電話	L.8
Chau (Chinese surname) (PN) Zāu¹ 周	L.1
Che Kung Temple (PN) a MTR station: Cē¹ Gūng¹ Míu² 車公廟	L.14
cheap (Adj) pèng⁴ 平	U.1
Cheaper, please! (SE) pèng⁴ dī¹ lāa¹ 平啲啦	L.13
chef (N) cèoi⁴ sī¹ 廚師；cỳu⁴ sī¹ 廚師	L.7
chemistry (N) fåa³ hōk⁶ 化學	L.5
Chen (Chinese surname) (PN) Càn⁴ 陳	L.1
Cheung (Chinese surname) (PN) Zōeng¹ 張	L.1
Cheung Sha Wan (PN) a MTR station: Còeng⁴ Sāa¹ Wàan⁴ 長沙灣	L.14
Chile (PN) Zǐ³ Lěi⁶ 智利	*
China (PN) Zūng¹ Gwỏk³ 中國	L.2
Chinese assorted cakes (N) Zūng¹ sīk¹ béng² sīk⁶ 中式餅食	L.13
Chinese clothing (N) Zūng¹ sīk¹ fūk⁶ zōng¹ 中式服裝	L.13

Chinese cuisine (N) Zūng¹ Gwők³ cỏi³ 中國菜	L.12
Chinese descent (N) Wàa⁴ jēoi⁶ 華裔	L.5
Chinese friend (N) Zūng¹ Gwők³ pàng⁴ jǎu⁵ 中國朋友	L.7
Chinese language (N) Zūng¹ Mán² 中文；Zūng¹ Màn⁴ 中文	L.6
Chinese mainland (PN) Zūng¹ Gwők³ dāai⁶ lūk⁶ 中國大陸	L.2
Chinese music (N) Zūng¹ Gwők³ jām¹ ngōk⁶ 中國音樂	L.5
Chinese origin (N) Wàa⁴ jēoi⁶ 華裔	L.5
Chinese restaurant (N) záu² làu⁴ 酒樓	L.7
Chinese style (N) Zūng¹ sīk¹ 中式	L.10
Chinese tableware (N) Zūng¹ sīk¹ sīk⁶ gēoi⁶ 中式食具	L.13
Chinese turnip cake (N) lò⁴ bāak⁶ gōu¹ 蘿蔔糕	L.12
Chinese Yuan; Renminbi (PN) Jàn⁴ Màn⁴ Bāi⁶ 人民幣	L.4
Chiu Chow style dumplings (N) cìu⁴ zāu¹ fán² gwó² 潮洲粉果	L.12
Chiu Chow style sweet paste bun (N) cìu⁴ zāu¹ séoi² zīng¹ bāau¹ 潮洲水晶包	L.12
chocolate (N) zȳu¹ gū¹ līk¹ 朱古力	L.11
chocolate drink (N) zȳu¹ gū¹ līk¹ 朱古力	L.11
Choi Hung (PN) Cói² Hùng⁴ 彩虹	L.14
Chow (Chinese surname) (PN) Zāu¹ 周	L.1
Christmas (PN) Sìng³ Dảan³ Zỉt³ 聖誕節	U.2
Chui (Chinese surname) (PN) Cèoi⁴ 徐；Cēoi¹ 崔	L.1
cinema (N) hẻi³ jýun² 戲院	L.9
Citibank (Hong Kong) Limited (PN) Fāa¹ Kèi⁴ Ngàn⁴ Hòng⁴ (Hōeng¹ Góng²) 花旗銀行（香港）	L.15
city (N) sǐ⁵ 市；sìng⁴ sǐ⁵ 城市	U.1
City Hall (PN) Dāai⁶ Wūi⁶ Tòng⁴ 大會堂	L.14
City One (PN) a MTR station: Dāi⁶ Jāt¹ Sìng⁴ 第一城	L.14
City University of Hong Kong (PN) Hōeng¹ Góng² Sìng⁴ Sǐ⁵ Dāai⁶ Hōk⁶ 香港城市大學	*
civil servant (N) gūng¹ mõu⁶ jỳun⁴ 公務員	L.7

classical music (N) gú² dín² jām¹ ngōk⁶ 古典音樂	L.5
clear (Adj) cīng¹ có² 清楚	U.1
clever (intelligent) (Adj) lēk¹ 叻；cūng¹ mìng⁴ 聰明	U.1; L.8
clinic (N) cán² só² 診所	L.7
close (Adj) kǎn⁵ 近	U.1
clothes (clothing) (N) sāam¹ 衫	U.1
coach (N) gǎau³ lǐn⁶ 教練	L.7
cocktail bun (N) gāi¹ měi⁵ bāau¹ 鷄尾包	L.10
coffee (N) gảa³ fē¹ 咖啡	L.11
coins (N) sáan² ngán² 散銀；ngāang⁶ bāi⁶ 硬幣	L.4
Coke (N) hó² lōk⁶ 可樂	L.11
Coke with lemon (N) níng² lōk⁶ 檸樂	L.11
cold (Adj) dủng³ 凍	U.1
colleague (N) tùng⁴ sǐ⁶ 同事	L.5
college (N) hōk⁶ jýun² 學院	L.7
Colombia (PN) Gō¹ Lèon⁴ Béi² Aả³ 哥倫比亞	*
colour (N) ngàan⁴ sīk¹ 顏色	L.13
come (V) lèi⁴ *(also "lài⁴")* 嚟	L.3
come home (VO) fāan¹ ūk¹ kéi² 返屋企	L.12
come in (Ph) jāp⁶ lèi⁴ *(also "jāp⁶ lài⁴")* 入嚟	L.3
come out from (V) cēot¹ 出	U.1
comfortable (Adj) sȳu¹ fūk⁶ 舒服	L.11
company (N) gūng¹ sī¹ 公司	L.7
computer firm (N) dīn⁶ nǒu⁵ gūng¹ sī¹ 電腦公司	L.7
congee with century egg and lean pork (Ph) pèi⁴ dáan² sảu³ jūk⁶ zūk¹ 皮蛋瘦肉粥	L.10
construction company (N) gin³ zūk¹ gūng¹ sī¹ 建築公司	L.7
continent (N) dāai⁶ lūk⁶ 大陸	L.2
convenience store (N) bīn⁶ lēi⁶ dim³ 便利店	L.9
convenient (Adj) fōng¹ bīn⁶ 方便	L.11
convert (currency) (V) wūn⁶ 換	L.4
cook (chef) (N) cèoi⁴ sī¹ 廚師；cyu⁴ sī¹ 廚師	L.7
cook (VO) zýu² fāan⁶ 煮飯	L.6
cooked rice (N) fāan⁶ 飯	L.12
cool (excellent, exact) (Adj) zẻng³ 正	L.11

corner (N) wāan¹ 彎	L.15
corporation (N) gūng¹ sī¹ 公司	L.7
corpse (N) sī¹ 屍	U.1
correct (Adj) ngāam¹ 啱	L.11
corridor (N) záu² lóng² 走廊	L.3
Court of Final Appeal (PN) Zūng¹ Sám² Fåat³ Jýun² 終審法院	L.14
country (N) gwŏk³ gāa¹ 國家	L.2
course (N) fŏ³ cìng⁴ 課程	L.1
crazy (Adj) cī¹ sìn³ 黐線	L.11
credit card (N) sêon³ jūng⁶ kāat¹ 信用咭	L.4
crow (N) āa¹ 鴉；wū¹ āa¹ 烏鴉	U.1
cup (N/M) būi¹ 杯	L.11
cute (Adj) hó² ŏi³ 可愛；dāk¹ ji³ 得意	*
cycling (VO) cáai² dāan¹ cē¹ 踩單車；jáai² dāan¹ cē¹ 踩單車	L.6
Czech Republic (PN) Zǐt³ Hāk¹ 捷克	*

<!-- D section -->
• 𝒟	
Dah Sing Bank Limited (PN) Dāai⁶ Sān¹ Ngàn⁴ Hòng⁴ 大新銀行	L.15
dance (VO) tîu³ mǒu⁵ 跳舞	L.5
dangerous (Adj) ngài⁴ hím² 危險	L.11
data SIM card (N) sôu³ gêoi³ sīm¹ kāat¹ 數據SIM卡	L.4
daughter (N) néoi² 女	L.12
day (N) jāt⁶ 日	U.2
day after tomorrow (N) hāu⁶ jāt⁶ 後日	L.8
day before yesterday (N) cìn⁴ jāt⁶ 前日	L.8
day of a month (N/M) hŏu⁶ 號	L.8
DBS Bank Limited (PN) Sīng¹ Zín² Ngàn⁴ Hòng⁴ 星展銀行	L.15
December (PN) sāp⁶ ji⁶ jyut⁶ 十二月	L.8
deep-fried breadstick (N) jàu⁴ zåa³ gwái² 油炸鬼；jàu⁴ tíu² 油條	L.10
deep-fried wonton (N) zåa³ wàn⁴ tān¹ 炸雲吞	L.12
deep fry (V) zåa³ 炸	L.12
deficient (Adj) kwāi¹ 虧	U.1
delicious (Ph) hóu² hóu² sīk⁶ 好好食	L.10
Deng Xiaoping (PN) Dāng⁶ Síu² Pìng⁴ 鄧小平	L.1
Denmark (PN) Dāan¹ Māk⁶ 丹麥	*

department store (N) båak³ fŏ³ gūng¹ sī¹ 百貨公司	L.7
Des Voeux Road (PN) Dāk¹ Fū⁶ Dōu⁶ 德輔道	L.15
descend (V) lōk⁶ 落	U.1
dessert (N) tìm⁴ bán² 甜品	L.12
dial (V) dáa² (dīn⁶ wáa²) 打（電話）	U.2
Diamond Hill (PN) a MTR station: Zýun³ Sēk⁶ Sāan¹ 鑽石山	L.14
diarrhea (N/V) ō¹ 屙	U.1
difficult (Adj) nàan⁴ 難	U.1
dim-sum (N) dím² sām¹ 點心	L.12
dim-sum menu (N) dím² sām¹ zí² 點心紙	L.12
dining room (N) fāan⁶ tēng¹ 飯廳	L.3
dinner (N) mǎan⁵ fāan⁶ 晚飯	L.12
discount (N) zǐt³ 折	L.13
discount of 10% (Ph) gáu² zǐt³ 九折	L.13
discount of 15% (Ph) båat³ nǧ⁵ zǐt³ 八五折	L.13
discount of 20 % (Ph) båat³ zǐt³ 八折	L.13
discount of 30 % (Ph) cāt¹ zǐt³ 七折	L.13
discount of 40 % (Ph) lūk⁶ zǐt³ 六折	L.13
discount of 50% (Ph) nǧ⁵ zǐt³ 五折	L.13
Disneyland Resort (PN) a MTR station: Dīk⁶ Sī⁶ Nèi⁴ 迪士尼	L.14
Disneyland Resort Line (PN) Dīk⁶ Sī⁶ Nèi⁴ Sin³ 迪士尼綫	L.14
dive (VO) cìm⁴ séoi² 潛水	L.6
do (work; engage in) (V) zŏu⁶ 做	L.8
do as one pleases (Adv) cêoi⁴ bín² 隨便	L.13
do homework (VO) zŏu⁶ gūng¹ fŏ³ 做功課	L.9
do physical exercises (VO) (zŏu⁶) wān⁶ dūng⁶ （做）運動	L.8
do shopping (buy something) (VO) mǎai⁵ jě⁵ 買野	L.8
do what (SE) zŏu⁶ māt¹ jě⁵ 做乜野？	L.8
Do you know... (Ph) něi⁵ zī¹ m̀⁴ zī¹... ? 你知唔知...？	L.14
doctor of Chinese medicine (N) zūng¹ jī¹ 中醫	L.7
dog (N) gáu² 狗	U.1
dollars (measure unit for money) (M) māan¹ 蚊	L.4
domestic helper (N) gūng¹ jàn⁴ 工人	L.7

Don't mention it. *(SE)* m̀^{4} sái^2 håak^3 he̊i^3 唔使客氣	L.9
don't move *(Ph)* mǎi^5 jūk^1 咪郁	U.2
Donald Yam-Kuen Tsang *(the Chief Executive of HKSAR, 2006)* *(PN)* Zāng^1 Jåm^3-Kỳun^4 曾蔭權	L.1
doorway *(entrance) (N)* mùn^4 háu^2 門口	L.15
dormitory *(N)* sūk^1 se̊^{3} 宿舍	L.3
double room *(room for two)* *(N)* sōeng^1 jàn^4 fóng^2 雙人房	L.3
double sunny side up *(Ph)* zīn^1 sōeng^1 dáan^2 煎雙蛋	L.10
double-boiled fresh milk and egg white *(N)* sōeng^1 pèi^4 nǎai^5 雙皮奶	L.12
downstairs *(N)* làu^4 hāa^6 樓下	L.9
drink *(V)* jám^2 飲	L.11
drink tea *(VO)* jám^2 càa^4 飲茶	L.12
drive *(a vehicle) (VO)* zāa^1 cē^1 揸車	L.6
driver *(N)* sī^1 gēi^1 司機	L.3
dry *(Adj)* gōn^1 乾	U.1
• *E*	
early *(Adj)* zóu^2 早	U.1
east *(N)* dūng^1 東	L.15
East Rail Line *(PN)* Dūng^1 Ti̊t^3 Si̊n^3 東鐵綫	L.14
easy *(Adj)* jī^6 易；jùng^4 jī^6 容易	U.1
eat *(V)* sīk^6 食	L.9
eat here *(Ph)* hái^2 dōu^6 sīk^6 喺度食	L.11
eat something *(VO)* sīk^6 jě^5 食嘢	L.8
economics *(N)* gīng^1 zåi^3 經濟	L.5
education *(N)* gåau^3 jūk^6 教育	L.5
Education University of Hong Kong *(PN)* Hōeng^1 Góng^2 Gåau^3 Jūk^6 Dāai^6 Hōk^6 香港教育大學	*
egg *(N)* dáan^2 蛋；gāi^1 dáan^2 雞蛋	L.11
egg custard tart *(N)* dāan^6 tāat^1 蛋撻	L.10
Egypt *(PN)* Āai^1 Kāp^6 埃及	*
eight *(Nu)* båat^3 八	U.1
elder brother *(N)* gò^4 gō^1 哥哥	L.5
elder sister *(N)* zè^4 zē^1 姐姐	L.5
electronic engineering *(N)* dīn^6 zí^2 gūng^1 cìng^4 電子工程	L.5

elevator *(N)* sīng^1 go̊ng^3 gēi^1 升降機；līp^1 𨋢；dīn^6 tāi^1 電梯	L.3
embroideries *(N)* ci̊^{3} såu^3 bán^2 刺繡品	L.13
emergency call *(Nu)* gáu^2 gáu^2 gáu^2 九九九	U.2
England *(PN)* Jīng^1 Gåak^3 Làan^4 英格蘭	*
English language *(PN)* Jīng^1 Mán^2 英文；Jīng^1 Màn^4 英文	L.6
enter *(go inside) (Ph)* jāp^6 he̊oi^3 入去	L.15
entrance *(N)* jāp^6 háu^2 入口	L.2
escalator *(N)* dīn^6 tāi^1 電梯	L.3
Europe *(PN)* Āu^1 Zāu^1 歐洲	L.2
Euros *(PN)* Āu^1 Lò^4 歐羅；Āu^1 Jỳun^4 歐元	L.4
evening *(N)* jē^6 mǎan^5 夜晚	U.2
everybody *(Pn)* dāai^6 gāa^1 大家	L.5
every day *(Pn)* mǔi^5 jāt^6 每日	L.14
evil-minded *(Adj)* sēoi^1 衰	L.11
excellent *(Adj)* sāi^1 lēi^6 犀利	L.11
excessively *(Adv)* tåai^3 太	L.13
exchange *(V)* wūn^6 換；*(V)* gāau^1 wūn^6 交換	L.4; L.5
Exchange Square *(PN)* Gāau^1 Jīk^6 Gwóng^2 Còeng^4 交易廣場	L.14
excuse me *(sorry)* *(SE)* m̀^{4} hóu^2 ji̊^{3} sī^1 唔好意思；m̀^{4} hóu^2 ji̊^{3} si̊^{3} 唔好意思	L.6
excuse me *[to draw sb's attention usually when one inquires sth.] (SE)* m̀^{4} gōi^1 唔該	L.3
Exhibition *(PN) a MTR station:* Wūi^6 Zín^2 會展	L.14
exit *(N)* cēot^1 háu^2 出口	L.2
expensive *(Adj)* gwåi^3 貴	U.1
extra-large size *(Ph)* gāa^1 dāai^6 mǎa^5 加大碼	L.13
extra-small size *(Ph)* gāa^1 såi^3 mǎa^5 加細碼	L.13
extreme, *terrific (Adj)* sāi^1 lēi^6 犀利	L.11
eyeglasses *(N)* ngǎan^5 géng^2 眼鏡	L.13
• *F*	
face to *(Prep)* ho̊eng^3 向	L.15
factory *(N)* gūng^1 cóng^2 工廠	L.7
faculty *(N)* hōk^6 jýun^2 學院	L.7
fairly *(Adv)* géi^2 幾	L.8
fall *(V)* lōk^6 落	U.1

family (N) ūk¹ kéi² jàn⁴ 屋企人	L.3
Fanling (PN) a MTR station: Fán² Lěng⁵ 粉嶺	L.14
far (Adj) jǘun⁵ 遠	L.11
fast (Adj) fåai³ 快	U.1
fast food shop (N) fåai³ cāan¹ dìm³ 快餐店	L.2
fat (Adj) fèi⁴ 肥	L.11
father (N) bàa⁴ bāa¹ 爸爸	L.4
February (PN) jī⁶ jǜut⁶ 二月	L.8
feces (N) sí² 屎	U.1
feel (V) gȯk³ dāk¹ 覺得	L.10
ferry (N) sỳun⁴ 船；síu² lèon⁴ 小輪	L.14
fetch (V) ló² 攞	L.9
few (a little) (Nu) síu² síu² 少少； (Adj) síu² 少	L.6; U.1
fifty cents (Ph) nǧ⁵ hòu⁴ 五毫	L.4
fifty dollars (Ph) nǧ⁵ sāp⁶ mān¹ 五十蚊	L.4
Filipino language (PN) Fēi¹ Lēot⁶ Bān¹ Wáa² 菲律賓話	L.6
finance corporation (N) gām¹ jùng⁴ gūng¹ sī¹ 金融公司	L.7
fine (okay) [used to express agreement] (SE) hóu² lāa¹ 好啦；hóu² åak³ 好呃	L.13
fine arts (N) ngài⁶ sēot⁶ 藝術	L.5
finish work at the end of the day (VO) fòng³ gūng¹ 放工	L.12
Finland (PN) Fān¹ Làan⁴ 芬蘭	*
fire station (N) sīu¹ fòng⁴ gúk² 消防局	L.9
fireman (N) sīu¹ fòng⁴ jǜun⁴ 消防員	L.7
firm (N) gūng¹ sī¹ 公司	L.7
first; in advance (Adv) sīn¹ 先	L.12
first (N) dài⁶ jāt¹ 第一	L.15
fish (N) jýu² 魚	U.1
five (Nu) nǧ⁵ 五	U.1
five dollars (Ph) nǧ⁵ mān¹ 五蚊	L.4
five hundred dollars (Ph) nǧ⁵ båak³ mān¹ 五百蚊	L.4
flatter (V) gwȯ³ zóeng² 過獎	L.8
floor (N) láu² 樓	L.9
flower (N) fāa¹ 花	U.1
follow (V) gān¹ 跟	U.2

food steamer (usually made of bamboo) (N) zīng¹ lùng⁴ 蒸籠	L.12
foot (N) gȯek³ 腳	U.1
foreign language (N) ngȏi⁶ gwȯk³ wáa² 外國話	L.6
foreign student (N) làu⁴ hȏk⁶ sāang¹ 留學生	L.3
fork (N) cāa¹ 叉	L.3
Fortress Hill (PN) a MTR station: Påau³ Tòi⁴ Sāan¹ 炮台山	L.14
Fo Tan (PN) a MTR station: Fó² Tȧn³ 火炭	L.14
four (Nu) sėi³ 四	U.1
fragrant (Adj) hōeng¹ 香	U.1
France (PN) Fåat³ Gwȯk³ 法國	L.5
free (not busy) (Adj) dāk¹ hàan⁴ 得閒	L.8
free size (Ph) fī¹ sāai¹ sí² *Free* 晒士； jāt¹ gȯ³ mǎa⁵ 一個碼	L.13
French language (PN) Fåat³ Mán² 法文；Fåat³ Màn⁴ 法文	L.6
French toast (N) sāi¹ dō¹ sí² 西多士	L.10
French Turk (Ph) Fåat³ zĩk⁶ Tóu² Jī⁵ Kèi⁴ jàn⁴ 法籍土耳其人	L.5
fresh milk (N) sīn¹ nǎai⁵ 鮮奶	L.11
Friday (PN) lǎi⁵ båai³ nǧ⁵ 禮拜五； sīng¹ kèi⁴ nǧ⁵ 星期五	L.8
fried noodle (N) cáau² mȉn⁶ 炒麵	L.10
fried rice (N) cáau² fāan⁶ 炒飯	L.12
friend (N) pàng⁴ jǎu⁵ 朋友	L.3; L.7
from (Prep) jàu⁴ 由	L.6
front door (N) cìn⁴ mún² 前門	L.3
front side (N) cìn⁴ mȉn⁶ 前面	L.3
full (Adj) báau² 飽	L.10
fun (Adj) hóu² wáan² 好玩	L.11
further (Adv) zȯi³ 再	L.15
future (N) zōeng¹ lòi⁴ 將來	L.7

● *G*	
garage (N) cē¹ fòng⁴ 車房	L.3
garbage room (N) làap⁶ såap³ fòng⁴ 垃圾房	L.3
garment (N) sāam¹ 衫	L.13
German language (PN) Dāk¹ Mán² 德文；Dāk¹ Màn⁴ 德文	L.6

Germany (PN) Dāk¹ Gwŏk³ 德國	*
get married (VO) gít³ fān¹ 結婚	L.12
get off a vehicle (VO) lŏk⁶ cē¹ 落車	L.14
get up (VO) héi² sān¹ 起身	L.8
girlfriend (N) něoi⁵ pàng⁴ jǎu⁵ 女朋友	L.4
give (V) béi² 俾	L.13
glass (N) būi¹ 杯	L.11
go (V) hèoi³ 去	L.2
go home (VO) fāan¹ ūk¹ kéi² 返屋企	L.12
go Dutch (SE) ēi¹ ēi¹ zǎi³ ＡＡ制	L.12*
go on duty (VO) fāan¹ gūng¹ 返工	L.8
go out (VO) cēot¹ gāai¹ 出街； hèoi³ gāai¹ 去街	L.10; L.12
go out from (V) cēot¹ 出	U.1
go to restaurant for dim-sum *(VO)* jám² càa⁴ 飲茶；sĭk⁶ dím² sām¹ 食點心	L.8; L.12
go to school (VO) fāan¹ hŏk⁶ 返學； *(V)* dŭk⁶ 讀	L.6
go to university (VO) dŭk⁶ dāai⁶ hŏk⁶ 讀大學	L.8
go to work (VO) fāan¹ gūng¹ 返工	L.8
gold colour (N) gām¹ sīk¹ 金色	L.13
gold jewellery (N) gām¹ sīk¹ 金飾	L.13
good (obedient) (Adj) gwāai¹ 乖	L.11
good (well) (Adj) hóu² 好	U.1; L.3
good day (SE) něi⁵ hóu² 你好	L.1
good morning (SE) zóu² sàn⁴ 早晨	L.9
good night (SE) zóu² táu² 早抖	U.2
good quality (Adj) lěng³ 靚	L.13
goodbye (SE) zŏi³ gin³ 再見	L.6
good-looking (Adj) lěng³ 靚；hóu² tái² 好睇	L.3
government departments *(N)* zíng³ fú² bōu⁶ mùn⁴ 政府部門	L.7
Government House (PN) Hōeng¹ Góng² Lǎi⁵ Bān¹ Fú² 香港禮賓府	L.14
great (terrific) (Adj) zěng³ 正	L.11
Greece (PN) Hēi¹ Lĭp⁶ 希臘	L.5*
green colour (N) lŭk⁶ sīk¹ 綠色	L.13
green tea (N) lŭk⁶ càa⁴ 綠茶	L.12
grey (N) fūi¹ sīk¹ 灰色	L.13
ground floor (N) dēi⁶ háa² 地下	L.9

Guangdong Province *(PN)* Gwóng² Dúng¹ Sáang² 廣東省	U.1
Guangdong speech *(PN)* Gwóng² Dūng¹ Wáa² 廣東話	U.1
Guangxi Province *(PN)* Gwóng² Sāi¹ Sáang² 廣西省	U.1
Guangzhou City (PN) Gwóng² Zāu¹ 廣州	U.1
Guangzhou dialect *(PN)* Gwóng² Zāu¹ Wáa² 廣州話	U.1
Guangzhou speech *(PN)* Gwóng² Zāu¹ Wáa² 廣州話	U.1
guesthouse (N) bān¹ gún² 賓館	L.3

● *H*

half-past three (Pn) sāam¹ dím² bŭn³ 三點半	U.1
ham (N) fó² téoi² 火腿	L.10
hangbags (N) sáu² dói² 手袋	L.13
handicrafts *(N)* sáu² gūng¹ ngāi⁶ bán² 手工藝品	L.13
Hang Hau (PN) a MTR station: Hāang¹ Háu² 坑口	L.14
Hang Seng Bank *(PN)* Hàng⁴ Sāng¹ Ngàn⁴ Hòng⁴ 恒生銀行	L.15
happy (Adj) hōi¹ sām¹ 開心；fūn¹ héi² 歡喜	U.1
harbour (N) góng² 港	U.1
hard (tough) (Adj) sān¹ fú² 辛苦	L.11
hardworking (Adj) kàn⁴ lĭk⁶ 勤力	L.11
hats (N) móu² 帽	U.1
have (possess) (V) jǎu⁵ 有	L.4
have a alcohol drink (VO) jám² záu² 飲酒	L.12
have a drink (VO) jám² jě⁵ 飲嘢	L.12
have a lunch (VO) sĭk⁶ àan³ zǎu³ 食晏晝	L.12
have a try (Ph) sĭ³ hǎa⁵ 試吓	L.10
have dim-sum (VO) jám² càa⁴ 飲茶	L.12
have free time (not busy) *(Adj)* dāk¹ hàan⁴ 得閒	L.8
have not (not to have) (V) móu⁵ 冇	L.4
have some tea (VO) jám² càa⁴ 飲茶	L.3
have to (need to) (AV) jiu³ 要	L.6
Have you got... (Do you have...?) *(QW)* jǎu⁵ móu⁵ ...àa³? 有冇...呀？	L.4
he (Pn) kěoi⁵ 佢	U.1

headquarters (N) zúng² hóng² 總行	L.14	*Hong Kong citizen* *(N)* Hōeng¹ Góng² jàn⁴ 香港人	L.6
hear (V) tēng¹ 聽	L.5	*Hong Kong currency (PN)* Góng² Bāi⁶ 港幣	L.4
heart (N) sām¹ 心	U.1		
hello (hi, good day) (SE) něi⁵ hóu² 你好	L.1	*Hong Kong dollars* *(PN)* Góng² Bāi⁶ 港幣；Góng² Jỳun⁴ 港元	L.4
hello (Intj) hāa¹ lóu² 哈佬；wǎi³ 喂	U.2		
help (S.O.S.) (SE) gǎu³ mēng⁶ åa³! 救命呀！	U.2	*Hong Kong Hotel* *(PN)* Hōeng¹ Góng² Záu² Dìm³ 香港酒店	L.2
Heng Fa Chuen (PN) a MTR station: Hāng⁶ Fāa¹ Cȳu¹ 杏花邨	L.14	*Hong Kong Island* *(PN)* Hōeng¹ Góng² Dóu² 香港島	L.2
Heng On (PN) a MTR station: Hàng⁴ ōn¹ 恆安	L.14	*Hong Kong people* *(N)* Hōeng¹ Góng² jàn⁴ 香港人	L.6
her (Pn) kěoi⁵ 佢；*(Ph)* kěoi⁵ gè³ 佢嘅	L.1		
here (Pn) nī¹ dōu⁶ 呢度	L.2	*Hong Kong Polytechnic University (PN)* Hōeng¹ Góng² Lěi⁵ Gūng¹ Dāai⁶ Hōk⁶ 香港理工大學	*
Here it is! (Intj) nàa⁴ 嗱	L.4		
hers (Ph) kěoi⁵ gè³ 佢嘅	L.1	*Hong Kong Shue Yan University (PN)* Hōeng¹ Góng² Sȳu⁶ Jàn⁴ Dāai⁶ Hōk⁶ 香港樹仁大學	*
hey (Intj) wǎi³ 喂	L.12		
hi (hello; good day) (SE) něi⁵ hóu² 你好	L.1	*Hong Kong speech* *(PN)* Hōeng¹ Góng² Wáa² 香港話	U.1
high (Adj) gōu¹ 高	L.11		
hike (VO) hàang⁴ sāan¹ 行山	L.5	*Hong Kong Station* *(PN)* Hōeng¹ Góng² Zāam⁶ 香港站	L.14
him (Pn) kěoi⁵ 佢	U.1		
Hin Keng (PN) a MTR station: Hín² Gìng³ 顯徑	L.14	*Hong Kong style (N)* Hōeng¹ Góng² sīk¹ 香港式；Góng² sīk¹ 港式	L.10
Hindi (PN) Jǎn³ Dēi⁶ Wáa² 印地話	*		
his (Ph) kěoi⁵ gè³ 佢嘅	L.1	*Hong Kong style café* *(N)* càa⁴ cāan¹ tēng¹ 茶餐廳	L.9
history (N) līk⁶ sí² 歷史；sí² 史	L.5		
HKID card *(N)* Hōeng¹ Góng² sān¹ fán² zìng³ 香港身份證	L.4	*Hong Kong University of Science & Technology* *(PN)* Hōeng¹ Góng² Fō¹ Gēi⁶ Dāai⁶ Hōk⁶ 香港科技大學	*
HKU (PN) a MTR station: Hōeng¹ Góng² Dāai⁶ Hōk⁶ 香港大學	L.14	*Hongkong and Shanghai Banking Corporation* *(PN)* Wūi⁶ Fūng¹ Ngàn⁴ Hòng⁴ 匯豐銀行	L.14
Ho (Chinese surname) (PN) Hò⁴ 何	L.1	*Horlicks (N)* Hóu² Lāap⁶ Hāk¹ 好立克	L.11
hobby (an interest) (N) hìng³ cěoi³ 興趣	L.5	*hospital (N)* jī¹ jýun² 醫院	L.7
holiday flats (N) dōu⁶ gåa³ ūk¹ 度假屋	L.3	*hostel (N)* lěoi⁵ dìm³ 旅店；lěoi⁵ sě³ 旅舍	L.3
Holland (PN) Hò⁴ Lāan¹ 荷蘭	*	*hot (in temperature) (Adj)* jīt⁶ 熱	U.1
Ho Man Tin (PN) a MTR station: Hò⁴ Màn⁴ Tìn⁴ 何文田	L.14	*hotel (N)* záu² dìm³ 酒店	L.3
home (N) ūk¹ kéi² 屋企	L.14	*horse racing track (N)* mǎa⁵ cèong⁴ 馬場	L.8
home telephone no. *(Ph)* ūk¹ kéi² gè³ dīn⁶ wáa² 屋企嘅電話	L.14	*hour(s) (Suff)* gò³ zūng¹ tàu⁴ 個鐘頭	L.15
		house (N) ūk¹ 屋	U.1
honey lemonade (N) níng² māt⁶ 檸蜜	L.11	*housewife (N)* gāa¹ tìng⁴ zýu² fǔ⁵ 家庭主婦	L.7
Hong Kong (PN) Hōeng¹ Góng² 香港	L.5	*how (QW)* dím² jóeng² 點樣；dím² 點	L.15
Hong Kong Baptist University (PN) Hōeng¹ Góng² Zåm³ Wúi⁶ Dāai⁶ Hōk⁶ 香港浸會大學	*	*How about you? (SE)* něi⁵ nē¹？你呢？	L.6
		How are you? (Q) něi⁵ hóu² måa³？你好嗎？	U.2

How is it called? *(QW)* māt¹ jě⁵ méng² 乜野名；mē¹ jě⁵ méng² 咩野名	L.5
how long *(QW)* géi² nǒi⁶ 幾耐	L.15
how many *(QW)* géi² dō¹ 幾多	L.3
how many people *(QW)* géi² dō¹ jàn⁴ 幾多人	L.4
How many years old? *(QW)* géi² dō¹ sėoi³ 幾多歲	L.4
How may I address you? *(Q)* dím² jóeng² cīng¹ fū¹ něi⁵ åa³? 點樣稱呼你呀？	L.15
how much *(money)* *(QW)* géi² dō¹ cín² 幾多錢；géi² cín² 幾錢	L.4
how much *(QW)* géi² dō¹ 幾多	L.3
How to get there? *(SE)* dím² jóeng² hėoi³ åa³? 點樣去呀？	L.15
however *(Conj)* bāt¹ gwó³ 不過	L.7
HSBC *(PN)* Wūi⁶ Fūng¹ Ngàn⁴ Hòng⁴ 匯豐銀行	L.14
hundred *(Nu)* båak³ 百	U.1
Hung Hom *[a major district in Kowloon]* *(PN)* Hùng⁴ Håm³ 紅磡	L.2
Hung Hom *(PN) a MTR station:* Hùng⁴ Håm³ 紅磡	L.14
Hungary *(PN)* Hūng¹ Ǹg⁴ Lěi⁶ 匈牙利	*
hungry *(Adj)* ngō̌⁶ 餓；tǒu⁵ ngō̌⁶ 肚餓	L.11
husband *(N)* sīn¹ sāang¹ 先生；lǒu⁵ gūng¹ 老公	L.5

● *I*

I *(Pn)* ngǒ⁵ 我	U.1
iced *(Adj)* důng³ 凍	U.1
ice-skate *(VO)* làu⁴ bīng¹ 溜冰	L.6
IFC *(PN)* Gwǒk³ Zåi³ Gām¹ Jùng⁴ Zūng¹ Sām¹ 國際金融中心	L.14
import-export corporation *(N)* cēot¹ jǎp⁶ háu² gūng¹ sī¹ 出入口公司	L.7
in *(a place) (Prep)* hái² 喺	L.3
in *(a place) (V)* hái² 喺	L.2
in advance *(Adv)* sīn¹ 先	L.12
in front *(ahead; the front side)* *(N)* cìn⁴ mȉn⁶ 前面	L.3
in the middle of; *centre (N)* zūng¹ gāan¹ 中間	L.9

indeed *(Adv)* zān¹ hāi⁶ 真係	L.12
India *(PN)* Jản³ Dōu⁶ 印度	*
Indonesia *(PN)* Jản³ Nèi⁴ 印尼	*
Indonesia language *(PN)* Jản³ Nèi⁴ Wáa² 印尼話	*
Industrial and Commercial Bank of China (Asia) (ICBC Asia) (PN) Zūng¹ Gwǒk³ Gūng¹ Sōeng¹ Ngàn⁴ Hòng⁴ (Åa³ Zāu¹) 中國工商銀行（亞洲）	L.14
inside; in *(N)* lěoi⁵ mȉn⁶ 裏面；jǎp⁶ mȉn⁶ 入面	L.9
instructor *(N)* gåau³ lȉn⁶ 教練	L.7
insurance company *(N)* bóu² hím² gūng¹ sī¹ 保險公司	L.7
intelligent *(Adj)* cūng¹ mìng⁴ 聰明；lēk¹ 叻	L.11
interest; hobby *(N)* hing³ cěoi³ 興趣	L.5
interesting *(Adj)* hóu² wáan² 好玩	L.11
international *(N)* gwǒk³ zåi³ 國際	L.2
International Finance Centre *(PN)* Gwǒk³ Zåi³ Gām¹ Jùng⁴ Zūng¹ Sām¹ 國際金融中心	L.14
invite *(V)* céng² 請	L.12
Iran *(PN)* Jī¹ Lǒng⁵ 伊朗	*
Iraq *(PN)* Jī¹ Lāai¹ Hāk¹ 伊拉克	*
Ireland *(PN)* Oi³ Jǐ⁵ Làan⁴ 愛爾蘭	*
Is it okay? *(SE)* dāk¹ m̀⁴ dāk¹ åa³? 得唔得呀？	L.13
Is it true...? *(Ph)* hāi⁶ m̀⁴ hāi⁶ 係唔係	L.6
Island Line *(PN)* Góng² Dóu² Sin³ 港島綫	L.14
Is that good? *(SE)* hóu² m̀⁴ hóu² åa³ 好唔好呀	L.12
Israel *(PN)* Jǐ⁵ Sīk¹ Lȉt⁶ 以色列	*
Italy *(PN)* Ji³ Dāai⁶ Lěi⁶ 意大利	L.5
it means... *(V)* zīk¹ hāi⁶ 即係	L.11

● *J*

jade *(N)* jūk⁶ hėi³ 玉器	L.13
January *(PN)* jāt¹ jÿut⁶ 一月	L.8
Japan *(PN)* Jāt⁶ Bún² 日本	L.5
Japanese language *(PN)* Jāt⁶ Mán² 日文；Jāt⁶ Màn⁴ 日文	L.6
Japanese nationality *(N)* Jāt⁶ zīk⁶ 日籍	L.5
Japanese speech *(PN)* Jāt⁶ Bún² Wáa² 日本話	L.6
Japanese Yen *(PN)* Jāt⁶ Jÿun⁴ 日元	L.4
Jasmine tea *(PN)* Hōeng¹ Pín² 香片	L.12

jewellery (N) sáu² sīk¹ 首飾	L.13
jog (VO) páau² bōu⁶ 跑步	L.6
Jordan (PN) a MTR station: Zó² Déon¹ 佐敦	L.14
July (PN) cāt¹ jỹut⁶ 七月	L.8
June (PN) lūk⁶ jỹut⁶ 六月	L.8
just arrived (Ph) sān¹ lèi⁴ gè³ 新嚟嘅	L.3
● 𝒦	
Kai Tak (PN) a MTR station: Kái² Dāk¹ 啟德	L.14
Kam Sheung Road (PN) a MTR station: Gám² Sõeng⁶ Lõu⁶ 錦上路	L.14
karaoke (VO) còeng³ kāa¹ lāai¹ ōu¹ kēi¹ 唱卡拉OK	L.5
Kennedy Town (PN) a MTR station: Gīn¹ Nèi⁴ Dēi⁶ Sìng⁴ 堅尼地城	L.14
key (N) só² sì⁴ 鎖匙；ì⁴ 匙	U.1
key holders (N) só² sì⁴ kåu³ 鎖匙扣	L.13
kill (V) såat³ 殺；sì³ 弑	U.1
kind (nice person) (Adj) hóu² jàn⁴ 好人	L.11
kitchen (N) cèoi⁴ fóng² 廚房；cỳu⁴ fóng² 廚房	L.3
know (V) sīk¹ 識	U.1
know about (V) zī¹ dòu³ 知道；zī¹ 知	L.9
known as (V) giu³ zōu⁶ 叫做；giu³ 叫	L.10
Korea (PN) Hòn⁴ Gwòk³ 韓國	*
Korean descent (N) Hòn⁴ jēoi⁶ 韓裔	L.5
Korean language (N) Hòn⁴ Mán² 韓文；Hòn⁴ Màn⁴ 韓文	L.6
Korean speech (PN) Hòn⁴ Gwòk³ Wáa² 韓國話	L.6
Kowloon (PN) Gáu² Lùng⁴ 九龍	L.2
Kowloon Bay (PN) a MTR station: Gáu² Lùng⁴ Wāan¹ 九龍灣	L.14
Kowloon Hotel (PN) Gáu² Lùng⁴ Záu² Dim 九龍酒店	L.2
Kowloon Tong (PN) a MTR station: Gáu² Lùng⁴ Tòng⁴ 九龍塘	L.14
kungfu (VO) dáa² gūng¹ fū¹ 打功夫	L.6
Kwai Fong (PN) a MTR station: Kwài⁴ Fōng¹ 葵芳	L.14
Kwai Hing (PN) a MTR station: Kwài⁴ Hīng¹ 葵興	L.14

Kwun Tong (PN) a MTR station: Gūn¹ Tòng⁴ 觀塘	L.14
Kwun Tong Line (PN) Gūn¹ Tòng⁴ Sìn³ 觀塘綫	L.14
● ℒ	
Lai Chi Kok (PN) a MTR station: Lāi⁶ Zī¹ Gòk³ 荔枝角	L.14
Lai King (PN) a MTR station: Lāi⁶ Gíng² 荔景	L.14
Lam Tin (PN) a MTR station: Làam⁴ Tìn⁴ 藍田	L.14
Lan Kwai Fong (PN) Làan⁴ Gwåi³ Fōng¹ 蘭桂坊	L.14
Landmark (PN) Zí³ Dēi⁶ Gwóng² Cόeng⁴ 置地廣場	L.14
Lantau Island (PN) Dāai⁶ Jỹu⁴ Sāan¹ 大嶼山	L.10
Laos (PN) Lǐu⁴ Gwòk³ 寮國	*
large size (N) dāai⁶ mǎa⁵ 大碼	L.13
last month (N) sõeng⁶ gò³ jỹut⁶ 上個月	L.8
last week (N) sõeng⁶ gò³ sīng¹ kèi⁴ 上個星期	L.8
last year (N) gāu⁶ nín² 舊年；gāu⁶ nìn⁴ 舊年	L.8
late (Adj) cì⁴ 遲	U.1
Latin language (N) Lāai¹ Dīng¹ Mán² 拉丁文；Lāai¹ Dīng¹ Màn⁴ 拉丁文	L.6
laundry room (N) sái² jī¹ fòng⁴ 洗衣房	L.3
law firm (N) lēot⁶ sī¹ làu⁴ 律師樓	L.8
lawyer (N) lēot⁶ sī¹ 律師	L.7
lazy (Adj) lǎan⁵ 懶	L.11
lean meat (N) såu³ jūk⁶ 瘦肉	L.10
lean pork (N) såu³ jūk⁶ 瘦肉	L.10
learn (V) hōk⁶ 學	L.7
leather goods (N) pèi⁴ gēoi⁶ 皮具	L.13
leave (V) záu² 走	L.6
leave first (Ph) záu² sīn¹ 走先	L.13
Lee (Chinese surname) (PN) Lěi⁵ 李；Lēi⁶ 利	L.1
left side (N) zó² mīn⁶ 左面	L.9
leg (N) gŏek³ 腳	U.1
Lei Tung (PN) a MTR station: Lēi⁶ Dūng¹ 利東	L.14
lemon tea (N) nìng⁴ mūng¹ càa⁴ 檸檬茶；níng² càa⁴ 檸茶	L.11
lemonade (N) nìng⁴ mūng¹ séoi² 檸檬水；níng² séoi² 檸水	L.11

let me go through (Ph) zě³ zě³ 借借	U.2
let's go (SE) hàang⁴ làa³ 行喇	L.12
letter (N) sèon³ 信	U.1
Li (Chinese surname) (PN) Lěi⁵ 李	L.1
Li Yuen Street East & West (PN) Lěi⁶ Jyun⁴ Dūng¹ Sāi¹ Gāai¹ 利源東西街	L.14
library (N) tòu⁴ sȳu¹ gún² 圖書館	L.3
lift; elevator (N) dīn⁶ tāi¹ 電梯；līp¹ 軐	L.3
light rail (N) hīng¹ tit³ 輕鐵	L.14
like (V) zūng¹ ji³ 中意 / 鍾意	L.7
Immigration Depatment (PN) jì⁴ màn⁴ gúk² 移民局	*
Lingnan University (PN) Lǐng⁵ Nàam⁴ Dāai⁶ Hōk⁶ 嶺南大學	*
lion (N) sī¹ zí² 獅子	L.15
listen (V) tēng¹ 聽	L.5
listen to music (VO) tēng¹ jām¹ ngōk⁶ 聽音樂	L.5
little (a few) (Nu) síu² síu² 少少；(Adj) síu² 少	L.6; U.1
little more (Part) dī¹ 啲	L.13
little while (a moment) (N) jāt¹ zàn⁶ 一陣	L.11
live (V) zyu⁶ 住	L.3
living quarters (N) sūk¹ sè³ 宿舍	L.3
living room (N) hàak³ tēng¹ 客廳	L.3
Lo Wu (PN) Lò⁴ Wù⁴ 羅湖	L.14
local dialect (N) bún² dèi⁶ wáa² 本地話	L.6
LOHAS Park (PN) a MTR station: Hōng¹ Sìng⁴ 康城	L.14
Lok Fu (PN) a MTR station: Lōk⁶ Fù³ 樂富	L.14
Lok Ma Chau (PN) a MTR station: Lōk⁶ Mǎa⁵ Zāu¹ 落馬洲	L.14
long (Adj) còeng⁴ 長	L.11
Long-jing tea (PN) Lùng⁴ Zéng² 龍井	L.12
Long Ping (PN) a MTR station: Lǒng⁵ Pìng⁴ 朗屏	L.14
long time (N) hóu² nòi⁶ 好耐	L.15
look (V) tái² 睇	L.13
lot (many; much) (Nu) hóu² dō¹ 好多；(Adj) dō¹ 多	L.13
lotus seed paste buns (N) lìn⁴ jùng⁴ bāau¹ 蓮蓉包	L.12

loud (Adj) dāai⁶ sēng¹ 大聲	U.2
love (V) òi³ 愛	U.1
low (Adj) dāi¹ 低	L.11

● M

Ma (Chinese surname) (PN) Mǎa⁵ 馬	L.1
Ma On Shan (PN) a MTR station: Mǎa⁵ Ōn¹ Sāan¹ 馬鞍山	L.14
Ma On Shan Line (PN) Mǎa⁵ Ōn¹ Sāan¹ Sin³ 馬鞍山綫	L.14
Ma Tau Wai (PN) a MTR station: Mǎa⁵ Tàu⁴ Wài⁴ 馬頭圍	L.14
macaroni in soup with ham (Ph) fó² téoi² tūng¹ fán² 火腿通粉	L.10
Macau (PN) òu³ Mún² 澳門；òu³ Mùn⁴ 澳門	L.9
maid (N) gūng¹ jàn⁴ 工人	L.7
mainland (N) dāai⁶ lūk⁶ 大陸	L.2
mainland China (PN) Zūng¹ Gwòk³ dāai⁶ lūk⁶ 中國大陸	L.2
Malaysia (PN) Mǎa⁵ Lòi⁴ Sāi¹ Àa³ 馬來西亞	*
manager (N) gīng¹ lěi⁵ 經理	L.7
Mandarin (PN) Póu² Tūng¹ Wáa² 普通話	U.1
mango pudding (N) mōng¹ gwó² bòu³ dīn¹ 芒果布甸	L.12
many (a lot; much) (Adj) dō¹ 多；(Nu) hóu² dō¹ 好多	U.1
map (N) dèi⁶ tòu⁴ 地圖	L.2
March (N) sāam¹ jyut⁶ 三月	L.8
market (N) gāai¹ sǐ⁵ 街市；sǐ⁵ 市	L.9
marketing (N) sǐ⁵ còeng⁴ hōk⁶ 市場學	L.5
Mass Transit Railway (N) dèi⁶ tit³ 地鐵	L.9
master (N) sī¹ 師	U.1
matter (N) sǐ⁶ 事	U.1
May (PN) ng̊⁵ jyut⁶ 五月	L.8
may I ask (V) céng² màn⁶ 請問	L.9
me (Pn) ngǒ⁵ 我	U.1
measure word [a bowl of] wún² 碗	U.2
measure word [a can of] gùn³ 罐	U.2
measure word [a cup of] būi¹ 杯	L.11
measure word [a pair of] dèoi³ 對	U.2
measure word [a piece of (clothes)] gìn⁶ 件	U.2

measure word [a plate of] dīp⁶ 碟	L.11
measure word [a pot of] wù⁴ 壺	L.12
measure word [for a person and a way to show respect] wái² 位	L.7
measure word [for books; magazines] bún² 本	U.2
measure word [for buildings; houses and rooms] gāan¹ 間	L.9
measure word [for most animals] zẹk³ 隻	U.2
measure word [for objects in a set, such as documents, newspapers; a sandwich or a job] fān⁶ 份	U.2
measure word [for objects that are cylindrical, rigid, long and thin, e.g. pencils, cigarettes, etc.] zī¹ 枝	U.2
measure word [for paper; cards; objects with a flat surface, such as chairs, tables or beds] zōeng¹ 張	U.2
measure word [for people; round objects or abstract things, such as questions or ideas] gọ³ 個	U.2
measure word [for streets or things with a long shape] (M) tìu⁴ 條	L.15
measure word [for vehicles; machines, e.g. cars, airplanes] gạa³ 架	U.2
meat (N) j̣ūk⁶ 肉	L.12
medical doctor (N) jī¹ sāng¹ 醫生	L.7
medicine (N) jī¹ họk⁶ 醫學	L.5
medium size (N) zūng¹ mǎa⁵ 中碼	L.13
meet (V) gịn³ 見	U.1
Mei Foo (PN) a MTR station: Mẹi⁵ Fū¹ 美孚	L.14
menu (N) cọi³ páai² 菜牌	L.13
Mexico (PN) Māk⁶ Sāi¹ Gō¹ 墨西哥	*
Middle America (PN) Zūng¹ Mẹi⁵ Zāu¹ 中美洲	L.2
Middle East (PN) Zūng¹ Dūng¹ 中東	L.2
Mid-Level (a district in HK Island) (PN) Bụn³ Sāan¹ 半山	L.14
midnight (N) nǧ⁵ jẹ⁶ 午夜	U.2
milk (N) ngàu⁴ nǎai⁵ 牛奶；nǎai⁵ 奶	L.11
milk tea (N) nǎai⁵ càa⁴ 奶茶	L.11
mind your step (SE) māan⁶ máan² hàang⁴ 慢慢行	U.2
mine (Ph) ngǒ⁵ gẹ³ 我嘅	L.1
mineral water (N) kwǒng³ cỳun⁴ séoi² 礦泉水	L.11
minibus (N) síu² bāa¹ 小巴	L.14
minibus station (N) síu² bāa¹ zāam⁶ 小巴站	L.14
minute (M) fān¹ 分	U.2
minute (of time duration) (Suff) ~ fān¹ zūng¹ 分鐘	L.15
Miss (N) mīt¹ sì⁴；síu² zé² 小姐	L.1
mobile phone (N) sáu² tài⁴ dīn⁶ wáa² 手提電話	L.4
Monday (PN) lǎi⁵ bạai³ jāt¹ 禮拜一；sīng¹ kèi⁴ jāt¹ 星期一	L.8
money (N) cín² 錢	L.4
money exchange shop (N) zạau² wūn⁶ dịm³ 找換店	L.2
Mong Kok (PN) a MTR station: Wǒng⁶ Gọk³ 旺角	L.2
Mong Kok East (PN) a MTR station: Wǒng⁶ Gọk³ Dūng¹ 旺角東	L.14
month (N) ǰyut⁶ 月	U.1
month after next (Ph) zọi³ hāa⁶ gọ³ ǰyut⁶ 再下個月	L.8
month before last (Ph) zọi³ sǒeng⁶ gọ³ ǰyut⁶ 再上個月	L.8
month(s) (of time duration) (Suff) gọ³ ǰyut⁶ 個月	L.15
moon (N) ǰyut⁶ 月	U.1
morning (N) zīu¹ tàu⁴ zóu² 朝頭早	U.2
most (Adv) zẹoi³ 最	L.8
mother (N) màa⁴ māa¹ 媽媽	L.4
motorbike (N) dīn⁶ dāan¹ cē¹ 電單車	L.14
mountain (N) sāan¹ 山	U.1
Mr. (N) sīn¹ sāang¹ 先生	L.1
Mrs. (N) tạai³ táai² 太太	L.1
MTR (PN) Góng² Tịt³ 港鐵；dẹi⁶ tịt³ 地鐵	L.9
MTR Corporation Limited (PN) Hōeng¹ Góng² Tịt³ Lòu⁶ Jǔ Hǎan⁶ Gūng¹ Sī¹ 香港鐵路有限公司	L.14
MTR station (N) dẹi⁶ tịt³ zāam 地鐵站	L.9
much (many; a lot) (Nu) hóu² dō¹ 好多；(Adj) dō¹ 多	L.13
mug (N) būi¹ 杯	L.11

music (N) jām¹ ngŏk⁶ 音樂	L.5
my (Ph) ngŏ⁵ gè³ 我嘅	L.1

• N

Nam Cheong (PN) a MTR station: Nàam⁴ Cōeng¹ 南昌	L.14
named; known as (V) gíu³ 叫；gíu³ zŏu⁶ 叫做	L.1
namely (V) zīk¹ hāi⁶ 即係	L.11
naughty (Adj) jǎi⁵ 曳	L.11
near (Adj) kǎn⁵ 近	U.1
nearby (N) fū⁶ gàn⁶ 附近	L.9
nearly (Adv) cāa¹ m̀⁴ dō¹ 差唔多	U.2
need to (AV) jíu³ 要	L.6
neighboring (N) gåak³ lèi⁴ 隔籬	*
Nepal (PN) Nèi⁴ Bŏk⁶ Jǐ⁵ 尼泊爾	L.4
nervous (Adj) gán² zōeng¹ 緊張	L.11
Netherlands (PN) Hò⁴ Lāan¹ 荷蘭	*
never (Adv) cùng⁴ lòi⁴ m̀⁴ 從來唔	L.7
never mind (SE) m̀⁴ gán² jíu³ 唔緊要	U.2
new (Adj) sān¹ 新	U.1
newspaper (N) bŏu³ zí² 報紙	L.8
new stuff (Ph) sān¹ jě⁵ 新野	L.11
New Year (PN) Sān¹ Nìn⁴ 新年	U.2
New York (PN) Náu² Jŏek³ 紐約	L.5
New Zealand (PN) Náu² Sāi¹ Làan⁴ 紐西蘭；Sān¹ Sāi¹ Làan⁴ 新西蘭	L.5
New Zealand Dollars (PN) Náu² Jýun⁴ 紐元	L.4
newcomer (Ph) sān¹ lèi⁴ gè³ 新嚟嘅	L.3
next month (N) hāa⁶ gŏ³ jÿut⁶ 下個月	L.8
next one (Ph) hāa⁶ jāt¹ gŏ³ 下一個	U.2
next time (Ph) hāa⁶ cì³ 下次	U.2
next to (N) gåak³ lèi⁴ 隔籬；zāk¹ bīn¹ 側邊；pìng⁴ bīn¹ 旁邊	L.9
next week (N) hāa⁶ gŏ³ sīng¹ kèi⁴ 下個星期	L.8
next year (N) cēot¹ nín² 出年；cēot¹ nìn⁴ 出年	U.2; L.8
Ng (Chinese surname) (PN) Ǹg⁴ 吳；Ǹg⁵ 伍	L.1
Ngau Tau Kok (PN) a MTR station: Ngàu⁴ Tàu⁴ Gŏk³ 牛頭角	L.14
nice person (Adj) hóu² jàn⁴ 好人	L.11

Nigeria (PN) Nèi⁴ Jāt⁶ Lèi⁶ Aå³ 尼日利亞	*
night (N) jě⁶ mǎan⁵ 夜晚	L.15
night(s) (of time duration) (Suff) ~ mǎan⁵ 晚	L.15
nine (Nu) gáu² 九	U.1
no (Adv) m̀⁴ 唔	U.1
no need (Adv) m̀⁴ sái² 唔使	L.8
no questions (Ph) mŏu⁵ mān⁶ tài⁴ 冇問題	L.4
noisy (Adj) còu⁴ 嘈	L.11
Non-Chinese descent (Ph) fēi¹ Wàa⁴ jēoi⁶ 非華裔	*
noodles (N) mīn⁶ 麵	L.10
noon (N) zìng³ nǧ⁵ 正午；zūng¹ nǧ⁵ 中午	U.2
north (N) bāk¹ 北	L.15
North America (PN) Bāk¹ Mĕi⁵ Zāu¹ 北美洲	L.2
Northern Ireland (PN) Bāk¹ Oi³ Jǐ⁵ Làan⁴ 北愛爾蘭	*
North Korea (PN) Bāk¹ Hòn⁴ 北韓	*
North Point (PN) a MTR station: Bāk¹ Gŏk³ 北角	L.14
Norway (PN) Nò⁴ Wāi¹ 挪威	*
not (Adv) m̀⁴ 唔	U.1
not at all (SE) m̀⁴ sái² m̀⁴ gōi¹ 唔使唔該	L.9
not busy (Adj) dāk¹ hàan⁴ 得閒	L.8
not quite (Adv) m̀⁴ hāi⁶ géi² 唔係幾	L.8
not up to standard (Adj) séoi² pìn⁴ 水皮	L.11
not yet (Adv) mĕi⁶ 未	L.12
November (PN) sāp⁶ jāt¹ jÿut⁶ 十一月	L.8
now (N) jì⁴ gāa¹ 而家	L.2
number (M) hōu⁶ 號	L.3
nunnery (N) ām¹ 庵	U.1
nurse (N) wū⁶ sī̌⁶ 護士	L.7

• O

oatmeal (N) māk⁶ pèi⁴ 麥皮	L.10
o'clock (basic time unit) (N) dím² 點；dím² zūng¹ 點鐘	U.1; L.6
obedient (Adj) gwāai¹ 乖	L.11
Ocean Park (PN) a MTR station: Hói² Jòeng⁴ Gūng¹ Jýun² 海洋公園	L.14
occasionally (Adv) gåan³ zūng¹ 間中	L.7

occupations (N) gūng¹ zòk³ 工作	L.7	
October (PN) sặp⁶ jŷut⁶ 十月	L.8	
Octopus card (PN) bặat³ dàat⁶ tūng¹ kāat¹ 八達通咭	L.4	
office (N) bãan⁶ gūng¹ sāt¹ 辦公室	L.3	
often (Adv) sì⁴ sì⁴ 時時	L.7	
okay [used to express agreement] (SE) hóu² lāa¹ 好啦	L.13	
okay; fine [used to express pproval] (Adj) dāk¹ 得	U.1	
old (not new) (Adj) gãu⁶ 舊	L.3; L.11	
old (not young) (Adj) lǒu⁵ 老	L.11	
Olympic (PN) a MTR station: Òu³ Wãn⁶ 奧運	L.14	
on (a place) (Prep) hái² 喺	L.3	
on (a place) (V) hái² 喺	L.2	
on foot (VO) hàang⁴ lòu⁶ 行路	L.14	
once (Nu) jāt¹ cì³ 一次	U.2	
once more (Adv) zòi³ 再	L.15	
one (Nu) jāt¹ 一	U.1	
one dollar (Ph) jāt¹ mān¹ 一蚊	L.4	
one hour (Ph) jāt¹ gò³ zūng¹ tàu⁴ 一個鐘頭	L.15	
one hundred dollars (Ph) jāt¹ bặak³ mān¹ 一百蚊	L.4	
one thousand dollars (Ph) jāt¹ cīn¹ mān¹ 一千蚊	L.4	
only (Adv) zỉng⁶ hãi⁶ 淨係	L.4	
Oolong tea (PN) Wū¹ Lúng² càa⁴ 烏龍茶; Cēng¹ Càa⁴ 青茶	L.12	
opposite (side) (N) dẻoi³ mĩn⁶ 對面	L.9	
or [only used in a question indicating options] (Conj) dĩng⁶ hãi⁶ 定係; dĩng⁶ 定	L.11	
or [used in a statement, not in questions] (Conj) wãak⁶ zé² 或者	L.12	
orange (N) cáang² 橙	U.1	
orange (N) cáang² sīk¹ 橙色	L.13	
orange juice (N) cáang² zāp¹ 橙汁	L.11	
Osaka dialect (PN) Dãai⁶ Báan² Wáa² 大阪話	L.6	
out of order (Adj) wãai⁶ 壞	U.1	
outside (N) cēot¹ mĩn⁶ 出面; ngõi⁶ mĩn⁶ 外面	L.9	

Ovaltine (PN) ō¹ Wàa⁴ Tìn⁴ 阿華田	L.11	
overseas Chinese (N) Wàa⁴ kìu⁴ 華僑	L.5	
over there (Pn) gó² dõu⁶ 嗰度	L.2	

● *P*

painful (Adj) tửng³ 痛	U.1	
Pakistan (PN) Bāa¹ Géi¹ Sī¹ Táan² 巴基斯坦	*	
Panama (PN) Bāa¹ Nàa⁴ Mãa⁵ 巴拿馬	*	
paper (N) zí² 紙	U.2	
parents (N) fũ⁶ mǒu⁵ 父母	L.11	
Paris (PN) Bāa¹ Lài⁴ 巴黎	L.5	
park (N) gūng¹ jýun² 公園	L.9	
particle (aspect) [used after a verb indicating an action in progress] gán² 緊	L.8	
particle (aspect) [comes after a verb to express the idea 'all, completely, entirely'] saai³ 晒	L.13	
particle (aspect) [used after a verb, indicating completed action whether in the past, present or future] zó² 咗	L.12	
particle (interrogative) [used at the end of a question to express an inquiry] ảa³ 呀	L.2	
particle (interrogative) [used to ask something that happened in the past or to require an answer straight away] gảa³ 㗎	L.6	
particle (interrogative) [used to form an elliptical question which is related to a previous question, statement or context] nē¹ 呢	L.6	
particle (modal) [accompanying the adverb "zūng⁶" to emphasize the idea of 'addition'] tīm¹ 添	L.12	
particle (modal) [meaning 'only' or 'just' to play down the extent or significance of sth.] zē¹ 啫	L.6	
particle (modal) [the emphasis form of "lảa³", used to indicate finality or exclamation] lảak³ 嘞	L.14	
particle (modal) [used at the end of a sentence to answer a question ending with "ga" or to give an explanation] gẻ³ 嘅	L.6	
particle (modal) [used at the end of a statement to form a supposition question seeking confirmation] àa⁴ 牙	L.10	
particle (modal) [used at the end of noun predicate sentences to give an explanation] lài⁴ gẻ³ 嚟嘅	L.10	

particle (modal) **[used at the end of sentence with the sense of request, suggestion or invitation]** lāa¹ 啦	L.1
particle (modal) **[used at the end of sentence, indicating suggestion]** āa¹ 吖	L.12
particle (modal) **[used to emphasize a point of current relevance]** lǎa³ 喇	L.3
particle (modal) **[used to indicate surprise, discovery or realization]** wǒ³ 喎	L.8
particle (modal) **[used to soften the tone of a confirmation in a statement]** åa³ 呀	L.3
particle (structural) **[meaning little more; used after adjectives to denote the comparative degree]** dī¹ 啲	L.13
particle (structural) **[used to indicate possession, similar to 's in English]** gě³ 嘅	L.1
pass by (V) gīng¹ 經	L.14
pass through (V) gīng¹ 經	L.14
passer-by (N) lǒu⁶ jàn⁴ 路人	p.50
passport (N) wū⁶ zỉu³ 護照	L.4
pay (V) béi² cín² 俾錢；béi² 俾	L.13
paying for the expenses, playing host (V) céng² 請	L.12
peak tram (N) sāan¹ déng² lāam⁶ cē¹ 山頂纜車	L.14
peak tram station (N) lāam⁶ cē¹ zāam⁶ 纜車站	L.14
Pedder Street (PN) Bāt¹ Dáa² Gāai¹ 畢打街	L.15
pomelo and sago in mango soup (PN) jòeng⁴ zī¹ gām¹ lǒu⁶ 楊枝甘露	L.12
pen (N) bāt¹ 筆	U.2
people (N) jàn⁴ 人	L.5
person (N) jàn⁴ 人	L.5
pharmacy (N) jŏek⁶ fòng⁴ 藥房	L.9
Philippines (PN) Fēi¹ Lĕot⁶ Bān¹ 菲律賓	L.5
pier (N) mǎa⁵ tàu⁴ 碼頭	L.14
Pi-luo-chu tea (PN) Bīk¹ Lò⁴ Cēon¹ 碧螺春	L.12
pineapple(-like) bun (N) bō¹ lò⁴ bāau¹ 菠蘿包	L.10
buttered pineapple(-like) bun with a slice of butter inserted in it (N) bō¹ lò⁴ jàu⁴ 菠蘿油	L.10
place of traffic light (Ph) dāng¹ wái² 燈位	L.14
plain rice congee (N) bāak⁶ zūk¹ 白粥	L.10
plain speech (PN) Bāak⁶ Wáa² 白話	U.1

plate (N) díp² 碟	U.1
play badminton (VO) dáa² jǔyu⁵ mòu⁴ kàu⁴ 打羽毛球	L.6
play ball games (VO) dkɑa² bí¹ 打波	L.8
play baseball (VO) dáa² lèoi⁴ kàu⁴ 打壘球	L.6
play basketball (VO) dáa² làam⁴ kàu⁴ 打籃球	L.6
play chess (VO) zūk¹ kéi² 捉棋	L.5
play football (VO) těk³ bō¹ 踢波；těk³ zūk¹ kàu⁴ 踢足球	L.6
play golf (VO) dáa² gōu¹ jĭ⁵ fū¹ kàu⁴ 打高爾夫球	L.6
play mahjong (VO) dáa² màa⁴ zŏek³ 打麻雀	L.5
play online games (VO) dáa² gēi¹ 打機	L.8
play piano (VO) tàan⁴ kàm⁴ 彈琴	L.6
play soccer (VO) těk³ bō¹ 踢波；těk³ zūk¹ kàu⁴ 踢足球	L.8
play squash (VO) dáa² bīk¹ kàu⁴ 打壁球	L.6
play table tennis (VO) dáa² bīng¹ bām¹ bō¹ 打乒乓波	L.6
play tennis (VO) dáa² mŏng⁵ kàu⁴ 打網球	L.6
play violin (VO) lāai¹ síu² tài⁴ kàm⁴ 拉小提琴	L.6
play volleyball (VO) dáa² pàai⁴ kàu⁴ 打排球	L.6
playing host (V) céng² 請	L.12
plaza (N) gwóng² còeng⁴ 廣場	L.14
please (V) céng² 請；(SE) m̀⁴ gōi¹ 唔該	L.11
P.M. (N) hāa⁶ zǎu³ 下晝；hāa⁶ nğ⁵ 下午	U.2
Po Lam (PN) a MTR station: Bóu² Làm⁴ 寶琳	L.14
poem (N) sī¹ 詩	U.1
police (N) gíng² cåat³ 警察	L.7
police station (N) gíng² gúk² 警局	L.9
beef (N) ngàu⁴ jŭk⁶ 牛肉	*
pork (N) zȳu¹ jŭk⁶ 豬肉	*
pork dumplings (N) sīu¹ máai² 燒賣	L.12
Portugal (PN) Pòu⁴Tòu⁴ Ngàa⁴ 葡萄牙	L.4
post office (N) jàu⁴ gúk² 郵局	L.9
postcards (N) mìng⁴ sėon³ pín² 明信片	L.13
pot (N) wù⁴ 壺	L.12
practice (N) lĭn⁶ zăap⁶ 練習	L.7
practice (V) lĭn⁶ zăap⁶ 練習	L.7

prefix to names (Pref) åa³ 阿	L.7
pretty (Adj) lěng³ 靚	L.13
preserved egg (N) pèi⁴ dáan² 皮蛋	L.10
Prince Edward (PN) a MTR station: Tåai³ Zí² 太子	L.14
problem (N) mǎn⁶ tài⁴ 問題	L.4
professor (N) gåau³ sǎu⁶ 教授	L.7
psychology (N) sām¹ lěi⁵ hŏk⁶ 心理學	L.5
Pu'er tea (PN) Póu² Léi² 普洱；Bóu² Léi² 普洱	L.12
Pu'er tea with chrysanthemum (PN) Gūk¹ Bóu² 菊普	L.12
Putonghua (PN) Póu² Tūng¹ Wáa² 普通話	U.1
public light bus (N) síu² bāa¹ 小巴	L.14
pudding (N) bǒu³ dīn¹ 布甸	*
purple (N) zí² sīk¹ 紫色	L.13

● *Q*

Quarry Bay (PN) a MTR station: Zāk¹ Jy̌u⁴ Cūng¹ 鰂魚涌	L.14
question (N) mǎn⁶ tài⁴ 問題	L.4
quick (Adj) fåai³ 快	U.1
quiet (Adj) zǐng⁶ 靜	L.11
quite (Adv) géi² 幾	L.8
quite good (Ph) géi² hóu² 幾好	U.2

● *R*

Racecourse (PN) a MTR station: Mǎa⁵ Còeng⁴ 馬場	L.14
railway station (N) fó² cē¹ zǎam⁶ 火車站	L.14
rarely (Adv) hóu² síu² 好少	L.7
raw (Adj) sāang¹ 生；měi⁶ sūk⁶ 未熟	U.1
read (V) tái² 睇；dūk⁶ 讀	L.13
read books (VO) tái² sȳu¹ 睇書；dūk⁶ sȳu¹ 讀書	L.5
read newspaper (VO) tái² bǒu³ zí² 睇報紙	*
real estate company (N) dēi⁶ cáan² gūng¹ sī¹ 地產公司	L.7
really (Adv) zān¹ hǎi⁶ 真係	L.12
receptionist (N) zip³ dōi⁶ jy̌un⁴ 接待員	p.50
red colour (N) hùng⁴ sīk¹ 紅色	L.13
Renminbi (PN) Jàn⁴ Màn⁴ Bǎi⁶ 人民幣	L.4

restaurant (N) cāan¹ tēng¹ 餐廳	L.7
restricted area (N) gåm³ kēoi¹ 禁區	L.14
return; go/come back (V) fāan¹ 返	L.9
Ribena (PN) Lěi⁶ Bān¹ Nāap⁶ 利賓納	L.11
rice congee (N) zūk¹ 粥	L.10
rice noodle rolls (N) cóeng² fán² 腸粉；zȳu¹ còeng⁴ fán² 豬腸粉	L.10
rice noodles (N) fán² 粉	L.10
ride (a mode of transportation) (V) cǒ⁵ 坐；dåap³ 搭	L.14
ride a car; by car (VO) cǒ⁵ cē¹ 坐車；dåap³ cē¹ 搭車	L.14
right side (the right side) (N) jǎu⁶ mǐn⁶ 右面；jǎu⁶ 右	L.9
room (N) fóng² 房	L.3
run (VO) páau² bǒu⁶ 跑步	L.6
Russia (PN) Ngò⁴ Lò⁴ Sī¹ 俄羅斯	L.4

● *S*

safe (Adj) ōn¹ cy̌un⁴ 安全	L.11
sago in coconut milk (N) sāi¹ mǎi⁵ lōu⁶ 西米露	L.12
Sai Wan Ho (PN) a MTR station: Sāi¹ Wāan¹ Hó² 西灣河	L.14
Sai Ying Pun (PN) a MTR station: Sāi¹ Jìng⁴ Pùn⁴ 西營盤	L.14
sale (SE) dāai⁶ gáam² gåa³ 大減價	L.13
salesperson (N) sǎu⁶ fo³ jy̌un⁴ 售貨員	p.50
sandwich (N) sāam¹ màn⁴ zī⁶ 三文治	L.10
Saturday (PN) lǎi⁵ båai³ lūk⁶ 禮拜六；sīng¹ kèi⁴ lūk⁶ 星期六	L.8
sausage (N) hōeng¹ cóeng² 香腸；cóeng² zái² 腸仔	L.10
say (V) wǎa⁶ 話；góng² 講	L.14
scented tea (N) fāa¹ càa⁴ 花茶	L.12
school (N) hŏk⁶ hǎau⁶ 學校	L.1
Scotland (PN) Sōu¹ Gåak³ Làan⁴ 蘇格蘭	L.5
scrambled egg (N) cáau² dáan² 炒蛋	L.10
seafood rolls (N) hói² sīn¹ gýun² 海鮮卷	L.12
second (N) mǐu⁵ 秒	U.2
second floor (Ph) jī⁶ láu² 二樓	L.9

second(s) *[of time duration]* (Suff) mǐu⁵ zūng¹ 秒鐘	L.15
secondary school (N) zūng¹ hŏk⁶ 中學	L.3
see (V) gin³ 見；(V) tái² 睇；(Ph) gin³ dóu² 見到	U.1; L.15
see you later (SE) jāt¹ zǎn⁶ gin³ 一陣見	U.2
seldom (Adv) hóu² síu² 好少	L.7
September (PN) gáu² jÿut⁶ 九月	L.8
servant (N) gūng¹ jàn⁴ 工人	L.7
seven (Nu) cāt¹ 七	U.1
Seven-up (PN) Cāt¹ Héi² 七喜	L.11
Seven-up with lemon (N) níng² cāt¹ 檸七	L.11
Shanghaiese dialect (PN) Sōeng⁶ Hói² Wáa² 上海話	L.6
Shau Kei Wan (PN) a MTR station: Sāau¹ Gēi¹ Wāan¹ 筲箕灣	L.14
Shatin (PN) a MTR station: Sāa¹ Tìn⁴ 沙田	L.14
Shatin to Central Link (PN) Sāa¹ Zūng¹ Sin³ 沙中綫	L.14
Shatin Wai (PN) a MTR station: Sāa¹ Tìn⁴ Wài⁴ 沙田圍	L.14
she (Pn) kěoi⁵ 佢	U.1
Shek Kip Mei (PN) a MTR station: Sěk⁶ Gip³ Měi⁵ 石硤尾	L.14
Shek Mun (PN) a MTR station: Sěk⁶ Mùn⁴ 石門	L.14
Shenzhen (PN) Sām¹ Zan³ 深圳	L.14
Sheung Shui (PN) a MTR station: Sōeng⁶ Séoi² 上水	L.14
Sheung Wan (PN) a MTR station: Sōeng⁶ Wàan⁴ 上環	L.2
shoes (N) hàai⁴ 鞋	U.1
shop (N) pòu³ táu² 鋪頭	*
shop (VO) hàang⁴ gāai¹ 行街	L.5
shop assistant (N) zīk¹ jÿun⁴ 職員	L.13
short *(in height)* (Adj) ái² 矮	U.1
short *(in length)* (Adj) dÿun² 短	L.11
Shou-mei tea (PN) Sāu⁶ Méi² 壽眉	L.12
shower (VO) cūng¹ lòeng⁴ 沖涼	L.8
shrimp dumpling (N) hāa¹ gáau² 蝦餃	L.12

shrimp dumplings served with salad dressing (N) hāa¹ gȯk³ 蝦角	L.12
Shum Shui Po (PN) a MTR station: Sām¹ Séoi² Bóu² 深水埗	L.14
shuttle bus (N) cÿun sō¹ bāa¹ sí² 穿梭巴士	L.2
Si *(Chinese surname)* (PN) Sí² 史	L.6
siblings (N) hīng¹ dāi⁶ zí² mūi⁶ 兄弟姊妹	L.5
sick (Adj) bēng⁶ 病	U.1
sign (V) cīm¹ méng² 簽名	L.3
signature (N) cīm¹ méng² 簽名	L.3
silly (Adj) sò⁴ 傻	L.11
silver (N) ngàn⁴ sīk¹ 銀色	L.13
sing (VO) cȯeng³ gō¹ 唱歌	L.5
Singapore (PN) Sān¹ Gȧa³ Bō¹ 新加坡	L.4
Singapore Dollars (PN) Sān¹ Gȧa³ Bō¹ Jÿun⁴ 新加坡元	L.4
singer (N) gō¹ sáu² 歌手	L.7
single (N) dāan¹ 單	U.1
single room (N) dāan¹ jàn⁴ fóng² 單人房	L.3
Sir (N) ȧa³ sòe⁴ 阿 Sir	L.1
sisters (N) zí² mūi⁶ 姐妹	L.11
sit (V) cȯ⁵ 坐	L.3
Siu Hong (PN) a MTR station: Sīu⁶ Hōng¹ 兆康	L.14
Siu-Ping Chan *(Chinese name)* (PN) Càn⁴ Síu² Pìng⁴ 陳小平	L.7
six (Nu) lūk⁶ 六	U.1
size (N) cėk³ mǎa⁵ 尺碼；sāai¹ sí² 晒士	L.13
ski (VO) wāat⁶ sÿut³ 滑雪	L.6
sleep (V) fȧn³ 瞓；fȧn³ gȧau³ 瞓覺	L.15
slow (Adj) māan⁶ 慢	L.11
small (Adj) sȧi³ 細	U.1; L.3
small size (N) sȧi³ mǎa⁵ 細碼	L.13
smart *(intelligent)* (Adj) cūng¹ mìng⁴ 聰明	L.11
smelly, *stench* (Adj) cȧu³ 臭	L.11
smoke (VO) sīk⁶ jīn¹ 食煙	L.5
so... (Intj) gám² 噉	L.1
social worker (N) sě⁵ wúi² gūng¹ zȯk³ zé² 社會工作者	L.7

socks (N) māt⁶ 襪	U.1
soft drinks (N) hěi³ séoi² 汽水	L.11
some (Nu) jāt¹ dī¹ 一啲	L.4
sometimes (Adv) jǎu⁵ sì⁴ 有時	L.7
son (N) zái² 仔	L.12
sore (Adj) tǔng³ 痛	U.1
sorry (SE) dèoi³ m̀⁴ zỳu⁶ 對唔住； m̀⁴ hóu² jì³ sī¹ 唔好意思	U.2
so-so (Adv) màa⁴ máa² déi² 麻麻哋	L.8
soup dumplings (N) gǔn³ tōng¹ gáau² 灌湯餃	L.12
sour (Adj) sȳun¹ 酸	U.1
south (N) nàam⁴ 南	L.15
South Asia (PN) Nàam⁴ Aå³ 南亞	*
South Asia origin *(Ph)* Nàam⁴ Aå³ jēoi⁶ 南亞裔	*
South Africa (PN) Nàam⁴ Fēi¹ 南非	L.4
South America (PN) Nàam⁴ Měi⁵ Zāu¹ 南美洲	L.2
South Horizons (PN) a MTR station: Hói² Jì⁴ Bǔn³ Dóu² 海怡半島	L.14
South Island Line (East) (PN) Nàam⁴ Góng² Dóu² Sìn³ (Dūng¹ Dỳun⁶) 南港島綫（東段）	L.14
South Korea (PN) Nàam⁴ Hòn⁴ 南韓	L.4
South Korean Won *(PN)* Nàam⁴ Hòn⁴ Wàan⁴ 南韓圜； Nàam⁴ Hòn⁴ Jỳun⁴ 南韓元	L.4
soya bean milk (N) dāu⁶ zōeng¹ 豆漿	L.10
Spain (PN) Sāi¹ Bāan¹ Ngàa⁴ 西班牙	L.4
Spanish language *(PN)* Sāi¹ Bāan¹ Ngàa⁴ Mán² 西班牙文； Sāi¹ Bāan¹ Ngàa⁴ Màn⁴ 西班牙文	L.6
Spanish speech *(PN)* Sāi¹ Bāan¹ Ngàa⁴ Wáa² 西班牙話	L.6
spare ribs (N) pàai⁴ gwāt¹ 排骨	L.12
speak (V) góng² 講	L.7
Special Administrative Region of Hong Kong *(PN)* Hōeng¹ Góng² Dāk⁶ Bīt⁶ Hàng⁴ Zǐng³ Kēoi¹ 香港特別行政區	U.1
Special Administrative Region of Macau (PN) Où³ Mùn⁴ Dāk⁶ Bīt⁶ Hàng⁴ Zǐng³ Kēoi¹ 澳門特別行政區	U.1

sports (N) wǎn⁶ dūng⁶ 運動	L.6
spring rolls (N) cēon¹ gýun² 春卷	L.12
Sprite (PN) Sỳut³ Bīk¹ 雪碧	L.11
square; plaza (N) gwóng² còeng⁴ 廣場	L.14
Sri Lanka (PN) Sī¹ Lěi⁵ Làan⁴ Kāa¹ 斯里蘭卡	*
staircase (N) làu⁴ tāi¹ 樓梯	L.3
stamp collecting (VO) zāap⁶ jàu⁴ 集郵	L.5
Standard Chartered Bank *(PN)* Zāa¹ Dáa² Ngàn⁴ Hòng⁴ 渣打銀行	L.15
Star Ferry Pier *(PN)* Tīn¹ Sīng¹ Mǎa⁵ Tàu⁴ 天星碼頭	L.14
station (a stop) (N) zāam⁶ 站	L.9
statue (N) zōeng⁶ 像	L.15
Statue Square (PN) Wòng⁴ Hāu⁶ Zōeng⁶ Gwóng² Còeng⁴ 皇后像廣場	L.14
steam (V) zīng¹ 蒸	L.12
steamed bean curd rolls *(N)* sīn¹ zūk¹ gýun² 鮮竹卷	L.12
steamed chicken feet (N) fūng⁶ záau² 鳳爪	L.12
steamed salted egg yolk custard buns *(N)* làu⁴ sāa¹ bāau¹ 流沙包	L.12
stench (Adj) cǎu³ 臭	L.11
stewed beef tripe (N) gām¹ cìn⁴ tǒu⁵ 金錢肚	L.12
sticky (Adj) cī¹ 黐	U.1
sticky rice dumplings with meat *(N)* hàam⁴ séoi² gǒk³ 咸水角	L.12
sticky rice dumpling (N) zúng² 糭	L.10
sticky rice with chicken, wrapped with lotus leaf *(N)* zān¹ zȳu¹ gāi¹ 珍珠雞； nō⁶ mǎi⁵ gāi¹ 糯米雞	L.12
still; also (Adv) zūng⁶ 仲	L.12
St. John's Cathedral (PN) Sìng³ Jòek³ Hōn⁶ Zō⁶ Tòng⁴ 聖約翰座堂	L.14
stop (like a car, a train) (Ph) tìng⁴ cē¹ 停車	L.3
stop to get off (SE) jǎu⁵ lōk⁶ 有落	L.14
store room (N) zāap⁶ māt⁶ fóng² 雜物房	L.3
street (N) gāai¹ 街	L.15
street intersection (N) gāai¹ háu² 街口	L.14
street junction (N) gāai¹ háu² 街口	L.14
stroll (VO) sǎan³ bōu⁶ 散步	L.8

student (N) hŏk⁶ sāang¹ 學生	L.1	

English	Cantonese	Lesson
student (N) hŏk⁶ sāang¹ 學生		L.1
student hostel (N) hŏk⁶ sāang¹ sūk¹ sẻ³ 學生宿舍		L.13
study (V) dūk⁶ 讀；hŏk⁶ 學；(VO) dūk⁶ sȳu¹ 讀書		L.5
study in school (VO) dūk⁶ sȳu¹ 讀書		L.5
study room (N) sȳu¹ fóng² 書房；jẏut⁶ dūk⁶ sāt¹ 閱讀室		L.3
stupid (Adj) céon² 蠢		L.11
submit homework (VO) gāau¹ gūng¹ fỏ³ 交功課		L.12
sugar (N) tòng⁴ 糖		L.11
sun (N) jāt⁶ 日；tảai³ jòeng⁴ 太陽		U.2
Sunday (PN) lǎi⁵ bảai³ jāt⁶ 禮拜日；sīng¹ kèi⁴ jāt⁶ 星期日		L.8
Sung wong Toi (PN) a MTR station: Sủng³ Wòng⁴ Tòi⁴ 宋皇臺		L.14
Sunny Bay (PN) a MTR station: Jān¹ Ổu³ 欣澳		L.14
supermarket (N) cīu¹ kāp¹ sỉ⁵ còeng⁴ 超級市場		L.9
surf the Internet (VO) sǒeng⁵ mǒng⁵ 上網		L.8
surname (N) sìng³ 姓		U.1
surroundings (N) zāu¹ wài⁴ 周圍		L.9
Sweden (PN) Sēoi⁶ Dín² 瑞典		L.4
sweet black sesame soup (N) zī¹ màa⁴ wú² 芝蔴糊		L.12
sweet dumpling in soup (N) tōng¹ jýun² 湯圓		L.12
sweet egg custard buns (N) nǎai⁵ wòng⁴ bāau¹ 奶皇包		L.12
sweet ground almond soup (N) hāng⁶ jàn⁴ lòu⁶ 杏仁露		L.12
sweet ground walnut soup (N) hāp⁶ tòu⁴ lòu⁶ 合桃露		L.12
sweet mixed beans soup with taro (N) zāa¹ zàa⁴ 喳咋		L.12
sweet mung bean soup (N) lūk⁶ dáu² sāa¹ 綠豆沙		L.12
sweet red bean soup (N) hùng⁴ dáu² sāa¹ 紅豆沙		L.12
sweet sponge cake (N) mǎa⁵ lāai¹ gōu¹ 馬拉糕		L.12
swim (VO) jàu⁴ séoi² 游水		L.6
Swiss Francs (PN) Sēoi⁶ Sī⁶ Fảat³ Lòng⁴ 瑞士法郎		L.4
Switzerland (PN) Sēoi⁶ Sī⁶ 瑞士		L.4
Szeto (Chinese surname) (PN) Sī¹ Tòu⁴ 司徒		L.1

● 𝒯

English	Cantonese	Lesson
T shirt (N) tī¹ sēot¹ T 裇		L.13
Tai Koo (PN) a MTR station: Tàai³ Gú² 太古		L.14
Tai Kwun (PN) Dāai⁶ Gún² 大館		L.14
Tai Po Market (PN) a MTR station: Dāai⁶ Bỏu⁶ Héoi¹ 大埔墟		L.14
Tai Shui Hang (PN) a MTR station: Dāai⁶ Séoi² Hāang¹ 大水坑		L.14
Tai Wai (PN) a MTR station: Dāai⁶ Wài⁴ 大圍		L.14
Taiwan (PN) Tòi⁴ Wāan¹ 台灣		L.4
Taiwan Dollars (PN) Sān¹ Tòi⁴ Bāi⁶ 新台幣		L.3
Tai Wo (PN) a MTR station: Tàai³ Wò⁴ 太和		L.14
Tai Wo Hau (PN) a MTR station: Dāai⁶ Wō¹ Háu² 大窩口		L.14
take a taxi; by taxi (VO) dảap³ dīk¹ sí² 搭的士		L.14
take a train; by train (VO) cǒ⁵ fó² cē¹ 坐火車		L.14
take an aeroplane; by aeroplane (VO) cǒ⁵ fēi¹ gēi 坐飛機		L.14
take away, "to go" (V) nīng¹ záu² 拎走；nīk¹ záu² 搋走		L.11
take; get (V) ló² 攞		L.9
taking photographs (VO) jíng² sóeng² 影相		L.5
talk (V) góng² 講；kīng¹ 傾		L.7
tall (Adj) gōu¹ 高		L.11
Tang speech (PN) Tòng⁴ Wáa² 唐話		U.1
taro dumplings (N) wū⁰ gòk³ 芋角		L.12
tasty (for drinks) (Adj) hóu² jám² 好飲		L.11
tasty (for food) (Adj) hóu² sīk⁶ 好食		L.10
tasty (Adj) hóu² mēi⁶ 好味		L.10
taxi (N) dīk¹ sí² 的士		L.2
taxi driver (Ph) dīk¹ sí² sī¹ gēi¹ 的士司機		p.50
taxi stand (N) dīk¹ sí² zāam⁶ 的士站		L.14
tea leaves (N) càa⁴ jīp⁶ 茶葉		L.13
teach (V) gảau³ 教		L.7

teacher *(N)* lŏu⁵ sī¹ 老師；sīn¹ sāang¹ 先生	L.1
tears *(N)* ngǎan⁵ lēoi⁶ 眼淚	U.1
telephone *(N)* dīn⁶ wáa² 電話	L.2
telephone number *(N)* dīn⁶ wáa² hōu⁶ mǎa⁵ 電話號碼	L.3
telephone no. for police *(Nu)* gáu² gáu² gáu² 九九九	U.2
teller *(N)* ngàn⁴ hòng⁴ cēot¹ nāap⁶ jyun⁴ 銀行出納員	L.7
teller machine *(N)* gwāi⁶ jyun⁴ gēi¹ 櫃員機	L.9
ten *(Nu)* sāp⁶ 十	U.1
ten cents *(Ph)* jāt¹ hòu⁴ 一毫	L.4
ten dollars *(Ph)* sāp⁶ mān¹ 十蚊	L.4
terminal station *(N)* zúng² zāam⁶ 總站	L.14
terminus *(N)* zúng² zāam⁶ 總站	L.14
terrific *(Adj)* zěng³ 正；sāi¹ lēi⁶ 犀利	L.11
Thai Baht *(PN)* Tàai³ Zyu¹ 泰銖	L.4
Thai language *(PN)* Tàai³ Mán² 泰文；Tàai³ Màn⁴ 泰文	L.6
Thailand *(PN)* Tàai³ Gwók³ 泰國	L.5
thank you *(many thanks)* [express one's gratitude] *(SE)* dō¹ zē⁶ 多謝	L.5
thank you [for a small ravel] *(SE)* m̀⁴ gōi¹ 唔該	L.4
thank you in advance *(SE)* dō¹ zē⁶ sīn¹ 多謝先	L.12
thank you very much! *(SE)* m̀⁴ gōi¹ sǎai³ 唔該晒	L.13
thanks for asking *(SE)* jǎu⁵ sām¹ 有心	U.2
that *(Pn)* gó² dī¹ 嗰啲	L.10
that person *(Pn)* gó² wái⁴ 嗰個	L.10
The Chinese University of Hong Kong *(PN)* Hōeng¹ Góng² Zūng¹ Màn⁴ Dǎai³ Hŏk⁶ 香港中文大學	*
them *(Pn)* kěoi⁵ dēi⁶ 佢哋	L.1
then [used in a clause to indicate the consequence or result of an action] *(Conj)* zāu⁶ 就	L.14
then that's fine *(SE)* zāu⁶ dāk¹ lāak³ 就得嘞	L.14
there *(Pn)* gó² dōu⁶ 嗰度	L.2
therefore *(Conj)* só² jǐ⁵ 所以	L.14
these *(Pn)* nī¹ dī¹ 呢啲	L.10
they *(Pn)* kěoi⁵ dēi⁶ 佢哋	L.1

thin *(in contrast to fat)* *(Adj)* sáu³ 瘦	L.11
think *(V)* gǒk³ dāk¹ 覺得	L.10
thirsty *(Adj)* géng² hót³ 頸渴；hót³ 渴	L.11
this *(Pn)* nī¹ dī¹ 呢啲	L.10
this month *(N)* gām¹ gǒ³ jyut⁶ 今個月；nī¹ gǒ³ jyut⁶ 呢個月	L.8
this one *(Pn)* nī¹ gǒ³ 呢個	L.10
this pair of shoes *(Ph)* nī¹ děoi³ hàai⁴ 呢對鞋	L.10
this piece of clothes *(Ph)* nī¹ gīn⁶ sāam¹ 呢件衫	L.10
this week *(N)* gām¹ gǒ³ sīng¹ kèi⁴ 今個星期；nī¹ gǒ³ sīng¹ kèi⁴ 呢個星期	L.8
this year *(N)* gām¹ nín² 今年；gām¹ nìn⁴ 今年	L.8
those *(Pn)* gó² dī¹ 嗰啲	L.10
thousand *(Nu)* cīn¹ 千	L.13
three *(Nu)* sāam¹ 三	U.1
three years *(Ph)* sāam¹ nìn⁴ 三年	L.15
Thursday *(PN)* lǎi⁵ bǎai³ sěi³ 禮拜四；sīng¹ kèi⁴ sěi³ 星期四	L.8
Tie-guan-yin tea *(PN)* Tit³ Gūn¹ Jām¹ 鐵觀音	L.12
time *(N)* sì⁴ 時；sì⁴ gåan³ 時間	U.1
Tin Hau *(PN)* a MTR station: Tīn¹ Hǎu⁶ 天后	L.14
Tin Shui Wai *(PN)* a MTR station: Tīn¹ Séoi² Wài⁴ 天水圍	L.14
tired *(Adj)* gūi⁶ 攰	U.1
Tiu Keng Leng *(PN)* a MTR station: Tǐu⁴ Gíng² Lěng⁵ 調景嶺	L.14
to *(Prep)* zǐ³ 至；dōu³ 到	L.8
To Kwa Wan *(PN)* a MTR station: Tóu² Gwāa¹ Wàan⁴ 土瓜灣	L.14
toast *(N)* dō¹ sí² 多士	L.10
today *(N)* gām¹ jāt⁶ 今日	L.8
tofu pudding *(N)* dāu⁶ fū⁶ fāa¹ 豆腐花	L.12
together *(Adv)* jāt¹ cài⁴ 一齊	L.7
toilet *(N)* sái² sáu² gāan¹ 洗手間；ci³ só² 廁所	L.2
tomorrow *(N)* tīng¹ jāt⁶ 聽日	L.8
tonight *(N)* gām¹ mǎan⁵ 今晚	L.8
too; also *(Adv)* dōu¹ 都	L.7
too; excessively *(Adv)* tåai³ 太	L.13

top (N) sōeng⁶ mĭn⁶ 上面	L.9
total (Adv) jāt¹ gŭng⁶ 一共； hăm⁶ bāang⁶ lāang⁶ 冚嘛呤	L.11
toward (Prep) hŏeng³ 向	L.15
trademark (N) pàai⁴ zí² 牌子	L.13
train (N) fó² cē¹ 火車	L.14
tram (N) dĭn⁶ cē¹ 電車	L.14
tram station (N) dĭn⁶ cē¹ zāam⁶ 電車站	L.14
translate (V) fāan¹ jĭk⁶ 翻譯	L.5
translation (N) fāan¹ jĭk⁶ 翻譯	L.5
transport/freight corporation (N) wān⁶ sȳu¹ gūng¹ sī¹ 運輸公司	L.7
translation (N) fāan¹ jĭk⁶ 翻譯	L.5
travel (V) lĕoi⁵ hàng⁴ 旅行	L.5
ravelling (N) lĕoi⁵ hàng⁴ 旅行	L.5
treat (V) céng² 請	L.12
treat a meal (VO) céng² sĭk⁶ fāan⁶ 請食飯	L.15
trousers (N) fŭ³ 褲	U.1
try (V) si³ 試	U.1
Tseung Kwan O (PN) a MTR station: Zōeng¹ Gwān¹ Ŏu³ 將軍澳	L.14
Tseung Kwan O Line (PN) Zōeng¹ Gwān¹ Ŏu³ Sin³ 將軍澳綫	L.14
Tsim Sha Tsui (PN) a MTR station: Zīm¹ Sāa¹ Zéoi² 尖沙咀	L.2
Tsim Sha Tsui East (PN) Zīm¹ Dūng¹ 尖東	L.2; L.14
Tsing Yi (PN) a MTR station: Cīng¹ Jī¹ 青衣	L.14
Tsuen Wan (PN) a MTR station: Cȳun⁴ Wāan¹ 荃灣	L.14
Tsuen Wan Line (PN) Cȳun⁴ Wāan¹ Sin³ 荃灣綫	L.14
Tsui (Chinese surname) (PN) Cèoi⁴ 徐；Céoi¹ 崔	L.1
Tuen Ma Line (PN) Tȳun⁴ Măa⁵ Sin³ 屯馬綫	L.14
Tuen Ma Line Phrase 1 (PN) Tȳun⁴ Măa⁵ Sin³ Jāt¹ Kèi⁴ 屯馬綫一期	L.14
Tuen Mun (PN) a MTR station: Tȳun⁴ Mùn⁴ 屯門	L.14
Tuesday (PN) lăi⁵ bǎai³ jī⁶ 禮拜二； sīng¹ kèi⁴ jī⁶ 星期二	L.8

Tung Chee-Hwa, the first Chief Executive of HKSAR (PN) Dúng² Gin³ Wàa⁴ 董建華	L.1
Tung Chung (PN) a MTR station: Dūng¹ Cūng¹ 東涌	L.14
Tung Chung Line (PN) Dūng¹ Cūng¹ Sin³ 東涌綫	L.14
tunnel (N) sēoi⁶ dōu⁶ 隧道	L.14
Turkey (PN) Tóu² Jĭ⁵ Kèi⁴ 土耳其	*
twenty cents (Ph) lŏeng⁵ hòu⁴ 兩毫	L.4
twenty dollars (Ph) jī⁶ sāp⁶ mān¹ 二十蚊	L.4
two (Nu) jī⁶ 二；lŏeng⁵ 兩	U.1; L.5
two dollars (Ph) lŏeng⁵ mān¹ 兩蚊	L.4
two months (Ph) lŏeng⁵ gŏ³ jȳut⁶ 兩個月	L.15
type (VO) dáa² zī⁶ 打字	L.6
● *U*	
U.S. Dollars (PN) Mĕi⁵ Gām¹ 美金；Mĕi⁵ Jȳun⁴ 美元	L.4
ugly (Adj) cáu² jóeng² 醜樣；cáu² 醜	L.11
uncooked (raw) (Adj) sāang¹ 生	U.1
under (N) hāa⁶ mĭn⁶ 下面	L.9
underground (N) dēi⁶ hāa⁶ 地下	L.9
under the bridge (Ph) kìu⁴ dái² 橋底	L.14
understand (V) mìng⁴ 明；mìng⁴ bāak⁶ 明白	U.2
United Kingdom (PN) Jīng¹ Gwŏk³ 英國	L.6
United States of America (PN) Mĕi⁵ Gwŏk³ 美國	L.5
university (N) dāai⁶ hŏk⁶ 大學	L.3
University (PN) a MTR station: Dāai⁶ Hŏk⁶ 大學	L.14
University of Hong Kong (PN) Hōeng¹ Góng² Dāai⁶ Hŏk⁶ 香港大學； Góng² Dāai⁶ 港大	L.1
university's hostel (N) dāai⁶ hŏk⁶ sūk¹ sĕ³ 大學宿舍	L.3
until (Prep) zi³ 至；dŏu³ 到	L.8
upstairs (N) làu⁴ sōeng⁶ 樓上	L.9
Urdo (PN) Wū¹ Jĭ⁵ Dōu¹ Wáa² 烏爾都話	*
us (Pn) ngŏ⁵ dēi⁶ 我哋	L.2

● 𝒱	
vegetable (N) cỏi³ 菜	U.2
vegetarain food (N) zāai¹ 齋	L.12
very (Adv) hóu² 好	L.3
very good (Ph) hóu² hóu² 好好	U.2
vicinity (N) fū⁶ gān⁶ 附近	L.9
Vietnam (PN) Jỳut⁶ Nàam⁴ 越南	*
visa (N) cīm¹ zing³ 簽證	L.4
vision (N) sī̍⁶ 視	U.1
visit a friend (VO) tǎam³ pàng⁴ jǎu⁵ 探朋友	L.8
● 𝒲	
wait a moment (Ph) dáng² dáng² 等等	U.2
wait for (V) dáng² 等	U.1
waiter; waitress (N) sī̍⁶ jing³ sāng¹ 侍應生	L.7
Wales (PN) Wāi¹ Jǐ⁵ Sī¹ 威爾斯	*
wallets (N) ngàn⁴ bāau¹ 銀包	L.13
walk (on foot) (VO) hàang⁴ lōu⁶ 行路	L.14
walk (V) hàang⁴ 行	L.15
walk straight on (Ph) zīk⁶ hàang⁴ 直行	L.15
walkaround (VO) hàang⁴ gāai¹ 行街	L.5
walnut sweet soup (N) hāp⁶ tòu⁴ lōu⁶ 合桃露	L.12
Wan Chai (PN) a MTR station: Wāan¹ Zái² 灣仔	L.2
want (something) (V) jiu³ 要	L.3
want to (do something) (AV) sóeng² 想	L.3
want to have (something) (Ph) sóeng² jiu³ 想要	L.3
washroom (N) sái² sáu² gāan¹ 洗手間；cì³ só² 廁所	L.2
watch (V) tái² 睇	L.13
watch movies (VO) tái² hėi³ 睇戲	L.5
watch TV (VO) tái² dīn⁶ sī̍⁶ 睇電視	L.15
watches (N) sáu² bīu¹ 手錶	L.13
we (Pn) ngǒ⁵ dēi⁶ 我哋	L.2
Wednesday (PN) lǎi⁵ bǎai³ sāam¹ 禮拜三；sīng¹ kèi⁴ sāam¹ 星期三	L.8
week after next (Ph) zǒi³ hǎa⁶ gȯ³ sīng¹ kèi⁴ 再下個星期	L.8
week before last (Ph) zǒi³ sōeng⁶ gȯ³ sīng¹ kèi⁴ 再上個星期	L.8

week(s) (of time duration) (Suff) gȯ³ sīng¹ kèi⁴ 個星期	L.15
week; day of a week (PN) lǎi⁵ bǎai³ 禮拜；sīng¹ kèi⁴ 星期	L.8
weekend (N) zāu¹ mūt⁶ 週末	L.8
weight lifting (VO) géoi² cǔng⁵ 舉重	L.6
welcome (V) fūn¹ jìng⁴ 歡迎	L.1
welcome for coming (SE) fūn¹ jìng⁴ gwōng¹ làm⁴ 歡迎光臨	L.1
well… (Intj) gám² 噉	L.1
west (N) sāi¹ 西	L.15
West Rail Line (PN) Sāi¹ Tit³ Sin³ 西鐵綫	L.14
Western style (N) sāi¹ sīk¹ 西式	L.10
Western style barbecue pork buns (N) cāa¹ sīu¹ cāan¹ bāau¹ 叉燒餐包	L.12
Whampoa (PN) a MTR station: Wòng⁴ Bȯu³ 黃埔	L.14
what (QW) géi² dō¹ 幾多；māt¹ jě⁵ 乜嘢；mē¹ jě⁵ 咩嘢	L.3
what kind of (QW) māt¹ jě⁵ 乜嘢；mē¹ jě⁵ 咩嘢	L.6
what kind of company (QW) māt¹ jě⁵ gūng¹ sī¹ 乜嘢公司	L.8
what kind of language (QW) bīn¹ zúng² jǔ⁵ jìn⁴ 邊種語言	L.6
what kind of vehicle (QW) māt¹ jě⁵ cē¹ 乜嘢車	L.14
what mode of transportation (QW) māt¹ jě⁵ cē¹ 乜嘢車	L.14
what name (QW) māt¹ jě⁵ méng² 乜嘢名；mē¹ jě⁵ méng² 咩嘢名	L.5
what nationality (QW) māt¹ jě⁵ jàn⁴ 乜嘢人；mē¹ jě⁵ jàn⁴ 咩嘢人	L.5
what number (QW) géi² dō¹ hȯu⁶ 幾多號	L.3
what on earth is this/that? (Q) māt¹ jě⁵ lài⁴ gåa³? 乜嘢嚟㗎？	L.10
what subject (QW) māt¹ jě⁵ fō¹ 乜嘢科	L.5
what's your surname? (SE) něi⁵ gwåi³ sing³ åa³? 你貴姓呀？	L.6
what time (QW) géi² dím² 幾點	U.2; L.6
when (QW) géi² sì⁴ 幾時	L.8

where (QW) bīn¹ dōu⁶ 邊度	L.2
which (QW) bīn¹ dī¹ 邊啲	L.10
which building (QW) bīn¹ gāan¹ 邊間	L.10
white (N) bāak⁶ sīk¹ 白色	L.13
whole (Pn) hām⁶ bāang⁶ lāang⁶ 冚唪唥	L.11
wicked (evil-minded) (Adj) sēoi¹ 衰	L.11
wide (Adj) fut³ 闊	U.1
wife (N) tàai³ táai² 太太；lǒu⁵ pò⁴ 老婆	L.5
will; would (AV) wǔi⁵ 會	L.15
window-ledge (N) cōeng¹ tòi⁴ 窗台	L.3
wind-surfing (VO) wāat⁶ lōng⁶ fūng¹ fàan⁴ 滑浪風帆	L.6
wine (N) záu² 酒	U.2
with (Prep) tùng⁴ 同	L.7
withdraw money (VO) ló² cín² 攞錢	L.9
Wong (Chinese surname) (PN) Wòng⁴ 黃／王	L.1
Wong Chuk Hang (PN) a MTR station: Wòng⁴ Zūk¹ Hāang¹ 黃竹坑	L.14
Wong Tai Sin (PN) a MTR station: Wòng⁴ Dāai⁶ Sīn¹ 黃大仙	L.14
wonton (N) wàn⁴ tān¹ 雲吞	L.10
wonton noodles (N) wàn⁴ tān¹ mīn⁶ 雲吞麵	L.10
work (N) gūng¹ zòk³ 工作	L.7
work (V) zòu⁶ 做；(VO) zòu⁶ sī⁶ 做事；zòu⁶ jě⁵ 做嘢	L.8
worker (N) gūng¹ jàn⁴ 工人	L.7
worth buying (SE) dái² mǎai⁵ 抵買	L.13
worthy (Adj) dái² 抵	L.13
would like (something) (V) jiu³ 要	L.3
would like to (do something) (AV) sóeng² 想	L.3
would; will (AV) wǔi⁵ 會	L.15
Wow! [express surprise or wonder] (Intj) wàa³ 嘩	L.13
write (V) sé² 寫	L.15
wrong (Adj) cò³ 錯	L.11
Wu (Chinese surname) (PN) Ǹg⁴ 吳；Wù⁴ 胡；Wu¹ 鄔	L.1
Wu Kai Sha (PN) a MTR station: Wū¹ Kāi¹ Sāa¹ 烏溪沙	L.14

● Y

Yau Ma Tei (PN) a MTR station: Jàu⁴ Màa⁴ Déi² 油麻地	L.2
Yau Tong (PN) Jàu⁴ Tòng⁴ 油塘	L.14
year (N) nìn⁴ 年	L.8
year after next (N) hāu⁶ nín² 後年；hāu⁶ nìn⁴ 後年	L.8
year before last (N) cìn⁴ nín² 前年；cìn⁴ nìn⁴ 前年	L.8
years old (N) sèoi³ 歲	L.5
yellow (N) wòng⁴ sīk¹ 黃色	L.13
Yellow tea (PN) Wòng⁴ Càa⁴ 黃茶	L.12
yellowish green (N) cēng¹ sīk¹ 青色	L.13
yesterday (N) càm⁴ jāt⁶ 噚日；kàm⁴ jāt⁶ 琴日	L.8
Yogoslavia (PN) Nàam⁴ Sī¹ Lāai¹ fū¹ 南斯拉夫	*
you (plural) (Pn) něi⁵ dēi⁶ (also "lěi⁵ dēi⁶") 你哋	L.1
you (Pn) něi⁵ (also "lěi⁵") 你	U.1
you're welcome (SE) m̀⁴ sái² m̀⁴ gōi¹ 唔使唔該；m̀⁴ sái² dō¹ zě⁶ 唔使多謝	L.9
young (Adj) hāu⁶ sāang¹ 後生	L.11
young lady; Miss (N) síu² zé² 小姐	L.1
younger brother (N) dài⁴ dái² 弟弟	L.5
younger sister (N) mùi⁴ múi² 妹妹	L.5
your (Ph) něi⁵ gè³ 你嘅	L.1
yours (Ph) něi⁵ gě³ 你嘅	L.1
youth hostels (N) cīng¹ nìn⁴ lěoi⁵ sě³ 青年旅舍	L.3
yum-cha (VO) jám² càa⁴ 飲茶	L.12
yuanyuang (PN) Jīn¹ Jōeng¹ 鴛鴦	L.11
Yue language (PN) Jy̌ut⁶ Jy̌u⁵ 粵語	U.1
Yuen Long (PN) Jy̌un⁴ Lóng² 元朗	L.14

● Z

Zee (Chinese surname) (PN) Cèoi⁴ 徐	L.1
zero (Nu) lìng⁴ 零	U.1
Zing-Zing Wong (Chinese name) (PN) Wòng⁴ Zīng¹ Zīng¹ 王晶晶	L.1

Glossary & Abbreviations of Grammatical Terms

- **Classification of Words/Part of speech** (詞類 cì⁴ lēoi⁶)

  In modern Chinese, according to their nature, words are classified into nouns, adjectives, verbs, etc. which are known as "詞類 cì⁴ lēoi⁶ *(parts of speech)*".

  Here are the twelve common categories:

  1) **Nouns** (名詞 mìng⁴ cì⁴) – Nouns are the words that denote people, things or places and time.

  2) **Pronouns** (代詞 dōi⁶ cì⁴) – Pronouns are words that stand for nouns, verbs and adjectives.

  3) **Verbs** (動詞 dūng⁶ cì⁴) – Verbs are the words that express the existence, action, behaviour, will or change of a person or a thing.

  4) **Adjectives** (形容詞 jìng⁴ jùng⁴ cì⁴) – Adjectives are words that describe the nature or condition (the shape, quality or state) of a person or a thing.

  5) **Numerals** (數詞 sŏu³ cì⁴) – Numerals are words that express numbers.

  6) **Measure words** (量詞 lōeng⁶ cì⁴) – Measure words are words that express a unit of a thing or an action.

  7) **Adverbs** (副詞 fŭ³ cì⁴) – A word that generally proceeds a verb or an adjective to express time, degree, scopes, repetition, negation, possibility or tone of speech, etc. is called an adverb.

  8) **Prepositions** (介詞 gåai³ cì⁴) – Prepositions are words that are placed before nouns, pronouns or phrases to form a prepositional phrase and are used together to express the direction, object, time, place etc. of an action.

  9) **Conjunctions** (連詞 lìn⁴ cì⁴) – Conjunctions are words that connect words, phrases, clauses or sentences.

  10) **Particles** (助詞 zō⁶ cì⁴) – Particles are words that are added to words, phrases or sentences to express some additional meanings.

  11) **Interjections** (感歎詞 gám² tåan³ cì⁴) – An interjection is an exclamation, a crying out or a response.

  12) **Onomatopoeia** (象聲詞 zōeng⁶ sīng¹ cì⁴) – An onomatopoeia word is one which imitates the sound of a thing or an action.

- **Word** (詞 cì⁴) –

  The smallest meaningful unit of language, which can be used independently.

- **Phrase** (詞組 cì⁴ zóu² / 短語 dýun² jŭu⁵) –

  Two or more words together may be a word group, which is generally called a phrase.
  e.g. jāt¹ bún² sān¹ sȳu¹ *(a new book)*

- **Sentence** (句子 gĕoi³ zí²) –

  A phrase or combination of phrases that can stand independently and express a definite idea is a sentence.

● **Abbreviations of grammatical categories**			
Adj	= adjective	jìng⁴ jùng⁴ cì⁴	形容詞
Adv	= adverb	fů³ cì⁴	副詞
AV	= auxiliary/optative verb	zŏ⁶ dūng⁶ cì⁴ / nàng⁴ jẙun⁶ dūng⁶ cì⁴	助動詞／能願動詞
Conj	= conjunction	lìn⁴ cì⁴	連詞
Intj	= interjection	(gám²) tảan³ cì⁴	（感）歎詞
M/MW	= measure word	lŏeng⁶ cì⁴	量詞
N	= noun	mìng⁴ cì⁴	名詞
	1) proper name (PN)	zȳun¹ jǎu⁵ mìng⁴ cì⁴	專有名詞
	2) time word (TW)	sì⁴ gảan³ cì⁴	時間詞
	3) localizer/place word (PW)	cẙu³ só² cì⁴	處所詞
	4) position word (PosW)	fōng¹ wái² cì⁴	方位詞
Nu	= numeral	sǒu³ cì⁴	數詞
Obj	= object	bān¹ jẙu⁵	賓語
Ono	= onomatopoeia	zŏeng⁶ sīng¹ cì⁴	象聲詞
Part (Pt)	= particle	zŏ⁶ cì⁴	助詞
	1) structural particle	gìt³ gảu³ zŏ⁶ cì⁴	結構助詞
	2) aspectual particle	sì⁴ tảai³ zŏ⁶ cì⁴	時態助詞
	3) modal particle	jẙu⁵ hẻi³ zŏ⁶ cì⁴	語氣助詞
	a) sentence/final particle	jẙu⁵ měi⁵ zŏ⁶ cì⁴	語尾助詞
	b) interrogative particle	jì⁴ mān⁶ zŏ⁶ cì⁴	疑問助詞
Ph	= phrase	dẙun² jẙu⁵; cì⁴ zóu²	短語；詞組
Pn	= pronoun	dŏi⁶ cì⁴	代詞
	1) personal pronoun	jàn⁴ cīng¹ dŏi⁶ cì⁴	人稱代詞
	2) demonstrative pronoun	zí² sī⁶ dŏi⁶ cì⁴	指示代詞
	3) interrogative pronoun/ question word (QW)	jì⁴ mān⁶ dŏi⁶ cì⁴	疑問代詞
Pred	= predicate	wǎi⁶ jẙu⁵	謂語
Pref	= prefix	cì⁴ tàu⁴	詞頭
	= specified prefix/specifier	zí² sī⁶ cì⁴ tàu⁴	指示詞頭
Prep	= preposition	gảai³ cì⁴	介詞
Pttn	= sentence pattern	gẻoi³ jìng⁴	句型
SE	= set expression	gwǎan³ jūng⁶ jẙu⁵	慣用語
Subj	= subject	zẙu² jẙu⁵	主語
Suff	= suffix	cì⁴ měi⁵	詞尾
Top	= topic	zẙu² tài⁴	主題
V	= verb	dūng⁶ cì⁴	動詞
	1) directional verb	cēoi¹ hǒeng³ dūng⁶ cì⁴	趨向動詞
	2) equative verb	sẙut³ mìng⁴ dūng⁶ cì⁴	說明動詞
	3) static verb	zīng⁶ tảai³ dūng⁶ cì⁴	靜態動詞
VO	= verb object structure	dūng⁶ bān¹ gìt³ gảu³	動賓結構

References

- Bauer, R. S. and Benedict, P. K. (1997) *Modern Cantonese Phonology*. Berlin: Mouton de Gruyter

- **Bruce Lee**. (2020) In *Wikipedia, the free encyclopedia*. Online: http://en.wikipedia.org/wiki/Bruce_Lee

- **Cantonese language**. (2007). In *Encyclopedia Britannica*. Online: http://search.eb.com/eb/article-9020079

- **Chinese Tea Culture**. (2001-2002) In *University Museum and Art Gallery*. Online: www.hku.hk/hkumag/teagallery

- **City Hall**. (2020) In *Leisure and Cultural Services Department, HKSAR*. Online: http://www.lcsd.gov.hk

- Crystal, D. (1991) *A dictionary of linguistics and phonetics*. 3rd edition. Cambridge, MA: Basil Blackwell.

- **Currencies**. (2020) In *Hong Kong Tourism Board*. Online: http://www.discoverhongkong.com; http://www.hkta.org

- **Deng Xiaoping**. (2020). In *Encyclopedia*. Online: https://www.encyclopedia.com/people/history/chinese-and-taiwanese-history-biographies/deng-xiaoping

- **Dim-sum**. (2020) In *Wikipedia, the free encyclopedia*. Online: http://en.wikipedia.org/wiki/Dim-sum

- **Fricative consonant**. (2020). In *Wikipedia, the free encyclopedia*. Online: http://en.wikipedia.org/wiki/Fricative

- Huang, P. and Kok, G., (1970). *Speak Cantonese, Vol: 1*. Newhaven: Yale University Press

- Linguistic Society of Hong Kong (2009) http:// lshk.ctl.cityu.edu.hk/

- Matthews, S. and Yip, V. (1994). *Cantonese: A Comprehensive Grammar*. London: Routledge

- **MTR** (2020) http:// www.mtr.com.hk

- The 100 Most-Spoken Languages in the world (2020) Visual Capitalist. Online: https://www.visualcapitalist.com/100-most-spoken-languages/

- **Transportation modes at Arrivals Hall**. (2020) In *Hong Kong International Airport*. Online: http://www.hongkongairport.com

- **Yum-cha**. (2020) In *Wikipedia, the free encyclopedia*. Online: http://en.wikipedia.org/wiki/Yum-cha

Scan the Master QR Code to assess MP3 audio files